# TANGLED

*Emerson Falls, Book 1*

## By Harlow James

Copyright © 2019 Harlow James

Tangled

Emerson Falls, Book 1

Cover Design: NET Hook & Line Design

*"Trust is like a mirror, you can fix it if it's broken, but you can still see the crack in that mother fucker's reflection."* — *Lady Gaga*

# CONTENTS

# CHAPTER 1

Kane

*3 Years Earlier*

My brown leather combat boot thumped steadily on the floorboard in the back of my Uber, keeping the rhythm with the song playing from the radio, but also the nervous beating of my heart in my chest. My left hand clutched my duffle bag next to me, fighting to keep the shaking at bay that I felt the moment I stepped off the plane and back on American soil.

"Coming home?" My driver asked, glancing back at me in the rear-view mirror.

"Yup," I curtly reply, too anxious to offer up more words.

It had been six months.

Six months since I'd been home—seen her face, kissed her lips, and felt like everything was right in the world. Natasha would be ecstatic to see me. I could already hear her scream of excitement, the jump in my arms she would complete the minute I opened the door and she saw my face, and the insane sex that would commence once we both came down from the thrill of the surprise and finally being back in each other's arms.

The brakes on the car screech as the driver eases to a stop in front of our apartment complex, the one I can't wait to leave in search of the home we'll raise our family in. My time away has been difficult, but the monetary compensation has been welcome as I've saved every dime I could for a down payment on our future home. The long list of things to accomplish now that I'm home for good has been running through my mind since I boarded the plane, but all of those things can wait until after I surprise my girl.

"Thanks for the ride," I acknowledge the driver, adding a more than generous tip for his time, reach for my duffle on the seat, and hoist myself up and out of the car, staring at the two-story building in front of me.

My palms are sweaty as I trek up the sidewalk and two flights of steps, the brush of my Army greens creating friction and background noise before turning the corner and gliding down the balcony of the tan building before arriving in front of our door.

I'm home, back in Oregon, a place I never plan on leaving again.

I put in my eight years in the Army but ultimately decided the military life wasn't for me. Natasha begged me to leave after four years, but I didn't feel like it was the right time. Plus, I wasn't finished with my teaching degree and my unit needed me still. We were knee-deep in operations overseas, and if I had left them four years ago, I know I would have regretted it and I would have let them down. Instead, I re-enlisted, much to the frustration of Natasha, but I promised her when those four years were up, so was my time in the Army.

And I kept my promise.

The only thing I asked for her was to understand and stand by my side, and also to marry me, so I knew she wouldn't doubt my commitment to her.

And here we are. I'm a bundle of nerves and longing as I find my key, turn it in the lock, and push open the door to the rest of my life.

The silence that fills the apartment is unsettling, especially because I know she's home. I checked to make sure her car was in her parking space as I walked up to the building. Then I think, she's probably in the bath or at least in our bedroom binge-watching a Netflix show in bed, so I set my bag down by the front door and make my way down the hall.

"Yes..."

I stop, dead in my tracks with the sound of her moans, the moans I know all too well with every touch I've given her body.

"You like that, baby?"

A man's voice rings this time, eerily familiar, yet equally unsettling. My stomach instantly drops, fearful that what I think I'm about to walk in on, is in fact, true.

"More..." Natasha encourages, letting out a small shriek that lets me know she's enjoying the activities that are ripping a gaping hole in my chest as I come up to the door to our bedroom and hear the unmistakable sounds of slapping skin.

"Take it all, babe.... Fuck yeah..."

That voice. I swallow hard, knowing now with no doubt that I'm about to walk in on my best friend fucking my fiancé.

Sweat beads on my forehead, my palms instantly fold into fists at my sides, and the war of emotion I'm feeling in my chest makes the thump of my heart shake my entire body.

*Do I let them finish? Or do I interrupt what I'm sure will be a blissful climax?*

*What do you think I did?*

I slam my fist into the door, the echo of my hand hitting the hardwood booming off the walls.

"What the fuck?!" I shout as I get an eyeful of my best friend's ass as he slams into my fiancé beneath him.

"Kane!" Natasha shouts, pushing T.J. off of her and rushing to find the blankets to cover her naked body. Sure, now she opts for modesty.

"What the fuck is going on here? Seriously? What the fuck, man?" My eyebrows draw together in confusion and rage, my hands are thrown up in the air in question, the adrenaline roaring through my body takes on a life of its own as I rush towards him while he's standing there butt-naked, and slam my fist into his jaw.

The crack of my knuckles hitting his face mimics my fist hitting the door just moments ago as he folds down onto the ground, clutching his jaw in his hands and curling up into the fetal position.

"Kane, stop!" Natasha yells as she scrambles out of the bed, wrapping the blanket around her, her long blonde hair a wild mess around her flushed cheeks.

I turn to her next. "Stop what? Sorry I didn't let you finish." I grit through my teeth as I watch her eyes fill with tears.

"I'm so sorry, Kane," she pleads as beads of moisture leak down her face.

"Sorry for what? Breaking your promise to marry me? Fucking my best friend? Sorry that you got caught?"

I look down at her hand clutching the sheet, the engagement ring I gave her shimmering in the light from the bedside lamp.

"You were gone. I got lonely. You brought this on yourself, you know! I asked you not to re-enlist, but…"

"So that gives you the right to cheat on me? Let alone, with my best fucking friend?" I turn and bend down to look T.J. in the eyes, right as he opens his to meet the rage on my face.

"You are a piece of shit!" I yell in his face while pressing my finger into his chest. "You are dead to me, you hear? Never contact me again. Both of you," I state finally, looking back at Natasha as I stand.

Her lips tremble as she studies me and then her eyes move to T.J., still cowering on the floor. She hurries to his side to check his face, which gives me no remorse in turning away and walking back down the hall.

"Fuck you both. Enjoy your life together," I wave over my shoulder with my hand as my boots stomp down the carpeted hall and back to the front door, retrieving my duffle and bursting through the door, leaving behind everything and everyone I've ever given two shits about besides my family and the men standing beside me in uniform.

I fumble to retrieve my phone from my pocket, my hands shaking so violently as the rush of emotions over what just happened flow through my mind and my body.

I order another Uber, the same driver as before since he's still close by, and wait on the curb, not bothering to look back at the apartment that I thought would hold a much different memory for me ten minutes ago.

I can't look back. I won't look back.

Only forward.

And I vow, right then and there, never to let anyone into my heart again.

# CHAPTER 2

Kane

*Present Day*

"Alright, class. Simmer down, please. The bell is about to ring, so please make sure your classwork is turned in and you've copied down the pages you need to read over the weekend," I project over the chatter filtering through my classroom.

"Mr. G., no one writes down the homework anymore. We just take a picture of it," Daisy replies with a roll of her eyes as she saunters up to the whiteboard and snaps a picture of the homework assignment written there with her phone.

I shake my head. I swear, these teenagers have been programmed to look for the path of least work possible in everything they do.

"As long as it gets done, I don't care how you remember," I tell her before making my way around the room to verify everything is in its place. Books are returned to the shelves, trash has been picked up off of the floor, and the desks are pushed into their rightful position.

The sharp ring of the bell through the speakers is like music to my ears as the kids beeline for the door, signaling the end of another grueling week. It's the end of September and we've been back in school for four weeks now. The honeymoon period has worn off, and the kids and teachers are all feeling the exhaustion.

"Have a good weekend, you guys. Make good choices," I

shout as my juniors in U.S. History filter out of the doors.

"Have a good weekend, Mr. G!" A few of them call out behind them just as the last kid leaves and I slump down in the chair at my desk.

I think back to three years ago when I first started teaching and how it was nothing like I thought it would be. Of course, I had just found my fiancé in bed with my best friend, so nothing in my life made sense. And even though that first year was hell, it gave me purpose at a time in my life when I really needed it. Everything I had been working toward was pulled out from underneath me, except for teaching. I always knew this was what I wanted to do, and the Army was a way for me to make it happen.

My parents—bless them both—were hardworking people, but couldn't afford to pay for me to go to college. And I didn't want to take out thousands of dollars in loans to then turn around and work to the bone to pay them off. So when the Army recruiters came to the high school and offered to pay for my degree in exchange for serving my country, I jumped at the opportunity. Most of my friends, T.J. included, didn't understand, but they didn't face the same monetary dilemma I did. And Natasha hated the idea of me leaving her after graduation, but she understood my reasons for the decision and promised to wait for me.

My high school sweetheart was supposed to wait for me and we were going to end up together... What a crock of shit that ended up being.

I stand from my desk, put out the papers I'll need for Monday, change the date on the board and erase the notes from today, grab my coffee mug and my lunch box, and head for the cafeteria where our principal has asked us to gather for a brief staff meeting at the end of the day.

Opening up the solid metal doors, I'm greeted with a gush of cool air and the faint scent of what the cafeteria served for lunch. My guess is pizza.

"Who schedules a staff meeting on a Friday?"

Mrs. Waterman sits down next to me on the bench of one of the cafeteria tables where I found a seat in the back, giving everyone the silent sign that says to leave me alone. However, I must have a beacon flashing above my head that says, *"Here! Come vent to me about how the entire world pisses you off!"*

"Mmmm," I mumble back, learning that fewer words in response to her make the conversation end much faster. I contemplate moving my seat just as she continues on with her rant.

"We spend all week at this damn school, so when two-o'clock on a Friday hits, we're done! The last thing we want to do is sit around and listen to an entire meeting that could have been summed up in an email."

I chuckle at that last point. The woman isn't wrong. I've lost count of how many meetings I've sat in that could have been communicated with a few sentences and the click of a button.

"Hey, Garrison." Drew comes up beside me, taking the seat to my right, giving me the perfect reason to turn my back to Mrs. Waterman. All that woman does is bitch about anything and everything related to her job and education. She's an emotional vampire and the type of teacher that gives good teachers a bad name. I can't believe she's married either. I feel terrible for her husband.

"Drew, how's it going, man? I haven't seen you much this week."

Drew Phillips is one of the most respected English teachers at Emerson Falls High School, and one of my best friends and colleagues. After what happened with my former best friend, I hadn't been too keen to extend olive branches of friendship. But Drew weaseled his way in during my first year of teaching, and the truth is, I wouldn't have survived without him.

"Yeah, well, between football practice and Tammy

ovulating, I haven't had much of a life," he sighs, running his hands through his blonde hair. The bags beneath his blue eyes only confirm his level of exhaustion.

"You guys trying again?"

"Yeah. After the miscarriage, I wasn't sure she'd want to. But we both agreed to keep trying to move forward. At least we know she can get pregnant. I just hope it sticks this time," he whispers, a hint of despair in his voice.

Drew's words hit me hard in the chest. His wife, Tammy, is one of the science teachers here at the school, and they've been married for a few years now. They met here when she got hired and Drew fell hard. A few months ago, they found out they were expecting and were beyond thrilled until she miscarried ten weeks in. It was a long summer for them, nursing the heartache of losing the possibility of the family they want so desperately. But they're both strong people and I have faith that things will work out for them.

But supporting Drew through his life challenges just reminds me that I should be in that same boat right now too —married, having children, being so disgustingly happy that nothing else matters in this world. Funny how things don't always work out the way we plan. I declared I would move on and not look back—that's what I vowed to myself to do three years ago. So why does it still feel like I'm hanging onto the pain like a grudge I refuse to drop?

"Everything will work out the way it's supposed to, man," I pat him on the shoulder. "You and Tammy are meant to be parents. I whole-heartedly believe that."

"Thanks, Kane. I just don't think I've needed sleep this badly in my life."

"Oh, come on. There had to be one point in college where you stayed up too late drinking and partying and didn't sleep until the next night?" I tease him, trying to distract him from the worry in his life, although I can't relate to the feeling of nursing a hangover and still having to function. I worked on my degree while stationed in a desert with limited wi-fi and no parties in sight. Sometimes I feel regretful that I didn't get the typical college experience, but I wouldn't change my time in the Army for anything.

He smiles at the thought. "Yeah, but I'm not twenty anymore. I'm thirty-one, and I swear, the thirties are great except for the depletion in your energy. If I didn't have to help coach a football game tonight, I'd be in bed at seven!"

"Just wait until you have a kid. I hear you really lose sleep then."

Drew stares blankly at me as he processes my words then mutters, "Fuck."

"Good afternoon, everyone!" Principal North addresses the room of disgruntled teachers, exhausted from another long week of work, effectively ending our conversation. "I'll try to make this quick since I know you're all eager to get your weekend started," she beams, surveying the teachers who look more like students trying to stay awake during class right now.

"Damn right. Make this quick, woman," Mrs. Waterman mumbles behind me, earning an eye roll from me that thankfully she can't see.

"As you know, Mr. Kirk left us a few weeks ago, leaving a huge vacancy in our math department."

"Yeah, well, if I'd won the lottery, I would have left too!" Another teacher shouts across the cafeteria, garnering murmurs of agreement and chuckles from the crowd of almost seventy of us.

"No judgment from me," Principal North replies with a wink. "I think we can all understand Mr. Kirk's choice. But I am happy to report we have found a replacement for him. Our new teacher will start on Monday, so please help her feel welcome. She has big shoes to fill, but she came highly recommended and knows her stuff."

"A woman, huh?" Drew whispers in my ear, causing me

to glare at him in wonder.

"Why does that matter?" I growl.

"Easy tiger. I wasn't insinuating anything. It's just not very often you hear of a woman teaching math. But maybe this one can end up being your Tammy."

"My Tammy?"

"In case you've forgotten, my wife was hired here and that's how I met her. Marrying a teacher is the best man. You both get the same time off, you understand what the job is like... it's the perfect relationship for men like us."

"That's pretty sexist, Drew, even coming from you. A woman who can teach math shouldn't be looked at differently. In fact, that's pretty hot. But sorry to burst your bubble, I'm not looking for a happily ever after. Knowing my luck anyway, she's probably in her fifties or something," I chide while Principal North drones on about the tardy policy.

I swear, with the way these kids are late to class, I wonder how any of them will ever hold down a job.

Drew holds his hands up in the air in defense. "Just sharing my thoughts. Although it seems to me like you could use the company of a woman right now. You're more surly than normal."

"I get plenty of company from women when I want it. And I'm not being any more of an asshole than normal, just tired," I grumble under my breath, knowing damn well that a wet and willing woman would be enough to snap me out of my funk.

It's been almost a year though since I've had the company of a woman in my bed. After Natasha wrecked our future, I sowed my wild oats for a while since she had been the only woman I'd ever been with. It got old really fast, so I called it quits and have only enjoyed the company of my hand for months now.

"The next item is the big rivalry game against Ashland High School next week," Principal North continues. "This is the biggest game of the year and we get to host. I would appreciate a few of you stepping up to help with taking tickets and just being present in the stands. Security will do the dirty work, but the more eyes we have in the stadium, the better things run. And of course, the kids loving seeing the teachers there."

The rivalry between Emerson Falls and Ashland High has been a long-standing one for over thirty years. I grew up in northern Oregon, so I was uneducated on the tradition, but the Emerson-Ashland rivalry has always been a brutal game and both towns take the competition very seriously.

"You're gonna be down on the field with us during that game, right?" Drew pulls my attention back to him while I survey the room. The soldier in me never stops observing my surroundings.

"Yeah, no problem. I can help in any way you need."

"Thanks. It helps to have another guy down there to keep the boys level-headed. Cory and Holt wanted me to remind you about it anyway, so now I've completed my job," he winks at me just as we hear Principal North end the meeting.

Corey Tanner and Holt Bennet are a P.E. teacher and athletic trainer respectively for the school, and two of the other men I've made friends with over the past few years. Drew, Corey and Holt coach the football team together, and I'll chip in sometimes when needed but couldn't commit to the team entirely. After one bad case of PTSD during a practice where the sound of the helmets hitting snapped me back to an IED going off in Afghanistan and I froze on the field, I realized coaching probably wasn't a good idea. I'm hoping one day that won't be the case anymore.

"Have a good weekend everyone! See you back here on Monday!" Principal North shouts over the noise of teachers making a mad dash for the parking lot.

"You going to Tony's tonight?" Drew asks as we grab our stuff and head for our trucks.

"Probably. Lord knows I've earned it after this week. It was a full moon and the kids were just more ornery than normal," I say while stroking my hand through my jet black hair and down the beard I'm obnoxiously proud of. After keeping a clean-shaven face in the Army for eight years, I was itching to grow a beard. So I did, and it looks damn good if I say so myself.

"Wish I could join you, but after the game, I'm headed home to pass out," Drew says through a laugh and I wish him luck before we both settle in our trucks and peel out of the parking lot.

Tony's bar is the local hangout for the working class. The younger crowd hangs out at Half Full, a hipster bar on the other side of town. Tony's is known for an older crowd who know how to keep to themselves and behave, which is fine by me since I don't really have much to say to anyone nowadays.

After I moved from my hometown to Emerson Falls and bought my house secluded in the thick forest on the outskirts of town, a trip to Tony's was the only interaction I allowed myself to unwind after a long week of teaching. Tony, the owner, became a close confidant I didn't know I needed, especially since he served in the Army as well. So most weeks, I take a trip to the bar, have a couple of beers with Tony, and then call it a night, retreating to my life of solitude that I've become accustomed to.

But if someone would have told me how my night would end when I made my way into Tony's later that evening, I would have laughed in their face and bet them a hundred bucks that it never would happen. Because there was no way that some woman would knock me on my ass and give me the best sex of my life. No way.

Good thing I never placed any bets against anyone else, because losing a bet to her took my evening in an entirely different direction.

# CHAPTER 3

Olivia

"Well, I think that's the last one," Clara exclaims as she sets the last box on my dining room table.

"Finally. I love you, Liv, but this moving thing is for the birds." Perry slides up next to her, slinging her arm around Clara's neck.

I sigh before turning around to face my friends. "I know, but you have no idea how much I appreciate your help. Believe me, if you asked me last week what I thought I'd be doing on Friday, I definitely wouldn't have described this," I gesture around my new apartment with my hands in the air.

Looking around the two-bedroom place, I'm hit with my new reality for the first time since I left northern California last week. Moving back to Emerson Falls was not on the agenda of my life. Of course, neither was catching my boyfriend fucking his secretary either.

*My heels click on the cobblestone floor that stretches throughout the entire winery, the mustard yellow walls and maroon accents surrounding me. The smell of oak and berries wafts up my nose as I inhale deeply, savoring the aromas only a true wine lover would appreciate.*

*Trevor said he would be working late trying to complete an order for next week. They have several tours coming through and wanted to make sure enough of their wine was bottled and the shelves in the gift shop were stacked and ready for purchases. So as I hoist the picnic basket in my hand and make my way down to* his office, I beam with pride that I took the initiative to surprise him with dinner so we could spend some time together. He'd been working late a lot lately and I missed him terribly.

I approach his door and notice it's slightly cracked open instead of closed as he'll normally keep it. He probably left to use the bathroom which would make my surprise even more worthwhile when he returned and I could see the expression on his face when he found me in his office. The sexy bra and panty set I wore underneath my dress would give me an even bigger pay-off as well.

Suddenly, heavy breathing and moaning fill my ears as I slowly push open the door and am granted with the vision of Trevor's bare ass thrusting into a woman who's heels I instantly recognize because I complimented them just last week.

I struggle to stay upright and not drop the basket from my shock, but the longer I stare without them aware that I'm watching, the more uncomfortable and emotional I become. I contemplate saying something, but then decide against it.

I knew in my gut something wasn't right between us. I'd been choosing to ignore the signs.

The lack of sex.

His need to work late lately.

The over-enthusiastic greetings I would get from his secretary every time I'd see her.

The last thing I wanted was for them to see the look of shock and disgust on my face, the confirmation that what they've done behind my back has affected me at all.

Fuck that. No one gets that satisfaction.

Instead, I quietly return the door to the cracked position I found it in, turn on my heels, and make my way back to my car.

Tears fall the moment I sit in the driver's seat. But they're not so much tears of sadness, but more of anger and regret, regret that I've spent almost the last entire year of my life with a man who couldn't see what he had in front of him.

I'm a catch, a well-educated woman who takes care of her body, a woman who loved him with every fiber of my being and *chose him over any other man.*

*Fuck this. I'm done.*

*I race home and find as many bags and empty suitcases that I can find in our townhouse. I shove clothing and dishes, movies and mementos from home, and anything else I can't live without into my car, and take off for the highway, never looking back.*

*"Mom," I choke through my tears when she picks up the phone.*

*"Baby, what is it? You never call this late," she whispers, making me think I woke her or Dad is sleeping there next to her.*

*"I'm on my way home," I say as I wipe the moisture from my face and merge onto the freeway.*

*"Okay..." She trails off, not sure of what I'm saying.*

*"Trevor and I are done. I caught him cheating on me. So I'm coming home... for good."*

*"Oh, Olivia. I'm so sorry, honey. Did you kick him in the balls before you left?"*

*That response earns her a chuckle through my cries, but sadly, the moment doesn't last too long.*

*"No, I didn't even let him know I saw."*

*"What? Why? I thought I taught you better than that, Olivia Jane. Always stand up for yourself!" The volume of her voice tells me she must have moved to another part of the house.*

*"I didn't want to give him the satisfaction of knowing I'm hurt. I just wanted out of there. I rushed home and packed up my stuff and started driving."*

*My mother lets out a long breath. "Okay, well, how long will you be?"*

*I glance down at my phone on the dash of the car. "GPS says I'll be there around one in the morning. I'm sorry, Mom. I just..."*

*"Don't you dare apologize, Liv. You know you can always come home any time you want. In fact, I just heard that Mr. Kirk retired from the high school. Maybe you should apply? Hell, the timing of this couldn't be more perfect."*

*Shit. My teaching job. I just up and left without thinking* twice. I guess I have a phone call to make in the morning. A sudden family emergency sounds like a legitimate excuse to leave my job without notice. I will miss my students though. Now the guilt of leaving my kids settles in my stomach along with the nausea and hurt.

"Mr. Kirk? The math teacher who was MY teacher when I went there?"

"Yeah. Word on the street is that he won the lottery and gave his notice. Can't blame the man. He's put in his time."

I laugh, the first genuine laugh I've felt in a while. "Yeah, I can't say I blame him either. Well then, I guess I'll call the school first thing in the morning."

"Liv..."

"Yeah, Mom," I clam up again, feeling the next wave of emotion come over me.

"I love you, baby. It's going to be alright."

I sniffle and wipe the snot from my nose with the back of my hand. I'm just all kinds of classy right now.

"I know, Mom. I love you too. I'll see you in a few hours."

"I'll be waiting for you."

I hang up the phone and search for the nearest gas station to stop off for coffee. I have a five-hour drive ahead of me and I'll need all the caffeine I can get.

My contacts stick to my eyes from the tears that keep falling, so I flip down the visor to extract them, then dig my glasses out of my purse. I glance in the mirror to wipe the mascara stains from my cheeks, blow my nose into a napkin I found in my glove box, and exit the car in search of caffeine and hopefully, some direction in my life.

I feel like I over-reacted, leaving my entire life behind in a matter of an hour, the life I've spent the last nine years building. Northern California was my home, the place I went to college, established my career, and where I ultimately thought I would build roots and start my family. But after seeing Trevor wrecking everything we'd spent the last year building, the last place I wanted to be was *there.*

*I guess it looks like Emerson Falls is calling my name again —my real home, the place I was raised in and grew up wanting to leave so badly. Hopefully, when I arrive, I'll feel some sense that this was the right thing to do.*

"Hey, baby," my mom glides through the door with bags of groceries, pulling me from my memory of last week.

"Hi, Mom. Here, let me help you," I offer while reaching out to relieve her of a few bags.

"Clara. Perry. So good to see you girls again." My mom smiles at two of my best friends. Getting to see these women more often is one of the few positive things to occur from my new circumstances.

"You too, Mrs. Walsh," Perry greets my mom with a hug, followed by Clara.

"We hate to run, but I've got to get back to my office for a conference call, and Perry has to go pick up her kids from school. But we'll see you and Amy at the bar later tonight, right?" Clara explains as they both go to gather their purses. Amy, the fourth leg of our pack, couldn't help this afternoon since her husband wasn't home and all of her kids aren't in school yet. But I know she'll be joining us for drinks later, more than eager for some adult interaction.

"Yes. I'll meet you there. I hope their tequila is stocked because I'm in the mood to forget everything right now."

"Don't worry. We'll help you forget that asshole," Clara confirms before kissing me on the cheek and following Perry out of my front door with a wave.

"It sure is nice to see those girls again. I can't believe how grown-up you all are now," my mom declares while starting to unload the food she bought for me. Even as a thirty-one-year-old woman, my mom still feels the innate need to take care of me.

I watch her move gracefully around my kitchen, stocking the cupboards and organizing fruits and vegetables on the shelves of my fridge. Her dark hair has streaks of grey in it and the lines around her eyes have become deeper since I'd seen her last. My parents are getting older and getting more time with them now that I'm home is something I can't complain about.

"Yup. Everyone's grown up and married and having children, and I'm running away from a man that couldn't keep his dick in his pants," I say sarcastically as I help my mom with the last few items to be put away.

"Liv, there's nothing wrong with where you're at in your life right now. In fact, I'm glad things didn't work out with Trevor."

"Really?" I question since this is the first time I've heard her speak negatively about him.

She nods in confirmation. "Yes. I didn't want to say anything while you were together because I trust you and know that if things progressed with you two, I didn't want you to feel uncomfortable about how your father and I truly felt about him. But deep down we kind of felt that something was off there."

I feel the tears threaten to rise again for the umpteenth time in the last week. My lips start to tremble while I fight for control, but ultimately the drops fall as I sag down onto a stool at my kitchen counter.

"Liv," my mom soothes me with her soft voice as she comes around the cabinets and wraps her arms around me. "Why are you crying?"

I sniffle and gain some composure before spilling my thoughts. "Because I'm mad at myself, Mom. I knew there was something off too, but I didn't listen to my gut like you've always taught me to do. I guess... I guess I wanted so badly to believe that it was all in my head, that the time I had invested in our relationship was worth trying to overcome the doubt I felt. But then when I saw him fucking her... I wasn't even angry with him... well, that's not true. I was and still am pissed at him. But I'm more angry with myself."

"Liv, you are human, baby. You're going to make mistakes…"

My tears are pouring now, emptying my sorrow and relinquishing the blame I've put on myself since that night. "I hate feeling like I failed, Mom. I mean, I tend to excel in everything else I do in life! I graduated at the top of my class in both high school and college. I kick ass at my job and have built a reputation as a strong teacher. I'm confident and work hard for everything I've ever achieved. I'm strong-willed and not afraid to stand up for myself. So why can't I succeed in love? Why am I thirty-one and still single? And why have I let a man's actions affect me this much?"

My mother wipes tears from my cheeks and brushes my deep red hair off of my face, staring down into my eyes in the way only a mother can. Her gaze offers me acceptance as I list my faults to the only person I know who won't judge me. I know I could vent to my friends, but they expect me to be the same Olivia I've always been… collected and focused, and definitely not one to cry over a man.

But here, right now—I don't feel like that Olivia. I feel like a woman whose fears are weighing on me. I feel like this unrealistic pressure I put on myself is making me crumble and shatter.

"Baby, this pain you feel right now is only momentary. This heartbreak you're feeling right now may have saved you from years of self-doubt and betrayal. Be grateful for the lesson that jerk has given you and move on with your life. He was a weed infiltrating your mind and heart. Rip him out and let the flowers continue to grow. You are a beautiful, intelligent, and generous woman who will find a man that cherishes you one day. Believe me—when you find that man, you'll want to get it right with him."

I struggle to smile at my mom, her words offering me some solace during my breakdown. Sometimes a woman can only handle so much before she breaks, before all the thoughts of self-doubt she's been tucking away are fighting to bubble up and over the threshold she keeps them buried under.

Being a perfectionist to the core, in moments like this where I feel like I'm failing, the anxiety and fear tend to overtake my mind. My battered heart and soul tell me that I'm not meant to walk this life alone. But I also feel this pressure from society and from myself to find that person. I think that's what kills me the most about leaving Trevor. It's not that I lost him, it's that I lost the time I invested in him. And I lost direction in my life.

Trevor and I met through his family's winery. I was there on a tour with a group of people from work. Teachers like to let loose on the weekends and have fun too, you know? We were buzzed and high on the smell of cedar and grapes when he walked into the tasting room and asked how our group was enjoying the wine. After small talk and a few more glasses, he offered me a private tour, showing me the behind-the-scenes look at the making of the deep red liquid. Being a wine connoisseur, I ate up the opportunity to absorb any information he shared, and then he asked me for my number before our group left.

He was charming, good-looking in that boy-next-door kind of way with dark hair and green eyes. But his smile was devious, in a way that was so alluring, yet also screamed of mischief.

I should have known he was capable of betrayal—of lying and cheating and wreaking havoc on my self-esteem.

"Thanks, Mom. I know you're right. I just really want to find me again. I feel like I've lost a piece of myself in the past few months, and I'm not sure how to rediscover it."

"You need to let loose, have some fun. Find joy in the little things again. Remember how much you loved to dance? Maybe find a class to take or... well, maybe just start by getting really drunk tonight and see how you feel in the morning." She shrugs her shoulders suggestively, which makes me laugh.

"Mom!"

"What? You're thirty-one, not fifty. And hell, even if you were fifty, I'd still say go for it. Get drunk. Flirt. Maybe have some hot revenge sex and take out your anger on another man's dick?"

My jaw drops to the floor. "Mother! When did you become so vulgar? I feel like I don't even know the woman who's standing in front of me right now!"

My mother chuckles while stepping away from me and opening the box with my dishes thrown inside.

"Your mom isn't as innocent as you might think, Liv," she teases while stacking plates in the cupboard.

"Oh, my God. Please stop right there before you tell me anything I can't unhear," I shake my head, about to plug my ears.

She comes back over to me and rests her hands on my shoulders.

"Be the woman I raised you to be. It's okay to cry, but don't live there in that pain. And don't punish yourself for not seeing who Trevor really was. You still need to trust your gut and keep an open mind. But right now, try to let the positive aspects of this shine through. You're back home, you're near your best friends and your family again, and you get to start a new job back where you went to school. You have so much to be proud of Liv. And don't forget that the people who truly love you will always have your back."

She kisses my forehead and brings a genuine smile to my face for the first time in days.

"I love you, Mom," I whisper through tears of happiness and gratitude.

"I love you too, Liv."

"And I plan on getting pretty drunk tonight and having fun as you said. I think I just really need to blow off some steam."

"I agree. Don't think, just feel. But remember, hangovers are way worse after thirty," she chuckles before resuming her task.

"Ugh. Don't remind me."

# CHAPTER 4

Olivia

"To having the gang all back together!"

The four of us—my best friends since high school—clank our shot glasses together before slamming the tequila back with full force.

"God, that crap is awful! How do you drink that?" Amy asks before gaging with her mouth closed, her fist closed over her lips.

"No one said it has to taste good," Clara replies. "It just needs to get the job done."

"That's right! Tequila always gets the job done. I know I'll definitely forget about that douchebag before the night is over," I add before taking a sip of my beer. I know I shouldn't mix beer and liquor, but tonight, I'm giving a big middle finger to all the rules.

"I can't believe you're back home. This is just so crazy..." Perry shakes her head while sipping her white wine. Her white satin blouse clings to her curves as she sits on the stool next to me. Her blonde hair is sleekly pulled back in a low bun with not one hair out of place, and her blue eyes sparkle from the dim light hanging above us. For a mom of two, she carries herself with such poise and always looks so put together that I wonder if she secretly cries in the pantry while eating Reese's peanut butter cups after her husband and kids have gone to bed.

"Yeah, well, I didn't think it would happen either... yet, here I am!" I exclaim while throwing my hands up in the air.

"Fuck him, Liv," Clara chimes in again. "That guy was a douche if he didn't know what he had and let you go." The tequila is definitely hitting us all as the honesty in our words becomes far too real.

"Correction. He didn't let me go. I left," I hiccup as I signal the bartender for another round of shots, twisting so quickly that my deep red hair almost smacks Perry in the face.

"Yeah, because you walked in on him banging his secretary!" Clara shouts so loudly that the entire bar turns their heads in our direction.

"Jesus, Clara! Shut the fuck up! I don't need the entire town to know why I'm home, okay? It's embarrassing enough that I couldn't keep a man happy... I don't need everyone else knowing that too."

I know the alcohol is hitting me hard when I start to drop F-bombs and feel the need to fight someone.

"Don't. Don't play that game where you put all the blame on yourself, Olivia." Perry cuts me off while pointing her finger in my face. The tequila is definitely hitting her too. "Trevor has control of where he puts his dick. And by him choosing to put it somewhere other than you, that's on him. That is *not* your fault."

I feel the tears start to bubble up again but decide to drown them in more beer. I've cried enough over the last week, mostly on the long drive home from northern California back to Emerson Falls, and I got the worst of it out earlier with my mom. But tonight, I refuse to give Trevor any more of my tears.

I stare across the bar, observing the surrounding crowd, wondering what demons everyone else in here is fighting tonight. Most people gravitate to alcohol for one of two reasons: to celebrate, or like in my case, to forget. I know I'll be okay. I'll land on my feet like I always do. But tomorrow I'll pull myself together. Tonight, I'm giving myself permission to ditch some of the pressure I feel pushing down on my shoulders, the pressure that's only there because of my own perfectionist tendencies and a ticking time clock.

"Earth to Liv! Are you still there?" Amy waves her hand in front of my face, trying to gain my attention back. "She looks like my kids right now when they zone out watching Paw Patrol," she turns and mumbles to Clara and Perry from the corner of her mouth, her light-brown shoulder-length hair swishing as she moves.

"Yeah, sorry. What did you say?" I shake my head and turn back to face the three people who know me better than myself.

Amy, Clara, Perry, and I met our freshman year in high school in our first-period Geography class. The four of us sat at the same table and instantly bonded. From that moment on, there was nothing that could have penetrated our friendship —not boys or money, or leaving to go to college.

Clara and Perry both left Emerson Falls for school, like me, but Amy stayed behind and married her high school sweetheart. She still went to college, but now she stays home and takes care of her three kids under the age of five. Her husband works in finance and can support the family on his income alone, but Amy rarely gets adult interaction. The fact that she came out tonight to support me is shocking in itself. Of course, the three of us won't mention the giant stain on her mint green shirt or the fact that she's wearing two different-ent colored socks, because Amy can barely keep her head on straight these days. She needs tonight out as much as the rest of us.

Clara is an advertising executive now who travels for work. She manages multiple accounts for her company and enjoys her never boring single life. She's also the most out-spoken of the four of us and will beat anyone to a pulp if our happiness is compromised. It's a good thing Trevor is still back in California, or she'd be on his front doorstep waiting to punch him in the balls like that girl in the movie, What Happens in Vegas... you know the one who's Cameron Diaz's best friend that punches her ex in the nuts when he answers the door and she yells in his face, "You know why!"? Yeah, that's Clara.

Perry majored in business and married her college sweetheart before returning to Emerson Falls to start their family. She's the typical type-A mom who always has her shit together and makes parenting and marriage look like a breeze. The woman could run the world from her phone, along with her parenting and lifestyle blog she runs from home. She's always put together, never shows her stress, and the three of us genuinely think she's a robot. But she's our robot friend who can seriously schedule or plan anything with the press of a button. And we love her for it.

"So what happens now, Olivia?" Amy continues, taking a sip of her strawberry daiquiri.

One of the cocktail waitresses comes by with another tray full of tequila shots.

"We drink... that's what happens now." I smile through clenched teeth, hoping the alcohol kicks in quickly to numb some of the pain. I certainly feel better after letting out my innermost thoughts with my mom, but a little alcohol will definitely speed along the process.

I know that leaving was the right thing because I would never tolerate being cheated on and sticking around. But it doesn't make the sting go away any faster. I'm a strong, confident woman who doesn't need a man to be happy. And realistically, Trevor and I haven't been happy for a few months now, mainly since we moved in together. It's not like I was asking for a ring, but I felt like maybe the commitment was too much for him. Whatever. I don't want a man who runs from commitment. In fact, I don't want a man for anything other than what's in his pants for a very long time. Maybe some time on my own, or some revenge sex, is exactly what the doctor ordered. My mother may be on to something.

The four of us toss back two more shots before the night really starts to turn.

"So you start at the high school on Monday then?" Clara slurs her words across the table at me.

"Yup. Mr. Kirk won the lottery and just quit. The timing couldn't have worked out better for me," I chuckle as I start to sway to the music while seated on my bar stool.

"No shit," Clara agrees. "If I won the lottery, you bitches would never see me again, that's for sure."

"Oh, don't act like you'd ditch us," Perry chimes in, a tad more drunk than I've seen her in years. She's mixing wine and tequila, so I can only imagine what she's going to feel like in the morning. "You'd have to give us all some of your winnings so we could travel around the world with you. You'd end up too lonely otherwise. You know you can't live without us," she blows a kiss in Clara's direction, as Clara reaches up to grab it and then smothers her mouth with her hand. The four of us burst out in laughter.

"You're right. I love you, bitches! In fact, I think I might miss you too much if I go to the bathroom by myself. Who's coming with me?" She shouts as she stands and tries to gain her balance.

Amy looks a shade of light green as she rises from her stool and grips the round table we're sitting around. She's only taken two shots, but I can't even remember the last time I've seen her drink.

"Oh no, I know that look. That's senior prom waiting to happen all over again. You guys better get her to the bathroom now," I say while pointing my finger at her.

"Shit. Come on, Amy. Let's hurry," Perry lures her away while Clara supports her on the other side by her arm.

I watch my friends usher Amy down the hall before I turn my attention back to the T.V. above the bar as today's headlines scroll across the screen from the local news.

It feels surreal being back in Emerson Falls. Besides coming home for holidays and the occasional vacation, my visits have been scarce since I left for U.C. Davis and never looked back. A full academic scholarship took me almost six hours away from home, but I loved every minute. College was the challenge I craved in high school, where I could finally channel my inner math nerd and find people who shared my passion for education. Becoming a math teacher was always my aspiration, and when an intern position opened up near Davis right after I graduated, I took it at the ripe old age of twenty-two.

I just never thought that fate would lead me back home to teach at my alma mater nine years later. But here I am, one weekend left between me and a new job, walking into a classroom full of kids more than a month into the school year. I certainly have my work cut out for me, even if this is my ninth year of teaching.

Suddenly, Jon Bon Jovi's 'You Give Love a Bad Name' blares overhead through the speakers, igniting a fire in my body as I bounce and sway to the music on my stool. Man, I love this song! And as I listen to the words, I can't help but laugh and think of Trevor and his stupid ass and how he's made me question falling in love again for a *very* long time.

Instead, I shove him out of my brain and all of his missed calls and pathetic text messages he's sent this week asking for me back, swearing that he's sorry and that he can't lose me. Too late for that buddy. I'm done. Fool me once, shame on you, and you'll never get the chance to fool me again.

I shove out the long to-do list lying on my kitchen counter in my new apartment, filled with boxes and suitcases thrown in every corner. I shove out the monumental task I have ahead of me on Monday of entering a new classroom with students I've never met and a month's worth of curriculum to catch up on.

Closing my eyes, I lose myself in the song, mouthing the words with a little too much animation, but whatever. I truly don't care what people might think. I just want to get lost in the words, shut out the distractions, and finish the song with no interruptions. I need to let loose, have some fun, and feel human again.

"You know people can see you, right?"

The rasp of the voice behind me sparks instant fury in my veins as my eyes pop open and I prepare to give this person a piece of my mind. I become keenly aware that someone thought it was so important to judge me that they interrupted my performance and interrupted my jam—and now thanks to the third and fourth tequila shot, I'm more than irritated.

"Listen buddy," I start to turn and give this guy a few choice words not suitable around the young children I teach every day—but as his face comes into view, I forget the anger and irritation I just felt as it's replaced with pure lust.

A wave of heat spreads over my entire body from my chest, where my heart is beating as fast as an elephant stampede, down to the tips of my toes.

*Holy shit! Where have men like this been hiding?*

*Apparently in Emerson Falls, Oregon.*

I swallow hard and then narrow my eyes back at him.

*Focus, Olivia. This guy just interrupted Bon Jovi. Let him have it!*

"Not that it's any of your business, but I don't care that people can see me. When Jon Bon Jovi sings, you dance, and you don't interrupt. This song is a classic," I lift my eyebrow at him in a challenge.

The man who was so eager to care about what I look like now has no words. He just stands there and stares, his jet black hair stuck up in that messy yet perfectly styled way, and his matching short beard frames his long face and perfect lips. His narrow eyes size me up as I lock my gaze with him intently, not blinking so he knows I'm up for a dispute. His dark brown orbs with flecks of gold flicker back and forth between my hazel eyes as we study each other.

I feel my heartbeat pick up rapidly again, hammering against my rib cage as I sit up taller to protect myself, hoping he can't see the effect he's having on me. My vagina clenches when his lips curl up on one side in a crooked grin, and that's when I surrender to the fact that this man is hot.

Not just nice to look at, but dangerous to your heart and mind kind of hot, full of the potential to shatter you into frag- ments of the person you were before him. Who knows what you'll look like after.

"You know, I'd have to agree with you," he says surpris- ingly, making me sit back in shock and confusion, even though I fight hard to hide that from my face. I really thought this guy was about to fight me on this.

"Glad we see eye-to-eye then," I say smugly, turning back around to grab my drink before realizing my beer is empty.

"Shit," I mumble before sitting up taller to get the atten- tion of the bartender.

"Here. Let me buy you a drink so then you can tell me just how many other songs shouldn't be interrupted," he teases before lifting his hand in the air and signaling the older man behind the bar who I can only assume is the owner.

"I can buy my own drink," I argue as he takes a seat at one of the empty stools at our table. I glance around him quickly to check for my friends, wondering what's taking so long in the bathroom. Amy must really be sick.

"Expecting your friends back?" He asks, lifting his beer to his lips as I watch them curl around the rim of his glass.

*Jesus, why do men always get the best lips? The ones that women pay good money for? I wonder what he can do with that mouth...*

"Yes, and they're very protective of me. I don't know if you have what it takes to take them on too," I shrug as the waitress sets down my beer. "Thank you," I kindly say in her direction before turning my daggered eyes back to the man who intrigues me more than he should.

"Are we about to fight? Because I really don't want to get my ass kicked by four women. That wouldn't bode well for my reputation, Red," he smirks as he calls me by a nickname I've heard one-to-many times.

"And what reputation is that?"

"How about we save that for the get-to-know-you portion of the evening?" He questions just as Perry, Clara, and Amy come staggering back to the table.

"I didn't realize we were going to get to know each other..."

He chuckles. "Oh, I think we're about to get to know each other *very* well."

# CHAPTER 5

Kane

"Well, if it isn't the greatest history teacher of all time!" Tony greets me with my signature IPA as I hoist myself onto my regular stool at the bar.

"You always say that Tony, but for all you know I could be the worst teacher on the face of the planet," I reply before quenching my thirst with that first sip of my beer.

"I seriously doubt that, Kane. I may not have seen you in action, but I know how much you love your job. And any teacher that loves that job has to be doing something right."

"Those kids might drive me nuts, but when I see the passion come alive, it's all worth it," I shrug. "And I have a project they're starting on Monday that I hope will spike their interest. Getting teenagers excited about studying history is a tough job."

Tony chuckles as he wipes down the counter in front of him, slinging the bar towel over his shoulder when he finishes. "I can only imagine. Any more nightmares?" He lowers his voice and flicks his eyes up to meet mine in a concerning manner.

I shake my head while downing more of my beer. "Not lately."

"Good," he grunts. "Just know they'll always pop up when you least expect them to."

I nod, choosing not to continue our conversation on that topic. Even though Tony understands what time overseas can do to a man, it's not something I like discussing in public, let alone a crowded bar on a Friday evening.

"The place is packed tonight, Tony," I say before spinning around to take in the crowd. Usually this many people would deter me from staying too long, but as my eyes move around the room, they pause on the deep red hair cascading down the back of a woman that I can only describe as mesmerizing.

Her back is to me of course, but her curves are on full display, cinching into a tiny waist before continuing down to an ass only a true man can appreciate. Dark blue jeans hug her legs and a simple black tank clenches her torso as she sways to the music all alone at her table.

"Yeah, plenty of people to talk to. You should go mingle." Tony nudges my shoulder from over the bar, pushing me off balance so I slide off my stool. Luckily, I land on my feet before I make a fool out of myself, turning around sharply to glare at him.

"Yeah, not interested," I grunt before fixing myself back on my seat, ignoring the inkling in my brain to turn around and look for the redhead again.

"You sure? 'Cause it seems to me you found something, or should I say, someone, that sparked your interest there for a minute."

"Yeah, well, women are trouble. And my life has been trouble-free for a while now, Tony. No sense in changing that."

"Her friends will be back soon. Go talk to her. That woman doesn't look like trouble. That woman looks like fun. Any woman who can move her body like that knows how to let loose. Lord knows you could use some fun, Kane."

I veer up at him with a glare. "I have fun," I say, trying not only to convince Tony but also myself of that fact.

Tony huffs. "Sure, okay. Name the last time you did something fun?" He challenges me, crossing his arms over his chest, resting on his gut.

I take a minute to study him, his dark grey beard and

matching hair slicked back on his head. His eyes framed by hard-earned wrinkles zero in on me like a father who's caught his son in a lie. Only I have a dad, but my dad doesn't scare me as much as Tony does.

I sigh. "Fine. You're right. I can't remember the last time I 'had fun'," I throw up quotations around the last two words, mocking him with a roll of my eyes. Normally, I would answer with riding my motorcycle—but after Natasha, I haven't even had the urge to do that.

Twisting around to glance in her direction again, I notice the woman moving even more suggestively now, igniting an interest in me even deeper than before.

As I stand, I grab my beer and turn back around to acknowledge Tony. "Here's to some fun." I raise my glass in my hand in his direction before heading towards the redhead. What the hell... what have I got to lose?

Reaching her table, I stand behind her and watch her for a moment, contemplating my opening line, and then I opt for teasing her a bit. I want to see just how fiery this woman can be.

"You know people can see you, right?"

Her hips abruptly stop and her shoulders tense as she turns around and shoots me a glare that only a pissed-off woman can perfect.

But when I see her face for the first time, I realize that this girl is more than just fun. She's exactly what I thought she'd be in the first place.

Trouble.

The deep burgundy of her hair shimmers in the light from the lamps above us as it frames her face. Forrest colored eyes narrow back at me above pursed lips, so full and plump that I wonder what they'd feel like against mine. Her chest is just as curvy as her body, showing a classy amount of cleavage from the top of her tank. Her shoulders are square and she straightens her spine before lacing her reply with venomous confidence.

"Not that it's any of your business, but I don't care that people can see me. When Jon Bon Jovi sings, you dance, and you don't interrupt. This song is a classic," she lifts her eyebrow at me.

Standing there watching her, I let her words sink in. Rarely do you see a woman so blatantly secure in who she is or how she feels. Granted, I've only known her for about thirty seconds now, but the energy she gives off is no bullshit. She's sure and confident, which is a total turn-on. I feel blood rush south as I offer her a sly smirk and steer the conversation in a different direction.

"You know, I'd have to agree with you," I reply, which catches her off guard. Her face immediately softens, but she recovers her icy glare.

"Glad we see eye-to-eye then," she fires back before turning around to grab her empty drink.

"Here. Let me buy you a drink so then you can tell me just how many other songs shouldn't be interrupted," I tease before lifting my hand in the air and signaling Tony behind the bar, whose eyes have been glued on me since I walked over here. A slight tip of his head lets me know he understands our need for a refill and catches one of the cocktail waitresses on her next trip.

"I can buy my own drink," she argues as I take a seat at one of the empty stools at her table. I know her friends will be back soon, but now that I've seen this woman up close, there's no way I'm ready for this conversation to end this quickly. Tony's right. I need to have some fun, and by the way this woman is so easily offended and quick to fight, I'd say she'd certainly entertain me for a bit.

"Expecting your friends back?" I ask as I take a sip of my

beer. I watch her eyes follow my glass and study my mouth while I sling back the last gulp and settle my empty glass next to hers.

"Yes, and they're very protective of me. I don't know if you have what it takes to take them on too." She shrugs as the waitress sets down our beers. "Thank you," she addresses Cindy the cocktail waitress in the sweetest tone I've heard from her yet, then turns her daggered eyes back to me. I can't tell if she's just really pissed off that I interrupted her or if she's just keeping her guard up.

"Are we about to fight? Because I really don't want to get my ass kicked by four women. That wouldn't bode well for my reputation, Red," I smirk as I call her by the first nickname that comes to mind. It's not original, but it fits her to a tee.

When you think of the color red, you think of fire and passion, lust and power. And this woman is putting off all of those vibes and more. Not to mention, the deep red of her hair is gorgeous—clearly not natural—but eye-catching, nonetheless.

"And what reputation is that?" She shoots back, watching my eyes as I peruse her face.

"How about we save that for the get-to-know-you portion of the evening?" I jest as her friends stagger back up to the table.

"I didn't realize we were going to get to know each other…"

I chuckle. "Oh, I think we're about to get to know each other *very* well." I raise my glass to my mouth as one of the women chimes in, interrupting our conversation.

"Hey, sorry it took so long, but Amy is in pretty bad shape," the professionally dressed blonde nods her head toward a woman who can barely stand.

"Shit, Amy. I'm sorry. I never should have made you do

tequila shots with us. I know you never drink," Red consoles her friend, which shows me yet another side to her. Nice to know she's not just pissed off at everyone in the world.

Her overly drunk friend just sways with her eyes closed, as the other two women hold her up.

"Hey, who's this?" The brunette turns to me, pointing a finger in my direction.

Red turns to me with her signature glare before twisting back to her friend. "This is someone who thinks it's polite to interrupt people while they're dancing to Bon Jovi," she juts her thumb in my direction, which makes me chuckle.

"Oh, shit, you interrupted her while she was dancing? Or singing?" The brunette leans into me, then throws her hand in the air. "Doesn't matter. No one interrupts her while she's jamming."

"See?" Red turns to me and smirks.

"Wait… you look kinda familiar. Do I know you?" The brunette points at me again.

I narrow my eyes at her and give her a once-over. Nope, definitely haven't slept with her. I've probably just seen her around town.

"Don't think so," I shake my head. "But I was just trying to get to know your friend here," I toss my noggin in Red's direction.

"Well, we need to get Amy home," the blonde pipes in.

"Yeah, and my boss just called and I have to get on an earlier flight tomorrow to be in Philadelphia by nine, so I need to jet too," the brunette adds, then turns to Red and covers her mouth with her hand to shield her words from me, attempting to whisper but failing miserably.

"You want me to call you an Uber too? Or are you staying?" She tilts her head in my direction, widening her eyes in concern.

*Subtle.*

Red turns to me, sliding her eyes slowly down my body and then back up to my face, peaking her tongue out slightly to lick her lips. The movement makes me swallow hard. Fuck, this woman is making my heart race and my dick wake up from his celibate slumber, which would be slightly embarrassing if I attempt to stand right now.

She turns back to her friends. "I think I'm going to hang out for a bit longer. I can get my own ride. Amy, feel better babe. Sorry again," she lifts her hand to caress her friend's shoulder before she mumbles something incoherent.

The brunette digs in her purse and grabs her phone and then holds it up to my face and snaps a picture of me with the brightest flash I've ever seen, leaving me dazed and confused as I sit back and lift my eyebrows at her.

"What the fuck was that for?" I growl a little too aggressively.

"That was in case she goes missing, so I know who to send the police after," she smiles evilly before gathering up their drunk friend and kissing Red on the cheek. "Be careful and have fun. You deserve it. Love you."

Red reciprocates the affection and nods at her. "Oh, I plan on it," she confirms and then turns back to me, lifting her beer to her lips. "Now where were we…"

# CHAPTER 6

Olivia

"Well, you were about to tell me about all the songs you should never interrupt..." Mr. Mysterious replies, holding his beer in his hands between his legs.

"That's easy. All of them," I shrug and then smile wide at him. I'm definitely buzzed, but the alcohol isn't the only thing that's making my mind fuzzy.

He laughs at me, a deep belly laugh that shows his brilliant smile as pearly white teeth peek out from under his perfect lips framed by that rugged beard. *God, that beard.* I'm not usually one who gravitates towards men with facial hair, but something about it makes me even hungrier for him.

The vibrations that resonated from the bottom of his stomach as he let out one of the most jovial but deep laughs I've ever heard traveled all the way down to the tips of my toes, making them curl just slightly in my black boots as my feet perch on the rungs of my stool.

This man—Mr. Mysterious—was like a sinful, fluffy, covered in maple syrup and sprinkled with a dash of cinnamon stack of pancakes—loaded with regretful carbs that you try to convince yourself you don't need, but have to have just one bite of.

Only these pancakes are covered in red and black checkered flannel, dirty washed jeans, the perfect amount of dark facial hair to constitute a beard, and served to you on a platter of thick muscle and corded forearms showcasing those sexy veins that really shouldn't be sexy but are, scented with the smell of pine and fresh rain, like he just stepped out of the forest.

Rugged, rustic, and enough to put you in a sugar coma if you decide to dive in fork-first, soaking up the sugary river of sweetness, basking in the flavor of the bronze liquid and meltiness of the cake as it hits your tongue.

All of a sudden I have the strongest craving for a stack of pancakes served up on the naked chest of the man in front of me.

I swallow hard, desperately trying to fight off the need to sink my teeth into his muscles, or better yet, that plump lip that's taunting me as he pulls it between his teeth, studying me while I study him. All I feel is a physical need, the need to forget everything that's gone wrong in my life this past week and lose myself in some much needed physical pleasure.

It's all there, and tonight, I feel like maybe—for once in my life—I might need to give in to the carbs.

This man is nothing like Trevor.

*No. Stop that, Liv.*

No comparing.

Not tonight.

*Go with your gut.*

Well, my gut is telling me I'd like to ride this man's face.

"So clearly this is some rule of yours then, Red?" He asks once our staring match has ended.

"I just hate when a good song gets interrupted, especially one you know all the words to. When that chorus comes on and you know you're going to nail it, but then someone or something cuts you off, it's more infuriating than getting interrupted during a good orgasm."

Mr. Mysterious chokes on his beer as he looks up and me

and laughs, shocked by the words that just came out of my mouth.

"Did you just compare singing a song to an orgasm?"

"I mean, everyone has the things that they feel passionate about. For me, that's music and orgasms."

My flannel-covered pal shakes his head and laughs at me before swallowing hard. His eyes peruse my body before settling back on my face.

"I guess I can appreciate that," he says, the deep rasp of his voice coating my body in tingles. I wonder what kind of orgasms this man can hand out.

*God, Liv. You sound like a slut right now.*

*No, I'm just drunk and horny. Sue me.*

*Shut up and for the love of God, stop drinking.*

*Mind your own business, sub-conscience. I have given myself permission to have fun tonight, and if that means straddling the man in front of me, then so be it.*

"So tell me something about you, since we're supposed to be getting to know each other," I tease. "Like, maybe your name?"

"Well, I don't know your name yet either," he fires back.

"True, but you gave me a nickname. It wasn't the most original one I've ever heard though."

"It just seemed appropriate," he says.

"So, what do I call you then?" I ask flirtatiously, the need to know more about him a sudden necessity I feel deep in my bones.

"How about you call me by a nickname too?"

I raise an eyebrow at him. "So, we're not going to exchange real names?"

He nods. "Seems more fun this way."

I smirk at him before taking a sip of my drink. "Okay then, what shall I call you?"

He looks away for a moment in contemplation before focusing back on me.

"Garrison," he says, which completely catches me by surprise.

"Garrison?" I ask, trying to clarify that I heard him right.

"Yup. It's what the guys called me from my time in the Army. It's uh... it's actually my last name."

"That's not a nickname then."

He grins in a boyish way. "Yeah, you're right, but it was the first thing I could think of."

"An Army man, huh? I can see that," I offer as I peruse his body again. The sight of him sitting casually in front of me is sending sharp pangs of desire between my legs the more I take in his entirety. You just don't see men like him anymore. And the thought of him dressed in Army greens and combat boots stirs up a fantasy I didn't realize I had.

"Yeah, I gave eight years, then got out," he says before looking away. I feel like he's done with the subject, so I let it go. I know little about that life, but I've heard countless stories about how serving affects the men and women once they're home.

"So, Garrison. What brings you into the bar then tonight?"

"The same thing that brings me back each week... having a few beers to relax after a grueling week."

"Yeah, I've had a tough week too. So what do you do that is so grueling?"

Before Mr. Mysterious can answer, a loud crash of glass booms through the bar. Both of us turn our heads in the direction of the scene, fixating on two servers who collided, their trays full of drinks smashing into pieces and leaving one hell of a mess.

"Wow, that sucks," I say just as the man in front of me goes to stand.

"Care to play some pool?" He offers his hand to me, which I take a little too eagerly. The connection of our skin touching sends a flutter to my belly, the tingles I felt before from just talking to him are now traveling all over my body with a fury. He takes my hand and leads me to the corner of the bar where four pool tables are situated. One table seems to have been recently abandoned, so we place our drinks on the high-top table next to it as my mystery man begins to rack the balls.

"You've played before, right?" He asks while hunched over the table. I watch the muscles in his forearms flex while he moves the balls into the plastic triangle. I've never been one to admire forearms before, but on this guy, they're quickly becoming one of my favorite features.

Little does this man know, but I was quite the pool shark back in college. Being a math person, I understand the geometry of the game. It's all about the angles, but he doesn't need to know that.

The last time I played pool was against Trevor, and I beat him so badly, I swear he was going to cry.

I shake my head, struggling to throw the thoughts of my ex out and focus and the perfect specimen of distraction in front of me. I've never been one to use one man to get over another, but hey, there's a first time for everything, right?

"Yeah, I've played before, but it's been a while."

"Care to make it interesting?" He glances up at me, smiling mischievously.

"What are you thinking?" I pop my hip out, resting my hand there with some much-added sass. This guy has no idea who he's up against.

"Next round of drinks is on the loser?" He stands once the balls are neatly tucked into a triangle, reaching around to grab two pool sticks from the rack.

I purse my lips in thought, then an idea pops into my head.

"If you win, I'll buy the next round," I nod, which he seems to like. "But if I win, you owe me a dance."

He instantly straightens his spine and then eyes me suspiciously.

"A dance?"

"Yeah. Since you were so intent on interrupting mine from before, I need a full song with no interruptions in redemption. And I only feel it's fitting for you to have to join me."

He takes a moment to mull over my suggestion before reaching his hand out to solidify our stakes with a handshake. His confidence is cute, and I can't wait to wipe that smirk off of his face in a moment.

"You can break," I offer as he hands me my stick.

"You sure?"

"Yup. Go for it, Garrison," I tease as he smiles over at me. That smile is making me warm and wet between my legs. But I have to give him a chance at least before I wipe the floor with him.

The delicious man in front of me bends over the pool table, tucking his stick in close to his body as he narrows his eyes in focus on the balls in front of him. All I can think about is what his face would look like staring down at me beneath him, or better yet, looking up at me from between my legs.

He pulls back and slams his stick into the cue ball, breaking the formation effortlessly as the balls scatter all over the green felt. A striped ball finds its way into a pocket as he declares he'll take stripes for the game.

I nod, watching him peruse the table searching for his next shot. Once he finds one he deems worthy, he hunches over again and pelts another ball into a corner pocket.

"Damn, looks like I might not get that dance after all."

He gazes over at me, shrugging with confidence. "I wouldn't make a bet I didn't feel confident about," he says as he takes his next shot, but misses.

Sauntering over to the table, I grab the chalk from the edge of the wooden frame, rubbing it on top of the nub on the end of my stick. Placing it back down, I lock eyes with him, searching for any indication that I shouldn't keep this game going.

"Neither would I," I fire back, turning to approach the table, adding a little more swing to my hips for his enjoyment.

I've never been a shy woman. I've never been one to feel intimidated by a man. But given everything that just happened with Trevor, my confidence is shaken. This man is slowly helping rebuild it though with every perusal of my body and bit of attention he gives me.

I don't even know this guy's entire name. I don't know what he does for a living, where he grew up, if he's respectful to his mom, if he's a serial killer, or if he secretly wears women's underwear for fun.

But if the way he makes my body all hot and bothered is any indication, I'd say my hormones may take the lead tonight. It's been a long time since I've had a down and dirty fuck. Maybe this guy *is* just what I need. And judging by the way he's been eye-fucking me for the past hour, I think we're on the same page.

I lean over to line up my shot, chuckling to myself at how easy this is about to be. I watch his eyes travel all over my body, zeroing in on the ample cleavage my shirt is offering. I laugh and then smack the cue ball, sending the solid ball to sink in the corner pocket.

"Nice shot," he offers while he observes my every move.

"Beginner's luck," I joke as I find my next shot and complete that one with ease.

Garrison watches me as I sink ball after ball, the smile on his face slowly falling as he realizes he's just been played. Once the eight-ball is all that's left, I take a break to gather a sip from my beer as he grins up at me from his seat.

"You hustled me," he confronts me as I stand before him.

"You're the one who raised the stakes. I was honest that it had been a while since I've played, but it's kind of like riding a bike. Well, that and understanding geometry. Playing pool is all about the angles."

"I've noticed. Personally, I like curves a lot more," he says as his eyes shift down my body. I feel the desire radiate from my chest as my heart picks up and beats frantically. God, this man is dangerous.

"Well, let me end this right now so we can get to our dance," I reply, sidestepping his comment, but peering back over my shoulder as I watch his eyes soak up all of my curves. I sure am glad I wore my favorite jeans tonight.

I sink the eight ball in the side pocket with little effort before Garrison grabs my stick and returns both his and mine to the rack.

"Time to pay up," I tease him as he circles his hands around my hips, pulling me in close to his body. The brush of his chest across my breasts make my nipples instantly harden. He leans down to whisper in my ear, the brush of his breath on my skin igniting goosebumps up and down my arms.

"I might have lost at pool, but I feel like I'm the real

winner really, now that I get to put my hands all over you as we dance," he growls as his words resonate in my ear like an aphrodisiac. He stands up tall and then takes my hand, leading me to the dance floor as my legs fight to keep up with him after turning to jello from his words.

The truth is, I feel like we're both about to win our little game tonight.

# CHAPTER 7

Kane

Fun. The whole point of approaching this woman tonight was from Tony's nudge to have a little fun.

But what's transpiring between me and Red is way beyond fun.

It's heat. Desire. Pure lust.

The fire of her hair and her confidence is burning me, but I'm welcoming it. It's been a long time since I've been tempted to touch a flame, and this woman is tempting me with every move she makes.

As soon as we hit the dance floor, Def Leppard's 'Pour Some Sugar on Me' filters overhead, granting me with the biggest smile from the woman that has stolen my attention for the night. I'm never here this late at Tony's, but right now, I'm oblivious to anyone and anything around me besides her.

"Ah! I couldn't have picked a more perfect song for you to owe me a dance to!" She shouts over the music, shimmying her hips to the beat as she approaches me. Her hands land on my shoulders and my palms instinctually find her hips, curving around her waist and following her lead to the beat. I don't consider myself a bad dancer, but it's not something I do very often.

"As long as I can watch you move like this, I'll dance with you all night," I confess, much to my own surprise. She smiles up at me with want in her eyes. I'm not gonna lie. I barely know this woman and I'm already scared of the effect she's having on me. "You've got rhythm, that's for sure."

49

"I used to be a dancer," she offers between her moves. "Now shut up and stop interrupting the song again. Remember, that's what got you into this mess in the first place," she teases before turning around to press her ass into my crotch while she continues to sway her hips.

I laugh. "So if I keep talking, I have to keep dancing with you?" I whisper in her ear as I pull her closer to me, one palm on her stomach and the other on her hip. I feel her fingers dig into my hands as she places hers over mine, clearly affected by my words.

"At this rate, we'll be here all night," she fires back, pressing her ass into me even further. My dick is painfully hard now, a development I'm sure she can feel through her jeans.

"Oh, I don't think we'll last all night. I have other plans for us."

She turns to face me, wrapping her hands around my neck this time. "Is that so? What plans are those, Garrison?" She bats her eyelashes a few times before staring me down.

I toy with how to approach the subject. It's clear there's sexual tension here. We're both feeling it. I know I'm not looking for anything serious, but I can't say she's thinking the same. Although the vibes she's been giving me would definitely suggest she's down for a good time. That's all this needs to be. A physical release. Two adults enjoying each other. A little fun.

"I'm gonna be honest, okay?" I stare down at her, those hazel eyes locked on mine as she nods.

"Please do..."

"I don't do this. I'm a simple guy that keeps to himself most of the time. But clearly there's something here. I'm not looking for anything serious, but if you're down to have some fun tonight, I'm game. From the moment I laid eyes on you, I haven't been able to stop thinking about what you'd sound like as I sink my cock into you. You're sexy, Red. A tease. And

I'd love nothing more than to fuck your brains out."

The corner of her mouth tips up as her eyes bounce back and forth between mine. She rises on her toes and presses her lips to my mouth, the gesture catching me off guard. But as soon as it registers in my brain, my other head takes over and I pull her to me, licking her lips so she'll open up to me.

I swirl my tongue with hers, the heat of her mouth makes my entire body temperature rise as my hands splay across her back and I press her tightly to my chest. Her hands weave up into my hair and pull me down to her so our lips are molded so closely together, it's hard to tell who's in control. And fuck if I care at this point because this woman tastes better than I could have imagined. The hint of beer on her tongue mixed with pent up sexual frustration is enough to make me groan out loud as I continue to assault her mouth with mine.

She claws at my neck, moaning seductively as we continue to kiss. I knew she was trouble. And now that I've tasted her, I need more. I want to see what kind of punishment she can dish out.

I break us apart, resting my forehead on hers as we both fight to refill our lungs with oxygen.

"I don't normally do this either. But fuck it. Tonight I want to play. Let's get out of here," she rasps from the overexertion of our kiss.

I stand up straight, searching for Tony, my eyes landing on him behind the bar as he shakes his head at me with a knowing smirk. Fucker. He knows he was right.

Whatever. I'll take his shit-talking later.

"Close out my tab, Tony," I yell over at him as he nods.

"We'll settle it next week. Have a good night." He waves over at me as I grab Red's hand and usher her out of the bar.

The moment we clear the door, I spin around and push her up against the side of the building, pinning her between the wall and my growing erection.

"How drunk are you?"

"I'm buzzed, but not so drunk that I don't know what I'm getting in to," she answers.

"Did you drive?"

"No, I Ubered with my friends, remember?"

"Right. So, your place?" I growl in her ear as she claws at my shoulders.

"My place is a disaster. I just moved in."

"My place is too far away. I need you. Now."

"If you don't mind the mess, then my place it is," she says before reaching up and taking my bottom lip between her teeth. The faint taste of blood fills my mouth from the deep penetration of her teeth on my lip, which both concerns me and turns me on like never before. There's nothing sexier than a woman who makes it clear what she wants, especially when it comes to sex.

*Fuck, I need this woman. NOW.*

I lead her to my truck, opening the passenger door for her and helping her up inside.

After we're both buckled in, I peel out of the parking lot and follow her directions to an apartment complex I'm vaguely familiar with.

The charcoal blanket of the sky dotted with twinkling stars rests above us, framing the trees that line the roads of this sleepy forest town.

Once we arrive, I follow her up the steps to her door, holding her hips in my hands from behind, kissing and sucking on her neck as she fiddles with her keys to unlock the handle. Once she turns her key and leads me inside, she throws her purse somewhere to the left and then jumps in my arms, wrapping her legs around my waist. I waste no time pinning her up against the door and grinding my erection between her legs as my mouth claims her in a heated and desperate kiss.

It's messy, hot, wet, and wild. Everything I knew this woman would be and more.

Damn, I'm so glad I listened to Tony right now because

watching this woman come undone beneath me will definitely be *fun*.

# CHAPTER 8

Olivia

*Don't think. Just feel.*

Well, I'm pretty sure I couldn't try to *unfeel* the raging hard-on of the man between my legs grinding up against my clit even if I tried. Jesus. With what he's packing, I might not be able to walk tomorrow.

Pressed up against my door, my legs circling his waist, I surrender to Garrison and his mouth, plunging my tongue into his with severe desperation. Hell, the man can kiss and the way his hands feel squeezing my ass as he holds me up makes me itch with anticipation for the way our bare skin will feel against each other in a moment.

"Fuck, Red. Ditch the clothes. Now," he orders, lowering me to the ground as I bend down to unzip my boots, throwing them across my living room full of boxes, the smack of leather against cardboard echoing in the empty space.

I watch him as he reaches down to pull off his boots as well, standing back up to observe me as we both remain there, panting wildly.

My arms reach out for his shirt, my fingers finding the buttons on his flannel as I frantically pop each button open one by one when his mouth finds mine again. I hear the whoosh of his inhale when he kisses me, his sudden intake of oxygen assures me he's fighting to keep some ounce of control right now.

We break apart as he growls, "Fuck it," and proceeds

to rip his flannel open as the few remaining buttons scatter across the floor before he whips the shirt across the room, standing there in a skintight black tank top and his jeans. The way the cotton molds to the boulders of his chest, showcasing the most massive shoulders and biceps I've ever seen on a man pushes my libido into overdrive.

It's been so long since I've been filled with this need to have a man so desperately, the adrenaline coursing through my veins has taken over and I react on pure instinct.

I reach for the hem of his shirt as he does the same on me, both of us pushing the fabric up and over our heads before slamming back together in a heated tangle of limbs. Garrison reaches down to unbutton my jeans, pushing the denim down my legs, grabbing a handful of my exposed ass in his hands as he kneels before me.

"God, your ass is amazing. One of my first thoughts about you was how this would feel in my hands," he murmurs looking up at me while he squeezes my cheeks and slaps them lightly. Next, he kisses a trail up my legs until he meets the juncture of my thighs, running his nose along my slit through the silk of my thong, which doesn't hide my insatiable need for him, the dampness of my arousal on full display.

Just when I think he's about to bury his face between my legs, he falls backward on to the floor, pulling me on top of him as he lies down. His hands grab the back of my thighs, pushing me up higher on his chest before he situates me right above his mouth, lining up perfectly with my pussy.

His hands pull on the strings of my thong, breaking the elastic in half, the snap of the material shocking me a bit as he lifts the fabric away from my body to expose my center right above his face.

"Hmmm... I'm going to enjoy this way too much," he declares before dragging the tip of his tongue through my wet slit, parting my lips and lapping up every drop of my wetness.

"Oh, God!" I shout, surrendering myself to the feeling

of his tongue diving in and out of me, listening to the groans coming from his mouth as he feasts.

I let my need take over, riding his face with no shame while falling forward to support myself on the floor below us, drowning in the ecstasy this man is giving me with his mouth. His tongue does wicked things to my clit, his lips suck hard and furiously on my bundle of nerves, drowning me in unadulterated pleasure.

God, I've forgotten how incredible sex can be when you let your inhibitions go.

Trevor rarely made me feel desired and wanted, even though I knew he was attracted to me. Still, when you're in a relationship with someone, it's important to let the other person know you still want them, even after the honeymoon period has diminished.

Before I let myself get too carried away, I spring up and twirl around above his head so my face lines up with his crotch when I bend forward.

"What are you doing?" He asks breathlessly while I undo the button on his jeans, reaching inside for his cock and freeing him from the confines of his boxer briefs.

Most women might argue that the penis isn't the most beautiful appendage. And most of the time, I'd have to agree. But my mystery man has—without a doubt—the most beautiful dick I've ever seen.

Long, thick, and hard as a rock---his massive erection stands proud in front of my face, making my mouth water with the thought of taking him inside.

"Oh, fuck," he says through gritted teeth when I bring him to my lips, licking around his head before taking just the tip in my mouth. He bucks up slightly, shoving his cock deeper in my throat as I hum in approval, increasing the wetness between my legs when his mouth finds my pussy again.

I rock my hips back and forth against his tongue as he pushes two fingers inside of me, the welcome invasion makes me clench and brings my orgasm forward so fast, I barely have time to prepare.

I continue to suck him hard, working my hand around the part of him I can't fit in my mouth when my orgasm slams into me with his stroke of my G-spot and the pressure of his tongue on my clit.

I scream, panting and gasping for air as I release his dick from my mouth and ride out the waves of my release, still running my hand up and down his shaft, spreading my saliva up and down his length.

"Oh, shit," I say exasperatedly, resting my head on his thigh while he continues to lick my lips with small strokes.

"Fuck you taste good, Red."

I sit up slightly to look back at him between my thighs, his face framed between my legs one of the sexiest sights I've ever seen. My arousal glistens on his lips and his beard from the light coming through the cracks in the blinds, which makes me smile and sigh with gratification. This man clearly enjoyed himself from the smirk he's giving me and the gleam in his eyes.

Suddenly, he lifts me off of him, sitting up and turning me around so we're face to face. Pushing my hair from my eyes, he stares at me before slamming his mouth down on mine, giving me a taste of myself—and fuck, if that isn't hot.

I get lost in his mouth again, our tongues moving together like the turns in a roller coaster—fast, hard, and suddenly without warning, you're falling down a hill, clutching your stomach from the uneasiness you start to feel.

I know this is just a hook-up, a one-night stand. Yet the feel of this man beneath my fingers and pressed up against my writhing body makes me crave more than just a one-time thing. Sometimes that physical connection between two people can be too strong to ignore. And if he continues to dish out orgasms like that one, I know I'll want more.

He moves to stand, hoisting me up by the back of my thighs so my legs wrap around his waist as he carries me over to the couch, depositing me softly on the cushions before he stands upright again. His dick is still hanging out of his pants, rock hard and dripping with pre-cum. I take the moment to savor every ridge of muscle on his chest and abdomen, mesmerized by the physical specimen of a man in front of me, covered in tattoos, exerting that bad boy vibe cliché, itching with the need to pleasure my body more.

I've already come once, yet my body is still humming with the need to lose control again, especially when the heat of his gaze tells me the pleasure is far from over.

Yup, this was exactly what I needed tonight.

# CHAPTER 9

Kane

This woman is addicting, her pussy hypnotizing me under a spell I'm not sure I'll ever break free from.

Watching her sitting on her couch, naked except for her bra—I'm confounded with how this was the direction in which my night turned.

But fuck if I'm complaining now.

"Take off your bra. I want to see your tits. I want you completely naked beneath my fingers," I demand as I shove my jeans and boxer briefs down my legs, effectively eliminating any more barriers between us. I grab my wallet from my pocket and retrieve a condom I keep for emergencies before throwing my pants across the room to join my flannel. The boxes stacked around the room offer many hiding places for my clothes, but my only thought at the moment is making this woman come again, and clothes only get in the way of that.

Her breasts heave with her strenuous breaths as she releases them from the black fabric, exposing her completely to me, and my dick gets even harder. Hardened, rosy nipples stand at attention on the most impeccable, round globes I've ever seen.

Fuck, her body is incredible. Curvy, yet lean—subtle muscle tone all over, but still enough meat to grab on to.

*She's perfect.*

I take a knee in front of her, pulling her face to mine to

kiss her again, losing myself in the feel of her soft skin beneath my fingers, squeezing her breasts and nipples while her wet tongue tangles with mine.

"Hmmmm," she moans as she reaches for my cock, pumping her fist around my rock hard length, making me fearful that I'll embarrass myself before I ever to get to fuck her like I promised.

Bringing our kiss to a halt, I lift her up and turn her around, pressing down on her back to bend her forward, presenting her ass to me like a prize. Because fuck yeah, I definitely won tonight.

Her forearms rest on the cushions, supporting herself while my hands caress the smooth skin of her lower half, my balls tightening just from the touch. I smack her ass, making her jump and moan at the surprise of my action, but she flicks her hungry eyes back to me and smirks.

"You like that, Red?"

"Maybe," she mewls, shaking her ass to taunt me again. I reach out and pinch her cheeks between my hands, rubbing her globes around in my palms while pushing my erection between her cheeks.

"I hope you're ready for a wild ride, Red," I promise while opening the condom and jacketing myself.

"Bring it on, Garrison. Show me your moves off the dance floor," she taunts as I bring my dick to her entrance, rubbing the tip through her wetness. I can see the glisten of her arousal on my cock, which ruins me— burning the image of her bent over like this with her thighs spread for me into my brain for all eternity.

I push inside of her with brute force, making her squeal from the intrusion until she moans deliciously when I start to set the pace. She meets me thrust for thrust, our grunts and moans filling the room as we lose ourselves in the physical indulgence.

"Fuck me," she urges me on, taking the beating I'm giving her with each slap of my hips against her ass. The jiggle of her body as I pound into her pulls me under her spell and testosterone pumps through my veins as caveman-like desire overtakes me.

I smack her ass again while I pump in and out of her, watching my dick disappear into her wet heat before re-appearing, over and over again.

"Oh, God! Yes! More!" She shouts and I don't ever think I've been this turned on by words in my life.

I lean forward, pressing my chest to her back as I reach around and palm both of her breasts in my hands, pinching her nipples between my fingers. Trailing kisses down her spine and across her shoulders, I continue to bury myself deep inside of her. If her moans and shrieks are any indication, I'd say she's enjoying herself as much as I am.

I feel like putty right now, melting into the feel of her body constrained by mine. At the same time, I feel equally strong with each flex of my muscles that give me the strength to support both her weight and my own as we race towards that ultimate physical release.

This woman makes me feel like a man, a man who knows how to please and worship the female form.

A man who's not haunted by his past, but truly indulging in his present.

I hear her breathing quicken, her pussy tighten around my cock, and with a few more thrusts she screams and then shatters again in my hands while I pound into her, withdrawing every last pulse of pleasure from her body. Feeling her clench around me almost pulls me over with her, but I'm not ready to bust yet. I'm so consumed in losing myself in this woman that all reality has escaped me.

The pain. The loneliness. The betrayal and hurt that I can't seem to forget or move past.

She stands up with me still inside of her, reaching her arm around my neck before turning her head and pulling my lips to hers. I continue to stroke her core as she presses her ass to my crotch, searing us together in a mess of sweat and her wetness.

I break free from her grip, the moan of her disapproval filling my ears when I turn her around and lay her down on the couch this time, kneeling above her while finding that sweet spot between her legs again.

I slide home once more, basking in how wet she is and how tight her pussy grips my dick. My body is running on sensation overload.

"God, you feel incredible, Red."

"You too..."

"This is..." I fight for the words to describe the most mind-blowing sex I've ever had. I never felt this sort of passion with Natasha, this downright primal need to be joined to a person this closely before for nothing more than pure physical satisfaction.

"Stop talking and just keep fucking me," she demands, gripping at my shoulders, digging her fingernails into my skin hard enough to draw blood.

"Ah, fuck!" I yell while picking up the pace, pounding her pussy into oblivion while reaching down to circle her clit with my thumb.

"Yes! Harder!"

*God damn, woman! You want harder?*

I hoist myself back and push forward with such brutal force, I'm afraid I might split her in two, but her shriek only confirms how much she needs this, and wants it.

Smack—my hips pummel her ass, her skin vibrating against my pelvis.

Pound—my dick reaches the very deepest depths of her pussy.

Thump—my heart rattles in my chest from the most grueling fuck of my life and the brutal intensity of this sexual encounter.

"Jesus Christ!" She screams as she comes apart beneath me again, the pure carnal expression on her face so passionate that I become entranced watching her lose control and race to join her at the finish line, filling up the condom with every drop of my cum until I can't possibly have anything left.

I collapse on top of her, our heavy breathing and panting providing background noise to the deafening quiet surrounding us. We lie there for what seems like minutes, but in reality, it is only a few seconds before I push myself up on my forearms and gaze down at the woman beneath me.

The smallest smile graces her lips with her eyes still closed as she basks in the aftermath of our fuck-fest. And suddenly her eyes pop open and meet mine, the intense green and brown hue glowing in the outside light filtering inside.

We stare at each other for longer than deemed comfortable, her eyes bouncing back and forth between mine before she shakes her head and then moves to push me off of her.

"Oh, God, I needed that," she says nervously, standing to search around frantically for her clothes.

I sit up on the couch and watch her, still stark naked and out of breath. The soft glow that highlights her curves lets me appreciate her body once more before I snap myself out of my ogling and join her on the hunt for my wardrobe. I pull off the condom and walk it over to the trash can in the kitchen before resuming my search.

"Yeah, no kidding. Looks like we both won tonight, huh?" I joke, locating my pants and underwear and pulling them on.

She pulls her tank top over her bare chest and then grabs a pair of shorts from a hamper sitting in a corner, pulling them up over her legs and onto her hips. The sight of her insane body covered up makes my dick slightly sad.

"Definitely. Well, uh... thank you, you know... for all

the orgasms," her eyes shy away from my face as she chuckles while looking around the room nervously, brushing her hair from her eyes. The woman looks thoroughly fucked and strikingly gorgeous.

I smile at her, enjoying how uncomfortable she seems after she screamed at the top of her lungs for me to fuck her as hard as possible. Sliding up next to her, I grab her hips and pull her to my body, tipping her chin up so her gaze meets mine.

"Tonight was fun, Red. I think we both needed that. Thanks for a good time and you're welcome... for all the orgasms," I whisper, pressing a light kiss to her lips. "I guess I'll see ya around," I say before walking away with my shirt in my hands and retrieving my keys from my pocket.

Reaching for the door handle, I turn the knob and prepare to leave, but something tells me to look back at this woman one more time.

Twisting around, I see her staring at me too. I can't quite decipher her expression, but she offers me a sweet smile and then a small wave of her fingers.

"Have a good night, Garrison."

"Night, Red."

I turn on my heels and exit her place, shutting the door behind me and finding my way back to my truck.

The pleasant surprise I found tonight leaves me with a smirk on my face on my entire drive home.

I had fun. I feel alive for the first time in I don't know how long.

And maybe it was from the redhead that lit a fire inside of me, bringing a part of me back to life that I didn't realize I was missing.

# CHAPTER 10

Olivia

"Please tell me you fucked the lumberjack!" Clara shouts into the phone the second I answer her call.

"Jesus, Clara. Stop shouting! Some of us are a little hungover this morning," I mutter while opening my eyes for the first time since my head hit the pillow last night.

"Sorry, but I'm dying here. Perry and I leave to take care of Amy and when we come back, you're talking to a man who looks like he just chopped down an entire forest, and then wanted to devour you for dinner. Forgive me, but I need to know what happened!"

I let out a long exhale, recalling every vivid detail of the night before in my mind.

Mr. Mysterious, or should I say Garrison, was the perfect way for me to wrap up the most life-changing week of my life—with life-changing sex.

I didn't know there were men out there who looked like him, let alone, a man who could fuck like him too. The man was a God, owning my body with every brush of his tongue, lips, and fingers... and I'd be lying if I said I wasn't disappointed that it was only a one-time thing.

"Well, I didn't come home alone, if that's what you need to know..."

"Ah! Yes, Liv! Good for you, girl! Please tell me it was hot... it's been a while since I've gotten any and I need to live vicariously through you right now," she beams through the phone, and I can only imagine the Cheshire grin on her face from my confession.

"It was... gosh, hot wouldn't even begin to describe it, Clara," I sigh, knowing that I definitely had the best sex of my life last night.

"Give me some details, woman!" I hear the clank of dishes in the phone's background.

"Are you at a restaurant right now?" I ask, sitting up in my bed, hit instantly with a pounding headache and the dire need to pee.

"Yeah, I'm grabbing breakfast before my meeting."

"And you're talking about sex out loud on the phone?"

"Whatever. It's not like I'm ever going to see these people again," she declares, and I can just imagine her waving her hand in the air nonchalantly.

"You really have no shame, do you?"

"Nope. Why worry about what others think of me? I don't have time for that. I'm too busy plotting world domination."

I laugh, knowing Clara could be plotting her own Pinky and the Brain scheme behind all of our backs. The woman doesn't take no for an answer and is always up for a challenge, a few of the many reasons she's so good at her job.

"So, do I get details?"

"Umm, I think I'm going to keep this specific encounter to myself, actually," I tease, knowing she's going to call my bluff right now.

"Ugh! You suck. But wait," she pauses, and I can hear the wheel turning in her brain. "Wow. Did you catch feelings, Liv? You know that's like breaking rule number one of one-night-stands..." Surprise fills her voice with the fact that I didn't spill.

Normally, I wouldn't have a problem sharing my sexual encounters with my girlfriends, especially Clara. Her, Perry, and Amy all knew about past men I had sex with, particularly Trevor and my disappointment with him at times. We're girls. We tell each other pretty much everything.

But something about my night with Garrison doesn't make me want to share. Bringing him home last night was one the most spontaneous and carefree things I've ever done in my life, and part of me wants to cherish that decision for what it is—a step in the right direction of moving on from Trevor and reclaiming myself and one of the few moments in my life where I gave myself permission to be carefree.

Plus, if I try to describe all the things he did to me last night, I'm going to end up all hot and bothered with no one to relieve the tension again.

"No, I didn't catch feelings. I just want to move on from last night, and last week for that matter, okay?"

She huffs. "Fine. It's not like you'll see him again anyway, right?"

Disappointment hits me in a sudden wave when I absorb what she just said. I know we went into last night knowing it was just for fun, a one-time thing. But part of me can't help but crave that physical connection again.

*Yeah, that's it. I'm just on a mind-blowing, post-sex high. I didn't catch feelings.*

*I simply caught multiple orgasms.*

"Right. I don't even know where he lives. He could have been in town for just one night for all I know. It was a one-night stand," I attempt to convince myself that I'm totally okay with what I knew I was getting myself into.

"It was fun, a great release, and now it's time to move forward. I have to make myself look somewhat human and go to the school today to get my keys. The principal said to call her when I was ready so she could meet me there. I'm ready to move forward, Clara. The lumberjack gave me some of the best sex of my life, and now it's time to slip back into Miss Walsh mode—math teacher extraordinaire and all-around bad-ass woman. Besides, you're right. I'll probably never see him again."

# CHAPTER 11

Kane

"I knew I shouldn't have washed my truck," I grumble as I hit yet another puddle from the rain last night, water shooting up and over the fender to pelt my windshield.

I swear, it's Murphy's law. As soon as you wash your vehicle, the rain Gods do a happy dance and literally, rain all over your parade. I guess that's what I get for not checking the weather before I turned the hose on.

It's Monday morning and still pitch black outside as I make my thirty-minute drive into town for work. The home I bought three years ago lies on the outskirts of town, deep in the trees, fulfilling my craving for isolation. I get privacy and land, but it makes for a slightly longer commute to Emerson Falls High School.

I'm an early riser by nature, so I tend to arrive at the school long before my colleagues, which also gives me ample time to prepare my lessons and necessary supplies for the day. Most people don't realize all the extra time that goes into teaching outside of the hours when the students are actually in the chairs. My colleagues and I spend way more time beyond our seven-to-two contract day to ensure our lessons are worthwhile and the students get the support that they need.

It's a little after six in the morning when I pull into the parking lot, securing my parking space and grabbing my thermos and lunch box before locking my truck and heading into campus. The smell of last night's rain still hangs in the air as I take in a deep breath and savor the aroma. I missed this while overseas—and even though it's been three years now since I've been home—I still remind myself to bask in the moments that make me feel grateful again. I swear, it's the little things you fail to appreciate until you can't experience them anymore.

I've spent a lot of time being angry and losing my happiness in reliving my failures and the ways in which other people have let me down. But over the past year particularly, I've tried really hard to focus on the positive, find the joy in the small pleasures that life brings us, and let go of the pain that weighs heavily on my mind and heart. At the suggestion of my parents, I started seeing a therapist three years ago to deal with the array of emotions I had trouble identifying and why. Therapy, along with having people like Tony and Drew, has helped me regain some control in my life. I'm a soldier who suffers from PTSD sporadically and whose life changed drastically when I came home—therapy was a necessary evil I'm not ashamed to admit that I needed.

Cracking a smile, I continue my trek onto campus. Mature trees line the sidewalks between buildings, the grey stucco with red accents paying homage to our school colors. My classroom is located in one of the two two-story buildings in the center of campus, which comprise the main offices in one of them and the English and History classes in the other. Beyond those are a few single-story pods that house the science, elective, and math classes. Our school grouped teachers from the same discipline in close proximity to maximize collaboration and support.

I also can't help but smile a bit as I replay my weekend while walking up to my classroom, the soft splash of water beneath my feet providing background noise in the eerie quiet of the morning. A hellish storm rolled through our town last night and the remnants of its torrential downpour will make for an interesting day as our students try to avoid getting wet. The change in the seasons is coming, and I can already see the wet footprints smeared across the tile floor in my classroom.

Ashamed to admit this out loud, I mentally chastise myself for how many times my thoughts veered to the red-head who blew my mind Friday night. I can't stop seeing her curves beneath my hands. I can't stop hearing her moans and cries of pleasure as I made her come three times that night (yes, I kept count). And I can't stop wishing that our sexual rendezvous could be a repeat. Not only had it been almost a year since I'd basked in the company of a woman, but I don't think I ever encountered a female who made me as sexually hungry and left me as sexually satisfied as she did.

However, I know that it's better this way. I got what I needed and so did she. I don't want complications in my life. I don't need a woman to rip my heart to shreds again. I'm finally starting to feel like me again and entertaining the thoughts of more with a woman will only set me back. All I needed was that release, and the fact that I got it with one of the sexiest women I've ever met makes me feel like I'm walking on air right now.

I arrive at my classroom, fiddling with my keys to unlock my door when I hear the most blood-curdling shriek I've ever heard in my entire life.

"EEEEEEKKKKKKK!"

My head twists so fast, I lose my balance and brace myself for the fall I know is coming. Luckily, I regain my footing before I hit the concrete and fall face-first into the behemoth of a puddle in front of my building.

"OH MY GOD!"

The voice squeals again as I drop my things, the clatter of my steel thermos rocking against the concrete and my lunch box slamming to the ground echoes behind me as I take off in the direction of the voice.

My heart is pounding in my chest, my feet slamming into the pavement and soaking up water from the puddles, my mind infiltrated with memories of women and children screaming after an explosive detonated in their village, the dust clouds powered red from blood spatter wafting through the air.

I feel my body react to danger, even though I have no idea what I'm running towards, but I'm preparing for the worst.

I feel the wetness of my shoes from soaking up the water under my feet and I hear the swish of my legs pumping fiercely as I run like a bullet shot from the barrel of a gun. My head twists and turns as I search for the person who sounds like they're about to die, just as I pummel into a warm body in front of me, my hands reaching to enclose the person in my arms as I fight for balance so we don't hit the wet pavement.

"Ahhhh!" She screams as we stumble and trip, her heels catching on the grass next to the sidewalk and my feet tiptoeing around, holding her to me as I bring us to a stop.

My eyes pop open and the shock registers instantly as I observe the person encased in my arms—and when I take in the red hair that's been taunting me for the past seventy-two hours, the sudden panic I felt is magnified and then quickly replaced with utter confusion.

"Red?"

Those hazel eyes pop up and lock with mine as the same shock I'm feeling is written all over her face.

"Garrison?" She asks before pushing herself out of my arms, shaking and breathing frantically, smoothing her hair down before continuing the motion over her sleek black dress that hugs every curve I've already committed to memory.

"What the fuck are you doing here?" I say a little too harshly, warranting a taken aback reaction from her.

"What do you mean? I work here!" She shouts at me, backing away and peering over her shoulder as if she was looking for someone.

"You work here?" I question, instantly running my fingers through my styled hair and then dragging my hands down my face and into my beard, absorbing the information that is quickly making the elation I felt just moments ago buried under a gut-wrenching reality.

*Holy shit! She works here?*

"What do you mean you work here?" I ask again, staring down at her while fury builds beneath my pulse.

"I start today. I'm replacing Mr. Kirk, the math teacher that left. What are *you* doing here?" She counters, still fighting to get her breathing under control.

Of course, this would happen! I finally let go, give myself permission to fuck a woman senseless after almost a year, and thoroughly enjoy myself, might I add—and the woman turns out to be my new co-worker.

I sigh while pinching the bridge of my nose, admitting defeat and cursing karma for rearing its ugly head. "I work here too."

"Oh shit," she whispers.

"What were you screaming about that made me think I was going to have to kill someone?"

She glances down at the ground before a shudder racks her body. "Ugh! There are a ton of crickets in my classroom right inside of the door. I got here early to finish up a few things before the kids arrive, and when I opened the door, they scattered everywhere! I HATE crickets, Garrison!"

"Are you fucking kidding me? You screamed like you were about to die because there are crickets in your classroom?"

She scowls at me and then turns on her heels, headed back in the direction she came from, I assume. The clack of her shoes against the wet cement ticks like a timer on a bomb —the bomb that just dropped between the two of us. This woman is now my colleague and I know what she looks like naked and what she sounds like when an orgasm racks her body.

"Where are you going, Red? The crickets might get

you," I tease, enjoying how ridiculous she looks right now as I follow her and thoroughly appreciate the view of her ass swaying in front of me.

"Screw you, Garrison," she spouts, as a rush of need glides through me. Like a freight train, the memory of what it's like to screw her slams into me and then blood rushes to my dick.

"It's Kane, actually," I offer as she leads me around the corner of the building while I discretely rearrange my junk, headed in the direction of the math classrooms.

A quick turn of her head over her shoulder tells me she does not find this as amusing as I do.

"Olivia," she says as we arrive at her classroom door, holding her hand out to me to shake while straightening her spine. Sure as shit, we're right at Mr. Kirk's old classroom.

*Olivia.* The name suits her and I let it swirl around in my brain and then roll off of my tongue. Classy, yet still fiery enough to match her personality.

"Olivia... I guess this makes sense why you kicked my ass in pool," I say while I study her now in better lighting, reaching for her hand and remembering what her skin felt like against mine, the tingles spreading down to my crotch as my erection grows harder. The sun is starting to come up from behind the mountains and the overhead light in the eaves of the building brightens the area around us.

"Are you going to help me, or not?" She fires back, releasing my hand and crossing her arms over her chest while avoiding my comment about her pool skills.

"Your cricket killer is ready to take down the enemy."

She rolls her eyes and then cautiously opens her door where I'm greeted with no less than fifty crickets, at least.

"Holy shit," I say louder than I intended.

"I told you! This is disgusting," she shudders before backing up.

"The rain must have brought them in. Is there a broom

or something?"

"Oh yeah. Let me just grab the one I rode in on."

"No need for the attitude, *Olivia*," I snap back at her as I step over the crickets and into her room. Pushing them out with the inside of my foot, the bugs begin to scatter and jump.

"Oh, God!" She squeals, running away from the door as they hop out of the opening and scurry on their way down the sidewalk, her hair flying up around her as she twists and turns amid her shrieks.

I joyfully laugh, relishing in the fact that this collected and fierce woman I fucked a few nights ago is losing her shit over a few bugs.

Once the bugs have been safely relocated—give or take a few that succumbed to my size thirteen shoes—I turn my focus back on Olivia, still reeling with how my casual one-night-stand is now my new co-worker.

"So... uh, thank you, Kane," she offers slightly less tormented now that the crickets are gone.

"You're welcome. This sure is a surprise, huh?" I say, trying to ease the tension.

"No shit," she says with a roll of her eyes, and then looks up at me beneath dark lashes.

Most of our interactions occurred in the dark the other night and the muted light in the bar. Absorbing her now as the overhead lights emphasize her face, I can see every fleck of color in her forest-colored eyes. Soft freckles dance across the bridge of her nose and those lips are painted a deep shade of red that makes her look even more powerful and strong than I sense she is. Her chest is completely covered by her dress, but I can still see her gorgeous tits beneath the fabric as if I have x-ray vision. My eyes travel down the length of her body to the tips of her heel-covered toes and back up before I register the look in her eyes.

There's a hint of fear there—what she's scared about I'm

not sure. And it irritates me that suddenly, I want to know what that fear is.

I shake off the thought as she stands up tall and then speaks up more confidently. "Well, we can either let this be weird, or we can act like two consenting adults who happened to sleep together and now plan to move on with their lives."

"Oh, I'm fine with that. I'm more worried about you," I point in her direction.

"Me? Why me?"

"Well, you're a woman. As a whole, you all tend to be the emotional ones. I can move past our little rendezvous, no problem. I'm just not sure you'll be able to contain yourself now that we know we work together."

Her jaw drops and then she scowls at me. "Excuse me? You don't think I can accept the fact that we had a one-night-stand without making it out to be more than what it was?"

I shrug. "In my experience, that's rarely the case."

"Well, *Kane Garrison*," she spits out my name like it's leaving a bad taste in her mouth. "Consider yourself lucky that your one-night-stand was with *me*. I know how to be professional and accept the consequences of my actions. It certainly was a surprise finding you here today, but rest assured, I'm not the one you should be worried about. Maybe you should look in the mirror on this one, and ask yourself if you'll be able to handle seeing *me* every day, given how you've been eye-fucking me since you eliminated my cricket infestation."

I chuckle and look away, wondering how my initial encounter with this woman has turned so sour in a matter of minutes. But I can't deny that watching her lose her cool is one hell of a turn on.

Giving her a sideways glance, I start to retreat to my classroom, aware of how much work I still have to do to be ready for the day. "Don't you worry, Olivia. You won't have to worry about me wanting to get to close to you. We're colleagues now, and I never sleep with my co-workers—well, with the exception of our little surprise. And if I ever get the feeling that you're overstepping your boundaries, I know that getting rid of you won't require more than a few crickets now, won't it?"

"Ugh! You're infuriating! Just... just do me a favor and stay far away from me, Garrison. I wouldn't want you to catch any of my emotions rubbing off on you!" She shouts while waving her hands up and down her body, a body that I'm having a hard time forgetting what it looks like naked.

I tip my head back in a laugh as I turn around, striding back to my classroom while shaking my head at how my morning has started—how in a matter of days, my quiet and uneventful life has been flipped upside down by a redhead with a body that is made to be worshipped and a mouth that doesn't have a filter.

And now I have to see this woman, day in and day out. I'll have to act like nothing happened between us, even though our mind-blowing sex has been on repeat in my brain far more often than I'll ever admit.

*It's alright*, I try to convince myself when I reach my door and gather my thermos and lunch box from the ground.

*No one has to know*, I remind myself as I open the door and flip on the lights.

*Olivia is just another woman you work with*, my thoughts travel as the vision of her in that sleek black dress bent over my desk infiltrates my mind the second I stop in front of my desk in my classroom.

*Jesus, I'm so fucked.*

# CHAPTER 12

Kane

"Come on, Bob. Level with me here?"

I coax the copy machine in front of me, smoothly rubbing the door that I just closed after clearing yet another paper jam.

"Is Bob jammin' this morning?" Drew comes up behind me, assessing the screen as I program the 175 copies I need, silently praying that the machine will work for me this time.

"You know Marley... always jammin'," I throw back at him as the machine fires up and starts spitting out papers.

"How was your weekend?" Drew asks as he collects his papers from his mailbox and strides over to the coffee machine, refilling his cup.

The teacher lounge in our building is our little cove of reprieve from answering emails and phone calls or dealing with brooding teenagers. A few copy machines line the far wall, cases of paper are stacked from floor to ceiling in one corner, and two round tables surrounded by chairs sit in front of a long counter to the left of the door, framing a refrigerator and housing our coffee pot and teacher-purchased supply of liquid caffeine.

"Uh, it was good. Uneventful," I shrug, feigning innocence as I avoid making eye contact. "How about you?"

"Man, I finally caught up on some sleep. Tammy let me

sleep in until almost noon on Saturday, then I graded some papers and took her out to dinner."

"Sounds nice, man."

"It was. So..."

Drew pauses mid-sentence as the clash of high heels on the tile floors pulls his attention to the doorway. As I turn, the air is sucked from my lungs when I see Olivia in a lavender dress, her vibrant hair pulled up off of her neck in a ponytail, and a soft pink dusts her lips.

*Fuck me.*

How on Earth are the teenage boys in her class able to learn anything when she looks like a walking teenage dream?

"Oh. Hi, there," she acknowledges us while making her way into the room, her hands filled with reams of paper and a file folder.

"Here, let me help you," Drew rises from his chair, looking back at me with intense eyes as I stay frozen to the ground in front of the copy machine, my back turned again to her and my best friend.

"Thank you. That paper is heavy," she chuckles while brushing hair from her face. I keep an eye on her from the corner of my line of sight.

"I'm Drew Phillips."

"Olivia Walsh. Nice to meet you, Drew. What do you teach?"

"English. Been here for eight years here now. And this is..." He turns to introduce me, but Olivia beats him to the punch.

"Kane Garrison," she spits out. "We've already met."

Drew flicks his eyes back and forth between us before he raises his eyebrows to me.

"Yeah. Olivia had a little run in with some crickets yesterday morning. I rode in on my loafers and saved the day."

She sighs with a roll of her eyes before gliding over to the copy machine to program the copies she needs.

"Crickets?" Drew asks while he gives me a look that says he's thoroughly confused. "Good thing Kane was there to help then, I guess. Aren't crickets supposed to mean good luck though?"

Olivia gives me a side-eye glance before pushing a few buttons. "That's still debatable."

I huff and then shake my head, gathering my papers that just finished on the tray at the end of the machine as I prepare to make my way back to my classroom.

"What the?" Olivia says as the paper jams yet again in the same copy machine I just used.

"Oh, yeah. We call that one Bob, as in Bob Marley, because it 'always be jammin',"" Drew laughs while giving his best Jamaican accent.

"Well, it seemed to work fine just a minute ago. Is there some trick to this, Kane? You got your copies made. You mind helping me out here?"

I shrug and then start to walk backwards towards the door. "Well, apparently my help isn't that impressive. Maybe you need more crickets to give you some luck with getting Bob to cooperate."

If looks could kill, I'd be pierced by the daggers Olivia is throwing my way with her eyes.

"Here, I'll try to help," Drew offers just as I head out the door and back to my classroom, leaving the two of them to tackle the dreaded copy machine that haunts any teacher's dreams at night.

Five minutes later, there's a knock on my door as Drew

pushes his way in and shuts the metal barricade behind him.

"What the fuck was that, Kane?"

"What do you mean?" I ask, playing stupid while organizing stacks of papers on my desk to prepare for my next class. Drew and I have the same prep period, and with a glance at the clock, I realize it will end in about ten minutes. And now I know that apparently Olivia has that same hour too.

"Don't play stupid with me, man. I know you generally give off the surly, 'leave me the hell alone' attitude, but something's going on here with Olivia. Do you know her or something? Did something happen yesterday morning that has you acting like a complete ass to her?"

"Besides the fact that I saved her from a swarm of crickets and she was less than grateful? Nope."

Drew eyes me with that look that indicates he knows I'm full of shit.

"Kane, please remember that we both teach teenagers, so I know if someone's lying to me. Give me more credit than that. What are you not telling me?"

A lump forms in my throat before I blow out a long breath and lean forward, bracing my hands on the edge of my desk. If there is anyone I can trust with the truth, it's Drew.

"Dude... I kinda hooked up with someone Friday night..." I glance up at him with my body still hunched over.

"Okay, that's nice. I mean, actually, that's great, Kane. Good for you getting back out there, but I don't understand what that has to do with Olivia..."

And then the light bulb clicks on.

"Oh, fuck," his hands drop to his sides and then the biggest grin spreads across his face.

"Don't smile like that, Drew," I point in his direction as I stand up tall again. "This is all kinds of fucked up. I work with the woman now. I never would have taken her back to her place if I knew we were colleagues. You know me, I have a strict policy against that. Hell, Misty Chambers is still trying to get in my pants and it's been three years since I started here."

"Yeah, but Misty is Misty. She's not very particular about who she invites in her bed."

"No kidding. I just... hell. I actually allow myself to have fun, have sex for the first time in almost a year, and then this happens. Obviously, it can't happen again and no one needs to find out."

"Fuck, a year? And I here I complained that I only get it twice a week," he jokes, but his laughter falls on deaf ears. I do *not* find this funny.

Drew rubs his chin in thought as he circles around my classroom, pushing his glasses up the bridge of his nose before trying to reason with me.

"I agree no one should know, but does that mean it has to be just a one-time thing? There's obviously something there between the two of you. She may have looked like she wanted to murder you, but all I felt was sexual tension."

Yeah, I felt it too. The woman may be trying to convince me and herself that she can't stand me, but all I feel is her denying her attraction. I mean, we obviously slept together already, so there's no doubt that she felt the same way about me physically that I did about her. The woman was fire and ice, singing my flesh before offering relief in the form of a mind-numbing orgasm.

And that night I had no other thought than to accept that it was a single occurrence. But now that I know who she is and we'll obviously be near each other, I can't help but wonder if she'd be down for a repeat. I'm definitely not looking for a relationship, but the sex was too good to pass up again.

"Nah, I get the feeling she's more angry that we ended up being co-workers, and then I saved her from some bugs."

"Why is she here anyway? I mean, math teachers are scarce, especially ones that know their stuff and look like her. There has to be a reason why she took a job this far into the school year."

Drew has a point. It's not very often teachers change jobs in the middle of the year, or any time into a school year. Something must have happened that brought her to Emerson Falls. But no sooner do I realize that, I shove the thought from my mind.

It's not my business. She's not my business. I may want to fuck her senseless again, but no good can come from digging deeper than that. I learned my lesson with letting women in.

"I hate to burst your bubble, Sherlock, but I have no desire, nor the time, to figure out why she's here," I say, glancing up at the clock as I realize the bell is about to ring, signaling the start of our next classes.

"Well, shoot me for trying to nudge you in the right direction."

"And what direction is that?"

Drew tilts his head at me. "Come on, Kane. It's been three years since Natasha. I know she fucked you up, but are you going to just be alone forever because one bitch broke your heart?"

"I didn't know you cared so much, Dr. Phil."

Shaking his head, Drew begins to retreat from my room. "I'm not saying it has to be with Olivia—although, you could do a lot worse," he wiggles his eyebrows at me. "I just hate to see you waste the best years of your life because you're punishing yourself and anyone else for what your ex did to you."

One drunken night I divulged the entire history of my

relationship with Natasha to Drew. I barely remember the conversation, but I'm pretty sure I threatened him within an inch of his life if he brought it up again.

"You'd better go before I make it so you and Tammy can never have kids, Drew."

He laughs at me while walking out of my door. "She'd kill you before you ever got the chance to touch me. Don't be a dick, Kane. It's not becoming of you."

"Kiss my ass, Drew," I fire back, just as the bell rings and students infiltrate the halls.

I know Drew is right, but fuck if it doesn't make me apprehensive about letting a woman get further than just sex. Sex is easy. Sex is safe. I can shut off my feelings and just focus on the wet heat of a woman clenching my dick.

But that was before Olivia Walsh sucked me in and spit me out. I wasn't ever supposed to see her again.

Funny how the universe had different plans.

# CHAPTER 13

Olivia

"Okay, you know it's a school night and I had to rip the talons of my offspring off of my legs to get here, so this better be good," Amy says as she grumbles through my front door and throws her purse on my couch. Her oldest just started kindergarten this year, which I've heard changes the parenting game tremendously.

"Oh, it's good alright," Clara declares from the kitchen where Perry, her and I are huddled around a pitcher of margaritas and chips and salsa.

"I at least made you food. And I have margaritas," I try to soothe my friend as she makes her way into the kitchen to join us.

"No tequila for me, thanks. I think I've learned that lesson."

"It's different when you take shots. Mixed in a margarita with the combination of all the sugar, it won't hit you as hard," Clara pipes up while taking a long draw of the frozen concoction and then smacking her lips in appreciation.

"John had to take care of the kids on his own until noon on Saturday so I could sleep off my hangover. When I finally emerged from our room, the house looked like the Tasmanian Devil paid us a visit. I went from hungover to fully enraged. Then John and I got in a huge fight. I can't handle that again."

"It won't kill John to have to play Dad once in a while,

Amy," Perry says while dipping a chip into my homemade salsa.

Amy sighs. "I know."

"And you need a break sometimes. Don't let one bad experience and fight with your husband deter you from getting your mommy time."

"Fine. One. Drink," Amy caves as Perry pats her on the back and fills up her cup.

"Okay, so spill, Liv. Why the hell are we gathered here tonight, on a Wednesday?" Clara demands as my three best friends shift forward in their stances, leaning on the kitchen counter, waiting for my answer.

I take a deep breath and then a long sip of my margarita before placing my drink down and running my sweaty palms over my leggings.

"So, you guys remember the man I was talking to at the bar before you left?"

"The lumberjack," Clara says.

"The lumberjack?" Perry and Amy ask at the same time.

Clara nods. "Yeah. He was decked out in flannel and jeans, looking like Paul Bunyan's long-lost son. If Liv hadn't seen him first, I would have climbed him like the tree he probably chopped down before entering the bar."

The three of us silently chuckle at our blunt and hilarious friend.

"Okay, so what about him?" Perry asks.

"They slept together," Clara answers for me, as I swat her arm.

"Jesus, Clara. This is my story, right?"

"You slept with him? Was it good? Please tell me it was good," Amy asks, more than interested in my sex life. She's told us on more than one occasion that her and John barely have sex because they're always tired by the time the kids are in bed. Poor girl. I almost don't want to share how mind-blowing the sex was so I don't make her feel bad.

Side-note: here's a common misconception. Married people assume that single people are out having wild and crazy sex all the time, filled with multiple orgasms and abundantly attractive people. This cannot be further from the truth. Those of you who are married should know, being single sucks. My encounter with the lumberjack was pure luck, the exception to the rule. You're lucky to get regular sex, and if you are, it's usually in some friends-with-benefits type of situation where the sex is great, but everything else is lacking.

Single people—at least most I've talked to—are generally envious of married people. Remember, if you're single, that means you haven't found that person that you want to spend the rest of your life with yet. That person who makes you laugh and accepts you for who you are—quirks, flaws and all. The person who loves you without make-up, when you're carrying around a few extra pounds, or when you have such bad gas, you're running each other out of rooms from how bad you both smell.

We're all looking for that, the person you feel so comfortable with that you can have the toe-curling sex, but still wake up to your best friend each day.

So when you hear stories of your single friends having mind-blowing sex, please know that this rarely happens. The grass isn't always greener on the other side.

The grass is greener where you water it.

Don't search for something beyond what's right in front of you. There's a reason you chose that person, so remember that and fight for it. (Solid advice from my parents who still look at each other like the other one hung the moon.)

Otherwise, you could end up in a situation like mine right now, where my incredible one-night-stand is actually my new colleague and I want to pound his face in right after he gives me a few more orgasms.

"Uh, yeah. It was good," I say, glancing away from my friends.

"I believe you told me that hot wouldn't even begin to describe it." Clara opens her big fat mouth again.

Amy fans herself while Perry shakes her head with a grin.

"Okay, fine! It was the best sex I've ever had, okay?" I shout at my three friends before pounding my margarita.

They stand there in utter silence, waiting for me to speak again, I'm sure. Clara has a wicked grin, Perry is looking away embarrassingly, and Amy looks like she's about to hump the counter.

"Why are you yelling, Liv?" Perry breaks the quiet before making her way around to me, placing her hands on my shoulders.

My eyes are closed, my head hung low while I find the courage to share the truth bomb dropped on me two days ago that has continued to rattle my brain.

"Because," I say, still looking down at the ground. "I work with him now."

Clara spits her mouthful of chips and salsa across my kitchen floor while Amy knocks her margarita over, pink slushie sliding across the granite counters.

"What?" Clara asks once she's cleared her throat, still leaving her mess everywhere. Amy frantically searches for a towel to clink up her drink and Perry rushes to help her, sopping up the pink liquid with paper towels.

Sighing, I brace myself for explaining our encounter. "I

went to work early Monday morning to finish up a few things before the kids arrived, and when I opened my classroom door, there were a bazillion crickets all over the floor."

"Okaaaaay," Perry drags out, motioning us all over to the couch and loveseat so we can get more comfortable while I re-live my mortification.

"I screamed when I saw them, of course... you guys know, I hate crickets."

Amy and Perry nod while Clara rolls her eyes.

"Anyway, I screamed and then started running away..."

"That's a bit dramatic," Clara teases as I shoot her a death glare.

"And with my head turned, I ran into someone and almost fell over, but he caught me. When I looked up at who it was, it was him."

"The lumberjack?" Amy asks, sitting on the edge of her seat with drool dripping from the corner of her mouth.

"Yup. Only he wasn't dressed in flannel and jeans this time. Nope. He was wearing a dark grey button-down shirt with a black tie, black slacks, and tan dress shoes." I distinctly remember thinking that the look of him dressed professionally could easily rival the lumberjack look. The man is downright sexy in anything he wears, apparently.

"So what happened?" Perry urges me to continue.

"Well, once we realized who each other was, he teased me about the crickets before he helped extricate them from my room. I thanked him and then told him things didn't have to be awkward, given that we slept together before knowing we were colleagues. And then he proceeded to tell me he was fine with it, but he was more worried about *me* making it a big deal," I roll my eyes before taking a sip of my drink.

"He said that?" Perry asks, her nose scrunching up.

"Yup. Said women are too emotional, so I'd better check my feelings."

"Ugh, what a pig."

"Then I ran into him in the teacher's lounge yesterday and he acted like an ass when I asked him for help unjamming the copier. One of the other teachers helped me, but not before apologizing for Kane."

"Kane? Mmmm, that's a yummy name," Clara points out. Believe me, when he told me his name, that was the first thing that came to my mind too. It suits him, and I couldn't help but want to shout it while he plowed into me again.

"So, he's being a dick. Is that really that big of a problem? I mean, you probably won't see him that much, right? Teachers are usually so busy during the day, they rarely interact with each other," Perry adds.

"Well, yes, and no. I mean, we will see each other at meetings and sporting events, fundraisers, and other stuff. But God! The man made me so pissed that he couldn't just remain civil. Just because I'm a woman doesn't mean I can't have a one-night-stand and detach feelings."

I say the words, but my heart doesn't believe them. The truth of the matter is, even though I wanted to so badly to believe that my night with Kane was just me trying to move past Trevor and have fun, I've never been the type of girl to just sleep with a guy one time. I've always been either dating the guy or in a committed relationship. I had *one* one-night-stand back in college and cried for three days afterwards, swearing I would never do it again. Sex has always been emotional for me, so I don't know why I thought that now, at thirty-one, I would feel any different. Believe me, Sunday I was nothing more than a jumble of emotions as I rearranged my classroom and then vegged out on the couch before work on Monday. I was trying to process all of my thoughts by distracting myself and eating my feelings.

But then once I saw Kane again and he started acting like an ass, I had to accept that the emotion I couldn't put a label on, was in fact, disappointment.

I was disappointed in myself for doing something so out of character. I was disappointed in him for not being able to act like an adult about it. And in turn, I guess I felt a tad rejected, especially when he looked at me like I was a mistake.

I'm tired of feeling like a mistake, like I'm second best. Trevor chose someone else over me. And another one of my exes married the woman he dated right after me, which definitely dwindled my confidence and made me feel less than good enough.

I may look confident and collected on the outside, but right now, I'm swimming in a sea of self-doubt.

"Well, I'm gonna be honest here," Perry chimes in. "It seems you do have some feelings about this. Was it *just* sex for you?"

I glance away, focusing on the TV stand, where pictures of my family and friends are on display. The frame holding a picture of my parents at their thirtieth wedding anniversary catches my attention, the two of them gazing at each other like they were still teenagers in love—I want that. And I thought that having casual sex would help me move on from that longing, accept the fact that I'm starting over again at finding my person.

I guess I was wrong.

"I wanted it to be just sex, but you guys know me. I'm not wired that way."

"Well, was it because you liked him more than just for the physical? Or are you still nursing your broken heart?" Amy finally speaks up, and I hate her questions because I don't know how to answer them.

"I guess a little of both. I mean, the thing with Trevor

sure has rattled me. I never thought I'd be that woman who was cheated on, which I think hurts my ego more than anything. But when I was with Kane the other night, we had more than just a physical connection. I think if the alcohol hadn't been involved, we probably would have gotten to know each other a bit more. At least, I wanted to."

It's the first time I've resigned myself to the fact that seeing him again made me even more curious about him. I know he was in the Army, and now I know he's a teacher too. But there is definitely more to him, the pain in his eyes I saw clearly telling me there's a story there.

He's sexy and charming—when he's not acting like an ass—and the man definitely has moves on and off of the dance floor. I just wish the circumstances in which we met were different now, my mind reeling with the possibilities.

"Okay. So don't smack me until I've finished," Clara says, scooting forward on her couch cushion. "But it's clear to me that you felt more than just sex. And maybe the reason Kane is acting this way is because he felt the same way too. What if you actually tried to get to know him?"

I shake my head at her before shooting her down. "I seriously doubt it. You should have seen the way he looked at me. Plus, we're co-workers now. It could get even messier than it already is."

"Men act like assholes when they like you, right?" Amy asks, her lack of experience in dating makes her question things in our love lives quite a bit.

"Yeah, in elementary school maybe," Perry replies with a roll of her eyes. "Sometimes, yes that's the case. But most of the time, men are just dicks to be dicks."

"True. But I saw the way he was looking at her Perry," Clara speaks up, defending her position. "Sure, there was lust there. Hell, he probably would have mounted her right then and there if we hadn't returned from the bathroom. But there was something else there too."

"Okay, before we all start sharing theories on whether Kane actually liked me more than for sex, can we focus back on the problem, please? I have to work with him. How do I make this less awkward?"

"Well, I really see that there are only two options here," Clara provides. "One, you try to be his friend, move past the uncomfortableness and tension. Or, you channel that sexual tension and have sex with him again."

Perry shakes her head, Amy laughs, and I stand, throwing my hands up in defeat.

"You guys are useless. I need new friends," I say while making my way back to the kitchen, taking the stuff out of the fridge for the pork tacos I made in my crock-pot.

"Hey, we're the best friends you could want, Liv," the three of them follow me, Clara pulling me into her for a side hug.

"I know. I just hate this. My entire life has been turned upside down, and the one spontaneous thing I do to let go and try to move forward comes back and bites me in the ass."

"Did he bite your ass? Oh, that's hot," she says, which makes me question how this woman can be taken so seriously in her job. She must put on one hell of filter when she's wheeling and dealing.

"No, he didn't bite my ass. But, there may have been a spank or two," I say with a glance over my shoulder and a Cheshire grin while I dig through the fridge.

"Lord almighty," Clara fans herself while Perry giggles and Amy's jaw is dropped.

We feast on tacos and a few more margaritas before they all call it a night, early wake-up calls for all of us pending in the morning.

While snuggling into my bed that night, I think about what my friends said. Clearly, I'm not separating my feelings about the one-night-stand as well as I thought I could. But the question is: is that because I felt more with Kane? Or am I just an emotional mess right now about everything in my life?

Succumbing to sleep, I remind myself that I don't need to have answers right now. I just need to focus on my job, myself, and try to avoid getting involved with any of my other coworkers. Maybe I should just ask any man I meet at this point whether we work together before I pursue a conversation so there are no more surprises thrown my way.

# CHAPTER 14

Kane

It's Friday and my guilt has been eating away at me for the way I treated Olivia the other day. Well, it's more like Drew laying on the guilt, but I guess it's finally hit me. To make matters worse, Drew told his wife Tammy about our situation (why must married couples tell each other everything), so she's been on my case too.

When I was in the drive-thru for Starbucks this morning—my Friday morning treat—I decided that maybe a peace offering was necessary. Contrary to how surprising it was to see her here as my colleague, it's not her fault that things between us played out this way. In fact, I can't help but smile at the fact that I ended up seeing her again. I sure as hell know that once I left her place Friday night, I wished there would be a repeat. But now that she's working with me, I know I can't continue to punish her for the surprising twist to our encounter.

I pull into the parking lot, shutting off the engine and grabbing my stuff, including the two venti coffees I purchased, hoping to deliver the sustenance before class starts. If she's a creature of habit like I am, I know she'll be in her classroom early like she was that first day.

I stop by my room to drop off my lunch box and finish setting up my plans, then grab the coffee and head for her room. I'm not going to lie and say I don't feel nervous for what I'm about to walk into. Given our few interactions since Monday, I'm going to say she's not a huge fan of mine right now, and I can't really blame her. I was an ass, even though the woman gave it back to me. And I'm not going to lie and say that that side of her isn't hot as hell, because it is. It's the side I got in the bar that night—full of sass and fire, not afraid to speak her mind and stand up for herself.

So now I hate the fact that I can't stop wondering what other sides there are to her—the sides that aren't full of pissed off energy directed at me. The woman I caught a glimpse of Friday night has held more of my mental attention than I care to admit over the past week, and the fact that I want to know more about her makes an uneasy feeling settle in my stomach.

I don't let myself care about women. I know, I know... that makes me sound like even more of an ass. But after what Natasha did to me, I couldn't let myself care. I promised myself I would never let someone have that hold on me again. I gave her everything. I loved her and wanted to spend my life with her, and she threw me away.

But then here comes Olivia in my life, the bold and beautiful redhead that mesmerized me and made me think with my dick for a night, and suddenly I can't stop thinking about her. It scares the shit out of me. And especially since we work together, I know I can't just shut her out. I can't act like the dick I usually am. She doesn't deserve that because it's not her fault that we're in this mess.

Hence, the peace offering. I don't know of any mishap that can't be smoothed over by a surprise Starbucks coffee.

It's still dark outside when I approach her classroom, the glow of the lights through the windows helps to light up the sidewalk as I stride along. The small rectangular window on her door gives me a sneak peek into her room, where I'm greeted with her back to me, those curves that drove me insane covered in dark denim and her body draped in an Emerson Falls grey and red staff t-shirt. Her long red hair is softly curled and falls down her back, which sways ever so slightly as she writes something on her whiteboard.

The memory of her bent over in front of me from Friday night wakes up my conscience, instantly rushing blood to my crotch.

Fuck. I can't go in there with a semi. I close my eyes and think of my wrinkly old Grandma, butt-naked.

*Yup, that will do it.*

Fully flaccid again, I twist the handle of her door and step inside, glancing around the room. The space is so much brighter than it was when Mr. Kirk was here. She's obviously spent time in the last week making her classroom look appealing and functional, full of bright colors and features in the room that help a classroom run efficiently. Only another teacher could appreciate her file folders on the wall for missing assignments, the baskets for collecting work, and the station full of staplers, three-hole punches, and hand sanitizer for students to use.

"Hey, Theodore. Let me finish this really quickly and then I can help you with your Calculus," Olivia shouts over her shoulder with her back to me, finishing up a graph that she's drawing on the board.

She's obviously expecting a student right now, not me —but that just gives me the opportunity to surprise her a bit.

"Nice curves," I tease as she flips around so fast the marker flies out of her hand, her eyes wide when she takes me in.

"What?" She looks at me like I'm crazy, but then her eyes narrow into those slits that she gave me that first night. There's the fire again.

"Are you serious right now? Are you actually hitting on me after the way you acted the other day?"

I shake my head, grinning from ear to ear. "No, actually I was complimenting your graph. Even as a history buff, I can appreciate the curves on a polynomial function."

The disgust on her face quickly falls away, replaced with astonishment. "You know what a polynomial function is?"

"Yup. Contrary to what you might think, I was actually quite the brilliant math student. But history just seemed like more fun to teach."

"I can't argue with that. Sometimes I wonder what the hell I was thinking choosing to teach math. The pressure, the kids that come in lacking basic number sense, the tests and impossible standards to cover... I should have just taught P.E."

Her sarcasm makes me laugh, clutching my stomach a bit while I take her in some more. Then I remember the reason why I'm here.

"Um, this is for you." I offer her the coffee, reaching out to meet her hand while she takes it from me. Our fingers lightly brush against one another as she receives the cup, looking down at our connection, then back up at me. There's no denying the spark we both feel. I remember vividly what it was like to be skin-on-skin with this woman.

"Thanks?" She says as more of a question, clearly confused about my gift.

I clear my throat before standing up tall so she takes me seriously. "I, uh, owe you an apology."

"Really?" She lifts an eyebrow at me while placing a hand on her hip.

"Yeah. I was an ass the other day and I'm sorry." I let out a long breath before continuing. "You didn't deserve that. And leaving you with a jammed up copy machine is like the worse thing a teacher can do to another teacher."

She chuckles and then takes a sip of the coffee. "I expect you should know better than that. The rage that overcomes you when the copier isn't working is a feeling only another teacher can understand."

"Yes, I know. So, again, I'm sorry. I figured some extra caffeine on a Friday should help smooth things over between us."

"It's definitely helping. Although," she turns and walks away from me towards her desk in the front corner of her classroom, picking up her own Venti Starbucks cup. "I always get myself Starbucks on Friday too... so I guess I'll just be extra energized today."

"Shit. I'm sorry..."

"No, don't apologize, Kane. You didn't know. But hey, I guess great minds think alike. I always treat myself to Starbucks on Fridays. The extra caffeine is necessary to get through the last day before the weekend."

"Exactly," I agree while appreciating the small smile on her face.

"Thank you... for this," she gestures with her cup and then lets out a long sigh. "I'm sorry I wasn't very nice to you too. Seeing you here was the last thing I was expecting." She directs her gaze away from me, showing me yet another side to her—remorse.

"Psh... tell me about it. So, you were expecting Theodore this morning? Is that Theodore Scranton?" I ask, desperately wanting to change the subject and move on.

"Yes. He's such a nice boy. A little awkward, but borderline super-genius."

"Tell me about it. I have him in AP US History this year. The kid is like a human encyclopedia."

Olivia laughs and then walks back to her desk to set

down her coffee. "Well, you should see his math work. It's beautiful... well-organized, clearly explained, every step is shown... he's a math teacher's dream," she beams, the sparkle in her eyes when she talks about a student is breath-taking.

*Breath-taking? Where the hell did that come from?*

One moment I'm enjoying actually having a conversation with this woman, and the next my throat feels like it's about to close up when I find myself taken with her eyes.

*Her eyes? What the hell, Kane? When's the last time you found yourself enamored with a woman's eyes?*

Before I make myself look like a pussy, I turn on my heel and make my way back to her door.

"Yeah, I can only imagine. Well, uh, I have to get back to my room. Still have a few things to get done, you know, before the bell rings. Enjoy the uh, coffee, and I'll, uh, see ya around," I say, attached with an uncoordinated wave.

"Okay..." She drags out, clearly confused about how I'm acting right now. I was fine, perfectly content with offering an apology and making things less weird, and then I got caught up in her eyes and pussyfied thoughts started swirling around in my brain, which caused me to panic.

Olivia is just a co-worker. A colleague. A woman that I had a one-night-stand with and nothing more. She can't be anything more.

*I can't want anything more.*

"Thanks again, Kane," she calls out as I push open her door and speed walk back to my room, running my hand down my beard as I will my heart to stop racing.

"Fuck," I mumble when I reach my room, pacing across the floor while I breathe deeply and count to ten. I feel the panic attack coming on, which concerns me since I have to teach in a matter of minutes.

It's been months since I've felt my anxiety rear its ugly head, the pulsing in my veins making my brain fuzzy and the desire to pass out rings hard. Sweat breaks out on my forehead and my breathing is shallow, despite how hard I'm willing my body to take a deep inhale of oxygen. I hunch over in my chair at my desk, and hug my body tightly, knowing that the pressure will help calm me down quicker.

*Anxiety is just your response to a lack of control, Kane.*

*You're living in the future right now, instead of the present.*

*Nothing is going to hurt you. Just take a deep breath and count down from ten.*

I hear my therapist's voice in my head, telling me these statements over and over again, following her advice for dealing with the feeling of losing control over your own body. This isn't my first panic attack, but it certainly is the first one I've had in months.

When I got back from Afghanistan and Natasha ripped my heart out, I started experiencing waves of fear about the unknown of my life. I've always had a plan. I've always known what I wanted and felt in control about that.

And then everything burned up in flames, and suddenly, I had no direction to follow. The only thing I knew for certain was teaching. I knew I was supposed to teach.

But now even my job is being compromised by the sultry redhead that I slept with and now work with.

*Fuck my life.*

A few more deep breaths and I can feel my pulse returning to normal, the fuzziness leaving my head, the heightened temperature of my body slowly falling. I wipe the sweat from my forehead and glance in the mirror next to my desk that I keep there to check for food in my teeth or marker on my face throughout the day.

Yes, I walked around with marker on my face one day for four hours before one of my students said anything to me. Hence, the mirror. I'm not a pre-Madonna, if that's what you're thinking.

"Fuck," I mumble to myself again before shooting off a text to my therapist, asking to see if she has an opening soon. It's been months since I've felt the need to see her, but maybe a quick visit will help me process the sudden fear I felt when Olivia looked at me.

One thing's for certain: whether we're mad at each other, fucking each other's brains out, or attempting to remain civil—the woman is definitely having an effect on me.

And I'm not sure that I like it.

# CHAPTER 15

Olivia

"So, he brought you coffee?" Clara asks as her and Perry follow me down the steps into the football stadium to take our seats. Amy couldn't make it tonight since her husband wasn't home from work yet.

It's the night of the rivalry game between Ashland High School and Emerson Falls High School, and since all of us went to Emerson and I now work there, I felt a deep-rooted obligation to attend.

"Yes. It was surprisingly sweet."

"It was just Starbucks," Perry says, unimpressed. The woman doesn't understand how all of America has become consumed with overpriced coffee full of chemicals and sugar. She actually has a post on her blog about making your own specialty coffees at home for a fraction of the price and calories.

"Yes, but it's the thought that counts. And he was actually pleasant to talk to this time," I defend as we find an empty row of seats pretty close to the field. Kickoff is in about ten minutes and the stadium is filling up quickly, so I'm surprised we found seats this close.

Our conversation earlier was actually going somewhere before he started stuttering and retreated like a kid who got caught with his hand in the cookie jar.

"Hey, Olivia," a blonde woman waves over at me down

our row and her familiarity hits me. "It's Tammy Phillips. I'm married to Drew and teach biology at Emerson," she adds and then her placement clicks.

"Oh, yes. Hi!" I say a little too enthusiastically. I've only been at the school for a week, so it's impossible to know everyone yet. But I do remember Drew and his heroic rescue with the copy machine, so this is apparently his wife.

She scoots down the bench so she's seated closer to us.

"Tammy, this is Clara and Perry, two of my best friends. Tammy is another teacher at Emerson."

My girls both shake her hand and offer her a welcome feeling. "Nice to meet you. So, Olivia, how has this week been? You like things so far? The students haven't been giving you too much trouble, have they?"

I laugh and then look out on the field as the team jogs on before turning back to her. "No, things have been pretty smooth, despite walking in to a room full of students who haven't had a teacher for a month. My fifth period is a little rowdy, but it's nothing I can't handle. I've been doing this for a while."

She nods and then screams down on the field, her hands cupped around her mouth. "Go Drew! Love you!" Turning back to me, she continues. "Sorry, just have to cheer on my hubby. He's the head coach."

"Oh, I didn't know that."

"Yeah, he, Holt, and Corey coach the team together. Football season is always the craziest time of year for us, but he loves it. And Kane Garrison helps from time to time. I heard you actually know Kane already," she winks, which catches me off-guard.

Clara snorts next to me and Perry elbows her in the ribs.

"Uh, yeah. I've met Kane."

"Oh, yeah, they've met alright," Clara mumbles under breath as Perry smacks the back of her head. "What the hell, Perry? Don't think I won't fight you just because we're at a high school football game."

"Shut up. You're making this awkward for Liv."

"Did I miss something?" Tammy asks, her eyes bouncing back and forth between the three of us.

I clear my throat and quickly think of something to divulge about how I know Kane without revealing the truth, but then decide to fish for information.

"How do you know that I know Kane?"

"Well, Drew and he are best friends, and he might have shared your little copier incident with me. Seems Kane was quite the ass to you," she quirks her eyebrow.

I fiddle with my fingers just as the announcer asks the crowd to stand for the National Anthem. Once the choir has finished a beautiful rendition of the song, the four of us take our seats and resume the conversation.

"Yeah, he wasn't very pleasant."

"Well, Drew made him feel like shit afterwards, just so you know."

"Really? Is that why he brought me coffee this morning then? Because Drew told him to?"

Tammy blinks at me a few times before the corners of her mouth curl up into a devious smile. "Nope. He just told him not be to a dick. If he brought you coffee, that was all on his own accord. Hmmm..." she hums while turning her attention to the field, and the four of us watch the kickoff, cheering when our team makes a killer thirty-yard return.

"What do you mean, hmmm?" Clara interjects as Tammy turns to us and shrugs her shoulders.

"Let's just say, I've known Kane for a while and I've

never known him to be one to apologize, let alone bring a woman a coffee."

"Interesting..." Clara chuckles while nudging me with her elbow.

"What?" I quickly turn my head in her direction, pulling my focus from the game I was just enriched in.

"Did you hear what Tammy just said?"

"No. Sorry, I was into the game."

Tammy laughs. "No worries. Just told your friends here that Kane isn't the type to apologize to a woman, especially with coffee."

I swallow hard, a lump forming in my throat and the need for a drink of water consuming me.

"Really?"

"Yup," Tammy nods smugly before taking a sip of her soda and changing the subject. "So, now that you're part of the Emerson family, I'll be the first to offer you an invitation to our house next weekend for our fall mixer," she smiles.

"Fall mixer?"

"Yeah. Each quarter, the staff organizes a mixer/party where we all get together and hangout outside of school. Drew and I usually host at our place, since we have a large property and no children yet," she looks down at her hands and then sighs.

"You okay?" I ask while placing a hand on her shoulder. When she looks up at me, I see tears in her eyes.

"Gosh, I shouldn't even be telling you this since we just met, but sometimes I can't control the wave of emotions that comes over me when I inadvertently bring it up." She takes a deep breath and then continues. "Drew and I were pregnant this summer, and then I miscarried."

"Oh, God, Tammy. I'm so sorry," I rub her shoulder as Clara and Perry offer their condolences as well. I can't imagine the pain she must feel. I don't have a family yet, obviously— but it's something I definitely want. And I couldn't imagine losing a baby I so desperately craved.

"Thank you. It's been hard. We're trying again now, but every time I'm reminded that we still don't have a family, it makes me burst into tears," she waves her hands in front of her face trying to calm herself. "Ugh! Sorry for putting a damper on the conversation."

"Hey, no judgment here from us. I promise." Clara and Perry both nod beside me.

"I had a miscarriage too between my two kids. It's a pain I've never felt before. Just try to remain positive and keep loving Drew. You'll get through it," Perry offers while taking her hand.

"Thanks. So anyway, back to the mixer… it's next weekend. You have to come! And you ladies can come too!"

"I'll be in New York," Clara answers.

"My daughter has a dance recital," Perry adds.

I turn from my friends back to Tammy. Her open heart is so visible, you can't help but want to be this woman's friend. And hey, maybe getting to know some of my new co-workers will help pull me out of my funk.

"Well, I will definitely be there."

"Great! Let me get your number," she digs through her purse to fetch her phone. We trade contacts and then turn back to the game.

"So why is Kane down there if he's not really a coach?" I ask, finding myself a little too curious about the man who gave me coffee this morning who doesn't normally give women coffee.

"Well, he tried coaching when he first started here, but uh… couldn't go through with it."

My eyebrows draw together as I question the reason.

"Why?"

Tammy shakes her head before meeting her eyes with my own. "Kane is a complex guy, Liv. He's been through a lot in his life and has some demons, although I think we can all agree that everyone does." We all nod at her in understanding. "But his demons are for him to tell, not me."

"I understand," I mumble and then search for the man in question on the field. His back to us, arms crossed over his body, his legs spread wide in his stance—he looks every bit of the coach, but also a man who's very guarded.

Even just in the brief interactions we've had—besides the primal sex—I can tell he's masking something. And the more I stare and the more I appreciate his physical form, the more I want to know about what's in his head—or even his heart.

The four of us watch the game on the edge of our seats, reminiscing about our high school memories of attending the same rivalry match but I was cheering down on the field. Tammy fits in perfectly with my friends, making me appreciate having another person on my side through this challenging phase of my life.

The older you get, the more you realize how hard it is to find people you click with. Everyone has their own agendas and problems. Some people are still drawn to the drama of life you find in your teens and early twenties. And once you hit a certain age, you realize you just want to be surrounded by people that bring out the best version of you. People who are like-minded, share some common feelings about life, and genuinely want to get to know the real you. Tammy is definitely one of those people.

The game ends with a victory for Emerson Falls, the crowd going wild beneath the florescent lights. The rumble of feet pounding the bleachers echoes in the stadium and fans and families rush the field to congratulate the players.

"Come on! Let's go congratulate the boys!" Tammy stands and pulls me up by my arm.

"Oh, I don't know..." I deflect, not sure if running into Kane right now is the best decision. After he left my room this morning in a funk, I'm reluctant to make it seem like I'm chasing after him. I know he said he was sorry, but then he got all weird and stuttered and left in such a hurry, I wasn't sure what to think.

"Hey, we're gonna head out. But go, Liv. Go see the boys," Clara wags her eyebrows at me while Perry nods in agreement. Whispering in my ear, she adds, "Go talk to him. Keep this momentum going. I know I'm right. I think that one night was more to him too. You can keep convincing yourself otherwise, but my gut is telling me you need to make a move."

I shake my head at my friend as a slight grin dances on my face. "You're crazy, Clara. But fine, I will go congratulate the *team*. You girls be careful getting home, okay?"

"Always. Love ya, Liv," Perry kisses me on the cheek before they stomp up the staircase in the opposite direction of where Tammy is now leading me.

"So, are you sure we're allowed to be going down here?" I ask in trepidation, the nerves from seeing Kane again making my hands tremble.

*But sure, you don't feel anything for him. Keep lying to yourself, Liv.*

"Uh, do you see the hundreds of people on the field right now? Yes, I'm sure it's alright," Tammy laughs at me as we push through the gate and stride across the dirt track to the edge of the football field.

"Congrats Coach! What a game!" She shouts as she runs up to Drew and tackles him, jumping in his arms as he catches her with the biggest smile on his face.

"Does that mean I'm getting lucky tonight?" He whispers a little too loudly in her ear, making me chuckle behind my hands.

"Oh, shit. Sorry, Olivia," he laughs when he sees me while setting Tammy back down. "I take it you met my wife finally," he pulls Tammy into his side, kissing her on the head.

*That right there. That's the kind of love that I want.*

"Yes. We actually watched the game together and talked a bit."

"Yup. I invited her to the mixer next weekend too. She's got to meet more of the staff. I kind of have a girl crush on her," she winks at Drew, just as Kane comes up behind him.

"Good game, man," he pats Drew on the shoulder with the most genuine smile on his face, before he turns and locks eyes with me, his smile falling almost instantaneously.

*Wow. Well, there's a boost to my ego if I ever needed one.*

*Not.*

Drew watches Kane's face fade, then elbows him in the rib cage hard, causing him to buckle over as a giggle escapes my lips. The pain etched on Kane's face isn't funny, but Drew catching him off guard was.

"You think that's funny?" He asks, popping his head up far enough to watch my face.

"Well, from what I know of you, you probably deserved it," I shrug as Tammy bursts into a fit of laughter.

"Oh, now I like you even more, Olivia. Smart, classy, and can give Kane the shit he deserves."

"Told ya," Drew whispers in her ear while they both fixate on me.

*Okay, kinda creepy.*

"Fuck man, what the hell was that for?" Kane finally stands back up, rubbing at his rib cage where Drew clocked him. His shirt rides up just enough to offer a peek at the tan and ink-covered skin I remember so vividly from a week ago.

Those toned abs, that well-defined chest, those tattoos I wish I had time to trace with my tongue... I can feel my cheeks turn red as I stare, so I turn around quickly to hide my face.

"Olivia, are you okay?" Tammy comes up behind me, circling to my front to take in my expression.

"Yup, just fine," I mumble behind my hands covering my cheeks and part of my mouth.

She narrows her eyes at me and then smiles that knowing smile.

"What's going on?" She asks, searching my eyes for a clue.

*Shit, does she know? Did Kane tell Drew, and Drew tell Tammy?*

I spin back around, glaring at Kane and searching Drew's face before I grab Kane's hand, dragging him across the field, away from the students and families, and away from prying ears and eyes, around the corner into a dimly lit tunnel between the locker rooms where we can speak in private.

"What the hell?" He grunts when we finally stop, yanking his hand back from my grasp.

"*What the hell*? Do Drew and Tammy know about us?"

Kane's silence is enough of an answer.

"Seriously? I thought we were trying to keep this between us?" I'm exasperated and the fury I felt towards him earlier this week is back with a vengeance.

"Hey! You can't tell me that you didn't tell your girl-friends about what happened between us, right?"

I shake my head. "That's different! They don't work with us!"

"Well, Drew is my best friend, and he just happens to work with us. Plus, he kind of put two and two together after how we acted towards each other in the teacher lounge. And if anyone was watching the way you dragged me across the field just now, I'm sure suspicions are already starting to fly."

I sigh and then turn around, my hands running along my scalp as I pull on my hair in frustration.

"Great! It's only a matter of time before the whole staff knows now..."

Kane steps forward, his hands gripping my shoulders so I'm forced to face him and can't move.

"No. Drew and Tammy are good people and they wouldn't do that. Believe me. Plus, I don't know if Drew actually told Tammy we slept together. All she knows is that I was an ass to you. Drew told me that much. So stop stressing and take a deep breath."

Surprisingly, with Kane's grasp on my body, I do feel calmer, more at ease. His large hands make me feel capable of handling this, knowing he's holding me up.

And maybe he's right. All Tammy said earlier was that she knows Kane was a dick to me. Maybe she doesn't know the whole truth.

When Kane's hands leave my shoulders, I sink back, remorseful for the lack of contact now and embarrassed for my overreaction.

"I'm sorry. I shouldn't have overreacted."

"Yup."

"*Yup*? That's all you're going to say?"

"Yes. I agree. You *way* overreacted."

"You really are a dick, aren't you?"

He laughs and then looks back over his shoulder to the field. When his head moves back in my direction, there's a glint to his eyes that reminds me of what he looked like that night in the bar. The carnal lust that poured out of this man as he offered me a good time and then fucked me into oblivion.

My pulse is racing as he takes a few steps to me, my feet retreating until my back hits the brick wall of the tunnel we're still encased in.

Leaning down while his hands on the wall lock me in place, Kane runs his nose along the column of my throat before lining up his mouth to my ear. I can hear my own breathing as I wait for his words.

"This is me, Olivia. I am a dick, a man who doesn't know how *not* to be honest and sugar coat my words."

I swallow hard as I feel the pounding of my pulse beneath his nose on my throat. "What about that sweet side you showed me earlier? Bringing me coffee? That doesn't seem like a dick move..." I whisper, my hands reaching up to hold on to his broad shoulders, reminding me of what it felt like to grip them while he fucked me.

"That was a rare move for me, I promise you. But then I rushed out this morning in the middle of our conversation... see? Dick move."

I lean back so that I can search his eyes, desperately seeking some answers to this puzzle of a man in front of me. First, he offers himself up on a silver platter for one night of fuckery—and boy, did he deliver. Then when we meet again, he acts like an ass when he claims I can't keep my emotions in check about our one-night-stand. Next, he apologizes with a coffee—which I found utterly sweet, yet confusing. And then he runs out of my room in the middle of a conversation that actually felt like we were two normal people who could possibly be friends.

Now, he has me pressed up against a wall, the sexy rasp of his voice filling my ears and the gold flecks of his eyes glowing like the eyes of a wolf who's stalking its prey.

*See my confusion here?*

"What do you want from me, Kane?"

I watch Kane study me, his eyes bouncing back and forth between mine and my lips. I can smell the scent of his laundry soap, mixed with that woodsy smell of his cologne from the other night.

He smells like a man, a man that has put my mind in more of a tailspin than Trevor ever did. When Trevor cheated, it definitely stung. But it didn't confuse me. In all actuality, I think I kind of expected it.

But nothing that Kane has done since our night together is something I would have expected. I feel whiplash from the way he's dragging me in and throwing me back out. I need some answers.

I watch his Adam's apple bob as he swallows hard, clearly waiting to respond so he can choose his words carefully.

"I... I don't know..." He growls, pushing himself up off of the wall and turning his back to me, pulling on his hair.

"What?" I ask, even more confused than I thought I was before.

"I don't know what I want from you, Olivia. You and I were supposed to be a one-time thing. But now you're here and I... I feel..."

Anger floods my veins as I watch him throw blame on me once more. "Well, I'm sorry I've come along and wrecked your life. Don't worry, Kane. Our secret will stay a secret and

I'll leave you alone," I chide, pushing myself off of the wall and turning for the exit, making my way out to my car.

"Olivia!" He shouts after me, but I don't turn around. I feel the sting of tears hit my eyes when I realize that trying to reason with him is just a waste of time. From our few brief encounters, it's obvious we can't have a normal conversation. Maybe sex is all we were ever meant to be.

And I'm stupid for thinking it could ever be something more.

The slap of my boots on the pavement mimics the slam of my heart in my chest. My tears threaten to fall, but I hold them inside until I reach my car door and begin to fish my keys from my pocket, the saltiness of the droplets hitting my lips as I let my frustration out in the form of crying.

"Hey, sis," a low voice catches me off-guard as I spin around and hoist my keys up in the air, prepared to do as much damage as the jagged pieces of metal will allow.

"Whoa there! Easy tiger. Liv, it's me."

My brother Cooper stands there before me in his sheriff deputy uniform, one hand on his gun while the other is high in the air.

"Jesus, Coop. You scared the shit out of me!"

He laughs as he lowers his hand and reaches both arms out for me, pulling me in for a hug. I've been home for over a week now, but this is the first time I've seen my younger brother. Cooper is three years younger than me and a newbie sheriff deputy in town. His shifts have been opposite of my schedule so we haven't been able to meet up with each other.

Even though he's younger than me, Cooper towers over my five-eight frame. At six-three and two-hundred some odd pounds of muscle, he makes me feel safe in his arms, in a brotherly way, of course. His dark brown hair and matching eyes make him look just like a younger version of our dad.

"You working the game tonight?" I ask as we break apart.

"Yup. You know this game can get out of hand sometimes. The crowds are insane, so the school district always calls in to the department for added security."

"It's so good to see you. I'm sorry I haven't made an effort to catch up yet. It's been crazy with starting my new job and getting settled in. You're going to mom and dad's for dinner on Sunday, right?"

"Yeah, I'll be there. I'll have to leave a bit early to start my night shift, but I'll be there. Are you okay?" He searches my face, which I'm sure is three shades of red with mascara running down my cheeks.

"Oh, yeah. I'm fine," I lie, looking away to swipe at my face.

"Hey. Did something happen?" He asks, pulling my chin so my face meets his again.

"Just stressed and tired. And these shoes are killing me. I'm ready for bed," I shake him off, unlocking my car and opening my door.

"You're a horrible liar, Liv."

"It's nothing you need to concern yourself with, Coop. I'm good. I'll see you Sunday."

He shakes his head at me before leaning down and kissing the top of my skull. "Whatever you say. Love you. See you Sunday."

I give him a tight-lipped smile, then slide into my car and pull out of the parking lot, leaving the night and all the confusion behind.

The day started out promising and then quickly went to shit. Is this just the new theme of my life now? If that's the case, I demand a do over! Thirty-one years on this earth and my world has never been shaken like this before. This better not be the Trevor effect. Or some weird Mercury retrograde that's making my universe teeter off of its axis.

Sleep. That's what I need. Sleep, a good book, and as little interaction with Kane as possible.

# CHAPTER 16

Kane

"So what brings you in today, Kane? I haven't seen you in a few months."

It's three in the afternoon on a Wednesday and I'm hunched forward, arms resting on my knees on my therapist's couch. My chest is tight and my mind is exhausted ever since my panic attack on Friday and then my confrontation with Olivia that night. I ran several miles trying to work off the adrenaline. I even thought maybe a ride on my motorcycle would help clear my head. But I couldn't muster up the courage to jump on my bike in the state of mind I was in.

So when my therapist responded to my text on Monday that she had an opening today, I took it. I know that therapy has helped me learn much more about myself than I could have realized, and it helped me through one of the most difficult times of my life.

Surely it can help me through whatever the fuck this is that I'm feeling.

"I, uh, had a panic attack on Friday."

"Really?" Dr. Martinez perches in her chair, sitting up taller and eager to take notes with her pen and paper in hand. This Hispanic woman in her fifties may look sweet, but she's made me face my demons harder than Tony ever could. I love her and borderline hate her at the same time.

I sit up and wipe my hands down my slacks, itching to

get rid of the moisture that has been gathered there for days.

Sweaty palms, increased heart rate, a tight chest—all indicators of my anxiety flaring up.

"Yeah. It happened in the morning before school started. I was able to talk myself down, used some of the breathing techniques we've discussed. But the truth is, it scared me."

"Scared you? How so?"

I clear my throat before answering. "It happened after speaking with a colleague of mine. A woman..."

Dr. Martinez lowers her head so she can peer at me above her teal-rimmed glasses.

"A woman?" The look on her face is all-knowing, yet she's still waiting for me to say the words.

"Yeah. I, uh, kind of slept with her."

She sits back in her chair and clicks her pen, placing the ballpoint on the paper, ready to document. "Let's start at the beginning...."

• • • • • • • • • • • • • • • • • • • • • • • • • • • • • • • •

"So, you surrendered yourself to the physical connection you felt with this woman, but what you're feeling is beyond physical?"

I nod. "Yeah, and it freaks me the fuck out."

"Language, Kane," she scolds me.

"Sorry. I just... it's been three years since Natasha and not once have I felt the desire to get to know a woman beyond what will make her come. And even when I took a break from sex, there wasn't a woman who caught my eye like Olivia has. It's... I'm terrified."

"Terrified is a strong word to use. Why choose that

one?"

I sit back and think about what she's asking. Terrified, by definition, means to 'fill with terror or alarm; to make greatly afraid.' And the thought of opening myself up to someone again makes me feel just that.

"Because all I feel is an extreme fear at the thought of trying to have a relationship again. But for the life of me, I can't get this woman out of my head. Even when I thought it was just going to be for the night, by the time I left, I wondered if there was a chance we could make it more than a one-time thing. Our physical connection was insane, obviously. But there was more there. I want to explore it. I want to see if there could be more... but I'm not sure I'm ready for that commitment again. However, I do know that she's the first person who's made me think about it."

"I think that's definitely something to consider. For the three years that you've been coming to me, you've never mentioned a woman before, besides Natasha, of course. If you're here because of her, I think that's worth exploring."

"But... how do I do this? I mean, think about it... the only person I've ever been in a relationship with was Natasha. She was my high school sweetheart. I never dated. I never wooed anyone but her. I don't know where to begin. I've been out of the game my whole adult life pretty much. I'm going to fuck it up."

Dr. Martinez shoots me a scowl at my language again, but I ignore it.

"You start small. You simply vow to get to know her and try to be honest with her about your intentions. If she's the woman you describe her to be, she will appreciate your honesty and hopefully give you the chance to prove yourself. The only way you can move past Natasha, Kane, is by putting yourself out there. You have come so far since your time overseas and after what not only Natasha but T.J. also did to you.

You experienced a deep-rooted betrayal that has made you question your trust in people, yet you've let people in since then."

"Who? Who have I let in, because all I can think about is how many people I've pushed out?"

"Drew and his wife, Tammy, the other men you work with..."

"But they're all my friends, not someone I'm interested in romantically..."

"Beneath every true romance is a foundation of friendship. Friendship you are capable of, so you start there. And as the intimacy grows, you'll find yourself more willing to open up your heart."

I sit back against the couch, a deep sigh leaving my nostrils as the weight of my anxiety starts to leave my chest. This was the clarification and direction that I needed.

I know that I have opened myself up to other people since being bitch-slapped by my best friend and fiancé. And if I don't want to lose my chance with Olivia, I have to be willing to do that with her too.

"My greatest fear is ending up alone..." The words leave my mouth before I can stop them, and finally voicing them out loud feels freeing, like a bird escaping a cage and spreading its wings for the first time in an eternity.

"Because you know that's what you fear, you won't let it happen," the woman sitting across from me says, letting me know that the hundred dollars an hour that I pay her is worth every penny.

# CHAPTER 17

Olivia

High school. I work at one every day and the emotional distress I'm currently feeling makes me believe I'm reliving it.

It's been almost a week since the Ashland-Emerson game where I stormed off and left Kane behind. But sadly, the only way I retreated from him was physically. He's still very much present in my thoughts.

It's like having a crush on a boy back in high school. You get dressed that day with the thought of running into him in the halls, wanting to leave a killer impression on his memory of your aptitude for fashion sense. You avoid locking eyes with him at the same time, pretending you both weren't searching each other out in a crowd. And any conversations you absolutely *have* to partake in, you over-analyze every word you speak in fear of looking stupid.

Well, I've managed to bypass any interaction with him so far, until today. It's Thursday, which means the restaurant class bakes treats for the teachers and leaves them in the lounge for us to pick up at our convenience. After the sample I devoured last week, let's just say I set a reminder on my phone to make sure I got one of each pastry this Thursday.

"Good morning, Olivia," Drew greets me as I step through the door to the lounge, the overpowering smell of sugar and cinnamon wafting through the air.

"Hi, Drew. How's it going?"

"Oh, you know... just living the dream," he chuckles and then shoves the rest of his scone in his mouth. "I swear, these kids might not remember to bring a pencil to class, but they sure can bake the hell out of some flour and sugar," he mumbles around a mouthful of food.

I chuckle as I watch the crumbs fly out of his mouth, preparing to agree when someone else joins our conversation.

"Jesus, dude. Finish chewing before you speak."

*That voice.* I don't even have to turn around to know who that deep rasp and sinful body belongs to. My entire body stiffens, my senses heighten, and my pulse spikes knowing Kane and I are in the same room since our encounter Friday evening.

"Sorry, Mr. Etiquette. But dude, seriously... these things are amazing. It's a snickerdoodle scone! And there's blueberry lemon, raspberry and white chocolate, and pumpkin. You and Olivia better grab some before I eat them all."

"If you do, I'll tell Tammy. I know she's making you watch what you eat, man."

Drew narrows his eyes at Kane. "You wouldn't dare."

Kane snickers. "Try me."

"Fine. I'll just take one more," he reaches through both of us and grabs a blueberry lemon scone and then another, offering it to me. "Want one, Olivia?"

I snatch that scone right up, trying not to act too eager. "Thanks."

"How about a pumpkin one?" Drew grabs one to offer it to me again, as if I can't serve myself.

I crinkle my nose in disgust. "Eck! You can keep all the pumpkin ones far away from me, sir. I don't understand the hype about pumpkin-flavored everything in the fall."

"Dude, that disgusting. Don't offer people pumpkin,"

Kane chimes in, surprising me.

"Really? I thought all women were in to pumpkin. Candles, decorations, pumpkin spice lattes? You chicks usually eat up all that fall shit, right?" Drew asks before turning to Kane for support.

I still haven't turned around to register the look on Kane's face. Obviously he knows I'm here, but he hasn't addressed me either. Then I think he's got a perfect view of my backside right now, and I wore my black slacks today that hug every curve on my lower half. Point for Olivia.

"The decorations I can handle, but the pumpkin flavor is way overdone."

"See, told you," Kane says before he grabs a few scones for himself on a napkin, then proceeds to make another stack.

Drew smirks while slyly reaching for another snickerdoodle before he makes his way to the door. "Seems to me you two share a lot more in common than just a hatred of one another."

"I saw that, Drew. Don't forget, I'm friends with Tammy now too. So don't think I won't squeal as well."

"You both deserve each other then," he waves at us from over his shoulder with his back turned. "And who's to say this one isn't for my lovely wife? I am a gentleman, after all. Hey, don't kill one another before the next class starts."

I shake my head as I laugh at Drew, only to turn back around to find Kane staring down at me now, penetrating my mind with his gaze, holding out the napkin full of scones to me.

"Thank you," I say shyly, accepting his offering and finding a seat at one of the tables.

"You're welcome," he says, shifting his feet, heading to the coffeemaker to refill his thermos.

Silence fills the room as I pick at the raspberry scone —which is wickedly delicious, crumbling and melting on my tongue while a savor every calorie. The slow trickle of Kane pouring coffee into his cup is the only noise.

"So, I've finally met another person who hates pumpkin flavored shit as much as I do," Kane breaks the silence after clearing his throat, startling me.

"Uh, yeah. I only eat one slice of pumpkin pie a year and that's on Thanksgiving. Other than that, I could live without it," I nervously reply, waiting for him to turn around so I can read his face again.

Kane turns and glides over to the table, standing before me, studying my face while his eyebrows draw together in thought.

"Can I help you with something?" I ask curiously, wondering how this man can be so hot and cold. There has to be demons he's fighting to be so wishy-washy with me. How is it we've gone from attacking each other, to him saving me from crickets, to screaming at each other, to frozen in place, talking about pumpkin flavored foods?

"I don't hate you, Olivia," he confesses, astonishing me with directness.

"I don't hate you either, Kane." Our two sets of eyes remained locked on one another, the hammer of my heart in my chest picking up relentlessly as I wait for him to make the next move.

"Olivia, I..." He speaks just as the bell rings and he darts his head to locate the sound, signaling the end of our prep period and the impending start of the next.

The skid of my chair against the tile rings through the room as I push it back to stand, grabbing my scones and keys from the table.

"Have a nice day, Kane," I offer as I scoot around him, my

head held high, not allowing his uncertainty to rock me any more than it already has—at least not in front of him.

"You too, Olivia," he calls out after me, his voice fading away as I turn the corner and battle the students through the halls to get back to my classroom in time for the next period.

# CHAPTER 18

Kane

"I swear, at this point, she probably thinks I can't finish a goddamn sentence," I mutter to Tony as I sip my IPA, hunched over on his bar like I usually find myself on a Friday night.

I needed someone to talk to who wasn't Drew—who's trying to play matchmaker along with his wife—or my therapist, who already gave me the direction I needed to move forward with Olivia. I don't also need to pay her to listen to me bitch about what an idiot I looked like.

Tony just smirks at me with his arms crossed over his chest, that knowing look in his eyes.

"Just say it, Tony...."

"I never thought I'd see the day that you would be this torn up about a woman," he chuckles, making the sound of drowning myself in beer even more appetizing.

"Psh... you and me both, Tony. This is all your fault, you know," I say while pointing a very strong finger in his direction.

"Me? What the hell did I do?"

"You're the one who told me to go have fun that night. You're the one who pushed me towards her. If I hadn't listened to you, none of this would be happening right now!"

"So? If I had to do it all over again, I would. You needed

that, Kane. And now the more I see you up in arms about this woman, the *more* I think you need her," he says while pointing his finger back at me.

"I don't *need* a woman..."

"You may not think that now, but trust me... no man is meant to walk this Earth alone. As much as we don't want to admit it, a good woman makes life worth living, son. Trust me... when I found Georgia, life had a new meaning after her. If anything can help heal you, it's love."

"Hey, I'm not saying I'm in love with the woman. I'd say it's more along the lines of infatuation. Love is what got me in this mess to begin with, Tony. Loving Natasha ended up being the catalyst to a nuclear bomb. Everything and everyone was destroyed in my path after that..."

He nods and then leans in closer to me, his eyes level with mine. "Because you let it. Eventually, you have to re-build, Kane. It's been three years, and I've never seen you like this before. You and Red obviously had more than just a physical connection. Explore it. You owe it to yourself."

My eyes drop to my hands holding my glass, the condensation running down the sides, my thumbs erasing it with each pass of my fingertips. Tony is right, yet another person in my life pushing me to break past this fear I have, and with each piece of advice, I feel myself getting closer to breaking through the barrier.

"Olivia," I state.

"What?"

"Her name is Olivia... and fuck me, Tony... she's everything right and infuriating in a woman. She's intense and passionate, intelligent and witty, beautiful and also kind. She's stubborn, yet sexily confident. She's classy, but wild. And every time I talk to her, I fuck it up by saying the wrong thing —or like yesterday, not being able to finish a thought."

"The bell rang, Kane. That's not your fault. When's the next time you'll see her?"

I sigh, knowing tomorrow night is the best opportunity I have to get us back on track. Tomorrow is the fall mixer at Drew and Tammy's house.

"Tomorrow. There's a party for all the staff at the school. I know she'll be there."

"Then use that time to lay it all on the line with her. I mean, you don't have to bare your heart and soul to the woman—not yet, anyway. But let her know that you want to pursue her, feel it out between the two of you to see if there's something more there."

I nod repeatedly, knowing that Tony's correct. Tomorrow is my perfect chance to push things with Olivia in the right direction. I just hope I can finish a sentence this time.

# CHAPTER 19

Olivia

"I'm pulling up to their house right now," I inform Clara on my Bluetooth speaker as I pull up to a front yard and a driveway full of parked cars.

"Will Kane be there?"

"I'm assuming so. He does work at the school, remember?"

"No shit, woman. I just thought maybe after what happened at the game, he'd chicken out about seeing you." Last weekend after Kane and I had it out in the tunnel, I called my friends and filled them in on the development.

"Yeah, well, *I* almost chickened out about coming here too. Especially after Thursday..."

"What the hell happened Thursday? Jesus Christ, Liv! You gotta keep a woman informed!" Clara shouts in the phone, making me cringe as I find a spot to park that won't leave me boxed in just in case I have to escape in a hurry.

"Sorry. I have this thing called a job, and so do you. It's hard to catch each other on the phone!"

"Yeah, stupid need for money to live and shit ruining our lives. Okay, so fill me in."

And I do in the cliff notes version, recounting the entire scone debacle in less than five minutes.

Debacle is a strong word to use to describe that event.

But right now, I feel like every interaction with Kane is a debacle. I just wish I knew where we stood.

Are we friends? Enemies? Just colleagues? Or is there a hope of more?

"Okay, well you'd better call me tomorrow and let me know what the hell happens tonight, or I will hunt you down at your parent's house for dinner tomorrow and unofficially invite myself."

"You know you're always welcome at my parent's house..." And it's true. My parents adore my three best friends. We spent so much time together in high school, especially at my house, that my parents joked they really had four daughters. My poor brother was surrounded by estrogen constantly.

"Well, I just might then. What's Mama Walsh making for the customary Sunday night dinner?"

"Chicken and dumplings, I believe."

"Oh, fuck me. Yeah, I'll be there," Clara moans in the phone, garnering a laugh from me as I check my face one last time in the rearview mirror.

"Okay. Well, here I go," I declare, taking a deep breath to quell my nerves.

"You've got this. Just have fun. Make some new friends. Don't drink too much, because you don't want to be that co-worker—the one who can't handle her liquor and gets overly friendly. Before you know it, you're walking around blindfolded trying to play pin the tail on the cock..."

"Dear lord, please tell me you're not speaking from experience?"

Dead silence echoes on the other end of the phone.

"Clara! You did not!"

"Ha! Oh no, not me. Sorry, my phone cut out. No, some

slutty secretary at my office lost her marbles at the Christmas party last year. Security had to usher her out."

I'm dying of laughter. "Oh, Jesus. Okay, not too much to drink. Got it."

"Go get 'em, Liv."

"Love ya!"

"Love ya, too!"

I end the call and gather my phone and lip gloss, depositing both items in the pocket of my new Calvin Klein coat I snatched up for dirt cheap at Marshall's. I shouldn't need a purse or I.D. This is a house party, not a bar or concert I'm walking in to.

Setting the alarm on my car, I head for the house, the chill of the fall air hitting my nose and ears, causing them to instantly freeze. The temperatures have already dropped below freezing a few times this year, which is normal for Oregon. Pretty soon there will be snow days and the holidays will be here.

The sound of chatter and laughter filters out from beneath the garage door that has been cracked. The front of the house is supremely lit with solar lights and hanging lanterns from the stucco. A giant red door is the only thing standing between me and a night of social anxiety. It's not so much the other people I'm anxious about seeing and meeting.

It's just one person in particular.

I don't bother knocking, knowing the chance of someone hearing it would be slim, so I turn the handle and push open the large barn door into a comforting home, charmingly decorated and open, the living room being the first thing you see. A giant brown sectional sofa curves around the room, facing a large flat screen anchored to the wall. Candles are lit on top of various surfaces and pictures frames filled with memories of Drew and Tammy's life adorn the walls. Looking around the room, you see the evidence of a life well-lived, a life joining two people who care deeply about one another.

Melancholy swallows me whole as I remember I am no closer to finding that myself. Hell, especially with all the drama surrounding my sexcapades with Kane, I'd say I'm three steps behind right now.

"Olivia! You're here!" An overenthusiastic and slightly drunk Tammy greets me, emerging from a hallway that must lead to the garage where the party is clearly gathered.

"I told you I would be here. Thanks for having me," I pull her into a hug where she almost takes me down to the floor in her excitement.

"Oops. Sorry," she laughs, righting herself as we both adjust our clothing from the close fall. "Come, come! Did you bring anything to drink?"

I shake my head, unaware this was a bring your own beverage type of party.

"No worries. We have beer and wine in the fridge in the garage. Typically, people bring their preferred drink of choice, but we always make sure to have stuff that anyone would like."

"Sounds great. I love wine," I answer, following closely behind Tammy as she escorts me out to the garage.

Filtering through the door, I'm surrounded by a room full of Emerson Falls High School staff. Many faces I recognize, some I've never seen, but I'd bet I only know a handful of names. When you're encased in your own four walls at school, it's hard to break free, let alone have time to mingle. Hence, the point of this party, I presume.

"Hey, everyone!" Tammy shouts over the low-playing music and cacophony of chatter. "This is Oliva Walsh, our new math teacher! Olivia, this is everyone!"

A collective "Hi!" rings out right before everyone resumes their conversations, a few people taking a moment to walk over and introduce themselves.

There's Harriet Tilman, our art teacher. She's a wiry old lady with long grey hair and turtle shell glasses, whose wardrobe looks like it's stuck in the sixties. But I know from the students that they love her, and after speaking with her, I can see why. She's so carefree and in tune with her surrounding energy... she'd make me want to take art and I can't draw a stick figure to save my life.

Sally Betts, one of the English teachers, comes up next to introduce herself. She's known for dressing up in a costume of the characters from whatever novel or play her classes are reading. I've heard she's channeled her inner Robin Williams and stood on her desk to recite lines before. The animation she uses when she talks definitely solidifies how charismatic of teacher she must be.

The other members of the math department stride up to me at various points to say hello as well. I know most of them now from the two meetings we've had since I arrived. It's always nice to have a group of people who get you. Few other people on the planet share a passion for math like I do, and physically, I definitely don't fit the stereotype. Math teachers have a bad rap for being middle-aged white men with receding hairlines and calculators in their pockets. Last time I checked, that wasn't me.

"So you're the newbie, huh?" I turn around, coming face to face with Mrs. Waterman, or what some other teachers have referred to as 'the succubus.'

"Uh, yes. Hi, I'm Olivia. It's nice to meet you," I offer while extending my hand. She inspects my palm before barely placing her fingers in mine, half-heartedly shaking my hand in reciprocation.

God, I can't stand it when people can't give a proper

handshake. Didn't anyone teach them how important a strong greeting is? How pivotal that first impression can be?

One of these flimsy handshakes I'm receiving right now just irritates my soul.

"Alice. So, how have the little punks been treating you?" She grits out while taking a sip from her red wine. She's got that saliva build-up in the corners of her mouth that is making me want to gag.

"Uh, just fine actually. I really love my students."

"Ha. Just give it time," she snarks, and I immediately know I need to get as far away from this woman as I can before she wrangles me into her cult of teachers who stick around in the profession for the summers off and full benefits.

I know teachers like her. There are a few at every school. They hate their jobs and really don't like kids, yet they've been there for so long, there's no reason for them to leave. It's so unfair to the students who end up in their class-rooms. I vow to never be one of those teachers.

"Olivia, there you are," the voice I hear immediately pulls my attention as I twist around and am greeted by Kane, dressed in dark jeans and a black pea coat, his hair perfectly tousled and his beard neatly trimmed, framing that rugged jaw and highlighting those whiskey-colored eyes. Damn, why does he have to be so freaking sexy?

"Yes, uh, here I am," I answer timidly, not really sure where he's going with this.

"Sorry, Alice, but I need to steal Olivia away. There's a situation I need her assistance with. You have a great evening," he politely dismisses her while reaching for my hand, inter-lacing our fingers together before pulling me behind him out of the back door of the garage and onto a large patio, overlook-ing a forested field, the music from inside the garage becoming just a distant sound.

The feel of our hands entangled together makes butterflies take flight in my stomach, the warmth of his skin on mine helps heat me up as the frigid air hits my face. Kane takes the lead as he walks us past a few people sitting at a steel patio table and around the corner where a standing swing sits under the eaves of the porch, overlooking a different side of the property.

"Take a seat," he urges me and I comply, even though I'm completely confused as to why he pulled me away from everyone. This is the man that now, on more than one occasion, I have vowed to stay away from—for his benefit—and yet, he's the one making it a mission for us to be alone.

The side of the house we're perched up against is dimly lit, only the residual light cast from the front and back of the house providing enough glow that I can still see the features of Kane's face, the same ones that pulled me in that first night and I haven't managed to forget.

"Sorry to pull you away, but believe me, I was saving you from a torturous conversation with Alice."

I chuckle as I realize Kane was protecting me, an unfamiliar feeling hitting me in my chest. If you would have asked me last week if I thought Kane would come to my rescue again, I would have laughed in your face. He saved me from crickets already, but after our encounters since then, I assumed our relationship was headed in a very different direction.

"As soon as she opened her mouth, I knew I was in for a world of hurt."

"Yup. That woman will suck you in and spin a web around you of venomous thread, and before you know it, you'll start believing everything she says."

"You forget, Kane. I've been a teacher at another school before this. I know about the Alice's of the educational world."

He gives me a half smile before realizing he's still holding my hand, releasing mine gently as he turns to face me more. Propping one foot on his other knee, he tilts his head in my direction.

"Where did you teach before this?"

"Uh, in Northern California, a little outside of Napa. Being that close to wine country sure had its perks," I jest while adjusting my hair behind one of my ears.

"So what brought you to Emerson Falls then?" Kane's eyes are studying me, making me even more nervous about this conversation. I have so many questions for him about why he suddenly seemed intrigued by me, but I can't help but relish in the feeling of being normal with him right now, talking like two human beings who genuinely want to get to know each other.

I debate how much to divulge before opting for vagueness.

"I needed a change, so I came home. I actually grew up here. I went to Emerson Falls High, believe it or not."

Kane's eyebrows shoot up in surprise. "No kidding? How did it feel sitting in the stands the other night then?"

"It was odd, to say the least, but obviously I'm no stranger to that stadium. Emerson is just where I work now," I answer, giving him a small glance into my past.

"What's your favorite color?"

I'm taken aback at his abrupt change in topic and more than innocent question.

"Uh, teal."

"Nice. Favorite food?"

"Sushi," I answer, pondering this inquisition even further.

"Never had it. When's your birthday?"

"July sixteenth. Kane," I begin to stop him, but he cuts me off.

"Sweet. Mine's the tenth of April. Any siblings?"

I scrunch my face at him, irritation clouding my mind as I realize he's sitting here and drilling me and I have no idea why.

"I'm sorry, but are we playing twenty questions here?" I ask, sarcasm lacing my words.

Kane retreats, scooting back along the swing, increasing the distance between us.

"What's going on, Kane? Forgive me for being curious, but the last time we spoke you made it clear you didn't know what you wanted from me. Before that, I thought we had agreed to stay away from each other. And now, you're acting like we're best buds and interviewing me like I'm in the running for your new best friend. I'm... I'm just confused," I confess, my inquiry causing a shift in the conversation between us.

Kane's head lifts now, but he's staring out into the yard, not at me. After what feels like the longest silence of my life, he finally speaks just loud enough for me to hear.

"I'm sorry. I wasn't trying to make you feel uncomfortable. Shit..." He turns away, pinching the bridge of his nose in frustration. "I... I don't know how to do this, Olivia..."

"Do what, Kane?"

Turning to face me now, I can see the fear in his eyes. This dominant and headstrong man I met just a few weeks ago looks like he's on the verge of tears, or at least some sort of revelation.

"I don't know how to date..."

"Date?" I ask in shock, completely flabbergasted that

Kane's thoughts regarding us were about dating.

He lets out a long breath before reaching for me, pulling my icy fingers into his warm palm, rubbing his thumb over the top of my hand. The warmth is not only counterbalancing the coldness of the air but also the frigid air between us.

"Yes, date. Christ, Olivia. You and I were supposed to just be a one-time thing, right? But when I saw you again, I couldn't stop thinking about you. Hell, I couldn't stop thinking about you when I left that night. It's been a long time since I've been interested in a woman... and I guess I'm just trying to get to know you. Hence the questions... I'm sorry. I didn't mean to make you feel uneasy."

The intensity of my pulse right now only makes my head spin that much faster. He wants to date me? Or get to know me? So all of these hot and cold signals he's been giving me is because he doesn't know how to handle what he's feeling?

"Wow. Okay... I guess I understand. I mean, Kane... I'm not going to lie and say that I wasn't thinking about you too after our night together. But when we ran into each other again—literally," he chuckles as I continue, "You seemed so upset to see me again. I thought you wanted nothing to do with me."

Kane's thumb continues to stroke my hand as he watches our connection. Looking back up to me, he continues. "I didn't know how to process seeing you again. I know I didn't handle it appropriately, but the more we ran into each other, the more I realized that getting to know you better is something I definitely want."

Who would have known that this man could actually confess his desire to me without acting like a child?

"You continue to surprise me, Kane."

He cracks a smile. "Oh yeah, how's that?"

"I don't know. I guess I just had you pegged for this guy that wasn't very in-tune with his feelings and wanted to just be left alone."

He huffs. "Yeah, well, if you'd met me three years ago, that's exactly the man you would have encountered. I've come a long way since then."

"Is that how long it's been since you've been interested in someone?" I ask, hopeful he'll continue to be honest with me.

I see his jaw clench and then his eyes retreat from mine as he drops my hand, his face turned back to looking out over the yard. "Yeah, something like that."

Okay, not the most detailed answer, but hopefully he'll open up to me, eventually.

"Well, I don't know who taught you how to date, or woo a woman, but drilling her with random questions is not the best approach," I joke, hoping to lighten the mood.

The slightest smile tips up on the sides of his mouth, his eyes bouncing back and forth between mine when he focuses back on me. "I was told to try to establish a friendship with you, and I thought asking you a bunch of questions would help me do that. You gotta admit, I did learn some interesting facts about you."

"Okay, yes, that's one way, I suppose. So is just having a natural conversation. Getting to know someone doesn't have to just consist of facts about the other person. Getting a glimpse into your mind and how you think about the world tells me way more about you than your favorite color."

"Which is red, by the way," he answers back, making me smirk.

"Good to know," I say, immersing myself in this euphoric feeling of how ecstatic I am that the night turned out this way. I came into this party not knowing what the repercussions would be when I ran into him, because I knew we would cross paths. Naturally, this conversation is surpassing my assumptions immensely.

"So who told you to drill me with questions?"

Kane shakes his head and then laughs.

"It was Drew, wasn't it?" I lean forward, itching for information.

"No, it wasn't Drew. No one actually told me to just start drilling you. I made that mistake all on my own."

"Wow, so you really must have been out of the dating world for a while then, huh?"

Kane's face falls as he clears his throat and then nods. Suddenly, a rush of fear zips through me as I wait for his answer. Based on his reaction, nerves spike in my chest, bracing myself for a confession that might make me run.

"The last time I pursued a girl I was sixteen," he finally states, rocking my mind and causing my stomach to plummet.

"Sixteen?" I whisper, afraid to show my true shock and concern. That means he was a teenager and now he's gotta be in his late twenties at least. Holy hell! What the heck happened there?

"Yeah. She was my high school sweetheart. Things didn't work out, obviously," he declares in a way where I sense the conversation ends there.

"Well, don't worry. I'll coach you along the way," I tease him, winking in his direction when he locks eyes with me again.

"I just might need that Olivia. I'm way out of my comfort zone here."

Reaching for his hand, it becomes my turn to soothe and comfort him. I close the distance between us, scooting close enough that I get a whiff of his scent now, his cologne mixed with the smoke from the bonfire out back transporting me to another place entirely.

"So where do we go from here?" I ask as this elated feeling overcomes me. I don't think I realized just how much I wanted to see this side of him until he just gave me a glimpse of it. Clara was right. There is definitely something here between us, besides the physical.

Although, as I study him, admiring his strong face and eyes and the way his entire body eats up the space on the swing, I'm only reminded of our sexual rendezvous from before, and suddenly my entire body becomes hot.

"Well, I have more questions I'd like to ask you, if you're game?"

I smile, admiring how boyishly cute he sounds right now. It's like the sixteen-year-old innocence he still possesses is the only way he knows how to interact with me right now.

"Sure," I agree, the tingles of excitement I feel makes me itch with anticipation for more. The truth is, I think I've always wanted more from him since that first night. And now I'm getting it.

"Okay, let's do this."

# CHAPTER 20

Kane

I swear, I don't think I even felt this nervous when I was trekking across the desert trying not to get killed in Afghanistan.

No, that's a lie. Avoiding death is definitely the most nerve-wracking thing I've ever done. But knowing that I had to make a move tonight with Olivia is definitely a close second to that level of anxiety.

Yet, here we are, sitting on the porch swing, isolated from the crowd so the only two people who exist at this moment are her and me. She looks stunning tonight, wearing dark blue jeans and a puffy cream-colored coat, her stark red hair cascading down around her face in soft waves. Every time her eyes meet mine, I get that same spark of need I felt in her classroom that day that made me run. But tonight, I'm welcoming it.

Obviously, I've always found her beautiful—but something about how the tip of her nose is slightly red from the cold, or the way she's finally opening up and letting me in without all the bullshit sexual politics in the way—makes her even more desirable.

Reaching in the pocket of my coat, I fetch my phone where my list of questions is typed out. I prepared in advance for my goal this evening. Little did I know that it would slightly backfire. But then again, here we are, Olivia agreeing to continue my inquisition. I guess this idea wasn't all bad.

"Oh, my gosh... do you have notes on your phone?" She peers over into my lap, and the closeness of her body spikes my heart rate to unhealthy levels. I've already been inside this woman, but now that our relationship has shifted, she makes me even more nervous than I was that first night. When all I considered we would be was casual sex, the pressure was off. I could immerse myself in the experience and own it. Sex is easy, that's something I've never struggled with.

But now we're crossing into an unfamiliar territory for me, the process of getting to know each other beyond the physical. The last time I did this was with she-who-will-not-be-named anymore. I refuse to dwell on her when I have this gorgeous woman in front of me, her head mere inches from my crotch.

"Yes, I have a list. I wanted to be prepared," I fire back, retracting my phone from her eyesight, making her sit back and fake a pout, crossing her arms over her chest.

Fuck, she's cute when she's mad—even if it is fake.

"Come on. I worked hard on this. Let me be bask in my effort?" I ask, hoping she'll see that I'm putting in an abundance of effort where she's concerned.

"Fine," she huffs and rolls her eyes, making me grin at her reaction. I sit up tall against my side of the swing as my foot on the ground pushes off the deck, propelling us back before we rock forward in a slow, rhythmic glide. "But if you ask me a question, you have to answer it too."

"That seems fair. Okay, here goes. Let's start with an easy one. What is your favorite thing about your career?"

She doesn't pause to think at all before she declares, "The kids." Only a teacher who truly understands the meaning of the job would offer that answer. Not summers off, not paid vacation. Nope. An irreplaceable teacher is the one who shows up every day for their students, despite the bullshit that goes along with the job.

"I wholeheartedly agree."

"I should hope so, and that you aren't just copying my answer to score brownie points with me," she teases.

"No, I really do agree. I knew I wanted to teach since high school, and the Army helped me pay for my degree. Knowing when I was out I would finally get to make a difference in the classroom was the only thing that kept me going some days. Well, that and..." I stop myself before I utter her name. Because after what she did to me, it doesn't matter that she was who I would dream about at night to remind me of the sacrifice I made for our future. She burned that dream up in flames as soon as she touched T.J.

"And what?" She asks curiously.

"Never mind. It's not important," I shake it off and glance back down at my phone for my next question. "Okay, I'll answer this one first so you know I'm not just copying you this time. Sound good?"

Her smile says it all. "Learning to compromise already. I'm impressed."

"I'm not a stubborn, spoiled brat, Olivia. I know how to play fair... well, most of the time," I say, feigning innocence but sending her a vibe that I hope she picks up on. By the narrow pinch in her eyes, I can tell she senses where I'm going with this.

I can't wait to get her beneath me again so I can tease her and bring her to the brink of an orgasm before working her back down and up all over again. Yeah, I can play fair... or I can make her question her sanity as I edge her up to an orgasm repeatedly before she explodes. Usually, I win either way.

"Okay," I clear my throat while trying to discretely reposition myself on the swing to ease the friction on my growing dick in my pants. "What celebrity would you like to meet at Starbucks for a cup of coffee?" I tilt my head in thought, even bringing my hand to my chin to accentuate my deep reasoning. "I'd have to say... Ryan Reynolds."

"Oh! Interesting... Do explain..." she says as she pulls her jacket tighter around her body.

"I hate to admit this, but you'll find out, eventually. I have a bit of a man crush on him."

She laughs at me, the sound like music to my ears. Olivia should laugh more, the full-bodied, natural, mesmerizing laugh that sounds like pure joy. Why haven't I heard that sound before? Oh, probably because I was too busy acting like an ass which didn't warrant her laughter. I do know what she sounds like when she comes though, if that's any consolation.

"Please elaborate," she says as her laughter winds down.

"Well, for starters, the man is just good-looking. He's got the hot nerd thing going for him, and his body is fit. I'm not gay, I swear. I can just appreciate the dedication it takes to look like that."

She giggles and then waves her hand in front of me to continue.

"Second, he's funny as hell and wickedly charming. And, he's a great dad. He worships his wife, and you can tell the relationship they have is built on the fact that they are best friends. The way they troll each other on social media has me dying of laughter all the time. And she's gorgeous too. He has it all, and I would love to know what his secret is."

Oliva stares with this childish smirk on her face. "That's a really great answer. I agree, Ryan Reynolds is hot as hell, but everything else you said is also dead-on."

I welcome her appreciation of my answer, but now it's her turn. "Okay, okay... who's your person?"

"Hands down, Ellen DeGeneres."

"Oh, yeah... great choice."

"She is my human crush. It has nothing to do with male versus female. I just think she's one of the best people to walk the planet. I mean, her show brings so much joy and positivity in this world. I just want to be her, or at least be surrounded by her so I can absorb some of her awesomeness. She preaches kindness over everything. Her bravery is admirable, and she isn't afraid to speak her mind."

"That's a fine answer, Olivia," I reply in a weird British accent. *Where the hell did that come from?*

"Excuse me?" She giggles again and fuck, if it doesn't make my dick twitch.

"Just pretend that didn't happen. Okay, last one for now..."

"What? Last one? This is fun," she pouts, making me want to suck that bottom lip in my mouth and worship her tongue with my own.

"Oh, look who likes the questions now?" I tease. "We need to save some for next time."

"Next time?" Her voice sounds surprised, but seriously —did she not think I'd want to take her out?

"Yes, next time. There will be a next time for us, Olivia. Now that I finally got you to talk to me, I'll be damned if I let my momentum slow down," I wink at her.

Her cheeks flush with bashfulness as she looks down at her hands, fidgeting with the sleeves of her coat. "Okay, I'm ready for my last question," she says peering up at me, her long lashes framing her eyes and the soft glow of the light around us bringing out the subtle green hues that get lost in the browns.

"Okay. This is a good one. What's your biggest fear?"

She ponders her response for a moment, then provides

me an answer I wasn't expecting.

"Snakes. But crickets are definitely a close second."

I throw my head back in laughter, my entire body shaking as I process her words.

"Snakes and crickets? Really?" I fire back through my chuckles. "I already knew about the crickets, but snakes? Not death? Or public speaking? According to the internet, those are the top two fears of most people…"

"Nope. Snakes are disgusting! They have no limbs! And yes, crickets terrify me, but you already knew that. Public speaking doesn't bother me too much, seeing as how I stand up and talk in front of people virtually every day. And I don't fear death. I guess I more fear the idea of dying before I've felt like I've lived and loved wholeheartedly."

Her candidness hits me hard as I realize I agree. When I was overseas, it terrified me to think that I could die before marrying she-who-will-not-be-named, or getting to have children and raise a family. After hearing Oliva phrase it like that, I realize she's right. It's not death that I fear—It's *not* living a life well-lived, void of someone who you want to share all the good and bad with. It's taking for granted the people who are there for you, day in and day out. It's the fear of being alone, just as I voiced to Dr. Martinez the other day.

"When you put it that way, I guess I'd say I would have to agree with you. Although, I suppose you could say my biggest fear then is ending up alone." It's the first time I've ever uttered the words out loud to someone besides my therapist. "There was a time a few years ago when I thought being alone was what I wanted. Then I realized that you don't have to let everyone in, but you can't go through life shutting everyone out either."

"Exactly," she agrees before smiling up at me, the bright white of her grin turns my insides to putty. "For what it's worth, Kane... thank you for finally letting me in a little. I don't think I've had this much fun getting to know someone in... well, I don't know how long."

"I feel the same, Olivia," I reply as I watch her shiver on the swing beside me. "But I think I'd better get you near the fire or back inside soon before you turn into a popsicle." Gathering myself to stand, I turn around to assist her, reaching for her hand again, pulling her in closer to me than I intended, but fuck if the feel of her pressed up against me doesn't feel right. It did that night we spent together too, but this is different—more intimate if that's possible. Before it was all about the physical connection. But now I know more about the woman standing in front of me, which makes our proximity even more influential.

When I look into her eyes now, I see a woman with a heart who cares deeply about her students, who values kindness in others above what they can offer her, and who ultimately wants a life filled with love and people that make her feel fulfilled. Those are things I never knew about her before we slept together. And hell if it doesn't make me want to learn more.

"Come on," I lead her back around the house along the back porch, passing by the patio table again where a few of our colleagues are seated, drinking and playing cards. A small staircase descends off of the wooden platform, leading to a fire pit in the middle of the only open clearing in the yard, as trees surround every other surface of the property.

Giant logs are situated around the fire, contained by a circular structure of rocks. The heat of the flames instantly warms me, but so does the thought of spending more time with Olivia. I motion for her to sit on one of the tree trunks, her hands reaching out in front of her to absorb the heat from the fire.

"Oh, yes, that feels good," she moans as the heat from

the flames highlight her face and begin to defrost her features. Being the man that I am, her words instantly spark the memory of her saying something along those lines while I was buried inside of her.

*Shit. The last thing I need right now is a raging hard-on.*

"Are you thirsty?" I offer before taking my seat.

"A glass of wine would be great, actually," she smiles up at me, and the more often I see this content side of her, the more I want to be the one to bring it out.

"Sure. Red or white?"

"White is perfect. Thanks," she states as I nod and turn in the direction of the house, entering back through the garage and into the kitchen where Drew is leaning over the counter, his face stuffed full of chips and dip.

"Hey, man. Where have you been? I didn't even know you were here," he mumbles around a mouthful of food. I swear, I don't know how he eats the way he does and stays in shape.

"Oh... I was actually with Olivia," I discretely answer while reaching for a bottle of white wine from the counter and pouring a glass.

"No shit. How'd it go?"

I smirk up at him while pouring the crisp liquid, the sweet smell of grapes hitting my nose. "Really well, actually."

"Fuck yeah, Kane. Good for you, man!"

"Jesus, Drew. Pipe down. I don't need everyone knowing I'm pursuing a woman for the first time since I was a teenager," I grit through my teeth.

"Fuck man, I'm sorry. The beer is hitting me hard. I haven't been this drunk in a long time," he hiccups while shoving more chips in his mouth.

I shake my head at him. "Just remember you'll pay for it tomorrow."

"So, did you make a move?" He asks as crumbs fly out of his mouth. The man really needs to wear one of those bibs that catches the food that trickles out.

"Uh, not really. I mean... fuck, should I?"

Drew eyes me suspiciously. "Haven't you already slept together?"

I drop my voice lower as a few teachers walk by on their way back to the garage. "I mean, yeah. But now things are different. I don't want her to think I just want to get in her pants again. I mean, Christ. I definitely do eventually, but that will take time."

Drew nods. "That a boy. Take it slow. Make her work for it," he winks.

"You really are a douche, you know that? How Tammy ever saw marriage potential in you, I'll never understand," I rib my best friend, grabbing a beer for me out of the fridge and the glass of wine I poured.

"The ladies dig the asshole vibe, Kane," he belches, and then takes a drink from his beer.

"Sure, 'cause the asshole thing was getting me really far before."

Drew stumbles over to me, grasping my shoulder with his empty hand. "Seriously, bro... take it one day at a time. I... I love you, man."

*Oh, Jesus Christ. We're at that level of drunk now, are we?*

"I love you too, Drew. Now I'm going to go find Tammy so she can cut you off. Behave yourself and lay off the chips."

Drew glides back around the counter, lifting the bowl and pouring it into his mouth, crumbs flying everywhere. "Never!" He shouts as chips soar through the air.

I laugh my ass off as I amble down the hallway back to the garage, making small talk with a few people on my way back out to the fire.

And when I see her—Olivia hunched over and bundled in her coat, a joyful smile spread wide across her face as she speaks to the person next to her—I know she's worth the leap I'm taking. I just hope my past doesn't come back to haunt me and fuck this all up.

# CHAPTER 21

Olivia

"Mom, I'm here!" I shout as I walk through the front door of my parent's house on the chilly October afternoon. I barely defrosted this morning from the fall mixer last night at Drew and Tammy's, and then had to bundle up again to make the trek over to the home I was raised in for our weekly Sunday night dinner.

Before I moved to Northern California to go to college, Sunday nights were always reserved for a home-cooked meal from my mom. No matter what we had going on in our lives, my parents insisted we share dinner together at the end of each week. And now, being back home, my mother was elated to continue the tradition with me back at the table.

"In the kitchen!" She yells back as I remove my coat and hang it up near the front door. Adjusting my top and checking my appearance in the mirror in the entryway, I side-step the staircase right in front of me and make my way to the kitchen in the back of the house.

"Oh, it smells good, Mom," I greet her with a kiss on the cheek and probably a little too much enthusiasm. But hell, I can't help it. The perma-smile on my face won't leave after my night with Kane.

I left Drew and Tammy's last night full of optimism and giddy like a teenage girl with a crush. Kane's confession of how he truly felt about me finally made me more hopeful than

I've felt in a long time. Not only was he honest with me, but the fact that he put in so much effort with his list of questions solidified his intentions. Obviously, his lack of dating history is a bit concerning, but I know I can't doubt the fact that he's serious about moving forward. And now the anticipation of where we go from here is killing me.

"Go wash your hands so you can help me. I finally have my girl home and I need to remind you how to cook," she teases me as I reach for the faucet and lather up my hands.

"I haven't forgotten how to cook, Mom. But I'll be honest, I don't do it that often because cooking for one person is a lot of work."

"So how did last night go?" She asks, changing the subject and then directs me to mix the dough for the dumplings. Along with my four friends, I've kept my mother up to date on Kane developments as well.

I can't hide the mile-wide grin that spreads across my face and the blush I instantly feel come over my cheeks. I bend my head down to try to hide it, but nothing gets past my mother.

"That good, huh?" She laughs, stirring the pot of chicken and gravy on the stove. My mother makes the best chicken and dumplings you'll ever taste.

"Mom," I whisper, even though we're the only two people in the kitchen. "Kane was there, and he pulled me aside and...."

"Knock, knock!" A voice I'm all too familiar with interrupts my story as I turn around and search out Clara.

"You came?" I ask her as she makes her way around the corner and into the kitchen.

"Uh, yeah! You said Mama Walsh was making chicken and dumplings. I'm here!"

"Good to see you, Clara," my mom greets her and Clara hugs her from the side.

"I wore my stretchy pants just for this meal, Mama. I hope you made enough. Calories don't count tonight."

"There's plenty. So Liv, get back to your story," my mom prompts.

"Oh! Is Liv talking about what happened last night?"

I shake my head at her. Perry, Amy, Clara and I are all close, but Clara and I definitely talk the most, and she's the biggest cheerleader rooting for Kane and me.

"Yes, I was before you barged in."

Clara reaches for the veggies and dip my mom set out on the counter, chomping down on a carrot smothered in ranch. "Okay, please continue then. I'm dying to know what happened."

I let out a long sigh, but then that smile overtakes my face again. "You guys... Kane took me completely by surprise. I was talking to this evil witch of a woman that we work with, and he comes over and pulls me away from her. He led me to this porch swing on one side of the house, away from everyone else, and then started drilling me with all of these random questions, which completely threw me for a loop. When I asked him what he was doing, he got all awkward, which was charmingly adorable. And then... he told me he wants to get to know me. Date me. I... I still can't believe it."

"Eeeekkk! Oh my God, Liv! Yes!" Clara squeals and my mom and I both start laughing as I feel my cheeks get hot again.

"Well, is that what you want?" My mom chimes in.

I nod. "Yeah, I do. I mean, I never thought that dating him would be an option, given how we met and then finding out that we work together. But... he was so transparent last night. He really put himself out there and was honest, and it made me feel hopeful. I can't remember the last time I felt that way..."

And that's the truth. Even though things are new, there's something about Kane that has kept me intrigued since that first night. And after getting to know him better last night, I'm even more interested.

"This is crazy. You move back home after catching your ex banging his secretary, have mind-blowing sex with the hot lumberjack, find out you work with him, and then now you're dating him. Why can't things happen like this in my life?" Clara whines while I chuckle at her synopsis of my life in the past few weeks.

"Well, Liv. I'm happy for you and I can't wait to meet this man," my mom admits as I hand her the dough to drop in the gravy.

"Give me a little while before I throw him to the wolves, okay, Mom? You, I'm not too worried about. But you know Dad and Cooper... they'll drill him and chase him away."

Even though my brother is younger than me, he's always been massive, like my Dad. And any boy I dated in high school was terrified of both of them. It's a miracle I could keep any boy around for any length of time. My dating life didn't really take flight until I left for college. And the only guy they ever met after high school was Trevor, and well... we all know how that ended up.

"Speaking of your Dad and Cooper," Mom says as she looks over my shoulder, just as my father and brother walk in from outside.

"Just finished chopping some wood, hun. We should be good for a few weeks now," my dad tells my mom, as Cooper trails behind. "There's my girl! How is it you've been home for weeks now and I've only seen you once?" My dad greets me with a kiss on my forehead and a bear hug.

"Life has been crazy, Dad. It's difficult moving home and starting a new job in less than a week."

"Well, at least I know I'll see you every Sunday now, right?" He winks as Cooper comes around him and gives me a hug.

"You look better than when I saw you last, sis," he tells me before turning around and noticing Clara, who hasn't said a word since Cooper walked in. Clara looks stunned, her eyes bugging out of her head at the sight of my brother.

"Cooper Walsh? Is that you?" She finally speaks, faking innocence, but I caught the surprise on her face. "Gosh, you sure have grown up, haven't you?" She teases while reaching out to give him a hug, her hands lingering on his biceps a little too long for my comfort.

"Hey, Clara. Long time no see," he looks down at her, his dark hair falling forward on his face. The two of them hold each other's gazes for a minute before I clear my throat to interrupt.

"Clara, can you help us set the table?" I ask, as Clara spins around to face me, realizing I saw her perusal of my brother.

"Oh, yeah, sure," she stutters, looking flushed. Clara never ceases to appreciate a good-looking man. And even though Cooper is my brother, I can admit he's handsome. But the way she's reacting to him is far from normal for her.

I side-eye my brother, catching him staring at Clara's ass before shoving him out of the kitchen.

"Hey!"

"I saw that," I whisper through gritted teeth. "Go sit in the living room and wait for dinner."

Cooper chuckles and shrugs, before grabbing two sodas

from the fridge for him and my dad and making his way to the couch.

Once dinner is ready, the five of us sit down and dive in. I can't help the moans that escape my mouth as I devour my mom's cooking. It's been so long since I've enjoyed it—just another benefit of being home again.

"So, how's work going, Liv?" My dad asks around a mouthful of food.

"Great, actually. The kids are great, and I really like most of my colleagues."

"Yeah, one in particular," Clara mutters, causing me to throw an elbow to her rib cage and give her a wide-eyed warning.

"What was that?" Dad asks.

"Would you like more, Dan?" My mother distracts my father as I mouth a 'thank you' in her direction. She winks at me in that all-knowing way.

"Yes, hun."

"So, Cooper. You have to work tonight, right?" I ask, changing the subject and putting the attention on my younger brother.

"Yeah. The graveyard shift sucks, but that's what I've been assigned to. It's a Sunday night though, so hopefully it won't be too crazy."

"When did you become a sheriff deputy?" Clara pipes up, studying my brother across the table. I think she and I are going to have a little conversation later if she keeps ogling him like that. I love my friend, but Clara is a chew-them-up-and-spit-them-out kind of gal. Cooper is driven and focused, and Clara would only prove to be a distraction. She needs to stay far away from my brother, especially since he just started his career.

"A little over two years now," he answers before standing and clearing his plate.

"That's crazy. It's already been that long? I still remember you as the lanky little kid who used to torture us during sleep overs," Clara jokes, her eyes never leaving Cooper as he moves around. Cooper turns and leans up against the counter in the kitchen, crossing his arms over his broad chest. He's definitely not lanky anymore.

"Yeah, well, you girls drove me crazy. I had to get revenge somehow," he grins.

"We weren't that bad," I chime in, standing from the table and moving over to the sink to wash dishes.

"Weren't that bad? Do you remember the time you chased me around the house and pinned me down to paint my toenails?"

"Oh, God! I forgot about that!" Clara laughs.

"Well, I didn't. And there were four of you and only one of me, so it wasn't like I could fight you off."

"Well, I do believe you got your revenge when you put shaving cream in our hands while we slept that night. You tickled our noses with that feather so we would all smack ourselves in the face."

Cooper chuckles before making his way down the hallway. "And then you all chased me down again. Good thing we're not kids anymore, because I couldn't imagine the type of prank war that would commence now. And I definitely know you couldn't pin me down this time," he flexes his muscles before disappearing into his room.

"When did your brother get so hot?" Clara comes up behind me at the sink and whispers in my ear.

"Don't even think about it Clara," I warn.

"What? Ha, you're funny," she plays it off, but I know

the wheels are spinning in her mind.

"I'm serious. Cooper is off-limits, you hear me?"

Clara just stares at me, but then Cooper comes around the corner, dressed in his uniform and I see Clara swallow hard.

"Alright guys. I hate to eat and run, but duty calls," he says while kissing and hugging my parents goodbye. He comes over to me next and gives me a tight squeeze, before turning to Clara. "Nice to see you again, Clara," he winks while pulling her in for a hug.

"Yeah, you too, Cooper. Be safe," she says, watching him walk out the door.

Once the dishes are clean and we each inhale a slice of mom's fresh peach pie, it takes all of my energy to push myself off of the couch to leave.

"Thanks for dinner, Mom. I'll see you next week."

"I'm so glad to have you home, Liv," she says while hugging me close to her.

"Me too, baby girl," my dad says as he gives me another bear hug.

"Despite what brought me back, I'm happy to be home too."

"Thanks for having me, Mama and Papa Walsh," Clara adds while getting her own hugs. Clara's parents moved away right after she graduated from high school and left for college, so my parents are the closest thing she has to her own nearby.

"You're welcome anytime," my mom says as we gather our coats and walk out the front door.

"I'm going to have to run five miles to burn off that meal, but it was so worth it," Clara confesses, her usual snarky self returning.

"Me too."

"So, what happens now with Kane?"

I shrug. "I'm not sure. We exchanged numbers before we left last night. The ball is in his court, really. I mean, he doesn't have much experience dating, so I don't want him to feel pressured. But I'm excited to see where this goes."

"Well, you better keep me updated," she smiles before giving me a hug, hurrying our goodbye as the cold air and wind swirls around us.

"I will. Where are you headed for work this week?"

"Chicago and then Boston. But I'll be home by Friday. We should do something."

"Definitely. I'll let you know."

"Love ya, Liv."

"Love ya, too, girl. Goodnight," I say while closing my car door and making the short drive back to my apartment. As I get ready for bed that night, I can't help but feel anxious for seeing Kane again at work. I plan out my outfit so I look killer tomorrow and open up my book to quell my thoughts before I fall asleep.

Being home again brings a peace over me I was searching for when I first arrived. Even though I questioned everything that brought me back to Emerson Falls, I can't help but feel like things are starting to make sense.

# CHAPTER 22

Kane

I don't think I've ever been this eager to get to work before. After Saturday night with Olivia, I'm itching to make progress. I didn't officially ask her out on a date yet, but I know I need to soon. The more I stew on the idea of spending more time with her, the more anxious I am to move things along between us. She's the first person in a long time that makes me want more out of life. And I'm hoping the surprise I have for her this morning will help me score even more brownie points.

"Hey, Phil," I greet our morning custodian in the dark before the sun rises. Phil gets here before any of the staff, hosing down sidewalks, picking up trash, and restocking restrooms before the day begins. Custodians and secretaries are some of the most pivotal staff members of a school, and I was told early on to never get on their bad side or they could make your life a living hell. Lucky for me, Phil and I hit it off, and I always make sure to say hello to him in the morning when I see him, especially today since I need a favor.

"Garrison. Here earlier than normal today? What gives?" His deep voice resonates in the cold as I can see both of our breaths while we speak.

"Yeah. I uh, kinda need a favor. Could you let me into room 104 please?"

Phil eyes the coffee in my hand and then a knowing

smile creeps across his face.

"Is that coffee for her?" He asks, knowing who all the classrooms belong to.

"Yeah. I need to make sure I drop it off before she gets here."

Phil nods. "And the wooing begins," he chuckles as I follow him to Olivia's classroom.

Once the coffee and note are securely delivered, I thank Phil for his help and hightail it back to my room before Olivia arrives and can see me. I'm sure she'll know the coffee is from me as soon as she sees it and reads my message, but I don't want to blow my cover.

By the time my prep period rolls around, I haven't heard a word from Olivia. I know she was probably busy teaching, but I figured I'd get some sort of reaction from her—a text, an email, or even a phone call to say thanks. Just when I feel a wave of disappointment come over me, there's a knock on my classroom door.

Opening the steel barricade, I'm elated to see my beautiful redhead in front of me, holding up her cup of coffee with Ellen DeGeneres' face on it.

"Did you enjoy your coffee date?" I ask her, loving the smile on her face.

"Ellen was quite the company. Of course, we were interrupted by my students asking questions every five minutes. But it was definitely a coffee date for the books," she winks at me while taking a sip. "But she promised to bring Jennifer Aniston along next time, since they're best buds, you know."

"I figured I could help make some of your dreams come true," I say while opening the door wider and inviting her in. She glides in on her heels, her body draped in a navy blue pantsuit cinched at her waist that makes her look powerful and sexy as hell. The top half of her hair is pulled off of her face while the rest of it drapes down her back in soft curls. I take the opportunity to marvel at the way her ass looks in those pants before she turns around and gazes around my classroom.

"Well, I truly appreciated the gesture. Thank you," she beams. "So this is your room?" She searches the space, walking casually around to admire my walls.

"Oh, yeah. You haven't been in here yet, have you?"

She glares over at me. "Well, you weren't exactly welcoming me when I first arrived now, were you?"

"Got me there," I agree, placing my hands in my slacks to keep me from reaching out and grabbing her by the waist and devouring her mouth. I refrained from kissing her the other night, knowing that taking this slow would be the best route for starting over. But every time I see her, I recall the feeling of her beneath my fingers, and it makes the rule hard to commit to.

"Your room is great, Kane. I love the posters the kids created."

"Yeah, I had them pick a critical event in our country's history and then make their own political cartoon about it. They loved it and their creativity impressed me."

"I'm jealous. I rarely get to see that side of the students. Math is so black and white that I don't see the imaginative side of my students very often."

I take a few steps towards her, soaking up the features of her face. Oliva doesn't wear a lot of make-up, and quite frankly, she doesn't need it. But her dark lashes sure do bring out the subtle green hues in her eyes, and no matter what shade of lipstick she has on, it draws my attention to her perfectly plump lips—the lips I vividly remember wrapped around my cock.

Clearing my throat and willing my dick to calm down, I attempt to continue our conversation. "I've never thought of that."

"So, I really enjoyed Saturday night..." She trails off, looking away as if embarrassed by her confession. I reach for her chin to turn her head back to face me.

"Me too, Olivia. I thought about texting you yesterday, but I didn't want to seem desperate," I joke.

"I wouldn't have minded," she says as her eyes bounce back and forth between mine.

"Good to know," I answer as we stare each other down. I can feel the rapid fire of my pulse as I prepare myself to ask her my next question.

"So, I have another question for you, if you'll amuse me," I smirk as she cracks a cheesy smile.

"Okay..."

"Are you sure? Because it's a doozy."

She giggles. "Yup. I'm ready."

I take a deep breath and get very serious. I watch Olivia's face drop as she prepares herself.

"Olivia..."

She waits.

"Would you..."

"Yeah..." she stands there on pins and needles.

"Go on a date with me this Saturday?"

The laugh she lets out sends a flurry of excitement rushing through my body, her reaction everything I wanted from her.

"God, Kane," she playfully swats my chest. "I thought you were going to ask me something that would make me run for the hills."

I pull her by her waist, pressing my body against hers,

making her breath hitch. "You never know. It's still early. You might want to run away at some point."

Her eyes search mine, then bounce down to my lips. "I think I'm done running for now."

And if that doesn't light a fire under me, I don't know what will. It's definitely taken us a few miscommunications and obstacles to get here, but feeling her in my arms again and hearing her say that means we're finally both on the same page.

"Good. I'll pick you up at five."

"Can't wait," she almost whispers as we feel each other out. I want to kiss her, no doubt about that. But I feel like I should probably take her on a real date before that happens again. Knowing what she already tastes like though and the little sounds she makes when she's turned on helps me remember that our next kiss will be worth the wait.

"Well, I'd better get back to my room. I have some grading I should really catch up on," she says while backing away from me. I release her reluctantly, but I know the period is about to end.

"Yeah, me too. It never stops, does it?"

She chuckles. "No kidding. Well, have a good rest of your day, Kane."

"You too, Oliva," I say while watching her give me one more glance over her shoulder accompanied by a sweet smile before exiting my room.

I throw a fist pump in the air, celebrating my accomplishment. Dating is unchartered territory for me, but so far, I feel like I'm winning.

# CHAPTER 23

Olivia

All week long Kane left me little notes in my classroom in the morning, mostly filled with questions he wanted to ask me.

*Chocolate or vanilla?* Depends on my mood.

*Favorite flower?* Red roses

*Idea of the perfect date?* Any date that I don't want to end.

Each one I answered via text when I got a free moment from teaching or grading, running copies, or returning emails. And then Friday morning, there was no question, just a note from him that made my heart flutter.

*Can't wait for tomorrow.*

And truthfully, neither can I. I don't think I've ever been so anxious for a date in my life. Hell, Kane and I have already slept together, so it's not like I'm nervous about that, although the thought of that happening again is nerve-wracking. But I think it's more the reality that we mean more now than just a one-night-stand. And given how well Kane has been showing his interest this week, I'm dying to know what he has planned for our date. For a guy who hasn't pursued a girl since he was sixteen, he sure is doing a fine job. I wonder if Drew has been helping him.

By the time the last bell rings on Friday, I'm so exhausted from the week that I'm grateful Kane planned our date for Saturday instead of tonight. A twelve-hour coma will help me feel human again and fully awake for conversation tomorrow.

Tammy stops by my room with her arms full of bags, obviously on her way out for the weekend.

"Hey, girl," she greets me as I'm finishing grading a few tests at my desk.

"Hey, Tammy. How's it going?"

"Good. I was actually coming to ask you the same thing. A little birdie told me you have a date tomorrow night," she winks while setting down her bags on one of the desks.

"Is that little birdie named Drew?" I tease.

"I plead the fifth," she smirks. "So, I take it things went well the other night?"

I then realized that I haven't seen her since the mixer at her house. "Oh, yeah. Kane apologized for acting like an ass and we actually talked the entire night. It was like I got to see this whole other side of him..."

"That a boy! See, I told you he's really a great guy. He just needs some direction."

"Yeah, I gathered that. He was very honest that it's been a while since he's dated, but by the way he's been surprising me all week, I'd say he's better at this than he thinks," I smile elatedly.

"Oh, yeah? Do tell!"

So I do. I fill her in on Saturday and everything that's happened since.

"Yeah, sorry about Saturday. I tend to get drunk when we host since we don't have to drive and all."

"Hey, no judgment. I totally understand."

"But hearing you talk about Kane just reminds me of

when Drew pursued me back when I started working here."

"Oh, yeah, that's right. Was he an ass to you at first too?" I joke.

"No, the opposite actually. He was almost afraid to talk to me. I actually broke the ice with him."

I laugh trying to imagine Drew being too scared to talk to Tammy. From the time I've spent with him, I don't see him as anything but outgoing. "That's hard to believe."

"Yup, but true. Just don't risk having sex on campus, okay? Getting caught can be detrimental to your career."

I choke on my saliva with her confession. "Did you and Drew..."

"Almost, until I was the voice of reason and stopped it. Drew didn't care, but I did. I didn't work this hard for this job to give it all up for an orgasm or two."

Her bluntness makes me laugh. "No kidding. Well, thanks for the warning."

"What are friends for?" She winks. "Well, I hope Kane doesn't disappoint tomorrow night. You'd better fill me in next week."

"Definitely. Have a great weekend."

"You too, Olivia," she says before gathering her things and leaving my room.

After I finish my grading and inputting the scores into the computer, I shut down everything, lock my room, and head for my car. I grab some takeout on the way home, put my feet up on the couch and turn on Netflix, and gorge until I can't keep my eyes open any longer. I pass out on the couch and wake up in a panic Saturday morning when I realize I'm not in bed.

Chuckling to myself, I stand up and make my way to the bathroom, showering and pampering my body until I feel human again to prepare for my date. I do my laundry, clean around the apartment, and bask in the routine that I've created for myself over the past few weeks. But deep down I know that there's more to life than this. And I want more.

I want the husband and kids. I want the crazy, loud noise of a family spending time together on a Saturday morning, making pancakes and watching cartoons. I want a man beside me who is my best friend, but also the person I can't get enough of. And as I envision that scene in my mind, the face of the man I dream of as my husband looks like Kane.

Could he be that person for me? Am I putting all my eggs in one basket because he is the first man I'm dating after Trevor? Or does what I feel for him already honestly make me believe that this could be the real thing? I remind myself to take it one day at a time and try not to put pressure on this. But the ticking clock in the back of mind keeps reminding me that I'm not getting any younger.

Shaking off my insecurities, I put on a playlist on my phone while I get ready for my date. I curl my hair, opt for slightly darker make-up for the evening, and choose a body-hugging maroon sweater dress with cream-colored leggings, dark brown boots, and my heavy brown coat to complete my outfit. I give myself one last glance in the mirror before making myself comfortable on the couch to wait for Kane.

Three minutes before five there's a knock on my door. I stand, wiping my sweaty palms on my dress and smoothing the fabric over my curves. Taking a deep breath, I open the door to the vision of Kane in all his handsome glory, decked out in his black pea coat, dark denim, and a dark green Henley stretched across his muscular chest. The sight of him warms my insides, and a throbbing commences between my legs. He's so incredibly sexy and masculine, his beard trimmed to perfection and dark to match his hair—he takes my breath away.

"Hi, Olivia," he greets me as I usher him inside out of the cold.

"Hi, Kane," I say sheepishly, wondering how I could be even more nervous now that he's here.

His eyes dance up and down my body before landing on my eyes. The glint of approval shines just as he speaks. "You look incredible."

"Thank you. So do you," I reply, feeling the blush on my cheeks.

"Your place sure looks different since the last time I was here," he mocks while veering around the room, absorbing the home my apartment looks like now, instead of the heap of boxes that was here before.

"If you recall, Kane... I warned you to what you were walking into that night," I reply while remembering every vivid detail of that evening. When I make eye contact with him again, I can tell he's doing the same thing.

Clearing his throat, he continues. "Well, are you ready to go then?"

"Yup. Let me just grab my coat." Reaching for the jacket, Kane steps up behind me and grabs the material from my hands.

"Let me," he leans down and voices in my ear, causing goosebumps to erupt all over my skin, even though I'm warm all over from the heat in the apartment and his proximity.

He holds out my coat behind me as I locate the sleeves and slide my arms through, clutching the coat around my body as I hear him inhale behind me.

"You smell amazing..."

Turning around to face him, his face is itching with his need to control himself. With all the anticipation surrounding tonight, I want to see our date through. Although with the way he's looking at me right now, the thought of staying in and riding his face again seems fun too.

"You smell pretty good yourself there, Garrison," I joke while grabbing onto the collar of his coat, pulling him closer to me so our mouths are merely inches away from each other. "Now take me on a date before we never leave this apartment."

Kane throws his head back in a laugh, then leans down to kiss my forehead—the gesture so sweet and innocent, but it makes my heart come alive in my chest. The man has been inside me for Christ's sake, but something about that move is so much more intimate.

"Yes ma'am," he salutes before walking to my door and leading me out to his truck. He opens the door for me and helps me inside, like the gentleman he's proving he is. Once we're secured in our seats, Kane takes off for the highway and starts to drive out of Emerson Falls.

"Where are we going?" I ask once we're cruising along.

"Well, you're favorite food is sushi, right?"

"Yes..."

"Well, the closest sushi place is about forty-five minutes away."

"Kane, you didn't have to drive all this way just to get me sushi," I scold him. Hell, I would have been fine with just a steak dinner at Outback.

"I know I didn't, but I wanted to. And since I've never had it, I thought, what the heck?" He shoots me a crooked smile and a wink before focusing back on the road.

"Thank you, then. I've actually been craving it."

"Perfect."

While Kane drives we talk about music and he drills me with more questions—basic things about my likes and dislikes.

*Favorite season?* Spring.

*Favorite sport?* Football.

*Favorite holiday?* Thanksgiving.

The drive passes so quickly that before we know it, we arrive at the restaurant. Kane guides me inside and offers his name for the reservation he made. The hostess leads us through the restaurant that is actually a teppan-style dining establishment complete with a sushi bar. The walls are painted a deep red with bamboo accents throughout. Enormous hoods hang from the ceiling above the tables that accommodate ten people at a time. Chatter fills the room as families gather to celebrate birthdays and the cries of little children filter in and out of the noise created by food sizzling on the heated steel of the table tops.

"This is much fancier than just sushi, Kane," I state while following him, hand in hand, to our teppan table. Once the hostess hands us our menus and explains the ordering process, she leaves as we await our server for drinks.

"It is our first date, so that calls for something special. I've heard great things about this place, but never had a reason to come here... until now." His eyes sparkle from the overhead lights and the flicker of flames coming off of the tables nearby where chefs are busy preparing meals. His answer makes my pulse quicken, each glimpse of honesty from him making me fall just a little more.

"Thank you for bringing me here then," I smile at him, reaching for his hand. He grabs mine and brings it to his mouth, pressing the softest caress of his lips against my skin, making my nipples harden from his touch. I feel my entire body warm and anticipate even more hints of his lips on my body later.

"Let's figure out what to eat." I shake off the moment,

opening the menu in perusal of our options. Kane decides on the steak and shrimp dinner and I opt for chicken and calamari, deciding we'll share our plates so we can sample everything. He urges me to choose a few sushi rolls to share before dinner is served, and we place our order once the server arrives. The rest of our table fills up in a matter of minutes. Two more couples join us and a family of four celebrating the oldest son's birthday.

Even though it's not an intimate setting, I'm situated so close to Kane to accommodate all the people at the table, I don't feel a lack of affection from him.

Taking a sip of my wine, I turn to Kane while we wait for our food. "So, have any more questions for me tonight?"

Kane tips up the corner of his mouth while he drinks his beer. "You should know by now I come fully stocked with a list of questions."

"Bring it on then," I tease while placing my wine glass back down so I can give him my full attention.

Kane reaches for his phone from his coat pocket on the back of his chair, lighting up the screen and searching out his list from before. "Okay," he clears his throat, which makes me chuckle. "If you could live anywhere, where would that be?"

"Hmmm. That's a good one. I think I'd have to say somewhere tropical. I'm not a fan of the cold weather, and there is nothing more peaceful to me than turquoise blue water. Belize. Tahiti. Hawaii. I'm not picky, just somewhere where I can see straight down to the bottom of the ocean and live in a bikini all year round."

Kane's eyes are filled with lust when he hears my answer. "I think if you're wearing a bikini every day, I'd want to live there too." I swat him playfully in the chest before he grabs my hand and caresses my fingers with his.

"Okay, what about you?"

"I'd probably stay in Emerson Falls, if I'm being honest. I don't mind the cold, and Oregon is home. I love the trees and hiking. I enjoy living in the wilderness, far enough away from people, but close enough not to be off the grid. After spending years in a desert in that heat, I don't know that's something I would want to deal with every day."

"That's fair. So where is your house exactly?"

"I live about thirty minutes out of town, north of Emerson Falls. I bought a cabin style home up there three years ago and have slowly been making it my own."

"I'd love to see it one day."

Kane kisses my hand before opening his phone again. "Don't worry. You will. Next question—who is your hero and why?"

"You have to answer first this time," I remind him of our rules the other night.

"I know, I know. I guess, I don't have any one person in particular, but would say any man or woman in the armed forces. I spent so much time with men and women who sacrificed their lives and time away from their families to serve their country. It made me realize that there are so many things people take for granted every day. Any person who can be that selfless for the safety of others is a hero in my book," Kane finishes while reaching for his beer. I study his face as he looks away, the sharp lines of his jaw barely hidden by the short scruff of his beard, the lines around his eyes that show his age, but in a sexy way. He looks back at me, catching my perusal before flashing me a grin.

"What?"

"Nothing, just admiring you. I really loved your answer, by the way. Regardless of what you may think, you're a hero too Kane, for making that same sacrifice. I know that's not your life anymore, but the time you spent in the Army definitely made a difference, whether you believe that or not."

Kane remains silent for a moment, swallowing hard at my response before he speaks again. "Thank you, Olivia. So what about you?"

"That's easy. My grandma. She was the strongest woman I've ever known. She grew up during the Great Depression, learning to sew her own clothes because her family couldn't afford to buy things already made. She watched her younger brother get killed by a car in front of her when she was thirteen. My grandfather was a drunk and hit her a few times, but she stood up to him and eventually fought back, but she loved him with all of her heart and stayed married to him until the day he died. Her oldest son passed away from cancer and her other two children—my mom and her brother —had a huge falling out after their dad died. She raised a family and supported them through running her own porcelain business out of her garage. She was creative, talented, loving, and honest. I only wish I could be as strong as she was. And she was always so supportive of me. I miss her every day."

Tears start to fill my eyes as I recall everything about the woman who helped mold me into the person I am today. As a tear slips free, Kane reaches up to wipe it away with his thumb.

"She would be nothing but proud of you, Olivia," he says while penetrating me with his gaze.

"Thank you. Ugh, sorry for getting all emotional on our date."

Kane kisses my forehead again just as the chef arrives with the cart carrying the food for the table, preparing the hot surface for cooking our meal. "Don't apologize. The whole point of the questions is to get to know each other. And now, I feel like I know you a little better."

Giving him a soft smile, I turn my attention to our chef

and reach for my wine, savoring the crisp and sweet taste of the liquid on my palate. Kane drapes his arm over my chair while we listen to our chef recite our orders for clarification and then watch him put on a show—chopping, dicing, and searing meat, vegetables, and rice. He stacks the rings of an onion and pours oil in the center, lighting it to create a flame and mimic a volcano. The table applauds as he does trick after trick with his knife and food.

The server comes by with our sushi while the chef is cooking as Kane and I draw our attention to the raw fish and avocado draping over sticky rice, covered in eel sauce and spicy mayonnaise. Taking that first bite makes me moan, closing my eyes to savor the flavor and delicacy of the roll.

"That good, huh?" Kane teases me, while I hoist a piece of the roll and feed it to him with my chopsticks. Placing the bite in his mouth, Kane watches me intently while he chews and then swallows, leaning forward into my space before declaring his reaction with the most suggestive smirk on his face.

"Definitely worth the drive."

# CHAPTER 24

Kane

Tonight is going perfectly, except for making Olivia cry. That definitely wasn't my intention, but her answer was so raw and honest—It gave me a crucial glimpse into the woman who is quickly captivating me. Admiring someone like her grandma who can overcome obstacles like that in her life will definitely change you and give you strength to tackle your own. After hearing her grandma's story, it makes me feel stupid for reacting to being cheated on by Natasha the way that I have. But I guess everyone handles challenges in their own way, right?

Olivia and I barely put a dent in our food. The quantity is astounding, but we made sure to sample everything before we boxed most of it up to take home.

"I seriously don't think I've ever been this full," she moans while patting her stomach, drawing my attention to the curve of her hips as she sits next to me. The sweater dress she wore is sinfully tempting, hugging her in all the right places and reminding me of how voluptuous her body is.

"Yeah, I'm stuffed too. But if you're up for it, there's a courtyard on the other side of the restaurant we can walk around to try to burn some of this off."

"Yeah, that sounds great."

Once I pay and we drop off our leftovers at my truck, we head for the courtyard which leads out to a small pond of water, lit up by the lights reflecting off of the buildings surrounding it. This restaurant sits among several others around the water, collectively called The Cove, which is what I researched when I was planning our date. When I saw the pictures and dining options, I knew I wanted to take Olivia here.

"This is gorgeous, Kane," she says as we stroll hand in hand, overlooking the water and enjoying the scenery. You can see inside of the other restaurants as we glide along, people entrenched in conversation with a view of the glistening water as they dine.

"I agree. I wish it wasn't so cold, but I'm still enjoying this time with you," I declare while pulling her closer to me. We both grabbed our gloves from my truck when we went back, so at least our fingers aren't freezing.

"I know we're both stuffed, but there is a cupcake shop just over the bridge there that is supposed to have amazing cupcakes, according to the reviews online," I say while pointing in that direction.

"Someone did their research, didn't they?" She says and then leads me towards the bridge. "I'll need something sweet eventually, so let's check it out."

We walk along the wooden platforms of the bridge, turning to admire the surrounding view. Olivia's face is lit up by the glow of the lights, but also with her pure joy. That smile of hers is once again, lighting up my eyes. Hell, the woman is bringing light to my life.

When we reach the store, I open the door and guide her inside, both of us shaking off the chill of the night.

"Good evening!" A middle-aged woman with greying hair greets us as we enter.

"Hi, there," Olivia answers her as she admires the rows of cupcakes in the glass case. "What flavors would you recommend? We heard these are some of the best cupcakes money can buy." She looks over and winks at me.

"Well, as the owner, I'll say my favorite is our red velvet with homemade cream cheese frosting. And we have a peanut butter and jelly cupcake that is a crowd pleaser. But you can't go wrong with a classic vanilla with chocolate frosting either."

"We'll take one of each," I pipe up, causing Olivia to turn to me in surprise.

"Well, we do a special of buy five, get one free, if you can't decide."

"That's perfect. Olivia, you pick. I'll eat whatever."

Olivia grins and then turns back to the store owner, choosing six different flavors for us to take home. She puts as much thought into choosing cupcake flavors as she must into solving a math problem.

After I pay, which Olivia argues about but I don't give in to—I grab her hand and our box and make our way back to my truck. Once we settle inside and I fire up the engine to start the heater, she snatches the box from me and opens it, taking one of the forks and cutting off a piece of the red velvet.

"I have to try this one," she chuckles, licking her lips before placing the bite in her mouth. Her eyes close and she moans again—making my dick hard for the thousandth time tonight—before her lids pop open and she widens her gaze at me.

"Oh, my God, that's good!" She shouts, cutting off another bite before offering it to me. I stick my tongue out, noticing Olivia's focus drop to my mouth and the pupils of her eyes darken. The cake and frosting melt on my tongue, and I'd have to agree with the reviews—that's one of the best cupcakes I've ever had.

"Really good, and I'm not a sweets person."

"Well, as a sugar connoisseur, I will tell you that this here," she points down to the box, "Is one of the best cupcakes on the face of the planet!" Her words make me throw my head back in laughter as she joins me. I'll give her this—the woman sure is passionate about things she likes.

I pull out of the parking lot and head for home, making small talk with Oliva along the way. We talk about work and students we have in common. Even though it's the weekend, it's difficult to turn your brain off from the job. Teaching is one of those jobs that comes home with you mentally. There's always a kid you're worried about, a kid you know you need to talk to one-on-one, or a long to-do list of things you need to prepare for. It's one of the best and worst parts about the job—how much you end up caring about the kids.

When we arrive back at Olivia's apartment, I grab the cupcakes and her leftovers before I walk her to her door. She invites me inside, grabbing the boxes and placing them in the fridge before meeting me back at the front door, removing her coat along the way.

"Thank you for everything tonight, Kane. This was one of the best dates I've ever been on. I'm pretty sure I won't need to eat for a couple of days, but I seriously had the best time."

"Me too, Olivia. Are you free next weekend?" I ask, moving closer to her to thread a piece of her hair behind her ear. She leans into my touch, closing her eyes for a moment before peering back up at me, her hazel orbs sucking me in even further. This woman is beautiful, inside and out. It makes me crazy to think that she could have just been a notch on my belt. But here she is, right in front of me—making me want things I didn't think I'd ever want again.

"Yes, I'm free. What did you have in mind?"

"Don't worry about it. I'll surprise you," I say while reaching for her waist and wrapping her in my arms.

"Okay." Her eyes bounce back and forth between mine before she swallows hard and I know what she's waiting for. And hell, if I won't give it to her. I've been waiting all week and all night to kiss this woman again. I've been on my best behavior, but now the time is up.

Leaning down slowly, I reach for her neck, feeling the rapid fire of her pulse beneath my thumb as I stroke her soft skin. Her eyes are locked on mine, dropping to my lips for one quick second before flying back up. I waste no more time pressing my lips to hers, relishing in the feel of her mouth on mine again, and fuck if it isn't as good as the last time.

Olivia threads her hands behind my neck, her finger nails trickling through my hair at the back of my head, pulling me down closer to her as I memorize the way she feels in my arms. My thumb strokes her jaw as my other hand comes up and cradles her face just as I lick her lips, asking for her to open up to me.

And boy, does she comply. Olivia's lips open and her tongue searches for mine, as if we've been looking for one another for years and we finally found the other half of our souls. With smooth strokes, my tongue tangles with hers, immersing myself in the feeling of us connected again.

Olivia moans and fuck if that doesn't make my dick twitch and spur me on, tightening my grasp on her face while she meets me with every nip and caress that I offer her. Our lips remember how to move together. Our bodies recall what it feels like to touch.

I kiss her like it's the last time I'll be able to. I kiss her like the woman deserves to be kissed, full of passion and care. I kiss her like she's the last woman I'll ever kiss for the first time.

When we part, struggling to catch our breaths, her eyes fly open and meet mine. I struggle to form words, knowing that this physical connection we share is strong. I knew that the first night. But now, after getting to know this woman for more than just her body—that physical combustion is sizzling, and stronger than ever.

"Good night, Olivia," I finally muster, leaving one last kiss on her forehead before turning for the door.

"Good night, Kane," she replies as I open the door and walk outside, the smile on her lips tells me everything.

"See you Monday," I declare, closing her door and making my way to my truck. Once I'm seated and ready to drive, I lean my head back on the headrest, and close my eyes as I chuckle, recalling the entire evening.

"Man, I'm fucked."

# CHAPTER 25

Kane

"Alright, guys. It's time to make our way to the gym for the pep rally. Remember to behave yourselves," I eye my students as they roll their eyes and stand, making their way for the door.

"You act like we don't know how to sit and keep our hands to ourselves," Tristan says as he walks past me.

"Hey, I wouldn't put it past any teenager to make a rash decision in the heat of the moment. I know you guys are generally well-behaved, but there are always the few bad seeds who like to start crap. It's just a friendly reminder, kid."

"Yeah, you're right, Mr. G.," Tristan nods as he catches up to his buddies and heads for the gym.

It's a Friday, which means the football team is playing tonight. It's another big game for the school and ASB has really been trying to increase school spirit this year. The fact that our football team is actually winning games this season definitely helps the cause.

Slowly but surely, half of the students in our school filter into the gym, climbing the bleachers, and taking their seats in the designated class sections. Since I have primarily juniors, my class is attending the upper classmen assembly. Lower classmen attend their own rally earlier in the day.

I stand at the side of the room, greeting a few of my fellow colleagues as we all make our way in and wait for the students to get seated. School events like this offer the opportunity to converse with some of the other teachers on the campus that I don't see on a regular basis and to watch the kids submerge themselves in the high school experience.

I think back to when I was in high school and on the football team. I lived for pep rallies—getting the school hyped for the game, sitting on the gym floor while watching the cheerleaders perform their routines, listening to the cheers from the other kids chanting my name. As one of the key running backs on the field, I had a stellar reputation for helping our team win.

Now as a teacher, I try to balance the need for structure and doing well in my class with enjoying these types of activities. I think the key is letting the kids have both.

"Hey, man," Drew comes up beside me, patting me on the shoulder.

"Hey. You ready for tonight?"

He nods. "Yup. This is going to be a defensive game, for sure. Tanner has been working with them all week. I'm pretty confident we have a great shot at a win, though."

"Well, after how well you guys played against Ashland, I think so too. Where's Tammy?" I ask, perusing the room.

"She came to the first assembly. She teaches mostly freshman this year. Poor woman," he shakes his head as I huff out a laugh. Drew slides closer to me, whispering in my ear. "But it looks like your woman has just arrived," he teases as my eyes lock on Olivia gliding into the gym. She's deep in conversation with a student, but her smile is still eye-catching and her deep red hair makes her stand out in the crowd.

It's been almost a week since our date and I've had the hardest time staying away from her, in fear of making myself seem too desperate to see her. I did text her though a few times in the evenings and I may have made some excuse to stop by her classroom during our prep period on Tuesday. Then I made sure to conveniently meet her in the teacher's lounge on Thursday for the baked goods from the restaurant class. Okay, maybe I haven't been as sly as I hoped, but she never seemed bothered with seeing me. In fact, her reaction was just as elated as mine. However, we do have plans tonight, which is the only reason why I think I've been able to talk myself down from stalking her *every* day this week.

"God, she's gorgeous," I say a little too loudly, which makes Drew break out in laughter beside me.

"Damn, man. Do you hear yourself?"

I shake my head. "I know. But seriously, Drew. Look at her..." I gesture with my hand, then quickly put it down. The last thing I need to do is draw attention to us and feed the rumor mill.

"I'm going to just agree without looking so I can appease you and avoid getting myself in trouble with my wife. But hey, keep putting yourself out there, man. This side of you since you started seeing her is refreshing," he clasps my shoulder again before walking away. Since Drew is the head football coach, he has to speak during the rally.

I find Olivia again just as she walks over to me, grinning from ear to ear.

"Hey, there, Mr. Garrison," she slyly speaks while turning around to face the gym, taking residence right beside me.

"Hi, Miss Walsh," I reply, chuckling as I feel like we're trying to maintain our composure next to each other without drawing wandering eyes to us.

"How has your week been?"

I turn to her, searching for her gaze. Just as she faces me, I speak.

"Long," I answer honestly, knowing that looking forward to our date tonight has made time pass so slowly.

"Mine too," she says while her eyes bounce back and forth between mine.

Before I can speak again, the band starts playing and the football teams runs out to the middle of the gym floor, shouting and jumping up and down as the crowd of students and teachers cheer. I clap my hands while watching the spectacle, catching a glimpse of Oliva smiling and cheering beside me from the corner of my eye.

"Man, Emerson sure does know how to do a pep rally," she says as the noise starts to diminish, her eyes surveying the decorations in the room. Banners of red and gray fabric drape from the center of the gym, balloon structures line the floor and seats where the athletes are seated, and hand-painted banners in the school colors with positive slogans hang on the walls. "My last school was definitely lacking in the school spirit department."

"Really? That's a shame."

"Yeah. This rally reminds me a lot of the ones we had when I was in school."

"Oh yeah? And were you involved in them?" I ask, curious to know more about her in high school. I'm sure Olivia was just as big of a knock-out back then as she is now.

"Yup. You're in the presence of the cheerleading captain here, Kane," she beams. And just as she says the words, the vision of Olivia in a cheerleading uniform, skipping and jumping around makes my dick swell in my jeans.

"Fuck, Olivia. Why did you have to tell me that here?" I growl, placing my hands in my pockets, trying to discretely change my stance to adjust my erection in my pants.

She chuckles. "Are you having a problem right now?" She whispers, her eyes glancing briefly to my crotch before finding mine again, her face alive with mischief.

"Yeah, which is extremely inappropriate given we're around hundreds of students right now."

Olivia's hand comes up to cover her mouth as she shakes from her laughter. I can't help but join her, because this situation is pretty funny. But fuck, this woman gets a reaction out of me every time we're near each other. At this rate, I might not allow myself to be near her at school functions any more.

Once Olivia composes herself, she avoids looking at me while speaking. "I'm sorry, I know it's not funny..."

"It's okay, I know you didn't do it on purpose. But maybe refrain from telling me details like that about you while we're at work and there are hundreds of pairs of eyes on us, alright?"

She chuckles again. "Okay."

"So, we still on for tonight?" I say from the corner of my mouth. It seems we're both trying to make it look like we're not dating in front of everyone. The less eye contact, the better.

"Definitely. I may not be able to stay up too late, but I'm excited to spend some more time together."

"Yeah, I'm usually pretty beat on Friday's too, but I know you have plans tomorrow and I didn't want to go another week without a date with you."

That declaration causes her to turn to me, searching my face for something.

"That's really sweet, Kane," she smiles up at me, her eyes shining from the lights above us in the gym. I have the strongest urge to reach out and caress her cheek, but I refrain.

"Well, in case you haven't figured it out, I kind of like you," I wink, which makes the corner of her mouth tip up. She turns back to face the crowd before she replies.

"I kind of like you too."

My heart beat starts to pick up, my chest heaving from

the deep inhale I take as her words resonate with me. I honestly can't wait to spend more time with her tonight, and I'm starting to believe that she feels the same way.

# CHAPTER 26

Olivia

I rush home after work on Friday to change and fix my appearance—reapplying my make-up, re-curling my hair, and relaxing a bit before Kane picks me up for our date.

I've been anxious all week knowing I got to see him tonight. He originally asked me out for Saturday night, but my mom needs help with some event for the community center that night and asked me to assist.

So here I am, five o'clock on a Friday, waiting to hear the knock of the man who's been a constant thought of mine since our date last week.

I feel like someone needs to pinch me when I realize how much things have changed between Kane and me. I went from trying to avoid this man to searching for any opportunity to see him. Although, I think that's what he's been doing too. His need to borrow a stapler on Tuesday and conveniently running into me in the teacher's lounge on Thursday seems far too coincidental. His attempt to be sly made me laugh though, and actually started that flurry of excitement in my body whenever I got to see him. Now I get the entire evening with him, and I'm beyond ready.

Three minutes before five, there's a knock on my door. The fact that Kane is consistent in his timing makes me chuckle, thinking back to last week when he arrived at the exact same time.

"Hi, there," I greet him as I open the door, reading the smile on his face. He looks just as happy to see me as I am to see him.

"Hi, gorgeous," he says before stepping inside my apartment and reaching for my hand, drawing me in closer to him. His eyes stare down intently on mine before he presses a soft kiss to my lips. Just as I try to deepen the kiss, he pulls away.

"I've been wanting to do that all day," he says, leaning his forehead down on mine.

"Well, I'm glad you finally have the opportunity now."

"Yeah, damn jobs and students getting in the way of my game," he says with a wink as he backs up and pulls me behind him, his hand still clasped in mine.

"Awww, you poor thing," I tease as I grab my coat and purse on the way out and shut the door behind us.

Once we're settled in Kane's truck, I continue our conversation.

"So where are you taking me tonight?"

Kane's eyes are focused on the road, but his hand finds mine again, slowly rubbing his thumb along my skin.

"Well, are you in the mood for Italian?"

My eyes widen when I realize I think I know where he's going to take me. "Were you planning on going to Cristino's?" I say a little too loudly with my excitement.

"Yeah. I take it that's a good idea?" He asks, raising an eyebrow as he turns to me.

"Yes! I love that place! And I haven't been there since I moved back. Oh, my gosh, my stomach is rumbling at just the thought of their pasta and bread," I moan, which makes Kane laugh beside me.

"Alright then... Cristino's it is."

When we arrive at the restaurant, it's the same as it was when I left. The archways lined with vines and white lights encase the walkway leading up to the door. The Italian winery vibe you get when you walk in transports you to another part of the world, where food is everything and wine rules your palette. Cristino's is a staple in Emerson Falls, a family-owned and operated Italian restaurant that has been here for nearly thirty years now.

I search around the room, eyeing the painted grape vines on the walls, the black wrought-iron tables covered in red table cloths, and the stacks of wine bottles along the shelves behind the hand-carved wooden bar. The smell of garlic and roasted tomatoes makes me breathe in deeply, savoring the aroma just as I hear Kane speak next to me to the hostess.

"Reservation for Kane for two," he says.

"Absolutely. Your table is ready. Follow me this way, please," she smiles while grabbing two menus and then ushering us to the back of the restaurant.

I let Kane lead me, walking past the kitchen where the clatter of metal and glass ring in my ears, accompanied by the magnificent smells of hand-crafted Italian food.

When we make it to our table, I'm delighted to see we're in a little alcove, our rounded booth providing a little bit of privacy.

"Thank you," I say as I slide in and Kane follows, reaching for the wine menu as the hostess walks away.

"I know you love wine, so what would you recommend?" He asks, scooting closer to me so we can both read the list. His scent hits me when he closed the distance between us, making my heart kick start in my chest. I try to focus back on the list, but all I see are a bunch of letters and words that make no sense. Having Kane this close to me again is making my mind a jumbled mess.

I clear my throat and narrow my eyes, willing my brain to comprehend the choices of wine. When I see one I recognize from a winery near my home in California, I point it out.

"This one is fantastic. It's a cabernet, but it's fairly mild, not as meaty as they usually are. So if you're not usually a red wine drinker, that's what I would recommend."

Kane shuts the menu and then grabs the dinner one. "I trust you, so that's what we'll get. Now the real question is, what are we going to eat?" He grins over at me and wiggles his eyebrows, causing me to laugh at him before I search out the options.

Once the waitress comes by and takes our order, our wine arrives. Kane opted for a bottle, which was unnecessary, but he insisted. As I take the first sip, I hum in approval, making Kane freeze with his glass mid-air.

"Woman, can you please refrain from making noises like that in public? Do you not recall what I said to you today at the pep rally?"

I swallow and then smirk at him. "But we're not at work and there are no students around. Plus, there's a table blocking your lap," I argue.

"Still. What if there's a fire and we have to run out of the building? I can't do that with a raging hard-on," he fires back.

The thought of what Kane's raging hard-on looks like flashes through my mind, instantly heating up my body and commencing the throbbing between my legs.

"Fair enough. But it is a part of your body. I'd say the control lands on you."

Kane leans closer so his lips brush the shell of my ear. "I *can't* control myself around you," he whispers, making my breath hitch. I back away slightly so I can see his eyes.

"I feel like I'm having the same problem," I reply honestly as we stare at each other.

Just when I feel like we're about to jump each other's bones in this booth, the waitress comes by with our salads and freshly-baked bread, providing us with a welcome break in the sexual tension. I know I want Kane again, badly. But I'm reminding myself that he has to be the one to set the parameters here, knowing I want to make sure he's comfortable with how fast or slow we move. It took a lot of courage for him to put himself out there, and the last thing I want him to do is retreat because he feels like I'm progressing things too quickly. Plus, the idea of actually dating him and saving the physical stuff for later makes the anticipation build that much more. We've already slept together, and it was amazing—but I feel that now knowing that and prolonging the second time makes it even harder to wait.

"So, what questions are on the agenda for the evening? And please, nothing that's going to make me cry," I joke.

Kane finishes chewing before he answers. "I didn't plan on anything serious, but I don't know what may or may not make you cry, woman."

"Fair enough. So, lay it on me," I command as I see the twitch in Kane's jaw. I'm going to guess that his thoughts in response to my declaration were not of the PG-rated variety.

He clears his throat and then reaches for his phone, finding his list. I still think this is the cutest thing.

"Okay, what TV series can you watch over and over again and never get tired of?"

I snicker and then sit up tall. "That's easy. *Friends*, hands down."

He nods and then takes a sip of his wine. "Okay... elaborate please."

"I think something can be said that it's still one of the

most iconic TV shows of all time. Even the younger generations are discovering it now on Netflix and eating it up, just as everyone else did when it was on air. The characters are relatable and hilarious, and no matter what kind of day I've had, I know I can put on an episode of *Friends*, and my mood will instantly improve."

"Could you *be* any more right?" Kane attempts an impression of Chandler, and I struggle not to choke on my bread I just took a bite of.

"I take it you're a *Friends* fan too then?"

"Oh, yeah. Although, I will admit that for me, I was obsessed with WWE Smackdown when I was a kid, and I still will watch it if I'm flipping through channels and see that it's on."

"Oh, my God! That's... that's horrible!"

"Hey, don't knock it 'til you've watched it. It's highly entertaining," he challenges, reaching for his wine again.

I shake my head, imagining a boy version of Kane sitting cross-legged on the floor in front of the TV, cheering on his favorite wrestler.

"Alright. Next question..." I urge him to continue, just as our food arrives. The waitress tops our pasta with freshly grated parmesan cheese and asks us if we need anything else before she leaves. Kane offers me a bite of his veal parmesan and I reciprocate with a bite of my mushroom ravioli.

"This is the best idea ever," I mumble around a mouthful of food as I bask in the taste of eating at Cristino's again. I feel like every town has their own staple restaurant whose food you crave because you grew up with it. And if you ever go without it, you appreciate it so much more on that next taste.

Well, I'm drowning in the Italian goodness right now.

"You ready?" Kane teases as I turn to face him again, completely unaware of how long I've been stuffing my face.

"Yup."

"Okay. I have a few would you rather questions."

"Oh, fun!"

"Alright. Would you rather live full time in an RV or full time on a sailboat?"

"RV. I get sea sick."

Kane tilts his head at me in remorse. "That sucks. I'd pick the sailboat."

"Really?"

"Yeah, I love the ocean. We used to take a trip to the coast with my grandparents every summer and go out on a boat. It was one of the best feelings having the salty air hit your nose and feeling as if you could fall off the edge of the Earth."

"Huh. I like that. Did you channel your inner Jack Dawson and scream off the bow of the boat?"

Kane shakes his head and then looks away bashfully. "Maybe..."

I snort. "Yes! I love it! Okay, what's next?"

Kane looks back down at his phone. "Would you rather have an incredibly fast car or incredibly fast internet?"

"I'm ashamed to say, probably the internet. I'm an internet junkie. It's amazing how you can be online researching something, and suddenly you're stalking people on social media or watching cat videos on YouTube."

Kane laughs. "Yeah, it can definitely suck you in. And this may not surprise you, but I would pick the car."

"Shocker," I say sarcastically as Kane smiles wide.

"I love going fast. Even when I take my bike out, I like to press my luck sometimes to see how fast I can go."

"You have a motorcycle?"

"Yeah, I bought it while I was in the Army. I haven't been out on it in a long time though," he says, trailing off and breaking eye contact with me.

"Is there a reason?"

Kane doesn't say anything for a moment, which makes me nervous, thinking maybe I've overstepped a boundary.

"Sorry," he says while shaking his head. "I just… the last time I was on the bike was about three years ago…"

And that's all he has to say. I'm dying to know what happened to this man, why he's been so guarded and refused to let anyone in, but I have faith that he'll tell me when he's ready.

"Do you have any more questions?" I say, trying to change the subject.

"Yeah, how about one more?" His eyes finally meet mine again and I can see the gratitude there for not pushing him to elaborate.

I nod.

"Would you rather have true love or win the lottery?"

"I think you should answer this one first," I press a finger into his chest, but Kane doesn't even budge. Just that one little touch reminds me of how solid of a man he is.

"If you had asked me this three years ago, I definitely would have said win the lottery." His answer makes me instantly sad, desperate to hold him and prove to him that love is not evil.

"But now, after time has helped me see reason, I'd say true love."

The corner of my mouth tips up when I hear his honest words.

"True love for me too, hands down," I whisper. Kane

moves closer to me, pulling me into him by my waist, his eyes communicating something to me, but I'm unsure of exactly what that is. And before I can speak, he leans forward and kisses me, the taste of wine and marinara on his tongue as it tangles with mine.

I wrap my arms around his neck, pressing my chest against his as we continue to immerse ourselves in the kiss, showing our feelings physically instead of vocalizing them just yet.

Kane doesn't have to say everything he's thinking to me right now. I can be patient. I can be understanding that this man has been burned and it's going to take time for him to tell me everything I need to hear.

But if his kiss is any indication, I'd say we're both able to communicate our mutual attraction and pull through the touch of our lips. And for right now, that's enough.

# CHAPTER 27

Olivia

It's the week of Halloween, and this is by far my *least* favorite time to be a teacher. High school students are just as bad as the little ones. And hats off to those elementary school teachers who have to coordinate class parties, costume contests, and deal with the sugar-infested minions the day of *and* the day after. But in high school, some students still dress up, proving to be a distraction from learning. And then the day after, they're all zombies from staying up late the night before and bring all of their candy to school with them, snacking on the sugary treats all day so by the time the last period comes around, they're bouncing off of the walls just as bad as the little kids do. I'm all for teenagers trying to enjoy every minute of their youth—but their crazed mentalities those two days make it hard for me to teach.

"I can't believe you gave us a test on the day after Halloween," Daisy whines while I signal for students to turn in their homework.

"I know. I'm just the worst teacher ever, huh?" I mock her with a wicked smile while the students put away their bags.

"No, Miss Walsh. You're actually pretty awesome. But I'm gonna be real… I'm pretty annoyed with you right now."

I laugh at her. "Well, I appreciate your honesty."

Once everyone's ready, I wait for them to get silent

before passing out their tests. While monitoring the room, I catch myself sneezing repeatedly. After the symphony of bless-you's, I realize I think I'm getting sick. My nose is running, my throat is scratchy, and my head is pounding. Grateful that this is my last period, I hang on until the bell rings, then slump down in my desk chair.

"Oh, God," I whine while emailing the sub desk, knowing there's no way I'm going to be able to work tomorrow. I prepare lessons plans for my classes, grabbing some extra practice worksheets from my cabinet that I always have on hand for emergencies, leave a note of instructions for my substitute, and then grab my things and manage to drive home before beginning another sneezing fit. Seeing as how November is here, I guess cold season has arrived as well.

I change into pajamas, grab my blanket off the back of the couch, shove tissues up my nose, and melt into the cushions after drowning myself in cold medication.

The ring of my cell phone startles me awake, not realizing I drifted off. The meds must have hit me hard when I look at the time and notice it's after eight.

"Hello?" I answer, sounding more like a man than myself right now.

"Oh, no, are you sick?" Perry asks as soon as she hears my voice.

"Yes," I answer, trying not to cry. It seriously feels like an elephant is standing on my head and my chest.

"Oh, Liv. I'm sorry hun. Have you taken anything?"

"Yup."

"Okay, remember to put a humidifier in your room tonight and rub Vic's on the bottom of your feet, then put on your socks."

"Ewww, that's disgusting, Perry!" I choke out before

erupting into a coughing fit.

"I know it sounds weird, but trust me, it helps."

"Fine, *Mom*," I tease, but I know she wouldn't recommend it if she didn't believe it. It must be something she posted about on her blog.

"So, how are things going with Kane?" She asks, and I welcome the distraction from how horrible I feel.

"So great. Our date was phenomenal, and all week, he's been stopping by during our prep period to talk or give me a kiss, just because he was thinking about me…. Oh, shit!"

"What?" Perry reacts to my realization.

"I'm supposed to go out with him this weekend. I can't do that sounding and looking like this," I cry, more upset at the fact that I don't get to see Kane than how sick I feel.

"Hey, he'll understand. The man probably will thank you for not spreading your germs."

"I know, but I was really looking forward to our next date. I *really* like him, Perry…"

"I can tell, Liv. I'm truly happy for you. Who would have known this would happen after coming home, huh?" And she's right. The fact that this all occurred within a month of being home still shocks me.

"I know. He's surprised me in more ways than one, too."

"So when do the girls and I get to meet him? I wanna get a better look at this lumberjack. I vaguely recall him from that night."

I chuckle through a cough. "Let me get better first, and then I'll see what I can do."

"Sounds good, Liv. Get better soon," she says before we say our goodbyes and end the call.

The cold medication kicks in again, but I muster up

enough energy to make it to my room, plug in my humidifier, rub Vic's on my feet, and plop down in bed before I pass out.

The light from the morning doesn't even wake me up. It's the buzz of my phone on my nightstand that pulls me from my medication-induced slumber. Carefully propping my body up, I glance at the clock and notice it's ten in the morning, way past my normal four a.m. wake up time.

"Holy crap," I mutter while reaching for my phone. Swiping across the screen, I see a new message from Kane.

**Kane: Just went by your room and you had a sub. Is everything okay?**

My heart melts with his concern. And although the thought crossed my mind last night to text him and let him know I wouldn't be there today, I passed out before I remembered to.

I lay back and type out my response.

**Me: Yes. I'm home sick. It came on during sixth period yesterday. I'm sorry, but I don't think I'll be well enough for our date this weekend.**

My disappointment hits me hard because I really was looking forward to more time with him, away from the school. I wanted to kiss him more than just the few pecks and slips of tongue we've managed in our classrooms. I wanted more questions and more time studying every fleck of gold in his eyes.

**Kane: That sucks, but I completely understand. Do you need anything? Soup, medicine, soda?**

Oh, my heart. Kane is offering to bring me sickness supplies. Cue the heart-eyed emoji.

**Me: I think I'm okay. Plus, I don't want you to catch this.**

He texts back immediately.

**Kane: I don't give a shit about catching your cold. I just**

*want to make sure you're okay.*

Awww. This man is seriously dangerous to my heart.

*Me: I'm fine. Thank you though. I'll see you Monday, hope-fully.*

Today is Friday, so hopefully by the end of the weekend, I'll be normal enough to return to work. Let's face it, being gone is more work than being there for a teacher.

I don't get a reply from Kane, which makes me think he had work to do or something. I shrug it off and vacate my bed, taking a shower to clean off the stench and smell of Vic's, then stumble into the kitchen to make myself some hot tea and something to eat, even though nothing sounds good. I take residence on the couch and resume my Netflix marathon from last night. That Tom Ellis sure makes one handsome devil.

Before I know it, it's four o'clock and I haven't left the couch for anything except to go to the bathroom. The oatmeal I made myself for breakfast is barely touched and my stomach rumbles for sustenance.

Just as I stand, I hear a knock at my door. I remove the tissues from my nose, adding them to the growing pile on the coffee table, pat my hair down in the mirror by the door, adjust my glasses on my nose, and tie my robe around my waist before answering the door. It's probably Perry coming to check up on me. So you can imagine my surprise when I see Kane standing there, dressed in his Emerson Falls staff polo and jeans, dark brown boots and a matching jacket.

"Kane, what are you doing here?"

"I know you said you were fine, but I couldn't stop wondering if you were okay. So I brought everything I could think of to help you feel better," he says with a weak smile while holding up two bags from Target.

"Kane..."

"Olivia, just... let me do this, okay?" The look on his face is pained, and for whatever reason, I'm not sure. But he seems hard pressed to make sure I'm alright, and he obviously went to all this trouble to buy me things. It's seriously the sweetest thing any man has ever done for me.

"Okay, but I apologize for the mess—both my apartment and me," I say while gesturing down my body with my hand.

Kane chuckles and then kisses my forehead. "You look beautiful as always."

My heart thumps uncontrollably while I follow him into my kitchen where he proceeds to unpack the two bags full of goodies. Sudafed, Therma-flu, cough syrup and drops, Vic's Vapor Rub, ginger ale, tissues with lotion, and a carton of homemade chicken noodle soup from Penny's Diner, a local restaurant known for their home-style cooking. Kane must have cleared out the cold aisle at Target.

"Oh, my gosh, Kane. This is too much," I croak out, clearing the phlegm from my throat. "Sorry, I told you I wasn't in good shape."

Kane comes around the counter and grabs my face in his hands. "I know you're not used to someone wanting to take care of you. But this is something I really want to do. So stop apologizing and go sit down. I'll be right there," he demands with a kiss on my cheek, and that glimpse of his controlling side reminds me of his same demanding ways while we had sex. I know sex is the last thing I should be thinking about right now, but I can't help the fact that the man turns me on.

I nod and then he releases me as I amble over to the couch, picking up my snotty tissues from the coffee table and putting them in the trash before finally taking a seat. Kane comes in with one of my TV trays full of a bowl of soup, a stack of pills, and a can of ginger ale.

"Thank you, Kane," I say softly, peering up at him as he stands before me.

"You're welcome, Olivia. Now eat and hydrate. Take your pills. I'm gonna use the restroom really quick. I'll be right back."

Kane saunters down the hallway and I can't help but admire the view of his ass in those jeans as he walks away from me. If I was healthy right now, I'd be jumping his bones, no questions asked.

When he returns, he sits down next to me, putting his arm behind me on the couch. "So, what are you watching?"

"Lucifer. Have you heard of it?"

"Yeah, but I haven't watched it."

"We can watch something else if you'd like?" I offer as I take a sip from my soup. "Oh, God, that's good."

Kane glances over at me and grins. "How about a movie?"

"Sure, you pick."

Kane searches and then I know he found what he wants when his face lights up with the cheesiest smile.

"The Proposal?" I tease, knowing exactly why he picked this movie.

"It's one of Ryan Reynolds' best rom-coms, in my opinion."

I chuckle while finishing up my soup. "I agree. I love this movie. Press play."

Kane settles in to the couch and removes my tray once I'm finished. His arm finds its way around my body, hugging me tightly to his.

"You don't have to stay, you know. I don't want you to get sick, Kane."

"I'm fine. My immune system is killer and I'm not leaving you alone. I missed you today and I want to take care of you," he leans down and kisses the top of head, lingering longer than necessary, allowing me to melt even further into him with his touch and his words.

He cares about me. He's real. And he's choosing me.

I look up at him, waiting for his eyes to meet mine. And when they do, I speak. "I missed you too."

His smile returns before fading, his eyes drawing intensely together.

"God, I wish you weren't sick," he growls while resting his forehead against mine. "If you were well right now, I'd have you on your back and your mouth on mine so fast, you wouldn't even know what happened," he spits out, his grip on me tightening. I know he's feeling the same intense pull towards me that I feel for him. I want him so badly too, but it's obviously not the right time.

"You would do that and miss Ryan Reynolds?" I tease him which makes him laugh, pulling back away from me.

"If I had the chance to kiss you or watch Ryan, you'd win every time, Red."

Kane's words do nothing to quell my arousal, but him pulling me back into him as I rest my head on his chest while we watch the movie sure does something to my heart. I must doze off at some point because the next thing I know, I'm being carried down my hallway to my bedroom.

"Kane..." I stir as he carefully places me in bed.

"Shhhh. It's alright, Olivia. I'm gonna go. You get some rest and call me tomorrow, okay?"

I reach for his shirt, pulling his face close to mine. I want to kiss his lips so badly, thank him for being there and taking care of me, keeping me company when there were a million other places he could have been.

"Thank you," I whisper before placing a soft kiss on his cheek, the feel of his beard against my face sending a live wire of electricity over my body.

"Anything for you, Red."

I watch Kane leave and that's the last thing I remember before drifting off to sleep and dreaming of being in his arms again.

# CHAPTER 28

Kane

My usual sit-in at Tony's gets postponed after tending to Olivia last night, so when Saturday comes around, I decide to pay Tony a visit, and Drew's able to tag along.

Holding Olivia in my arms less than twenty-four hours ago calmed the ache in my chest I felt all day yesterday, knowing she was sick when I realized she wasn't at work. This innate need to take care of her kicked in—scaring me a bit—but also making me realize that I'm developing feelings for her, real fucking feelings, which makes my palms sweat, but also this sense of purpose come over me. The memory of what that feels like is fuzzy, but with each time I see her, the familiarity comes back.

The only other person I ever felt this for was she-who-will-not-be-named. Yet somehow, this differs from that. Maybe it's because I'm older now or I was so young with her that I can't remember entirely. But deep down I know that part of it is because it's Olivia that's sucking me into her world with her eyes and her smile, her quick wit and intelligence, and every morsel of information that I learn about her.

"I don't think I've ever seen you smile as much as I have in the past few weeks," Drew jests as we exit my truck and walk into Tony's.

"Believe me, you're not the only one who's noticed. Even my students said something to me the other day."

Opening the door, I usher Drew in first, then follow closely behind as we find my usual seat at the bar. Tony waves his hand over at us from the other end of the counter, letting us know he'll be with us soon.

"So, I take it things are going well, then?" Drew turns to me on his stool.

And I can't help but crack another smile. "Yeah, man. They are. The woman owns my mind right now. I… I can't get enough of her."

Clasping my shoulder, Drew shakes me in a brotherly manner. "That's great, Kane. Lord knows you deserve this. Hey, maybe the four of us can go out sometime? Tammy would love that."

"Sure, I'll ask Olivia," I say, just as Tony makes his way over.

"Well, if it isn't the two best teachers at Emerson Falls High School?" He mocks while giving us a shit-eating grin.

"Just changing the world one hormone-enraged teenager at a time," Drew replies.

Tony chuckles. "What'll it be tonight, boys?"

"The usual for me, Tony," I answer.

"I'll have the same, but add on two shots of whiskey," Drew adds.

"Shots? For what?"

"We're celebrating.."

I turn to Drew and narrow my eyes in confusion. "Celebrating what?"

"Kane's in *looovvveee*," Drew drags out, leaning over the bar to entice Tony.

"Shut the fuck up! Really, Kane?" Tony turns to me, his eyes wide, but that knowing smile accompanies his expression.

"I didn't say *love*, Drew. I'm just... quite enamored at the moment," I spit out, dropping my eyes to the beer Tony just placed in front of me.

Love is too strong of a word to describe what I feel for Olivia. Even I know that feeling anything like love for her this early on is impossible. I've only loved one woman. I can't possibly feel that way yet. I'm definitely interested in her. I want to see her all the time. And I care about her deeply... but it's not love yet.

Although I know that I could feel that way about her, eventually.

"Still, that is something to celebrate. Shots are on me, gentlemen," Tony winks while pouring the amber liquid and walking away to help another customer.

"To love and you finally getting laid regularly," Drew cheers, making me shake my head at him.

"Fuck you, man," I say before tipping back the shot, welcoming the burn as it flows down my throat.

"So, when are you gonna see her again? I know you're trying to take things slow and doing anything during the week is hard with our workload and stuff."

"Well, we were supposed to go out tonight actually..."

"Hold on! You ditched her to hang out with me? Uh, that's not how dating works, man," Drew scolds while sipping his beer.

"No, fucker. She's sick. She wasn't at work yesterday, so I texted her and she told me she was home sick. So I went over last night and brought her a bunch of medicine and some food and hung out for a while."

Drew's grin slowly spreads across his face before he takes a drink and then deposits his glass back on the bar.

"Okay, that's nice, Kane. But uh... if that doesn't sound like love, then I don't know what is."

"Shut up, man," I laugh while pushing Drew off of his stool.

"No, seriously. Taking care of her when she's all snot-covered and coughing up a lung... the only person I've ever done that for is Tammy."

"I just had to make sure she had everything she needed."

Drew pats my back, turning back to the bar in search of his beer. "I can't believe I was right."

"Right about what?" I ask, noticing Tony making his way back.

"She's your Tammy."

And I swallow hard. What if she is? What if Olivia is the woman I'm meant to be with?

Tony comes back over and starts drilling me about Olivia as Drew pipes in with details just to piss me off. I swear, if I knew I would get the dating inquisition tonight, I probably would have just stayed home.

After filling them both in on vague details of our time together—they don't need to know everything—I throw out an idea that I've been toying around with.

"I, uh, was actually thinking about inviting her over to my place next weekend..."

Drew spits out his beer and Tony stops cold as he wipes a glass.

"Seriously, Kane?" Tony speaks first, both of them clearly caught off-guard.

"Yeah."

"Dude, you've never taken a woman home. Are you sure?"

As Drew questions me, the only word that comes to mind is *yes*. It's true. Ever since I purchased the place, it's only been for me. Drew and Tammy have been by, and my parents when they were down to visit. But never once—in the last three years—have I brought a woman back to my house. I've never wanted to—until Olivia.

I nod. "Yeah, I think so."

"Fuck, he is in love," Tony declares, completely serious. I gaze up at him from my seat and don't have the desire to fight back this time.

Maybe he and Drew are right. Maybe I am on the way to falling in love with Olivia...

# CHAPTER 29

Olivia

Finally feeling human again after a visit to urgent care over the weekend, I saunter back into work on Monday to a heap of papers to be graded and a mile-long to-do list. I'm so entrenched in work and lesson planning for two days, I barely come out of my classroom and pass out on my couch as soon as I get home, still recovering slightly from my cold.

Despite a few texts here and there, I don't see Kane until Wednesday. Each night though, we talked on the phone or texted and he asked me more questions—the light ones that reveal more facts than anything. I love that he saves the deep ones for when we're together so I can embed myself in his warmth I've come to crave and see every emotion grace his chiseled face as we share more pieces of ourselves.

I insisted he stay away until I felt normal, but the man was relentless about seeing me, bribing me with cupcakes and coffee. I held him off, but by the middle of the week, I caved.

"Hey, beautiful," Kane greets me as he closes my classroom door behind him. He's dressed in a white button-down shirt with the sleeves rolled up to his elbows, the top two buttons open. Navy blue slacks hug his muscular legs and highlight that narrow waist I can't wait to explore again—knowing exactly what that sexy V leads to—and brown leather dress shoes skid across the floor as he makes his way over to me. His hair is casually styled and his beard looks better than ever. Damn, this man does things to my libido.

"Hi, handsome," I reply just as he finally reaches me, grabbing me by the hips and pulling me into him.

"Are you no longer contagious?"

"Nope. I even sound like myself again," I state while pointing to my throat.

"Thank God. I was beginning to think I was dating Kermit the Frog's long-lost cousin there for a while."

I suck in a sharp breath, playfully hitting him in the arm for his joke. "You take that back! I did not sound that bad. If anything, I sound more like a man when I'm sick, like my younger brother, or something."

"Speaking of which, when do I get to meet your family?"

His question throws me off-track because I didn't think we were at that point yet. Throughout our conversations this week, we talked more about our families. I learned he's an only child and his parents still live in northern Oregon. And I explained my family dynamic to him, including my four best friends that my parents pretty much adopted.

But the holidays are fast approaching. Thanksgiving will be here in a few weeks, and then Christmas and New Year's. I would love to introduce Kane to my family. I just didn't know that was something he was considering.

"You want to meet them already?"

"I mean, if you don't want me to, that's fine. I just thought, might as well. I'm curious about the people that made you who you are," he says while one hand comes up to caress my face, his calloused palm cupping my jaw as his thumb lightly touches my skin.

His inquisitiveness keeps taking me by surprise, coming from a man who was apprehensive about dating. He was the one I felt I would need to tread lightly around, ease gently into all of the steps of getting to know someone. Yet, suddenly, I feel like his increase in pace is all on his own accord. The look on his face solidifies his stance.

He's not wavering. He's not retracting. He's standing strong in his interest in me.

"I would love for you to meet them. We have dinner together every Sunday. Maybe one of these nights you can join us."

He kisses me on the nose and then retreats, leaving me desperate for more than just a peck. "Sounds perfect. So, what are your plans for this weekend?"

"Well, I do believe I owe you a date," I smirk.

"Agreed. How would you feel about me cooking you dinner at my place?"

"Your place? Are you sure?" I know how Kane feels about his home, his place of solitude that he is ornately proud of. Every conversation where he's told me about his house, he makes a point that it's his getaway—his one place to escape to when he needs space from the world.

"Yes. I want you there. I want to cook for you and then maybe we can watch a movie or something..."

*Or something.* Yeah, I'm definitely in the mood for *something.*

"I'll be there. Text me your address and what time you want me there," I say while trailing my hands up his arms, reaching to lock my fingers around his neck and pulling him down to me so our lips are but a whisper apart. I can feel Kane's pulse on my forearms, his chest rising and falling with each breath he takes as both of his hands circle my hips again.

"Good," he whispers before closing the gap between us and lowering his lips to mine. The soft brush of his mouth wakes up every inch of my body, searing our skin together in a blaze so hot, I feel like my fever from earlier in the week is returning.

Kane's hands move from my hips up my back, splaying across my body in a protective hold that is both powerful, but tender, drawing me closer to him. His tongue collides with mine in a dance that makes me forget we're at work, forget we once couldn't stand to be near each other—hell, he's making me forget my own name right now.

I soak up every touch of our mouths, every groan, every caress of finger tips across our bodies, reminding myself that it's only a matter of days before we can be completely immersed in each other again. I want him—all of him—but my professionalism is going to win this time.

"Kane," I exhale, cutting our kiss short while we both struggle to catch our breaths.

"Fuck. Sorry, Liv. I just... I've been dying to do that for days."

His confession makes me smile like a teenager. "Believe me, it was worth the wait. But we need to be careful at work. There will be more time for that this weekend," I look up at him from beneath my lashes, lacing my words with intention.

And by the way he's looking back at me, his eyes full of heat—he gets my message. "Without a doubt."

"Okay, well I need to get back to work," I stutter, trying to find my footing while escaping the confines of his arms, willing my heart and mind to stop racing and the normal color to return to my cheeks.

"Yeah, me too. I'll see you soon, Liv," he winks at me before turning on his heels and exiting my room.

The next two days crawl by as I anxiously await the next time Kane and I are alone, with only each other to hold our attention and not the needs of 175 teenagers, helicopter parents, and data-obsessed administrators breathing down our necks. Sometimes the stress of the job can be daunting. Grateful for our date to look forward to, it gives me the push to finish the week out strong and enjoy my night with Kane.

Saturday morning, I wake up later than normal to the sun peeking through the blinds and the hum of the heater coming through the vents of my apartment. I can finally breathe through my nose again and feel completely healthy. Stretching out my limbs in bed, I roll over to check my phone and see a text from Kane.

*Kane: Good morning, beautiful. Here is my address. Dress comfortably and bring your appetite. Can't wait to see you.*

His message instantly draws a smile from my mouth, making my entire body come alive with anticipation. I program his address into my GPS for later and then set about ticking off my chores as normal.

I brew myself some coffee, fry up a few scrambled eggs with cheese and avocado, get thirty minutes in on my elliptical, and finish all of my laundry before showering and relaxing before I have to get ready.

Choosing leggings and a long sweater, I get dressed before I pull my hair in a ponytail high off my neck and leave my make-up light. I check my appearance in the mirror one more time before leaving—nodding my head in approval—grab my coat from the hook by the door, and make my way to my car before sliding in, cranking the heater, and heading for Kane's home.

"Are you on your way there?" Clara's voice booms through the Bluetooth speaker as I cruise along the highway.

"Yes. Tell me why I feel so nervous…"

"Because you know you're going to have sex with him again tonight," she states firmly.

"Ugh, you don't know that. What if we're taking things slow?" I say, trying to convince myself. But it's a lost cause. If we don't sleep together again tonight, I might self-destruct.

She huffs. "Please. You've already slept together. What's the point? Now what you *should* be worried about is if it will be as good as it was last time."

Her words make my stomach feel unsettled. *Shit.* I didn't even think of that. What if the first time was a fluke? What if it was the booze and not this intense physical connection I thought we shared?

"Earth to Olivia..."

"Huh?" I answer, focusing back on our conversation and not the river of doubt swimming through my mind.

"Don't worry, Olivia. I'm sure you'll be fine. Hell, it will probably be better because you know each other now. One-night-stands are usually awkward, but from what you've told me... it seems like you both knew there was more there that first night. And I bet the sexual tension is so hot between you two right now, he'll jump you the second you walk through his door."

The image of Kane pressing me up against the door and having his way with me turns my insecurities completely around.

"That would be nice, but I'm not counting on it."

"Really? Tell me this... did you shave your legs, among other things?"

I pause, knowing my friend knows me all too well.

"That's exactly what I thought," she laughs through the phone, making me groan.

"Shut up. Okay, I need to get off of here. I'm almost there."

"You'd better come up for air at some point this weekend and let me know how it goes. You know, when your mouth isn't full of Kane's.."

"OKAY! I'm going! Love you!" I shout, cutting her off and ending the call before she can utter another word. Sometimes the woman can be the voice of reason I need to hear, and other times, she's the bane of my existence. She knows just how to ruffle my feathers and get a reaction out of me.

And after talking to Clara, I'm not sure if I feel better or more nervous about my night with Kane.

# CHAPTER 30

Kane

*Olivia: I'm on my way.*

Sitting on my couch, I stare at her text for the tenth time in the last five minutes, itching with anticipation for her to arrive. Prior to her message, I was staring up at the blades on my fan as they spun around, getting lost in the movement to calm my anxiety.

I shouldn't feel this unsettled at the thought of Olivia arriving. Hell, when I asked her to come over I was sure it was what I wanted. But now that it's happening, I'm fully aware of how monumental this is. I made a huge choice—a step forward with her—and it's both exhilarating and terrifying at the same time.

*"So how are things going with Olivia?" Dr. Martinez asked as I settled into her couch yesterday afternoon. After my self-appointed visit a few weeks ago due to my panic attack, she insisted I come back to check in with her sooner rather than later.*

*"Really well, actually. We're establishing a friendship. I've been asking her questions to get to know her, which kind of backfired, but then worked to my advantage," I chuckle. "I've taken her on a few dates and… we've kissed a few times. She, uh, got sick last week and I made sure to bring her medicine and food so she could recover quickly…"*

*"You seem shocked that you did those things, Kane. Why is that?"*

*Her question resonates with me as soon as she says it. Shocked? Am I startled by my actions?*

*Yes.*

*"I didn't realize it would be this easy. Moving on. Moving forward from Natasha. I've been so afraid for years to allow myself to let anyone else in. But it doesn't feel that way with Olivia."*

*"And why do you think that is?" She asks, straightening her back in her chair and pushing her glasses up the bridge of her nose.*

*Honestly, I'm not sure.*

*Is it because enough time has passed and in combination with seeing a therapist, I've been able to deal with my anger? Is it because I'm older now and have more life experience? It is because I've realized that Natasha and T.J.'s actions belong in the past and don't need to dictate my future?*

*Or is it her?*

*Is* she *the only reason this is easy for me? Is it because I'm genuinely attracted and drawn to Olivia, and no one else? Would I even be able to feel this way for another woman?*

*The thought of any other woman in my arms and against my lips makes my stomach turn.*

*"I think there are many reasons... but most importantly, I think it's just because it's her."*

*The smile that graces Dr. Martinez's face makes a wave of pride spread across my chest.*

*"When you find a person you feel is worth the effort, it makes moving on easier, Kane. I'm happy to see this side of you— the man who has patched up his wounds, owns his scars, and is now making progress in healing."*

Standing from the couch, I walk over to the large bay window that covers a good portion of the front of my house, flipping my fan off before watching the darkness overtake the sky and the stars appearing in the black blanket above us. My hands find the pockets of my jeans and I let out a long sigh, waiting for Olivia to arrive, knowing that slowly but surely, this woman is helping me heal.

The weight I've been carrying around on my shoulders is lightening, the anger I've been holding onto is dissipating, and the feeling of longing for someone again is returning full force the more time I spend with her. I've caught myself smiling, appreciating small moments throughout my day that I would never have focused on before—and I know that's because of her.

She's made life have meaning again.

I spent so much time today getting ready for tonight. I woke up early—as usual—got my workout in, showered, went grocery shopping, cleaned my entire house from top to bottom, and then showered again and got dressed for our date.

Just as I turn to assess my house one more time, I see headlights flash in the window, directing my attention back to the view of my front yard. The bounce of the white orbs mesmerizes me as my pulse picks up, knowing in just a few short moments, there will be a woman in my home—my place of reprieve—my sanctuary that no other woman has seen.

Her car stops and the headlights shut off just as the porch light activates from the movement of her standing from her car. And when I see her—her long, deep red hair pulled up off her neck, her eyes sparkling from the glow of the porch light, her long legs covered in black leggings and knee-high boots and a navy coat warming her body—all of my anxiety ceases to exist.

Instead, all I feel is need—a need for her to be right next to me—in my arms, in my home.

I gather my wits and race for the door, opening it before she has a chance to knock.

"Hi," she smiles as soon as she sees me and fuck, if it

doesn't send a dagger of hope to my chest.

"Hey, beautiful. Come on in," I say, holding the door open for her as she steps inside, shivering from the cold atmosphere outside. The rush of icy air offers a reprieve from the intense heat climbing in my body from my nerves, but I shut the door quickly as to not let the warmth of the house escape.

"Let me take your coat," I offer, helping her discard her jacket and hanging it in the closet by the front door. "Well, welcome. This is my home," I wave my hand through the air, directing her attention to the living area directly to the left of the door. The high ceilings with wooden beams create an open concept living area, connecting the living room, dining room, and kitchen. The couch and a recliner are situated around a handmade coffee table I built with my grandfather before he passed, directed at the flat screen TV hanging on the wall. Behind the furniture is a fireplace, roaring with flames from the logs I lit earlier today to warm up the house before the cold made it impossible.

I grab Olivia's hand as I lead her through the living room and into the kitchen which opens up to the living room space, directing her to take a seat at the island covered in white marble.

"Kane, your house is beautiful. Was it like this when you moved in?"

"Not everything. I've done a lot of the work myself or with help from Drew and the boys at school—Holt and Tanner that is, not our students."

Olivia laughs at my joke before turning back around to admire my house. I have to say—the fact that she approves makes my heart swell with pride.

"Well, it's amazing. Seriously—it's like a modern-day log cabin in the woods. And it's so quiet out here... no wonder you love it," she says before turning back to me. "Thank you for having me here."

I relish in the sincerity of her tone and then move the evening forward.

"You're welcome. So, I hope you're hungry."

"Always," she smirks, leaning forward on the counter, resting her chin in her hands propped up on her elbows. She looks adorable and I want to kiss that smirk off of her face.

*Focus, Kane. Food first, kissing later.*

"Okay, well the food won't take long. I have the rice in the rice cooker and I just have to throw the salmon and veggies in the oven to roast," I declare while moving around the kitchen to gather the ingredients. I purposely chose something quick and easy, and something I knew I couldn't fuck up, not wanting to risk the distraction of her while I was cooking, causing me to burn our meal.

"Oh, fancy," she teases. "Can I help?"

"You can pour us some wine," I nod in her direction, drawing her attention to the bottle and wine opener on the other side of the island.

"You got it. So, do you cook a lot? Or is this something you only do on occasion?" Olivia moves off of her seat, reaching for the bottle and twisting into the cork.

"Confession?"

"Of course," she gleams, fully intrigued by what I'm about to share with her.

"One of my guilty pleasures is watching cooking shows. Chopped is a personal favorite, but I really watch them all. One of my favorite things to do is try to recreate a recipe I see or fiddle around in here with what I have and see what I can make," I shrug while placing the two thick slices of salmon on a baking sheet, drizzling them both with olive oil.

"Oh my gosh, that's too cute, Kane," she laughs, handing

me a glass of wine as she makes her way around the island and closer to me.

"Cute?"

She nods. "Yeah, way too cute. I'd love to see you in action, prancing around your kitchen, whistling and probably cooking with your shirt off, right?"

I quirk my eyebrow at her. "Prance? I don't prance, babe. I fucking *own* this kitchen. And yes... there are no shirts involved," I say while leaning into her, the pupils of her eyes dilating the closer I get. I get a whiff of her scent, sweet and floral, and all I want to do is knock that wine glass out of her hands and crash my mouth down to hers.

I hear her gulp, then quickly draw a sip of wine from her glass, breaking our gaze. I know she can sense the sexual tension, which I plan on releasing soon.

I smile to myself as I turn back around to season the fish and veggies and pop them in the oven. "So, would you like me to show you the rest of the place while we wait for the food?"

"Absolutely," she nods. I reach out for her hand, interlacing our fingers together and walk her down the hallway to point out the bathroom and spare rooms—one operating as an office and the other as my home gym—before we make it to my bedroom.

"Wow. This is gorgeous, Kane," she gasps when she enters, taking in the matching high ceilings to the living room complete with sky lights that offer a breathtaking view of the stars when the sky is clear, like it is tonight. The oak four poster bed on the main wall takes up most of the space, accompanied by a matching dresser. Dark grey bedding and navy pillows are the only sources of color besides the light grey on the walls. A glass sliding door offers a perfect view of the backyard, providing just a slight view of the lake off the back of my property.

"And through there is the master bath," I point, just as Olivia turns and glides into my bathroom. The claw foot tub rests comfortably in its nook, away from the standing shower and across from the double sinks and full length mirror that spans the wall.

Olivia turns to me and shakes her head. "This is like a dream home, Kane. It's fabulous and very, you. I only hope to have a home this nice someday," she says so casually, I almost don't let her words hit me.

But then I see her back in my room, standing in the middle of the floor in front of my bed, and I feel this strong sense of belonging—like she belongs here. It's like staring at a painting or photograph that captivates your attention and leaves you speechless. All you can do is stare because there are no words to accurately describe the image in front of you.

It literally takes your breath away.

*Olivia takes my breath away.*

Clearing my throat, I move to speak, just as I hear the oven timer.

"Food's ready. Come on," I throw my head in the direction of the kitchen.

After I serve us both, we sit at the table and feast. Olivia makes little moans throughout dinner that test my restraint —my dick growing painfully hard with every noise and lick of her lips. Fuck, I can't wait to taste her again.

"That was delicious," she sighs, licking her fork clean and leaving not one grain of rice on her plate.

"Thank you. I'm glad you approved," I say, standing to grab both of our plates and depositing them in the sink. I did most of the clean-up beforehand, so the few dishes can wait until tomorrow.

"Is it movie time?" Olivia asks, reaching to refill her

wine glass as she arrives at the island next to me.

"Uh, sure," I say, just now remembering that I promised her a movie. Hell, did she not understand that movie is code for other things? Or is that just me, being a guy, thinking with my dick?

Resolving that the night is still young, I shove down my impatience and lead Olivia into my living room as she settles on my couch.

"Oh, my God, you do *not* have a shelf dedicated to Ryan Reynolds' movies in your cabinet!" She gasps, leaning over my shoulder as I hunch down and dig out a movie. I never heard her move from the couch before she popped up behind me.

"Damn right I do, woman. I told you," I say, pointing to myself, "Obsessed."

Olivia throws her head back in laughter before making her way back to the couch and removes her boots. That sound —her laugh—it's methodical and hypnotizing. I never want her to stop. I want to do anything in my power to make her laugh as much as possible.

"Well then, by all means... let Ryan entertain us tonight," she jests, tucking her legs underneath her as she sinks into the cushion. I stand tall and memorize her in this moment—so comfortable, so carefree, so completely perfect sitting there—on my couch, in my home.

I can't speak. I'm too overcome with the rush of feelings pounding on my chest. I toss the movie on the ground and stride over to her, leaning down and caging her in on the sofa as my arms rest on the back, her hazel eyes veering up to mine.

"What about the movie?" She whispers as I remove her wine glass from her hand and set it on the side table.

"I can think of things far more entertaining than Ryan Reynolds right now," I growl, the deep rumble of my voice so full of lust, there's no hiding it.

"I'm going to tell him you said that," she teases, biting her bottom lip and sending a strike of arousal to my dick. Fuck, I wanna bite that lip. I want to nibble on every inch of her skin.

"He'll understand. He's a guy. And if he saw the gorgeous and sexy-as-hell redhead sitting on my couch, he'd tell me to fuck the movie too and go after what I want."

Her eyes search mine before glancing down to my mouth and popping back up again.

"And what is it that you want, Kane?" She plays stupid, but we're both far too intelligent and turned on to play these games.

I've been drawing on the memory of her beneath me for weeks now, even before I realized I wanted more with her. I remember what she tastes like—her mouth, her skin, her pussy. I know the sounds she makes when she's about to come.

But nothing is better than the real thing. The images in my mind can only last me so long before I need my next fix. Before I feel the urge to bury myself so deep inside of her I lose all sense of reality.

"You, Olivia. I want you."

"Then take me, Kane," she whispers, and that's all the clarification I need.

# CHAPTER 31

Olivia

Kane leaves me no time to prepare—for the moment I give him permission, his mouth crashes down to mine, leaving me breathless and desperate for more of him.

My back arches off of the couch as I fight to situate my legs out from underneath me, propping myself up on my knees so I can be more level with his stance. Kane dives his tongue into my mouth, owning me more than he has before, a deep growl vibrating up his throat, making me crave more from him. A rush of memories flood my mind of our first night together—but this time is different. Clara was a fool to make me doubt that this time could be worse.

There is no denying the explosive chemistry between us.

My hands eagerly search for any part of Kane that I can grab onto to as he continues to kiss me with such passion that my knees become weak and I feel wetness pool between my legs—as if I haven't been wet for this man for weeks.

Our lips press tightly together as my hands meet behind his neck, pulling him down further to me. I feel his palms grace my hips before yanking me off of the couch and lifting my entire body in his arms. Instinctively, my legs wrap around his waist as he carries me away from the couch, our lips never parting.

I can hear my own heartbeat in my ears, I can feel Kane's

pulse beneath my fingers—and each thump of blood rushing through our veins drives us higher in our need for one another. I feel Kane's legs carry us to the back of the house, the warmth from the air in the living room slowly dissipating as we move further away.

And normally, I would protest. I hate being cold.

But there is nothing but heat permeating my body right now as Kane deposits me on his bed, hovering over me and finally breaking our lips free from each other.

"Fuck, Olivia," he growls, his nose trailing a path up the column of my neck until he reaches my ear, pulling lightly on my lobe between his teeth, igniting a flurry of tingles all over my skin.

"Kane..." I mewl, my hands caressing his shoulders and arms covered in a tight black shirt.

"I want to take my time with you tonight, baby. Last time we were rushed. We were so desperate for each other that I didn't take a moment to memorize every inch of your body." His words stroke a fire of arousal in my core—the heat so intense I feel like I'm about to explode.

"Yes... please touch me, Kane. Touch all of me," I surrender—ready and willing to hand my body over to this man.

Kane stands and reaches for my foot, removing my socks before his hands cascade up the buttery fabric of my leggings to the apex of my thighs, while his eyes never leave mine. He holds me in place with his intense stare, as if I would even consider moving from this spot. Who knew that a man taking off my socks could be so sexy?

He runs his thumb along my slit through my clothes, the friction just enough to relieve the throbbing in my clit for a moment until he moves his hand away, and I yearn for his touch again, moaning when his hands leave the area I need them in.

"Patience, baby," he smirks, reaching for the top of my leggings on my hips, tucking his thumbs in the waistband, and slowly pulling the stretchy cloth down my smooth legs.

Thank God I shaved. Let's be real, ladies. When the weather turns cold, we're not as diligent with leg shaving, am I right?

Kane leaves a trail of kisses up my calf to the top of my thighs, his face so close to where I need him to be—yet, he continues to tease me by brushing his fingers against the skin just above my thong and along the juncture where my leg meets my pelvis.

"Kane, please..."

"Mmmm, I can smell you, baby. Tell me how wet I make you..."

His nose presses against the silky fabric of my underwear this time as he drags it through my slit, inhaling my arousal deeply.

"I'm so wet, Kane. I need you..."

"I need you too, Olivia," he whispers—and somehow, by the tone of his voice, I don't think he just means right now.

Hooking his thumbs in the band of my thong, he drags the fabric down my legs so I'm left completely bare from the waist down.

"God, this pussy is amazing. I haven't stopped picturing you since that first night, exposed to me like this. I've been dying to taste you again," his voice rumbles between my legs as he pulls me to the edge of the bed and drops to his knees before I faintly feel the tip of his tongue glide through my wetness. The sensation sends me arching off of the bed, gasping for air, and moaning into the room.

"Oh, God," I sigh as Kane applies more pressure, circling my clit with his tongue, diving his mouth deep between my legs, tasting every inch of me and lapping up every drop of my arousal.

I climb, high and fast, the pressure and tightening in my stomach coming on strong with every move Kane makes with his mouth. I get lost in each twist and turn of his tongue as he alternates between short and long strokes and then occasionally sucks my clit between his lips.

It's amazing, electrifying, and yet not enough. I need more. I want more.

And just as the thought crosses my mind, I feel him stretch my opening as he pushes two fingers inside of me. I welcome the intrusion, reveling in the feel of him pulsing his fingers in and out of me, the sound of my wetness echoes in the room as he continues to work my clit with his tongue.

"Yes, right there," I declare as I feel Kane hook his fingers inside, rubbing that spot that sets me off. And after a few more strokes, the white hot heat of my orgasm slams into me, building like the crescendo of a song as I reach the peak, immersing myself in the feeling of losing control as my body rides out the waves.

But I'm not losing. And I'm certainly not fighting him. I handing myself over to him, trusting him to please my body—and slowly allowing him into my heart at the same time.

Kane rises from the floor, bringing his fingers to his mouth where he sucks them clean.

"Fucking perfect," he mumbles before reaching for his shirt, pulling the black fabric up and over his head, revealing that chiseled chest to me that should come with a warning label.

Warning: prolonged exposure to mountains of muscle covered in tattoos will result in wet panties and heavy panting. Possible side effects: not being able to control yourself and dropping to your knees at the first sight of them.

I push myself off of the bed, locking eyes with him as he watches me discard my sweater, leaving me in nothing but my bra. I push the straps down off of my shoulders and release the clasp so I'm completely naked, but his eyes never wander. They stay locked with mine until I drop to my knees and reach for the belt on Kane's pants.

"Olivia," his raspy voice calls to me, sounding like he's struggling to keep his cool.

"My turn to taste you, Kane," I smile while looking up at him again. And the way he's looking down on me makes me feel cherished, even though we're both insanely aroused right now. The bulge in Kane's jeans strains against the fabric, so I work quickly to release him and grant him some relief.

Pushing his jeans and boxer briefs down his legs, Kane helps me remove his pants completely so his naked body stands before me, like a Greek sculpture. The man has the body of a God. His muscles have muscles. I could spend all night licking every crevice of his physique and I still would want to do it again.

I reach for his length, hard and pulsing in front of me, wrapping my hands around him as I pump him in my palm.

"Fuck, Liv…"

His hands reach for my face, pushing my hair that fell from my ponytail out of the way so he can see me.

And when he looks at me again, he smiles—an innocent, pure, and soft lift of his lips that hits me hard in my chest.

I surrender myself to that feeling and then bring him to my mouth, dying to show him how much I want him, how much I need him, how much I care for him too. His reverent grin disappears as his eyes close and he moans in ecstasy.

"Fuck."

I flutter my tongue along the underside of his head and

then swirl it around, taking him deep in my throat, feeling him grow harder with each movement. Kane's hands find my head, guiding me up and down his length in a suggestive way, but never making me feel like I'm not in control.

I hear his breathing quicken, his inhales becoming short and sharp as I continue to pull him in and out of my mouth, using my hand to pleasure him simultaneously and cup his balls just as he pulls away.

"If you keep doing that, I'm never going to get to fuck you, Liv," Kane says as he helps me up and pulls my lips to his, kissing me intently before backing us up to the bed.

Kane motions for me to scoot back as he climbs on the bed, following me until my head hits the pillows. He moves one of his hands to my chest, pressing lightly between my breasts before dragging his fingers down my sternum and further to my belly button, swirling the tips of his fingers around the soft skin of my stomach and then back up to my breasts, circling my nipples.

"You're beautiful, baby. I could stare at you all night," he whispers while lowering his forehead to mine as he continues to caress my flesh.

"Please, Kane... you're driving me crazy," I whine, the pressure between my legs building again so intensely, I feel like I could come just from the soft touches he's giving my body right now.

Kane leans down to plant a soft kiss on my lips before reaching for his nightstand and fetching a condom. I watch him tear the foil with his teeth, sitting back on his legs to sheath himself. Once he's protected, he hovers over me again and locks his eyes with mine, the stars above us shining through the skylight in his bedroom.

Above me is this man, surrounded by darkness—yet all I see is the light he's brought back into my life.

He lines himself up to my entrance. "Look at me, Olivia. Don't look away... I want to see you when I take you this time."

I nod, my eyes never leaving his as he plunges into me, taking a few solid strokes before he bottoms out. Our breaths catch simultaneously when he reaches the furthest point inside, and I feel myself sigh in contentment—the feeling of being connected physically to Kane again almost too much to process.

"Fuck, baby. You feel incredible..." Kane says as he starts to move, setting a pace that is both intense yet luxurious.

My hands travel all over his shoulders and back as he moves inside of me, our bodies rocking together, feeding off of one another and pleasuring each other instinctually. His lips press to mine again, swirling our tongues together while he continues to fuck me.

Kane reaches down and hooks his arm under one of my knees, pulling the leg up and over his shoulder, sending him even deeper into my wet heat.

"Oh..." I moan, closing my eyes and relishing in the feeling of Kane's cock as he moves, hitting the furthest point inside over and over again.

"Fuck, baby..."

"More Kane..."

"Yes, Liv..."

"Harder..."

"God, woman..."

"Faster..."

"Fuck..."

"Oh, God!" I shout as my orgasm hits me, sharper and

more intense than the last. Kane's hand reaches between us to rub my clit while I climb high and then come again, making my orgasm double in one swift move. The man plays my body like an instrument, making sweet music with my strings, plucking me in the just the right way that I lose myself in his touch. I've never been with a man that can make my body sing like he does.

Once I start to come down, Kane flips us over, reaching up to pull my hair out of my ponytail, my long locks falling and framing my face as I hover over him this time.

"Ride me, baby," he grits out while grabbing one handful of my hair and the other handful of my ass.

And so I do. I rock and bounce, lifting up and down his length, which feels even bigger from this angle. Kane moves with me from below, meeting my thrusts and stroking my body up and down my curves as I move.

"Yes, baby... God, you look so beautiful when you ride my cock."

"It feels so good, Kane."

"Tell me how good it feels, baby."

"I'm so wet. I don't think I've ever been this wet in my life," I pant as I feel another orgasm come on. I clench around Kane's length inside of me, which ignites a growl from him.

"Are you gonna come again, baby?" He asks, guiding my hips to rub along him.

"Yes, but I need you to touch me, Kane..."

Not hesitating, Kane reaches between my legs and rubs my clit expertly, applying just the right amount of pressure so that it doesn't take long for me to reach the edge of the cliff again, falling over in an orgasm that drains every last drop of energy from me.

"Fuck!" Kane shouts as he sits up, wraps his arms around

my torso, and thrusts into me, stilling once his orgasm hits and squeezing me hard as he comes down from his high.

Sitting back slightly, he brushes the hair from my face so our eyes find each other—and we just stare, nothing but the sound of our breathing filling the room. I watch his dark eyes scan my face, softening as his hands caress my cheeks before pulling me to him in a soft kiss that melts my body into his. We hold each other, not speaking, not even thinking—just immersing ourselves in the feeling of our bodies connected to one another again.

• • • • • • • • • • • • • • • • • • • • • • • • • • • • • • • • •

"What's going on in that mind of yours?" I ask Kane, both of us resting on our sides facing each other in his bed after we cleaned up and relaxed from the mind-blowing sex.

Kane's hands trail up and down my body, soaking up every curve and inch of skin. I can't get enough of the way it feels to have his hands all over me. I'm addicted. And I don't know if I can ever live without his touch again.

"I'm thinking I really like having you here," he says on a slight smile, his eyes softening with his words.

"Does that surprise you?"

"Yes."

I notice a shift in his expression, so I force myself to push him further. Kane has already let me in more than I anticipated when he first made his intentions clear, but I know there's something he's not telling me—either by choice or because he's not ready to talk about it. But I desperately want to understand him. Ever since he told me he hasn't pursued a woman since he was sixteen, I've been dying to know why.

"Can I ask you something, and you'll promise not to get mad?"

"Just the fact that you prefaced your question with that

question alarms me."

"I just need to know something, but I'm afraid of how you'll react," I confess.

Kane sits up a bit more, propping his elbow further, his hand resting on his head so his entire body straightens. "I don't want you to be afraid to ask me questions, Liv. I just... there are some things that are hard to talk about."

"I understand that. But I need to know... why haven't you pursued someone since you were so young?"

And silence fills the room as Kane shifts his eyes from mine, hiding the pain there even though I can read him like a book. Whatever happened has to be a huge reason why he is the man he is today—guarded, a little off-putting, but secretly a man with a soft heart who cares about those close to him. He's shown me all three sides, but I can't help but feel like he's struggling to figure out which one he wants to be.

Kane exhales before lying back flat, staring up at the ceiling. I trace the lines of his chest and stomach with my fingertips while I wait for him to speak. Just when I think I'll let him off the hook, his voices fills the room.

"Her name was Natasha. We were high school sweet-hearts. We started dating when we were juniors and then I joined the Army after graduation to serve my country and get my degree paid for at the same time." He pauses and his eye-brows draw together as he gathers himself to continue. "She understood my choice and promised to stay with me while I was away. And for the first four years, things were fine. We made it work. But then I re-enlisted for another four years and she wasn't happy with my decision. I was just at a place where I felt like I couldn't leave, but I promised her that after those four years, I'd be done. I even proposed to her so she knew I was serious. I saw my future with her and I loved her."

He shifts again, back to facing me. The anguish in his

eyes penetrates my soul as I watch him struggle to continue. Instinctually, I reach for his hand, intertwining our fingers and caressing his, silently showing my support.

"I came home early, discharge papers in hand to surprise her, when..." he clears his throat of the emotion clouding his voice, "When I walked in on her fucking my best friend, T.J."

And my stomach drops, my heart breaks, and my eyes cloud with tears when I realize this woman shattered the man in front of me.

"Oh, Kane..."

"Don't, Olivia. I don't need your pity."

"It's not pity, Kane. I just can't imagine being betrayed like that," I argue, hoping he doesn't shut down on me now.

"It killed me, but I've been working past it. I just... I've never felt a betrayal like that in my life, and it made me want to shut myself away from the rest of the world."

"I can only imagine," I whisper, tracing the lines of his shoulders before cupping his face.

"It's been over three years, and even though the sting isn't as fresh... it still is something I struggle with accepting. The two people that I thought I could trust the most ripped my heart from my chest and left me a shell of the man I thought I was. It took me a long time to accept that their choices were their own, and I could either let them define me, or move on. I vowed to never let anyone in again... but then I met you..."

I swallow hard as he pulls me close to him, the full length of our bodies touching as his eyes search my face.

"Me?"

He nods. "You were the one thing I never thought I wanted again. Even though the night we met was more about letting go and trying to have some fun, there was something about you I couldn't stop thinking about. And when I saw you again, it made me feel things I hadn't felt since… well, since I wanted Natasha."

And right then and there, I surrender to this pull I've felt to him since that night.

"I understand completely, Kane. In fact, more than you probably think."

"How's that?"

"Well, that night was about me escaping betrayal myself. My entire reason for coming home was because I found my boyfriend fucking his secretary in his office. I was trying to surprise him, but it seems I'm the one who got the surprise."

Kane shakes his head and then presses a light kiss to my lips. "Why any man would want to cheat on you boggles my mind."

"Well, I could say the same thing about you. I thought I had it all. I thought I saw a future with my ex, but when I realized all the warning signs were there, I blamed myself for not seeing them."

"It's easy to take the blame for other people's actions, especially when they hurt you."

"I'm sorry you were hurt, Kane. I'm so sorry that the people closest to you made you question your ability to trust again. But thank you for opening up to me about it. Yet, I guess I should really be thanking Natasha…"

Kane chuckles. "Oh, yeah? Why's that?"

"Because if she hadn't messed up, you and I wouldn't be here right now."

The words leave my mouth before I thought them all the way through, yet the smile on Kane's face tells me he understands my confession as exactly what it was supposed to be—a clarification that things happened the way they were supposed to.

"Her loss, your gain, huh?" He teases, rolling me onto my back as he hovers over me.

"Definitely," the rasp of my voice comes through as I feel Kane's length harden against my leg. My entire body heats up in an instant at his touch, his hands traveling down to my thighs, pulling my legs apart so he can settle between them, rubbing his cock through my wetness.

"Christ, woman. What did I do to deserve you?"

"You killed all of those crickets," I joke as he throws his head back in laughter. "This is just my way of repaying you."

"You better not show your appreciation to anyone else who kills crickets for you in this way."

I shake my head. "Only the really good-looking men," I wink.

Kane smirks at me before kissing me deeply, teasing me with his lips and tongue.

"Thank you again for telling me, Kane. I know that can't be easy to talk about. But I feel like I understand you better now."

His eyes search mine, stalling in the moment before rubbing his hand along my face. "I don't want to live in the past anymore, Liv. I'm enjoying being here with you in the present far too much," he whispers while teasing my opening with his dick.

"Kane, I want you again. I don't think I'll ever get enough..." I mewl, wanting to so badly to feel Kane bare inside of me—a gift no other man has experienced. "I'm on the pill..."

His eyes dance between mine before he clarifies my request. "Are you sure?"

I nod. "Yes. I want to feel you... every inch."

"Fuck, Liv," he growls before diving his tongue in my mouth and pushing forward, claiming me as his. He dives into me, resting his forehead on mine while rocking us back and forth. My back arches with every drive as he leans down and pulls my nipples into his mouth, biting and sucking on the rosy buds while moving in and out of me.

My entire body comes alive as he ignites every nerve ending on my skin. His fingers, his mouth, his cock—he owns my mind and body tonight and probably forever, knowing I'll never feel this way with another man. No man will ever compare to him and I don't want any other man to try.

As Kane brings us both to orgasm again until we're both sated and surrender to sleep, I realize there's no turning back for me now. I'm falling and I don't want to get up.

# CHAPTER 32

Olivia

"When is he going to be here?" Clara whines as Perry and Amy both arrive from their trip to the bathroom and sit at our table.

"God, your patience is worse than that of a child," I scold her while nonchalantly scanning the crowd.

It's a Saturday night at Tony's and the place is packed. Yet as I sit here with my four best friends, the only person I'm anxious about seeing finally walks through the doors.

Kane stands there in his brown coat, brushing his hand through his hair as he takes off his beanie and searches the room momentarily before his whiskey-colored eyes find mine, lighting up his face with the most blinding smile I've ever seen from him before.

"My God. If a man ever looked at me like that, I'd ignore my friends for weeks too," Clara teases as I throw an elbow in her ribs. But the truth is, I haven't been the best friend lately, spending every moment of my free time I can with Kane. I've sent texts to let them know I'm alive, but most of my time and communication has been reserved for him.

Ever since our night at his house, we've been inseparable. We either stay at his place on the weekend or my place during the week. The only time we leave the bedroom is to eat or go to work. This is the first time in my life I've put a relationship above my job and friendships, and it's both scary, yet liberating.

The anguish and uncertainty I felt when I came back home has vanished, replaced with elation and lust, and I'm happily drowning in it. I don't feel like just Miss Walsh, the teacher, anymore. I feel like Olivia, this woman who finally feels like all of the puzzle pieces in her life are falling into place. And it's not just that there's this man now in my life that is making me feel things I never thought were real. It's that I've finally accepted the path I've taken to get here and I'm optimistic about the future direction of my life.

But that is in large part due to the man stalking towards me right now.

"Hi, handsome," I greet him just as he steps up to me and crashes his mouth to mine, in front of all of my friends, staking his claim and drowning me in one of his kisses that makes my toes curl.

Once he's satisfied with leaving me breathless, Kane breaks apart from me and turns to face my friends. I follow his lead and see the three of them—Amy with her jaw dropped, Perry with the widest smirk, and Clara wide-eyed and fanning herself.

"Hi, ladies. I'm Kane," he extends his hand to my girls, the three of them taking turns to shake his hand.

"Hi, Kane. I'm Perry. It's nice to formally meet you this time without tequila clouding our minds."

"Yeah, I barely remember that night," Amy adds. "Clara kept saying there was a lumberjack that evening, but all I remember is running to the bathroom."

"Lumberjack?" Kane asks, furrowing his brows as he turns to me.

"Don't you remember you were wearing that flannel the night we met, babe?"

Kane nods his head in recollection as he takes a seat. "Aw, yeah I guess I was."

"Hi, I'm Clara. And can I just say... I don't know what you're doing to my friend, but keep doing it. I've never seen her smile this much before," she teases him.

"Clara!"

"Oh, come on, Liv. Don't act like you're not completely smitten. I would be too if a fine piece of man meat like that was bringing me to orgasm every night." Clara rolls her eyes.

"Dear Lord," I lower my head in my hands while Kane's deep laugh rumbles beside me, his arms pulling me into him while we're both perched on our stools.

"Don't be embarrassed, babe. She is right, you know."

"Kane! Don't encourage her! If you accept her vulgar mouth, she'll never shut up and will keep pushing her limits with you."

Kane casts a gaze at Clara, and then focuses back on me. "There's nothing wrong with a woman who can speak honestly about sex. And hey, it's nice to know you're smitten with me... because I'm smitten with you too," he nuzzles his nose with mine as my friends collectively sigh beside me and my smile spreads wide across my face.

"Oh, my God, you guys are too cute!" Perry croons.

"That's it. I'm starting a fight with my husband when I get home so he knows he should act like that with me," Amy snarks.

"Hey, don't be jealous ladies," Clara argues. "Be happy for our friend. But Kane, if you have any single friends who know how to woo a lady such as yourself, you can send them my way," she winks just as the cocktail waitress comes over and takes our drink order.

"So ladies, what are the down and dirty stories I should

know about Liv here?" Kane drills my friends. It's his turn for my elbow in his ribs, which makes everyone at our table laugh besides me.

"This is not going to turn into a gang up on Olivia night, or I'm leaving."

"Oh, come on, babe. From what you've told me, these women know you better than anyone."

"Exactly, and if they wish to remain those women, they will keep their lips zipped," I shoot a warning look at all three of my friends.

"Don't worry. We'll just wait until you're in the bathroom to divulge all of your secrets," Clara waves me off, which entices a laugh from Kane, Amy, and Perry.

The five of us continue to talk, my friends sharing stories of their kids and husbands, and tales of our teenage years I deem acceptable.

"So Olivia thought a perm was a good idea..." Clara continues with her third story of the night.

"In my defense, it was the nineties and perms were all the rage."

"Uh, I think that was the eighties, babe," Kane pesters while whispering in my ear.

"Well, then I was born in the wrong decade."

"Anyway," Clara speaks, cutting off my protest. "She left the chemicals on too long and ended up looking like a cross between weird Al and Carrot Top," she snorts as Perry and Amy fall back in laughter as well.

"Curly hair was in and I was desperate to have it. I admit, it wasn't the best look on me, but I learned my lesson, okay," I drop my head in embarrassment as Kane pulls my face to his.

"Don't be embarrassed, babe. We've all been there. Hell,

I had bleached tips back in high school."

My eyes go wide with his confession, struggling to imagine Kane with bleach blonde hair on any part of his head given his jet black, dark and mysterious thing he has going on right now that makes my panties wet for him 'round the clock.

"Oh, God, no you didn't!"

He nods in confirmation. "Yup, and I thought I was the shit. Justin Timberlake and all the boy band members were doing it, so I thought I could too. Looking back on the pictures now, I wonder what the hell I was thinking. But hey, we were young and stupid, right?"

"Awww, it's like you two were bad hair soulmates," Clara bats her eyelashes at us.

"See, meant to be," Kane kisses my cheek before excusing himself to the bathroom.

"So what are the plans for Thanksgiving?" Perry asks once Kane walked away and we're knee-deep in our second round of drinks. He's currently leaning against the bar talking to Tony, who Kane told me is a close friend.

"Kane is coming over to my house. He wants to meet my family," I smile, watching him intently while he's focused on Tony and their conversation.

"Oh, girl, you've got it bad," Perry shakes her head at me, grinning like a fool over the rim of her glass.

"Seriously, Liv. It's written all over your face," Amy adds.

I exhale loudly. "I know, guys. He's been so amazing. I feel like I'm dreaming. He can't be this perfect, right? I mean, he finally opened up to me about his past, which helped me understand him so much more. And I can't get enough of him. He's thoughtful and caring. He's funny and makes me feel so safe. And the sex... my God. I've never had sex like this before,"

I confess as I close my eyes and replay the dozens of sexual positions and locations we've already explored.

"Girl, stop bragging!" Clara teases.

"It's obvious watching you two together that you're both completely entranced by each other. But what, Liv?" Perry asks, sensing there was a but coming.

"But... I don't know. I just feel like I'm waiting for the other shoe to drop. Everything is going so well. I leave a less than stellar relationship to come home and suddenly, I fall for a man and start a new relationship right away that seems too good to be true."

Perry's eyes search mine for clarification.

"The man hasn't had a serious relationship in years. He's only been in love with one woman. And yet, he's the perfect man with me. I feel like I'm waiting for something to happen to freak him out, or something to happen as I watch it all fall apart again."

Amy reaches out for my hand. "Man, Trevor really fucked things up for you, didn't he?"

"What?"

Clara chimes in. "Just because Trevor was an ass that cheated on you and couldn't appreciate what he had, doesn't mean that Kane is going to do that too. Liv, anyone would be blind if they didn't see the way that man looks at you. I know it's early, but he's in love with you, hun."

I turn to find him again just as he winks at me from across the room, sending a swarm of butterflies a flight in my stomach.

"You think so?" I whisper, refraining from voicing the reciprocal thought for the first time out loud. *I think I'm in love with him too.*

"Oh, Liv, it's so obvious. I just love seeing you this

happy..." Perry chokes out as her eyes water.

"And it's not that I think he's going to cheat on me. I don't get that feeling from him at all. I don't know... there's just some feeling in my gut that tells me there's a curtain pulled over my eyes and I'm afraid I'm blind to some warning sign. I ignored my gut with Trevor. Maybe I'm just being paranoid. He really is just so incredible, I'm afraid it's all a lie."

Clara smiles a shit-eating grin and Amy bites her bottom lip just as Kane comes up behind me.

"How's it going ladies? You need another round?"

Perry looks over at Clara and Amy, the three of them nodding silently towards one another before turning back to Kane and me.

"Actually, we'd better be going. The husbands are probably passed out on the couch already and the kids may or may not be running amuck in our homes."

"Yeah. And I don't have a husband or kids, but these two were my ride, so I have to leave too," Clara declares with a jut of her chin.

"Well, it was great to meet you all officially. Liv speaks very highly of you. It's clear that you're very important to her. She's lucky to have friends like you," Kane says while pulling each woman in for a hug.

"Oh, Kane. If you don't marry her or put a baby in her soon, I'll have to kick your ass," Clara says as she smacks his cheeks playfully, his eyes going wide before he cracks an uncomfortable smile.

"Oh, God, Clara," I sigh, pushing her away. "Go now before *I* kick *your* ass," I spit out as she throws her head back in laughter and I say goodbye to Amy and Perry. "I'll see you girls soon. I promise."

"Yeah, okay," Perry winks at me before the three of

them make their way out of the bar.

I turn back to Kane who's face has softened after Clara's declaration.

"I'm so sorry, Kane. Clara is out of control. I'm sorry if what she said scared you. Please don't freak out. I know we're far from that step...."

Kane cuts me off as he presses his lips to mine. The shock of his move hits me first, but only lasts a second as I melt into him. His kiss soothes my fears and gives me hope that this is the man I'm meant to kiss for the rest of my life.

When Kane releases his grip on me, staring down into my eyes, I sit there and wait for him to speak.

"Come on, babe. Let's get back to your place. I have some more orgasms to deliver," he wiggles his eyebrows at me, which sends a bolt of arousal between my legs and the corners of my mouth to tip up in anticipation.

"Yeah, I need a few after tonight," I tease as I follow Kane to his truck and he follows me back to my place.

Once we're inside, Kane pins me up against the door and makes good on his promise. Two orgasms later, I lie beside him in bed, curled up in his arms, basking in the satisfaction I feel while my world feels like it's finally coming together.

# CHAPTER 33

Kane

"I told you to let me sleep in this morning," a groggy Olivia answers the phone while I smile on my end.

"I know, but the high today is sixty, which is unheard of this time of year."

"You called to wake me up to talk about the weather? Kane, you're about to learn a valuable lesson from me about how much I like sleep..."

"Calm down, woman. I want to take you somewhere," I state, knowing it's one of our days off the week of Thanksgiving, but I can't waste this opportunity.

"Where could you take me on a Tuesday that is so important that you had to wake me up?"

I sigh in frustration, pinching the bridge of my nose. "Just dress warmly and be ready in thirty minutes. I'm picking you up," I demand and end the call before she can argue with me more. The woman is burrowing herself deep in my heart, but that doesn't stop her need to fight me still. Once I get some coffee in her and she sees my surprise, I think she'll turn around.

At least I hope. A grumpy Olivia is not a fun Olivia.

I step into my garage and pull the cover off of my bike —the motorcycle I haven't been on in almost three years. The last woman who rode with me was Natasha, and when that ended, I couldn't bring myself to get back on the horse, so to speak.

I wasn't in the right head space to ride, I didn't trust myself not to speed and careen uncontrollably down a windy road and lose myself off the side of a mountain—metaphorically speaking, of course.

I just knew that when I decided to get back on my Harley, I wanted it to be because something—or someone—told me it was time.

And now, since Olivia came into my life, I can't seem to get the image of her on the bike with me out of my head. And when I saw the forecast today, I knew it was the perfect opportunity to make that daydream become a reality.

After meeting her friends Saturday night, I knew that taking her for a ride was in our future, so I spent time on Sunday tuning up my bike, checking the engine and tires and giving her some TLC. Meeting the infamous Perry, Amy, and Clara definitely solidified our relationship. We haven't exactly put a title on things yet, but if our time spent together is any indication, I'd say we're committed. Hell, I'm spending Thanksgiving with her family. I'd say that's boyfriend territory I'm venturing into.

Once I put a few supplies in my side bag and grab my extra helmet, I fire up my Harley and listen to the thrum of the engine as I bring her back to life. When I re-enlisted, I used part of my signing bonus to put a down payment on this bike. Usually men wait until a mid-life crisis hits to make such a purchase, but I had spent years in the desert watching my friends and fellow soldiers lose limbs and their lives. So when I came home, I didn't hesitate to do something for me to remind me that I was still living—that I had a life and needed adventure and sometimes wanted to get lost with nothing but the road and wind guiding me. Natasha didn't understand, but she relented and let me take her out on a ride a few times. Ultimately it wasn't her cup of tea. But she was the only woman who's ever ridden with me—until today.

Securing my helmet on my head, I gas the throttle, the roar of the engine filling up my garage before I pull out and take off for the highway. The feel of the breeze hitting me makes my body come alive again as I weave along the asphalt, in and out of the thick forest headed back into town. It also reminds me that though the temperature is higher than it has been in weeks, the breeze is still cold as I fly along the road on the bike. I hope Olivia will endure the chill for our ride because I really want to spend the day with her and show her one of my favorite spots just outside of Emerson Falls.

As I close in on our town, I make a pit stop at Starbucks and secure us two coffees and muffins so I don't arrive at her place emptyhanded. The sputter of the engine quiets down as I pull into her apartment complex and shut it off, pulling off my helmet as I look up at her door and see her standing there, mouth open in shock.

"You've lost your marbles, haven't you?" She says as she makes her way down the handful of steps outside her door and across the sidewalk, stopping right in front of me while I still straddle the bike. Her pajama pants covered in math equations and the black camisole clinging to her torso do weird things to my mind, and my dick. She pulls her long sweater closer around her body while she looks at me like I've gone crazy.

"Nope. I've found a few more, actually," I grin up at her as she shakes her head. I extend my hand to hers and offer her the coffee that probably got cold on the way here.

Taking a sip, she closes her eyes in appreciation. "At least you had the good sense to provide caffeine after waking me up."

"I knew better than to come here without some sort of gift," I wink at her as she smiles. "So, wanna go for a ride?"

I throw my head in the direction of my bike and deepen my voice to entice her.

Olivia laughs at me while clutching her arms around her waist. "It's still pretty cold out, Kane."

"Wear some thick pants and a jacket. Come on. I haven't been out on this bike in a long time, Liv. And all I could think about was getting back on it with your arms wrapped around my waist," I pout while searching for her reaction.

"Man, you're really laying it on thick, huh?" The corner of her mouth tips up and lets me know I've got her right where I want her, until it falls just as fast. "I've uh, never been on a motorcycle before, Kane. The thought kind of scares me."

I reach for her hand and pull her close to me so I can encase her in my arms. "I'll do everything in my power to keep you safe, babe. But I'm telling you, it's one of the most exhilarating experiences you'll ever have."

Her eyes bounce back and forth between mine while she contemplates her answer. On a deep inhale, she gives in. "Okay, but don't do anything on purpose to scare me, or I will jump off."

Her threat makes me laugh and then pull her in for a kiss. "I wouldn't recommend that Liv, but okay. I promise."

Once Olivia retreats inside and changes, I can't help but soak her up as I watch her return to me in dark leggings and a thick jacket with a beanie in her hands.

"I said to dress warm and you come out wearing leggings," I scoff.

"I'll have you know, these are fleece-lined, so they're incredibly warm. And in case you haven't noticed, I live in leggings when I'm not at work. If you don't watch your tone, I will march right back inside and go back to bed."

Pulling her into me again, her eyes narrow at me while

she waits for my response. "I'm sorry. I just don't want you to be cold. And your ass in leggings is quite the distraction," I wiggle my eyebrows at her.

"Good thing my ass will be behind you then," she says while reaching for the helmet I hand her. She pulls it down onto her head and my stomach does a little flip when I take her in. The long red locks of her hair hang down over her shoulders under the helmet, her cheeks are pressed together from the foam inside, and her eyes sparkle in the sunlight raining down from the sky. She looks so fucking sexy and cute, I don't know whether I want to fuck her or kiss her senseless.

Both. I want to do both.

She throws one leg over the bike as she situates behind me and wraps her arms around my waist, holding on for dear life. This innate need to protect her comes over me, and it makes my chest tighten with purpose.

"Easy, babe. I still need to be able to breathe," I tease her.

"I'm scared, Kane," she whispers and my heart hurts at the fear I hear in her voice.

"I've got you, babe. It's going to be great," I console her by rubbing her hands with mine before giving her a pair of gloves to put on as I do the same. I turn to her and tell her to squeeze me twice if she needs to stop while we're on the road. Any other squeezes I will deem her reaction out of excitement.

Once we're settled in and ready, I fire up the bike, the sound so loud it makes it hard to hear her. I kick the stand up and show her where to put her feet before taking off slowly out of her apartment complex and onto the streets that lead to the highway.

Our town falls back behind us as we climb higher up the mountain, headed towards the lookout point I've been dying to take her to since I got this crazy idea in my head. Tall trees stretch towards the sky around us, blocking the sunlight and making the air colder than it was when the sun was beating down on us while patches of snow in the shade from the last storm spot the ground on the sides of the road.

Olivia continues to hold on tight, scratching my abs every now and again as we turn and glide along the road, the feel of her nails on my body causes my dick to strain against my jeans. Trying to drive my bike with a hard-on is definitely a challenge I've never faced.

We continue to cruise, taking each turn in stride, our bodies leaning together as I make the final ascent to the top of the cliff that overlooks the valley below us.

The feel of her behind me as I take the drive that leads us to our destination resonates in my chest. This is right. This is exactly where she belongs—with me, taking off on an adventure together, living life in the moment and holding on to one another through every twist and turn.

I slow the bike as we come to the area I targeted and as I bring us to a complete stop, I feel the warmth of Olivia's body relinquish from mine. Removing her helmet, she swishes her hair around like any woman would before finding my eyes as I stand before her and she flashes me the biggest smile, full of excitement.

"That was incredible! I mean, don't get me wrong, I was scared shitless the entire time. But the view, the feel of the wind, being able to hold on to you like that..." Her pearly whites continue to blind me as I soak up the euphoria on her face.

"I'm glad you liked it," I say, leaning down and taking her cheeks in my hands before pressing my lips to hers. I slip her my tongue just enough to tease her and then pull away as she moans in disappointment.

Olivia narrows her eyes at me in annoyance before she

stands from the bike and peruses the area around us. I parked in a little alcove off of the road so we have some privacy, but we're close enough to the clearing so we can experience the entire view.

I open up the bag on the side of the bike, retrieving the muffins from Starbucks and some cheese, fruit, and crackers that I prepared for us and a light blanket to sit on. Olivia shakes her head at me, finding humor in my picnic provisions.

"What? You didn't think I was going to bring you all the way up here and then not feed you, did you?" I mock while leading her to a flat spot on the ground where I set down the blanket and then arrange the food. Two blueberry muffins, cheeses, and crackers are spread out in a container, along with olives and peppers. I brought bottled water and a few squares of chocolate just in case since she always needs something sweet after she eats.

"Kane... this is so thoughtful," she murmurs as we both settle down on the ground, stretching our legs from the ride.

"See? Aren't you glad I woke you up?"

She bobs her head while gazing out over the cliff, soaking in the breathtaking view of Emerson Falls below us and a few other towns around ours.

"Definitely."

"Well, eat up. I know if I don't get some food in you, you'll be hangry."

Olivia reaches for the food. "You're learning, Kane. I'm impressed," she mocks me while popping a cheese and cracker in her mouth. I watch her chew and can't help but feel so damn content with her by my side.

"So how did you find this place?" She asks once she swallows, twisting the lid off of the bottle of water and taking a swig.

"It was actually one of the first places I drove to when I got my bike. I just took off on the highway and headed up the mountain. By the time I decided to stop, I turned around and saw the view below and felt like I found a little slice of heaven on Earth."

"It really is beautiful up here," she whispers, as if speaking at full volume will ruin the sight in front of us.

"Not as beautiful as the woman beside me."

Olivia turns to me, reaching for my hand and leaning into me. "That was cheesy, but I'll let it slide since you went to all of this trouble," she winks and the deep laugh that rips through me echoes around us.

"So, I have a few questions for you, if you're interested," I arch a brow at her as she nods with her mouth full.

"Yes! Oh my gosh, I feel like you've been holding out on me lately, Kane."

"Well, we have been preoccupied with other things," I tease her as I watch her eyes darken with lust. Last night was one of the few nights we spent apart these past few weeks and I dying to bury myself inside of her again. But first things first— I promised my girl some questions.

"Okay, well then I'm ready. Bring it on," Olivia challenges while sitting up taller and crisscrossing her legs in front of her.

"I'll start with an easy one. What is your favorite childhood memory?"

Olivia looks to the sky in contemplation before her eyes return to mine, reverent in her gaze as if she's right back in that moment in time. "Ah, it's kind of a compilation of ones, but when I was younger, I used to spend a lot of time at my grandma's house."

"Is this the same grandma you said was your hero?"

"Yes. I told you she owned her own porcelain business." I nod in recollection. "Well, there would be pieces she made—miniature birdhouses, teapots, or dolls—that she couldn't sell for various reasons. So she would let my cousins and me paint them and fire them off in the kiln so we could keep them." Her eyes move across the space as she regards the view before continuing. "I just remember sitting beside her in the garage at my own little painting station while she worked meticulously on her own pieces. She was so articulate in every flick of her brush and color choice. The woman was incredibly talented and I was always so in awe of her creativity. She could take something so plain and transform it into a piece of glass that suddenly had life. I've never considered myself a creative person. But any artistic bone I have in my body had to have come from her."

"I love that. What an incredibly gifted woman. She obviously meant a lot to you, Liv. Do you still have some of those pieces?"

Olivia's eyes find mine again as I see the tears forming. One drop falls down her cheek before she reaches up to brush it away. "Yes, I do. I keep them out so I can think back on her often. Sorry," she says before wiping her face. "You keep making me cry, Kane," she chuckles through her tears, looking away from me in embarrassment.

"I know. That's not my intention, I promise. But I love seeing you talk about her. You're entire face lights up. And I love learning more about you."

"I miss her so much," she whispers while taking another sip of her water, then shaking off her emotion. "Okay, your turn."

I sit up tall and pull her closer to me so our knees are touching. "Mine is sort of similar to yours. It involves my grandpa. He was a wood-worker, building all sorts of things in his spare time in his shop attached to his house. You know the coffee table in my house?" Olivia nods in acknowledgment. "Well, I helped him build that. It was one of the last pieces we made together before I left for the Army. He died during my second tour overseas. I was able to come back for the funeral, but then had to return almost immediately."

"I'm sorry, Kane. But that table is beautiful. *He* was obviously very talented."

"Yeah, he was. He taught me everything I know about building and fixing anything with my hands. My dad was always working, so I spent a lot of time with him. He taught me to fish and hunt, throw a football, and so much about being a man."

Olivia's tears return. "He would be nothing but proud of the man you are."

Her hand finds mine as we share a moment. "Your grandma would be proud of you too, Liv."

Olivia clears her throat and then takes a few bites of food. "Okay, next question. And please don't make me cry this time."

"I'll try not to," I say behind a small smile. "Alright. If you could go back in time and change one thing, what would it be?"

I have to admit that on some level, I'm more afraid to answer this question than ask it. I mean, I've already admitted my past to her, but I feel like there's something so meaningful about discussing your regrets.

I'd hate to say that I regret my time with Natasha or my friendship with T.J., but I do wonder how different my life would have been if I had never re-enlisted, or never pursued Natasha. Would T.J. and I still be friends? Would Natasha and I have gone our separate ways earlier and in turn, would I have saved myself the last three years of anger, resentment, and self-doubt?

I know I could sit here and play the "what if" game all day, but if I ever had a regret in my life, it would definitely be how that all played out. I feel like maybe I could have seen it coming, or maybe the writing was on the wall and I was too blind to notice. I think back over my relationship with her often and wonder how one different choice could have led me down a different path.

It's crazy how one event in our lives can feel like it dictates so much—like that single moment creates a divide in our mind—of the time before it and after it. The change it impacts is so monumental, we define our worlds with it.

Olivia ponders her answer for a moment before locking her eyes on mine.

"Nothing," she says, which completely catches me by surprise.

"Nothing?"

"Yeah, nothing," she shrugs. "I mean, there are obviously things that have happened in my life that were hard to experience. I've made mistakes and done things I'm not proud of. But if I changed any of that, I wouldn't be where I'm at right now. Coming home was such a rash decision I made out of anger—not my finest moment, by the way—but being back in Emerson Falls has sent me in a direction that I never could have imagined, and I'm grateful for that."

I swallow hard at her answer and realize this woman is so much stronger and wiser than I give her credit for. I mean, I knew she was strong-minded, which was one of the things that attracted me to her in the first place. But listening to her accept her life, endure it's developments so far, even with her losses and mistakes—it reminds me how incredible she is in her ability to move past the obstacles and disappointments she's faced and has vowed to continue to move forward.

"I'm jealous. I wish I had the confidence to answer the

same way."

"It's okay, Kane. If you would have asked me that question a few weeks ago, I probably would have answered differently."

"Really? Why?"

She stumbles for a moment before settling on her answer. "Because I hadn't met you."

And just like that, she penetrates those last few bricks structured around my heart.

"I feel the same, Liv," I say, reaching to pull her onto my lap. My lips seek hers out in desperation, yearning to feel her connected to me. I kiss her deeply as she surrenders to the moment—our two broken souls healing one another and fighting for the future I know we can have, the future that gets clearer every time we are together.

When we break, reclaiming our breaths, I lean my forehead down to hers and inhale her scent.

"Sometimes I still can't believe we got here," she whispers, running her hands through my hair as she holds on to my neck.

"Me neither. But I don't regret it for a second."

We sit there for a few minutes, encased in each other, soaking up the feeling of just being, before I move her next to me and reach for more food, feeding her seductively as the mood changes from reverent to heated.

Olivia licks her lips as I slide my fingers between them to pop an olive in her mouth, her mouth closing around my fingers as I pull away, sending a blast of arousal to my dick.

"You'd better watch it babe, or you're going to be on your back in the forest in no time."

"No, I have a better idea," she whispers, moving to stand and reaching for my hand to pull me up. Once we're both upright, she walks us back over to the bike and motions for me to sit before she straddles the bike in front of me so we're facing each other.

"What are you doing?" I ask as my hands run up along her thighs and onto her hips.

"I want you to fuck me on the bike, Kane."

And just as the words leave her mouth, my dick twitches in my jeans, making me painfully harder than I was just a few moments ago.

"Uh, I'm not sure how that's possible. Christ, do I want to, but you're going to get too cold, babe."

She shakes her head. "Not if you have easy access," she quirks her eyebrow while spreading her legs further, my eyes seeking out her crotch as she looks up at me. "Rip the seam, Kane," she points to her leggings between her thighs as I look up at her for clarification.

"Are you sure?"

She nods. "Yes. I can buy more leggings. But this moment, right here... this is the only moment we get like this," she declares confidently while leaning forward to suck my bottom lip into her mouth, biting it sternly before releasing it. And fuck if I needed another reason to submit to her requests—because if my woman wants sex on the bike, she's going to get sex on the bike.

I reach down and rub my fingers along her slit through her leggings, noticing how wet she already is as the fabric dampens. I situate my hands along the seam and tear, ripping the fabric farther than I intended. But when I see Olivia's bare pussy through the hole, I know there's no turning back now.

"You little minx. You're not wearing any underwear. Were you planning this the entire time?" I say through clenched teeth as my hands dig into her thighs and I feel my self-control fading.

"I wanted to be prepared in case the opportunity presented itself."

"Fuck, babe. You're soaked already," I say as my fingers thread through the opening in her leggings and run along her wet folds, enticing a moan from her.

"I'm always wet for you, Kane. Now fuck me, please," she cries as she leans back slightly along the body of the motorcycle.

I shuck my jacket off and lay it down under her for a little cushion and stand to release my cock from the confines of my jeans, grateful that we surpassed the need for condoms weeks ago as I stare down at Olivia's open legs and guide my dick to her entrance.

I veer up at her as I line us up and then reach around her body, enveloping her in my arms as I plunge into her.

"Yes," she exclaims as I set a punishing rhythm, losing myself in the fantasy of this woman beneath me on my bike, checking off a bucket list item, as well as a sexual first for the two of us. There are so many other firsts I want to experience with her—but I decide to just immerse myself in this one for now.

"God, baby. You feel good, so fucking good," I growl in her ear as she arches in my arms. My lips find her neck, leaving a wet trail of kisses in their wake as Olivia's head flies up and her eyes find mine—the forest green of her eyes is light, yet on fire, full of desire and need. And I see it there—the pleasure, the high, the ecstasy that's about to hit her.

"More, Kane," she shrieks as I pound into her, dragging my cock through her slick wetness with every thrust. This woman has ruined me, in the best way. There will never be another woman who can make me feel this out of control. I want to give her all of me, every last drop until we both see stars.

I sit back on the seat and bring her with me so my cock

hits every nerve ending deep inside of her.

"Oh, God," she moans as I lift her up and down, driving harder with each thrust up.

"I'm there, Kane," she breathes, her thighs clenching around my hips as I feel myself about to lose it as well.

"Come on my cock, Liv," I growl in her ear as she splinters above me, the pulse and force of her orgasm so brutal she brings me over with her, pulling every last ounce of pleasure from our bodies as she screams into the quiet surrounding us.

"Fuck, that was hot," I exhale, catching my breath as Olivia's head rests on my shoulder, her chest heaving with deep breaths.

"Hell yeah, it was. I was thinking about that all the way up the mountain," she confesses, which makes me laugh as she pushes up off of me to meet my eyes, my hand moving up to brush her hair from her face.

"You sure are a determined woman," I tease her and she smiles down at me, pure bliss in her expression.

"When I want something, I get it," she flashes me a devious grin. But I hear her loud and clear. And whether she realizes it yet, or not—she's definitely owning me.

"One thing you failed to consider here, Liv," I say as she waits for my rebuttal. "You're going to have quite the draft between your legs on the drive home," I motion with my eyes between her legs where we're still joined.

"Well, shit," she declares as a deep laugh rumbles in my chest.

"Not all ideas are good ones, babe," I run my nose along her neck before granting her a kiss on the lips, loving how we can go from fucking to laughing in an instant.

# CHAPTER 34

Olivia

"No, not like that," my mother scolds while I try to re-adjust the turkey.

"How many ways are there to do this, Mom? You're trying to shove a turkey into a brown paper bag."

My mother throws me a knowing glance and then turns the bag in my hands so it's more horizontal.

"There, now hold still," she says as she slides the bird into the bag and tucks the wings in before she pushes it all the way in. It's like seeing a baby being born in reverse and I'm not sure how I feel about it. Although my family has always cooked our turkey in a brown paper bag, so I guess I should be alright with it by now.

Except, all I have is babies on the brain in the last forty-eight hours—because I'm late. Like three days late. Which wouldn't mean much to me normally, except Aunt Flow visits my body like clockwork and I've never been this late before. A day or two, yes. But three? Never.

And I'm officially freaking out.

"Okay, put her in the roasting pan and wash your hands," my mother directs me as if I didn't know I need to remove the bird and butter juices from my palms.

"What's next?" I ask as I turn to her, drying my hands on the dish towel.

"We need to prep the stuffing and green bean casserole and start baking off the bread." My mother thinks she needs to feed a small army every Thanksgiving, but really it's just the four of us like any other Sunday dinner. Except this year, Kane is joining us.

Kane. My boyfriend, as he deemed himself after our motorcycle ride the other day. The man who is slowly burrowing himself in my heart.

And could be the father of my child.

*Oh, God.*

I knew it. I knew I was waiting for something to happen, something to pull me out of my sex-induced trance and bring me back to reality.

*Well, here's your reality, Liv—you might be pregnant. How's that for a smack in the face?*

"Earth to Liv," my mom waves her hands in front of my face, pulling me from the rambling of my inner thoughts.

I shake off the anxiety and focus back on her while she stares at me straight in the eyes.

"Are you okay? Did you just hear a word I was saying to you?" She gives me that knowing look that only a mom can pull off, searching the depths of mind, knowing there's something going on even though I haven't said a word.

My lips start to tremble and tears well in my eyes. And just as I gather myself to talk to my mom, the one person I should be able to speak to about this—the fear that is slowly crushing my chest—the doorbell rings.

• • • • • • • • • • • • • • • • • • • • • • • • • • • • • • • • • • • •

Kane

"I've got it!" I hear the muffled voice behind the door as

I straighten my spine and readjust the flowers and wine in my hands. I've never visited someone else's home on Thanksgiving before. Drew and Tammy have invited me over to their house the past few years, but I spent the day alone or at my parent's house. After Natasha and I split up and I moved south, I haven't seen my parents very often. Last Thanksgiving was actually the last time I visited.

Dad retired from his job and my mother got so involved in her crafting and reading groups, they pretty much leave me alone to live my life. I call them from time to time, just to check in, but we aren't super close. I was always closer with my grandparents.

The handle on the door turns and as it opens, I'm greeted with a younger man that matches me in height and build. I'm not a small guy, and neither is he.

"You must be Kane," he says, crossing his arms over his chest in an attempt to intimidate me, I suppose. It's cute, but it's not working.

"Yes, I am. Nice to meet you. You must be Cooper," I respond, instantly recognizing the family resemblance between him and Olivia now.

"Yup, that's me. So, what are you intentions with my sister..." he starts just as I hear the pitter patter of feet behind him, Olivia spinning around his frame and cutting him off.

"Dear Lord, Coop. Stop it," she shoves his chest. "Hi, Kane," she turns to me now, granting me with that smile that warms my entire body.

"Hi, beautiful," I greet her with a kiss on the cheek and then hand her the flowers and wine.

"You didn't have to do this," she admonishes while pushing Cooper out of the way more so I can step inside.

"Hey, Kane. Sorry about before," Cooper starts before Olivia cuts him off again.

"You are not. You're just warming him up before you and Dad start your real inquisition later."

Cooper nods in agreement and shrugs. "True. Be ready, Kane," he arches his brow at me before sauntering away.

"He seems protective of you," I whisper in her ear as I pull her into my chest. I see the goosebumps appear on her exposed skin, and fuck if I don't love how easily she responds to me.

"He is, even though I'm the oldest. He and my dad will drill you later, just so you're prepared."

"You already warned me, baby, remember? And it's fine. It's nothing I can't handle. I've had grown men scream in my face before. A little tough talk from your dad and brother ain't nothing."

Olivia kisses me on the cheek and then grabs my hand, leading me inside. Her parent's home is a shrine to a life well-lived—framed photographs decorating the walls and every flat surface, showcasing a family and the growth of its children over the years. The furniture is well worn and the space is warm and inviting, decorated in browns and greens with cream-colored walls. You can feel the love as you walk around, and you can smell it too. My God, that food smells amazing.

As I follow Olivia into the kitchen, I'm greeted with a slightly shorter and older version of her.

"Kane, this is my mom, Stacy. Mom, this is Kane."

The woman flashes me the same beautiful smile that Olivia must have inherited from her. "Mrs. Walsh, it's so great to meet you. Thank you for having me today," I reach out to shake her hand while Olivia locates a vase for the flowers and deposits the wine on the counter.

"Please, call me Stacy. It's so nice to meet you too, Kane. If her permanent smile is any indication, I'd say it seems my daughter is quite taken with you," she winks.

"Well, the feeling is mutual, I assure you."

"So, you two work together, right? How has that been going?"

Olivia and I glance at each other, realizing we should probably come forward about our relationship to principal North.

"We've been extremely professional at work, if that's what you're worried about, Mom. But we're going to say something to our boss once we get back to school next week."

I nod in agreement.

"I think that's wise. So Kane, why aren't you with your family today?" Stacy asks while gliding around her kitchen.

"My parents live up north, and Olivia invited me here. Plus, I really wanted to meet her family. We've gotten to know so much about each other over the past few months, I felt like this was the next step."

Olivia's mom looks me up and down before tilting up the corners of her mouth in a smile. "I couldn't agree more. I think it was time we met too."

I sit in the kitchen for a few minutes, watching Olivia and her mom move around, preparing dishes and cleaning as they go. The other night she got to peruse me while I cooked, and now it's my turn. I can't say I'm not enjoying it. I know Thanksgiving is her favorite holiday and you can see the serenity on her face as she mixes ingredients, teases back and forth with her mom, and looks so at ease—like she is one-hundred percent herself in this moment. And the image is captivating.

"Have you always helped your mom cook?" I ask while taking a sip from the glass of water Olivia filled for me moments ago.

"Yes, as soon as she would let me. My mom and my grandma used to bustle around each other in the kitchen every Thanksgiving and I wanted to be just like them so badly."

"Yeah, so we finally relented and let Olivia help us when she was about eight, I think," her mom continues. "But I believe that year we ate green bean casserole with Barbie shoes in it."

Stacy's story makes me nearly choke on my water. "Barbie shoes?"

Olivia rolls her eyes but there's a slight blush to her cheeks of embarrassment. "In my defense, Barbie was just trying to help, but walking around in heels is uncomfortable."

"So she kicked them off in a fit of joy and they landed in the green beans?" I tease her.

She shoots me an angry glare, but there's humor behind it. "Apparently so."

"So that year, we made it a game that whoever found Barbie's shoes got an extra piece of pie," Stacy chimes in. "I've never seen Cooper eat that much green bean casserole in my life. And then he almost choked on the shoe."

I laugh uncontrollably, loving hearing these stories about this woman.

The more I study her, watch her, get to know her—the more I'm falling and the more I see a future with her and can't imagine another day of my life without her in it. I can feel those three little words take shape in my mind, but something is holding me back from saying them. That fear that I'm putting all of my faith in what we have rings loudly, making me cautious that I might end up hurt again.

If you had asked me two months ago where I thought I would be right now—it sure as hell wouldn't be in the kitchen of a woman I'm falling in love with, getting ready to spend the holiday with her family. And at that exact moment that thought enters my mind, she looks up and wrinkles her nose at me, giving me a knowing grin and twisting my insides even more with the notion that I know without a doubt.

I love her.

"Hey, boys," Olivia says, catching me off-guard as I turn and see two men this time—her brother, Cooper, and another man who I can only assume is her father.

"Ladies," her father nods at them before focusing on me. "You must be Kane," his deep voice fills the room as I stand and motion to shake his hand. Olivia's dad is tall and built, an older version of her brother for sure. It's crystal clear her family has strong genes.

"Yes, sir. Pleasure to meet you."

"Likewise. Come on, Kane. Cooper and I were just hanging out in the garage and drinking a few beers. Come join us."

Even if I had a choice, the demand in his voice is one I comply to, following him outside but not before turning back to get one last look from Olivia. The worry on her face is unsettling, but she mouths a "Good luck" to me before I turn back around and walk into the lion's den. I take a deep breath and stand tall knowing no matter what they may ask me or test me with, Olivia is worth it all.

• • • • • • • • • • • • • • • • • • • • • • • • • • • • • • • • •

Olivia

"He seems like a wonderful man. And my God, he's gorgeous," my mom confesses once Kane shuts the door to the garage and my anxiety returns. But this time, it's more for him and what the hell my dad and brother are saying to him, than the thought that I'm still waiting on my period.

"Mom! Back off, he's mine," I tease which garners a laugh from her.

"Oh, I'm well aware. I completely understand the draw to him and why you decided to have fun with that one," she winks. "Have you noticed how he looks at you?"

I shake my head in distraction from my mother's bluntness. "What do you mean?" I ask curiously, knowing that my mother has a better instinct that I ever will.

"He looks at you like you hung the moon and the stars, baby girl," she says while reaching up to cup my face.

"Really?"

She nods. "Absolutely. He's in love with you, baby. And if those tears you were about to shed before he got here were any indication, I'd say you feel the same way."

"I do, but that's not why I was about to cry, Mom."

"Then what's the matter?" Her brows narrow as she sets down her spoon she was stirring a pot on the stove with.

I take a deep breath and close my eyes, bracing myself for her reaction.

"I'm late..." I whisper, even though I know the boys couldn't hear us in the garage if I was louder.

My mom's eyes go wide and her head drops closer to mine. "Are you sure?"

I nod. "And I'm never late, Mom. I keep telling myself it's stress or I'm just really tired. It is that point in the school year where I tend to get extremely exhausted."

"Olivia, I'm going to ask you something and it's not to make you sound stupid, okay?"

"Okay..."

"Haven't you been using protection?" My mother shakes her head at me like I should know better. And I do. I've been on the pill since I was eighteen. I know how to take it religiously and how other drugs can interfere with it....

"Oh, shit!" I whisper before throwing my hands over my mouth to prevent any more words from escaping.

"What?" My mother spits back, and if we're not careful, Cooper or my dad will come back inside to check on us.

"I took some anti-biotics when I got sick a few weeks ago. I went to urgent care when I started feeling worse and completely forgot. Oh, God! How could I have been so stupid," I shut my eyes and cry into my hands, my shoulders shaking as I realize that my fear could very well be a reality.

"Shhhh, it's okay, Olivia. You're not stupid, you're human. But are you sure? Could that be the reason you're late and not something else?"

"I can't think of another reason, Mom. Christ, what is Kane going to think?"

"Hey, calm down. First of all, you don't know for sure if you're pregnant, and you won't until you take a test. Second of all, I think you need to give him more credit than you are right now. This may come as a shock and be very soon considering how long you two have been together. But like I said, he obviously cares about you, hun. Get all the facts and then sit down and talk with him about it. But the sooner the better, Liv."

I pick my head up and feel the tears cascade down my face while my mom lovingly communicates her support through her eyes.

"Shit..." I mumble before removing my apron and heading to the bathroom.

• • • • • • • • • • • • • • • • • • • • • • • • • • • • • • •

Kane

"Take a seat, son," Olivia's dad directs me to a camping chair placed around a small heater in the center of the garage.

Tools line one wall and storage boxes are stacked along another, labeled with holiday decorations and various mementos. A flat screen TV is hoisted on the wall the chairs are facing and an ice chest rests between their two chairs.

I hunch down in a seat a little too small for my stature, but then notice Cooper and Mr. Walsh look very similar in theirs, so I make do.

"Mr. Walsh, it's really nice to meet you," I open up the discussion, not sure how to proceed.

"Dan," he replies and I nod.

"Dan."

"So, Kane. How old are you?"

"Twenty-nine."

"Never married? No kids?"

I shake my head. "No sir. I was engaged once though."

Cooper pipes up. "Really? What happened?"

I decide to go with brutal honesty, figuring it can't steer me in the wrong direction here. Olivia warned me they would do this. So it's best to present myself as the man I finally feel I am.

"She cheated on me while I was overseas serving my country, sir."

Cooper winces before taking a sip of his beer. "Damn, that's tough, Kane. I'm sorry to hear that. Did you know the guy?"

"Yup. It was my best friend."

"That's shitty, son. So, any other long relationships after that one?"

"No. Olivia is the first woman I've been interested in like that since that woman."

"Any warrants out for your arrest? Ever broken the law?" Cooper asks and I huff in amusement.

"You already know the answers to those questions, Cooper, seeing as how you're a sheriff deputy and all."

Cooper glares at me while Dan pipes back up.

"Ever done drugs?"

"I've smoked pot, but it was back before I joined the Army."

"Any siblings?"

"Nope, only child."

"You're a teacher like Olivia?"

I nod and set my jaw tightly. "Yes. Teaching was always in the cards for me. It's a calling. I joined the Army to help pay for my schooling since my parents couldn't afford to. But I take my job very seriously."

Cooper and Dan glance in each other's direction before focusing back on me.

"My daughter is extraordinary, Kane," Olivia's father leans in, resting his forearms on his knees. I want him to have no doubts about my intentions with her, so I mimic his stance —the only thing separating us is a few feet and a propane heater.

"Believe me, I know that, sir."

"And she's had her heart broken, too. She is intelligent and charismatic, sarcastic and loves with all of her soul. She's loyal to a fault and deserves someone who understands every facet of her."

"I agree, wholeheartedly. And believe me when I say this, Dan—even though I haven't known your daughter for very long, I sensed all of that within just a few encounters with her. She mesmerizes me. She makes me feel alive again. And I have no intention of hurting her or letting her go."

Dan leans back in his chair and Cooper follows suit before reaching down and grabbing a beer from the ice chest, popping the top off, and then handing it to me.

"Welcome to the family, son," he clinks his beer with mine, Cooper copies the movement, and the three of us turn our attention to the football game, acting like nothing ever happened.

# CHAPTER 35

Olivia

Getting through Thanksgiving dinner with my family was challenging given my emotional state. But seeing Kane come back inside from the garage with my brother and father, laughing and joking around with them, allowed me to postpone my freak out when I caught a glimpse of what our future could look like.

It made me think that maybe this could work, maybe this was it. *Our* story would be unconventional for sure, and backwards from how I thought my life would pan out—but Kane and I belonged together, that I was sure of. He fit in with my family seamlessly, my friends adored him, and he had made me feel a warmth and safety I've never felt with a man before.

The man had taken every doubt and insecurity I was feeling when I returned home from northern California and extinguished them, burnt them to the ground with every thoughtful question he asked, every kiss and reverent touch, and every mind-blowing orgasm. He'd restored my hope that there was someone out there meant for me. It's like what my mom said to me when I had my breakdown right after coming home—when you find the right person, you'll want to get it right with them. And I wanted everything right with Kane.

But now on the Saturday morning following Thanksgiving, I'm staring down at the two pink lines that have sealed our fate.

*Pregnant.*

"God, I knew it," I whisper out loud even though no one's around me and I am completely alone in my bathroom. My eyes shut as the tears threaten to start again. My mind is moving a mile a minute and my body is twisted in knots—I'm not even sure what emotions I'm feeling right now.

On the one hand, a part of me is excited to start a family and know that this baby is a part of Kane and me. I couldn't have asked for a better man to have a child with. I can picture Kane on the couch in our home, resting with a baby sleeping on his chest, his strong hands supporting and loving the life we created with no hesitation.

And on the other hand, I'm terrified—my entire body shaking at the thought of having to tell him I was careless and it's my fault this happened. I hope he doesn't see this as me trying to trap him. I hope he understands that although a family will happen faster than I wanted it to for us, I couldn't imagine doing this with someone else. My hands tremble with the possibility that although Kane has assured me it's *me* he wants, that a baby will push him over the edge and he'll retract his thoughts that he was ready to move on with his life.

Even though I know I need to tell him sooner rather than later, I'm desperate to confide in someone else.

"This better be good. I'm in the middle of a Netflix marathon," Clara answers my phone call on the first ring.

"Clara..." My voice is so flustered just speaking her name that she picks up on my distress immediately.

"Liv? What's wrong?"

"I... I'm..."

"Are you okay?" Clara sounds like she's on the edge of her seat while she waits for me to pull it together and utter the words I know I need to admit to someone else.

"Ugh, no..." I manage to get out before slinking down onto my couch and letting the tears fall.

"Liv, you're scaring me. Are you sure..."

"I'm pregnant," I blurt out before she can finish her thought.

"Oh, fuck. Are you positive?"

I nod even though she can't see me. "There are three tests in my bathroom that all say so."

"Fuck, Liv. Does Kane know?"

I shake my head. "No, I just took the tests and I had to tell someone. My mom knew I was late when I was stressing about it at Thanksgiving, but by today I was five days late, so I knew I couldn't procrastinate any longer. I had to know."

"Liv..."

"This is all kinds of messed up, right? I finally find this amazing man that allows me to see my entire future, everything I've wanted and feared I'd never have, and then I go and get knocked up after knowing him for only a few months. How do you think he's going to take it?"

Clara stays silent for a moment while pondering her response. "First of all, I'm impressed. I told him to put a baby in you and he did!"

"Clara..." I warn, which shuts her up fast.

"Honestly, I admit I don't know the guy as well as you do, but from what you've told me about him and how I saw him with you the other night, I actually think he'll be thrilled."

"Really? Because I'm terrified he'll think I trapped him, or he's not ready for that kind of commitment. I love him, Clara. I do. But this might be too much for him..."

"You won't know that until you tell him, Liv. And you

need to tell him everything—how he's going to be a father, how much you love him, and how you want the white picket fence and everything with him."

"What if..."

"Liv, stop. You can sit here and play the what if game with yourself until you turn blue in the face. Or, you can let him decide what he wants and just go from there. I know this is not even close to being the plan you wanted your life to follow. But maybe this is finally your wake-up call that life doesn't always work out like we plan. You need to take your type-A personality and tell it to fuck off. Sometimes we just have to roll with the punches and accept what happens. Hell, you never planned on moving home, but you did. And look what happened..."

I huff. "Yeah, I got knocked up," I say while wiping the snot and tears from my face.

"And you fell in love, a love you've always wanted. You were never this happy with Trevor. You never lit up around him like the way you do with Kane. And I know you've never had sex that great either."

Her bluntness makes me chuckle as I sink back into the couch. "Clara, I'm so scared. I have no idea what I'm doing..."

"Most people don't, Liv. Not with kids, not in life... we're all just faking it and making it look easy... but it's anything but easy."

I let out a long sigh, feeling an ounce of relief as I process this with Clara. But then I realize the person I should be processing this with is Kane.

"Okay, I need to call him."

"Oh, don't tell him over the phone," she reprimands.

"I'm not. I just need to ask him to come over so I can tell him in person."

"Yes, do that. And then call me and let me know how it goes. Are you sure you don't want me to come over?"

"No, I'm good. Thank you, Clara. I know you're a giant pain in my ass, but you really are the best friend when I need you."

"I offer many services, some more sexual for a small fee."

This girl. Always making something dirty. "I love you. Thank you."

"Anytime, momma-to-be."

"Oh, God..." I whine while Clara laughs on the other end.

"Good luck," she tells me before ending the call. Staring at my phone in my hands, I bring up a message to Kane and send him a text. There's no turning back now.

*Me: Hey you. Can you come over, please? I need to see you.*

His reply is almost instant.

**Kane: Missed me that much already? It's been less than forty-eight hours.**

After I stayed at his place the night of Thanksgiving, I told Kane I needed a day or so to take care of some things I had been putting off until the break, like cleaning out my closet. But in reality, I didn't trust myself around him until I knew for sure what our future held. The irony that I will now—in fact— *have* to clean out my closet, is not lost on me.

*Me: Always. Can you be here soon?*

**Kane: Leaving now. Gonna make a quick stop for food and then I'll be there. See you soon.**

Knowing I had a good forty-five minutes to an hour until Kane arrived, I mustered up enough energy to hop in the shower and wash off the grime of the day, tidy up my mess in the bathroom and hide the tests so I could show Kane when I was ready, and finish cleaning up my kitchen.

About thirty minutes later, I heard a knock at the door. I figured it was Kane, but if he's this early, he must have been speeding. Ready to give him a good teasing, I open the door with a smirk, but the person standing on the other side makes my face fall flat in a second.

"Hi, Liv," that voice that I swear would never utter my name again resonates in my ears as a wave of nausea hits me. It might be pregnancy symptoms, but more than likely, it's from facing my ex for the first time in months since I caught him with his dick in someone else.

"Trevor, what are you doing here?" I shake my head as I watch his eyes bounce back and forth between mine.

"I wanted to see you," he says, trying to sound sincere, but sounding more desperate.

"Really, it didn't seem like I was a thought on your mind while you were fucking Lexi?" I cross my arms over my body like a protective shield. Even though I'm one-hundred per-cent over him, I don't want him to think that I'm receptive to his groveling at all.

It's why I never responded to his dozens of texts or missed calls. It's why when he emailed me, I never thought twice about writing back. Because there was no way in hell I would give him another chance, let alone the opportunity to justify what he did.

"Why are you here?"

His head hangs low now between his shoulders as he takes a deep breath. "I fucked up."

"Yeah, no shit," I agree on a short breath. "Well, thanks for driving all this way to tell me that. Have a good night," I move to shut the door in his face, but he stops me before I'm successful.

"Can we talk? Please?" He begs as his eyes find mine and I see pain there. I don't think I've ever seen Trevor look distraught about anything.

"How did you even find me?"

He peers up at me again and stands tall. "Your Facebook. Plus, after you left I figured you must have gone home."

Fuck. Damn social media, always providing enough information to people when you don't want it to.

"So you're stalking me now? Pretty convenient given you had me near you every day for almost a year and didn't care that much."

"I'm not stalking you. Well, I kind of did for the past day or so. But I saw that you moved home and then you posted a picture of you and the girls with the apartment complex in the background. I waited around until I saw you so I knew which unit was yours."

"Christ," I roll my eyes. "Okay, so your stalker skills are up to par. What do you need Trevor?"

"Can I come in? I have a lot I need to say…" He's pleading, and hell if it's the pregnancy hormones or maybe just pity, but part of me can't turn him away. I sigh. He must have something important to say if he traveled all this way. Maybe this break-up will help him see what a pig he is and he can vow to be less of an asshole pig for his next lady. Because no matter what he says, that won't be me.

But Trevor was a part of my life for almost a year, a man I shared my life with and my bed with at one point. He must need someone to talk to, or at least my ears to hear his epiphany.

"Fine, but I'm expecting company, so you can't be here long," I open the door wider and motion him in, wondering how the hell this day could surprise me anymore.

# CHAPTER 36

Kane

When Olivia's text popped up on my phone, I felt re-
lieved to know that she missed me as much as I missed her. It
had been less than two days since I'd seen her, but after spending the holiday with her family, I had this urge to never let her
go. She insisted she had some things she needed to get done
before our break from school ended, so I relented and watched
her drive home, feeling like a piece of me went with her.

My future is so clear now. The idea makes me laugh
when I think about how differently I saw my life just a few
months ago. I was sure being alone was what I wanted. I was
sure there was no reason to open myself up to someone else
again.

And then a fiery redhead turned my world upside down
and flipped over everything I thought I knew. Heads was now
tails, dark was now light, and life without Olivia was something I never wanted to experience.

The speed at which I drove to her only solidified what
I knew. She owned me. I wanted it all with her. But before
I rushed into anything, I needed her to know how I felt. I
needed her to know that I loved her and I wanted a future with
her.

So when she sent me that text and sounded as desperate
to be with me and I was with her, I knew this was the night.
Eating dinner, watching a movie, and falling asleep with her

in my arms after worshipping her body was the agenda for the evening, and I couldn't fucking wait.

Olivia has a thing for burgers, so I stopped by one of her favorite places—Jack's Grill—for a classic burger that is infamous in Emerson Falls. As always, the drive-thru was insane, so it put me at her place a little later than I had intended.

I grabbed the food off the front seat, secured the sodas in my hands, and locked my truck before making my way to her door. The sound of two voices on the other side made me weary as I knocked on the door with my elbow since my hands were completely full.

"Just a second!" I hear Olivia shout before murmuring something else to the person on the other side. My heartrate picks up as I realize the voice is a man's.

Olivia wouldn't have a man in there with her, would she? No, she wouldn't have invited me over if she had company, especially of the male variety. There had to be an explanation.

I knock once more just as Olivia pulls the door open, looking flustered and surprised to see me.

"Kane..." she says, brushing her hair behind her ears. "I'm sorry. I had an unexpected visitor, but he's leaving now," her eyes move back into her living room.

"Hey, no worries. I brought dinner," I voice on a smile as I walk through the door.

And then the bags of burgers and fries along with our sodas, go crashing to the floor when I see who's in her apartment.

"What the fuck?" I shout as my blood pumps so furiously in my veins I think they might burst.

"Kane, what's the matter?" Olivia comes up behind me as she takes in the mess on her floor, but my eyes never leave the man standing across from me—the one person I thought I'd never see again after I found him the last time.

"Kane," he says as he stays put, afraid to move one inch in fear of the repercussions he'll experience from my fist.

"Kane, what is going on? This is..."

"T.J.," I manage to say, staring down the man who used to be my best friend.

"T.J.? No, this is Trevor... my ex," she answers full of confusion.

"Liv," T.J. starts to move just as I take a step back and put two and two together.

"This is your ex?" I choke out, turning to her and seeing the blind realization cross her face.

"Yes, but he was just leaving. I didn't invite him here Kane, I promise. I... I don't understand what's going on," she trembles as her eyes bounce back and forth between us.

"Yeah, well let me help you understand," I grit through my teeth, my fists clenching beside me, and the fire in my body about to ignite this room in flames. "That man over there *was* my best friend—Trevor Johnson, or T.J. as I called him—the one who fucked my fiancé behind my back while I was serving my country... and now apparently, he got to you too..."

I glare back over at him while T.J. remains rooted in place, his face almost white, his hair in disarray, and his eyes widen when he realizes our connection.

"Kane, I had no idea..." Olivia's voice sounds destroyed as everything clicks.

"No, you couldn't have, right? It's just a coincidence that my current girlfriend happens to know the man who wrecked my life...." I reply while fighting the urge to plow my fist into T.J.'s face.

"Kane," he starts, but I shoot him daggers with my eyes,

shutting him up effectively.

"Don't you even fucking *dare* say something to me right now! I can't believe this," I shout, pulling at my hair and retreating from the room.

I have to leave. I need to get out of here. The walls feel like they're closing in on me and my chest tightens—the first sign of an imminent panic attack.

"Kane, please. I'm so confused right now, let's just talk..." Olivia begs as I back up and turn for the door.

"Fuck, Liv. I just... I can't...I have to go," I manage to croak out before leaving the devastation behind me in a cloud of my dust.

I reach my truck, unlocking it and climbing in, firing up the engine and taking off, screeching the tires against the asphalt as I peel out of the apartment complex.

"Fuck! Fuck! Fuck!" I curse, slamming my fists on my steering wheel while I speed down the road, taking the first entrance to the highway to head for my house, the one place I go to escape reality, especially since my world is crumbling around me.

My phone starts ringing repeatedly, Olivia's name flashing across the screen. I can't talk right now and the distraction is blinding while I'm driving, so I silence my phone and turn it over so the screen stops illuminating the cab.

I just keep driving, lost in the fury racking my body and the fuzziness in my mind. I blank out so hard, I barely remember the entire trip as I pull in my driveway and shut off my engine. Slamming the door to my truck shut, I trudge inside and throw my phone across the room, stomp into my kitchen, and quickly locate the bottle of whiskey in my cupboard. I reach for a glass and fill it half full as my hand trembles and the bottle clanks against the rim. I shoot back the amber liquid and quickly refill it, throwing back shot after shot until my stomach turns and the ache in my chest starts to dull.

Once I'm satisfied with my level of inebriation, I stumble across my house and locate my phone that I tossed when I got home. Taking a seat on the couch, I unlock the screen and see the list of missed calls from Olivia, along with dozens of texts and voicemails.

And then the anger comes back and I chuck my phone across the room again, the thud of it hitting the wall and then the hardwood providing the only sounds besides the background noise of animals calling out into the night outside.

"Fuck! I... I just don't get it!" I shout into the room, throwing a pillow from the couch over my face as every emotion courses through my body.

I'm so goddamn angry, my skin is vibrating from my pulse.

My heart fucking aches in my chest as I picture the two of them together, and then realizing that he fucking cheated on her just like he did to me with Natasha, makes me want to bash his face in more than anything I've ever wanted to do in my life.

I feel tears threaten to fill my eyes when I think about how I had planned for the evening to go—the dinner we would share, my confession to her about how I truly felt.

And now all I can think about is the two of them together. How the fuck did this even happen? How did T.J. end up in northern California and woo Olivia, and then fuck it up— just like every other relationship he's ever had?

Did Olivia know who I was? Did T.J. ever talk about me? Was her coming home and weaseling her way into my world a plan the two of them had hatched together?

I had heard through the grapevine that T.J. left our town at the same time I did, his reputation destroyed when people found out about what he and Natasha did behind my back. I can't imagine they hid it all that well either, so I'm sure our neighbors and other people knew what was going on.

So did he find out Olivia and I were together and then came home to stir up some shit as some retribution for the direction his life took after he devastated mine? I wouldn't put it past him at this point. I always felt he was jealous of me, jealous of what Natasha and I had, jealous of my goals and aspirations when he had no direction of his own in his life. His dad had mapped out T.J.'s life for him before he graduated high school—securing him admission to Oregon State University and demanding he major in business so he could take over their drug store chain when his father retired.

And after he took the one thing from me that he didn't have—a woman to call his own, and his world shattered simultaneously with mine—was his goal always to get back at me? Was this the opportunity he saw and then pounced?

Some crazy shit is running through my mind as I remove the pillow from my face and inhale the oxygen I was lacking. This turn of events is so fucking crazy, I can't even form words or coherent thoughts that make any sense. The list of questions in my head is a mile long—as even more start to bellow in.

Is he here to try to get Olivia back? Is he still at her place? Fuck, I left her alone with him, not even contemplating what he's capable of. But if I know Olivia like I think I do, she wouldn't betray me—would she?

Hell, I thought Natasha would never cheat on me and look how that turned out.

And suddenly, every ounce of reassurance I felt just a few hours ago about my future with Olivia is drained from my heart and my mind. My ray of hope, the sunshine that brightened the darkened sky I was living in for years was just extinguished with one visit from a ghost of my past.

# CHAPTER 37

Olivia

"What the fuck just happened?" I shout at Trevor as he sinks back down in his chair and pulls on his hair right after Kane stormed off. I tried calling him a few times before I turned my attention back to Trevor, but the calls went unanswered.

"God, Olivia. I have no idea! How do you know Kane?"

I walk over to him as he looks up at me, and then I smack him across the face.

"What the fuck? What was that for?" He yells while rubbing the sting off of his cheek.

I bend down low and get right in his face, pointing a finger at his chest. "That was for Kane. You are such a selfish bastard, Trevor! Do you even know what you've done to him? You slept with his fiancé for crying out loud!"

Trevor moves to stand, which causes me to back up from him. I'm not afraid of him, but I can see the anger brewing behind his eyes.

"Natasha seduced me, Olivia. Not the other way around. And she was lonely, and my friend was a whole world away. We turned to each other and sought comfort in one another. But she wanted more, and I didn't."

"So you ruined your friendship for some convenient sex? God, you are one of the most self-centered people I've ever met! I can't believe I was with you for as long as I was!"

I study this man that I thought I wanted a future with and chastise myself for my naivety. My God, what would my life have ended up like if I had stayed with him and never caught him cheating on me?

"And apparently this is your M.O. since you fucked around on me, too. First you screw over your best friend, then you screw another woman behind my back. Tell me, Trevor. Was she the first? Or was I the first woman you were ever unfaithful to?"

His silence fills the room, and I know I have my answer.

"You're disgusting. I wish I never would have seen you in that winery..." I turn away from him, the mere sight of his face makes me want to hurl right now.

"I don't regret it, Liv. Moving to California and working for my uncle at his winery was the only thing I had going for me at the time, until I saw you that day. Falling for you was easy. But then I realized you were the type of woman who deserved it all—the family, the fancy house, the husband who worshipped you—and I realized I would never be able to be that man for you, not when I can't even stand to look at myself in the mirror."

"So that's why you cheated on me? Because you were so self-loathing, you figured, why not? There's nothing else you can do to make you hate yourself more?" I throw my hands up in the air for emphasis.

He shakes his head, dropping it down in defeat. "Pretty much. I felt like a piece of shit, so I acted like one too. God, Liv... I'm sorry I hurt you..."

"Yeah, you did. Did it ever occur to you that in inflicting your own punishment on yourself—which I think is bullshit by the way, but if that's what you think you needed to do, that's on you—did you realize that you would be inflicting self-doubt on me too? You made me question *my* self-worth, whether there was something I did or didn't do that caused you to stray. I never put pressure on you for a future, Trevor. I never demanded a ring, and it was your idea for us to move in together. If you knew that you didn't want or couldn't be with me, why didn't you say something sooner? Why did you allow me to waste that time with you and then shatter my confidence? I could have been with a man who cherished me and wanted a future with me—a man like Kane!"

The memory of meeting Trevor and falling for his charm makes my stomach revolt. Nausea hits me and I fight the urge to make even more of a mess on my carpet. I stare down at the spilled sodas, bags tipped over with food spilling out, and then my heart instantly breaks.

Kane was coming here, with dinner, and we were supposed to be discussing our future right now. I was supposed to be telling him that he was going to be a father, a life-changing detail that I hoped he'd be thrilled about.

Instead I'm face to face with the man that wrecked us both, the man responsible for hurting Kane so much more than he hurt me, which makes me tear up at the thought.

"You're right, Liv. I'm sorry. That's what I came to tell you. I swear, that was it. I know you'll never give me another chance..."

"You're damn right about that," I cut him off.

"Lexi is pregnant. I'm going to be a dad, and I just felt like I needed to clear my conscience of how I wronged you before I can move on with my life."

Trevor's desperation makes a lot more sense now, his shaking hands and the lump that I can hear in his throat. He's getting the future he didn't want with me and it terrifies him.

I take a seat on my couch across from where he's standing and look up at him.

"I'm sure I'm not the only person you own an apology to, but I can understand why you felt the need to give me that decency. Do you love her?" I ask, not sure why, but I guess it can't hurt at this point.

"I think I could at some point," he sighs as he takes a seat back in the chair next to the couch.

"Don't be with her just out of obligation. Don't do to her what you did to me, Trevor. Support her and be there for your kid, but stop doing things because you feel you have to. Figure out what you want out of life and stop wrecking the lives of others from your poor decisions."

He peers up at me, his forearms resting on his knees, looking utterly defeated. "I'm so sorry, Liv. You don't deserve what I did to you. *I never deserved you.* You deserve a man like Kane. He's one of the good ones. He was the best friend in the world to me, and I fucked up royally with him."

"You're right. You never deserved me, and I do deserve a man like Kane. What you did to him shattered him, Trevor. But he's become the most incredible man despite what you did to break him down. You need to apologize to him too at some point, but I'm pretty sure now wouldn't be a good time."

Trevor chuckles. "Yeah, no shit. He'd probably punch me again if I tried to get close to him right now."

"Yes he would, and I would let him."

"I'm sorry for wreaking havoc on your life again. I just needed to say my peace. Lexi actually encouraged me to do it."

I tilt my head in his direction and narrow my eyebrows as I study his face, realizing there's one more question I need to know the answer to before he leaves.

"How come I never heard anyone else call you T.J.? How did I miss this connection before?"

Trevor's head falls down in defeat as he takes a deep

breath before answering. "Kane was the only one who ever did. It was a thing between us—a nickname given and reserved by my best friend."

"I can't believe the thought never crossed my mind. He told me about you, and I know your initials. I guess I just thought never in million years that you could be the same person."

"Believe me. The last person I ever thought I'd run into in Emerson Falls was Kane Garrison. I know he left home after shit went down, but I never heard where he ended up. I just hoped wherever it was, he was happy," Trevor stares off to the side, avoiding my gaze until I yawn and draw his attention back to me.

I stare at him as the adrenaline depletes in my system and exhaustion kicks in. Great, one of the glorious side effects of pregnancy is already taking its toll. And then that fear hits my chest again as I realize I still need to talk to Kane. I have to make sure we're okay—that we're still as happy as I believed we were. A lump forms in my throat when I realize this crucial development could be a turning point for us. Will Kane ever be able to get past this?

"He is happy. *We* are happy. Go live your life, Trevor, and stay out of mine please. Kane moved to Emerson Falls to start over, and so did I. Go be a dad and be there for Lexi," I say as I stand and he follows closely behind me.

"Thanks, Liv. Good luck. I hope Kane can move past this weird coincidence. I swear, I had no idea."

"Yeah, me too," I say as Trevor turns and walks out of my door, and hopefully, out of my life for good.

"Oh, my God," I whisper as I turn around and replay the evening in my mind, reaching for the food on the floor as I attempt to clean up.

That was definitely not how I saw the evening going

and now my stomach is in knots as desperation fills my body to get Kane to talk to me. I call him over and over, each time the call goes to voicemail—he must have turned his phone off.

"Kane, please pick up," I cry into the speaker, leaving yet another voicemail that racks up a total of ten over the last hour. "Please don't let this ruin us. I need to talk to you. Please, Kane..." I croak as I end the call and throw myself into my bed, sobbing at the thought that I almost had everything I wanted, and then Trevor fucked it up again.

# CHAPTER 38

Olivia

I spent yesterday concealed in my apartment while I desperately tried to reach Kane. I considered driving to his house, but then my mom talked me out of it. Obviously if Kane wasn't answering my attempts at contact, he wanted to be left alone. But it killed me.

I was a problem solver by nature. Hell, that's what I did for a living. I solved math problems as a job. But the problem between me and Kane wasn't a simple equation with one clear-cut answer. That's the main reason I love math. It's black and white, a yes or no, a right or wrong that could rarely be disputed.

The issue with Kane was far more complex. Emotions were involved, people were connected, and suddenly I was in a state of panic looking at a problem that I couldn't solve, no matter what tool I tried to use.

My mom came over and I told her what happened while she held me as I cried. Even at thirty-one, the comfort of having my mother to cry with gave me some solace. But as soon as she left, I felt just as alone as I did before. As promised, I called Clara to fill her in, and true to her nature, she threatened to hunt down Trevor to unleash a world of hurt, and track down Kane to put me out of my misery. I declined both offers, praying that everything would work itself out eventually.

"What the hell happened, Olivia?" Drew whispers at

me when I see him back at work on Monday in the teacher's lounge. He's standing at my side while I fill my coffee mug with decaf coffee, resentful of the caffeine I now have to sacrifice.

The moment I meet Drew's eyes with my own, the moisture waiting on the edge of my lashes falls over.

"Drew," I breathe out as his arms encase me in a hug, consoling me through my despair.

"Olivia... Kane is a mess. I've never seen him like this."

My head pops up. "You've seen him?"

"Yeah, he came by my house yesterday to return a tool he borrowed and when I looked at him, I asked him why he looked like shit."

I wipe the tears from my cheeks, my voice hopeful that Drew has some morsel of promise I can cling on to. "What did he look like?"

Drew huffs. "Hungover as fuck. His eyes were bloodshot, he smelled like whiskey, and he looked like he didn't even sleep. I sensed it had to involve you, so when I asked, he told me to mind my own fucking business. I mean, I know we're men, but Kane has opened up to me before, so I was hoping he would this time too. But he threw my saw at me—which was hard to dodge, by the way—and then took off. And judging by the way you're crying right now, I think my intuition was correct."

I sigh as moisture clouds my eyes and falls repeatedly. Drew ushers me over to a chair so we can sit.

"Things were going so well, Drew. Well, except for..." I catch myself before I tell another person of our baby before Kane knows. I've accepted the life-changing development, but I still don't know how Kane will react—and the last thing I want is for him to find out from someone other than me. I already feel guilty that Clara and my mom know before him.

"Except for what?"

I wave my hand to push that little slip to the side. "Nothing. Anyway, I asked Kane to come over Saturday night so we could spend time together and when there was a knock at my door, I answered it expecting Kane, but it turned out to be my ex."

"Oh shit. Why was he there?"

I look down at my hands while gathering my strength to continue. "He drove all the way from California to apologize to me for being unfaithful. He was trying to clear his conscience, which I understood to an extent—but Kane showed up while he was still there."

Drew sits up as his eyes widen with fury. "Did he think you were cheating on him? If that's the case, I'll drive to his house and kick his ass right now."

"Wait, he's not here?"

Drew shakes his head. "No, he called out. Kane never gets a substitute to cover his classes, so I know something is seriously wrong."

"Shit, this is worse than I thought then," I tremble as tears continue to fall.

"Liv, what happened?"

I take a deep breath and fill him in. "When Kane walked in and saw my ex-boyfriend he flipped out...because my ex is his ex-best friend, T.J."

Drew's eyes bug out and his jaw becomes slack before he starts blinking repeatedly. "How the hell? Wait... I'm.... I don't even know what to say!"

"Yeah, you're telling me. So, not only did Kane meet my ex, but he realized we had one very horrible connection from our pasts—a past that he has been trying to move forward from for years and I brought it back to him."

And that's the reality that hurts me the most. When Kane divulged the betrayal he's been working so hard to overcome, I felt intense pride and adoration for him—of how strong of a man he was for mustering up the courage to move on—because he felt something deep inside saying that taking a risk with his heart again to pursue *me* was worth it. And that risk turned out to be catastrophic when Trevor waltzed back into our lives less than forty-eight hours ago.

Now, I can't even get him to talk to me. I know he's hurting, I know he's probably just as distraught as I am that our lives were so intertwined, yet we were miles apart from each other, but I don't know how much longer I'm supposed to wait. How long will he make me wait? Is there even an appropriate time frame to move past something like this? What if he takes off and I never get to tell him about his child—our child?

"Drew, he won't speak to me. I've tried calling and texting so many times, but I *need* to talk to him. I *need* to know if we're okay..."

Drew lets out a long breathe and then pauses before he hits me with the truth. "I wish I could tell you how to make that happen, but Kane does things in his own time. Hell, it took three years and meeting you to convince him to finally open up his heart and mind to the idea of dating again. The man internalizes everything, Liv. I can't imagine what's going on in his head, but I know he's a mess and probably just needs to sort it all out."

"But I want him to sort it out with *me*. I need him to know that I had no idea that Trevor was T.J.. I'm terrified of what he must be thinking about me right now, if he wonders if this was some twisted way to hurt him again. Can you talk to him?"

"I tried calling him, but he won't answer me either. Just give him some time. I know that must feel impossible. Hell, I can't stand when Tammy won't talk to me for a few hours. But Kane will come to you when he's ready, that I'm sure of."

"What if you're wrong? What if he can't move past this?" I whisper, afraid that if I speak my fear too loudly it will come true.

Drew just stares at me and swallows hard. "I... I don't know, Olivia. I hope he's the man I know he is and he can..."

I nod, accepting that I have no control in this situation —even though it is ripping my heart and mind to shreds—and then the bell rings, signaling the end of our prep period.

"Shit. Now I have to go teach like this," I sniffle while wiping my face again and righting my pants and sweater as I stand.

"Just have the kids work independently today or in groups. Tell them you're not feeling well. We're human too, Olivia, and teachers are allowed to have bad days."

"Thanks, Drew. If you do happen to speak to Kane, please tell him to call me or come see me."

"I will," he says before pulling me into a hug. I grab my coffee thermos and trudge down the hall and outside of the building, making my way back to my classroom. The chill of the wind bites my face, the cold borderline painful—but I welcome it. It's a momentary reprieve from the pain in my chest that only Kane can help diminish. My hand rubs over my stomach, remembering that it's not just me who will feel Kane's absence if he can't move past this. There's a whole other person who will miss him too.

# CHAPTER 39

Kane

My knee is bouncing up and down as I wait on the couch outside of Dr. Martinez's office. I texted her last night and told her that I needed to see her—that it was an emergency. The only appointment she had available was at eleven Monday morning, so I called for a sub, emailed sub plans into the secretary at work, and waited on pins and needles for my scheduled time to arrive, hoping I would leave this meeting feeling less turmoil than I've felt for the past day and a half.

The walls of her office are grey with a few paintings scattered around—watercolor depictions of ponds and flowers, places of serenity and beauty. I suspect those pictures and the color of the walls are supposed to offer a calming effect to patients, but all they're making me think of is Olivia and the grey cloud cast over our once serene relationship right now.

"Kane, come on in," Dr. Martinez calls me, pulling me from my mindless perusal of the walls and the tormenting thoughts running through my mind, forcing me to stand and follow her into her room. She turns on the noise maker outside of the door to help with privacy, then shuts the door quietly and faces me as I settle into the dark grey couch. What's with all of the grey in this place?

"So, I know you said this appointment was an emergency, Kane. I hope you're alright. You've been doing so well," she starts, grabbing her pad and pen and sitting snugly in her chair across from me. Her black hair streaked with greys falls around her face, a small clip pulling the bulk of it out of her dark brown eyes—those same eyes that took pity on me and helped change the man sitting before her.

"No, I'm not fucking alright," I grit out as she arches an eyebrow in warning at me for my language. "Fuck, I'm sorry. But Doc, there's no other word besides *fuck* to describe the turmoil I'm feeling right now."

She nods. "I can feel the anger coming off of you in waves, Kane, so do me a favor and try a few controlled breaths like we've practiced," she prompts, rolling her hand in front of her to usher me to start.

I inhale for five seconds and then exhale for the same length of time. I do this repeatedly until I feel some of the tension leave my shoulders and neck and feel calm enough to speak.

*In with the good, out with the bad.*

*Visuals of punching T.J. in the face still flash through my mind, but they're more like fuzzy pictures now, rather than vivid lines and clear images I've been envisioning since I saw him the other night.*

"Okay, that's better. Now, tell me what happened."

"I feel pathetic for being here," I confess, the defeat I feel overwhelming me at the moment.

"Why?"

"Because my anxiety and rage is so bad right now that I had to call my therapist for an emergency meeting," I fire off a little too harshly.

Dr. Martinez scolds me right away, throwing a stern gaze and finger in my direction. "Uh, uh… Kane, do not beat yourself up for being here. I wish half of my clients knew when to contact me like you do. You've learned the signs of an attack and when to listen to your mind and body. As a therapist, that's exactly what I wish for my clients. It takes courage to admit when we need help, when the weight of the world feels too heavy for us to bare alone. You are not pathetic. You are stronger than most."

The weight of her words sink in as I fall down on the back cushion, my hands wound so tight into fists to curb the urge I feel to destroy anything around me. I've come a long way from where I was three years ago when I first entered this office, but there are still times when I feel like that man again—the man that felt like he'd lost every ounce of control of his surroundings and his life.

"I know, but I sure don't feel that way right now."

Dr. Martinez tilts her head and flashes me a small smile. "That's okay, Kane. That's why I'm here. Sometimes we just need to process out loud so we can understand what's really going on—so we can pinpoint the source of our anxiety and move past it. Why don't you start by telling me why you came in today?"

I let out one more long breath and then hunch forward in my seat, ready to spill every thought that's been running on repeat in my mind. "I ran into T.J. this weekend."

Her eyebrows shoot up in shock. "Really? Where?"

"At Olivia's apartment."

And her eyes go even wider. "Okay... that's strange..."

"Not as strange as finding out that T.J. was her ex."

Dr. Martinez sets her pad and pen on her desk and then focuses back on me, reaching for my hands. And I let her hold them, her thumb brushing across my knuckles.

"Kane, my God. This is..."

"Un-fucking-believable, right?"

"For lack of a better word, yes," she huffs before releasing my hands and sitting upright again. "So how did you react?"

"Well, not very well. As soon as I saw him, I saw red. There was no stopping the thunderous rage that overcame me. I yelled at Olivia as she tried to process the connection. I ran when I started to feel the panic settle in. And I ignored her calls and texts all weekend because I don't even know what to say to her."

"I can imagine. So try to tell me what you're feeling."

I sigh. "Anger, obviously. Betrayal. Fear. Hurt."

"Okay, let's start with the anger. Who are you angry at?"

"T.J. for coming back and ruining what I had with Olivia."

"But did he ruin it?" She asks, reaching for her pen and the pad of paper again.

"What do you mean? He was there to see her, but I'm not sure why. I don't even know what happened after I left."

"Exactly. You don't know exactly why he was there, but does that change how you feel about Olivia?"

I clench my jaw as I realize I know the answer to that question with no hesitation.

"No, it doesn't change how I feel about her."

She nods and urges me to continue. "So what about the betrayal?"

"I just feel like he fucking betrayed me again. He slept with the last woman I loved, and now this one too."

"But he slept with her before she was with you, Kane. And you didn't meet her until after they were together. Is there a way they could have managed to put that connection together?"

I shake my head. "It's not likely," which is what I've been trying to convince myself of since that night. She never uttered his name and I never thought in a million years that T.J. would have been in northern California.

"Okay, what about the fear? What are you afraid of?"

I run my fingers through my hair and brush my clammy palms down my pants. "I'm afraid I've lost her. I'm afraid she'll go back to him and I'll lose yet another woman because of his selfish acts." My voice is beginning to choke as I finally say all the fears out loud.

"Okay. But did she say that?"

"Say what?"

"That you lost her? That she's going back to him?"

I think back as the night replays in my mind. "No, she didn't, but mostly since I didn't give her the chance to. She seemed just as confused as I did that we all were connected."

"And the hurt?" She presses again, calmly but firmly, directing me to keep talking.

I hear my breath catch in my throat and the sting of tears come forward. "My chest fucking aches. I'm so afraid to lose her because the pain I'm feeling right now is the worst feeling I've ever experienced—worse than when he ripped apart my life the first time, believe it or not. I'm hurt because the future I saw with Olivia is somehow tainted by my past, and I wanted so badly for those two things to be separate. There was supposed to be "before Olivia" and "after Olivia"," I say while weighing my hands in the air, "Not this weird limbo where those two parts of my life are tied together with a string. I guess I just feel like my past is doomed to repeat itself —T.J. playing his part in it again."

She scribbles a few notes on her paper before setting it down and facing me again. "That is a legitimate fear, Kane, given what you've experienced. But let me ask you this—who are most of those feelings directed towards? T.J. or Olivia?"

And when she says that, it finally hits me. The truth I needed to see, the clarification that I knew this appointment would help me find.

It's not Olivia I'm mad at. The fury I feel is not directed towards her, yet she's the one who's paying the price right now. She's the one I've been ignoring, not giving her a chance to reassure me that I'm the man she wants to be with. I haven't given her that opportunity because I've been too pumped with anger and fear to hear what she has to say.

"T.J., obviously," I answer as Dr. Martinez nods.

"Exactly. Your feelings are completely justifiable, but you need to remember who they're directed towards. And I hate to break it to you, but rarely in life can we avoid the connection between our past and our present. There's usually some experience before that leads us to the one we're living in, a tangled mess of interwoven plot lines and people. This woman obviously means a lot to you, and you don't want to ruin things with Olivia because you're mad at T.J. Plus, I think you owe it to her to hear her side of the story."

I let out a long exhale as the tightness of my chest dissipates and regret takes over.

"Fuck," I mumble.

"Kane, I really wish..." she pauses and then takes a deep breath. "You know what, I can't chastise you for using that word when I don't blame you. FUCK!" She exclaims, throwing her hands in the air, which makes my entire body bounce with laughter.

"God, it's crazy what processing that all out loud can do, Doc," I say as the adrenaline runs dry in my veins now.

"Exactly. Once we're able to take a step back and assess what's really causing the anxiety, we no longer give it power. Or at least, we give it less power. Living with this anger and anxiousness you feel may never completely go away. But you did the right thing by calling, Kane. I'm proud of you and I'm rooting for you and Olivia. Watching you transform into a man who opened his heart again has been a pleasure to witness. Please don't let her pass you by. You can move past this, I know you can."

Even though I hate to admit it, Dr. Martinez's words make my eyes well as a tear cascades down my cheek. Yes, I'm crying, but fuck... the past two days have sliced my heart and confidence in two. I told myself I would never care again, that I would never open myself up to the possibility to be hurt like I was before.

But my chest is wide open, and although this turn of events stings, I don't want to close myself off again because I know I would lose Olivia in the process. She's the woman I'm meant to be with, the one with the key to my heart. The only way I'll close myself up again is by her hands, because she's the only one that I want to let inside.

"Three years ago, I never thought I would get to the point I am today, where I finally feel at peace again. I never thought the idea of falling in love would cross my mind again after what Natasha and T.J. did. But you've helped me change my life, Doc. There aren't enough words to thank you."

Dr. Martinez's lip trembles through a smile, but she doesn't say anything. She doesn't have to. She looks at me with pride, which is enough for me—the woman has transformed my life. We both stand and give each other a heartfelt hug as I promise to check in with her soon once the dust has settled.

While driving back home, this intense wave of exhaustion hits me from the lack of sleep over the past few days and the adrenaline leaving my body. I make my way inside and head straight for bed, giving myself the permission to gather some energy, calm down, and put myself back together before making things right with Olivia. I want to make sure I am confident that I can move past this and explain my reaction clearly before I see her.

When I wake from my nap, it's late in the afternoon, the sunset blinding my eyes from between the curtains I accidently left open, and my appetite has returned. Trudging into the kitchen, I search for sustenance before I realize I have no food. So I fire up my truck and head into town. Since going to the grocery store on an empty stomach is not a good idea, I pull into the parking lot of Penny's Diner, deciding to eat before I restock my fridge.

The classic 50s diner transports you back in time with bright red booths, teal walls with giant black records painted on them, and chrome details along every surface. I glide over to a seat at the counter as a waitress greets me. Since I get the same thing every time I come here, I give her my order and wait for my food while sipping my iced tea and checking my phone.

There aren't any new messages or missed calls from Olivia, but there is one from Drew. I'm sure he's just trying to be a good friend, but I'm still not ready to talk to anyone yet. I know the only person I need to talk to is Olivia, but I need to get my head on straight. I need to make sure the words I want to say to her are clear and not misconstrued. As I start toying around with my speech in my head, a familiar voice comes up behind me.

"Hey, Kane," the timid rumble of T.J.'s voice startles me as I turn and take him in. His dark hair is a mess and the bags under his eyes indicate his lack of sleep and distress.

My jaw clenches tight and my heart jump starts while the distance between us closes as he takes a seat next to me. I don't speak; I don't react—because if I do, it's going to undo all the calm I finally found just a few hours earlier.

"I know I'm probably the last person you want to see

right now," T.J. breaks the silence, turning on his stool to face me. The waitress comes over at this moment to deliver my food, but I never acknowledge her face to face.

"Thank you," I say to her from the corner of my mouth, my eyes still locked on my ex-best friend.

"But I'm actually glad I ran into you. I'm... I just stopped for a meal before I hit the road again."

"What do you need, T.J.? Haven't you done enough damage in my life?" I finally manage to say even though my body is vibrating with my rapid pulse.

"I owe you a long overdue apology, Kane. I'm so sorry for the way things happened with Natasha. There's no excuse to justify what I did." His eyes plead with me for forgiveness as he waits for my response, but I remain silent.

"And I swear, I had no idea that you knew Olivia. Hell, I didn't even know you lived in Emerson Falls," he says, sitting up taller now.

"I moved here after I left home. I wanted a fresh start and they needed a history teacher."

"Seems like a great place to live and raise a family in."

I nod. "It is." And that's what I want for me and Olivia. "I still don't understand how you ended up in California though..."

"Well, after everything happened with Natasha, I had to leave. My parents couldn't even look at me, I lost my best friend, and I had nothing keeping me in our town any more. My uncle owns a winery down there and offered me a job and a fresh start, so I took it. I met Olivia while she was on a wine tour with some of her friends."

I shake my head. Fucking figures he would get the chance to start over and ruin it like he does to pretty much everything.

"I'm sorry I hurt you, Kane. I'm sorry that I wrecked your relationship and our friendship... but I'm glad to see you happy, at least—I guess you were before I came back here..."

I huff. "Yeah, I fucking was. Let me ask you something," I say, feeling more bold now to put him in his place. "How on Earth could you cheat on a woman like Olivia? When she told me her ex was unfaithful to her, I couldn't imagine any man that had her could be that fucking stupid."

T.J. hangs his head now, his eyes staying on the floor between us. "Because I'm not a fucking man. I knew I didn't deserve her, so I sabotaged the relationship. I know it's not an excuse, but that's the best explanation I have."

"You *are* fucking stupid and not even close to being a man good enough for her," I growl. "But you know what, thanks to you and your cowardness, she moved back here and I met her."

"She deserves someone like you, Kane. I could see it on your face when you came into her apartment. You care about her the way I knew I never could."

"Damn right I do, and you coming back here made me question what we had."

"I only came back to clear my conscience, I promise. My life has taken an unexpected turn and I'm trying to right my wrongs and be a better person. But please don't let the fact that she and I have a past dictate your future with her."

I laugh. "Thanks for the pep talk, but I wasn't planning on it. Stop fucking tormenting other people, T.J., and be the man I always believed you were. You aren't this guy—this pathetic man who leaves a path of destruction everywhere he goes. You were my best friend, the guy I thought would always have my back." My eyes survey his body, dropping from his face to his toes and back up. "But really, you just turned out to be the man behind me, digging the knife in deeper. You make shitty decisions and hurt others in the process. It's time to grow the fuck up, T.J." I shake my head at him before delivering that last bomb of truth. "And know this—you may have had Olivia first, but *I* will be her last. *I will be her fucking everything*," I declare, standing up tall in front of him, looking down on the pitiful shell of man I used to know.

"Good. Take care of her, Kane. I, uh, need to get going. I have a long drive," he moves to stand as well so we're eye-to-eye now, his face clearly showing his embarrassment and disgust in himself. The green of his eyes stare back at me, and in that moment I realize I have to forgive him—not for him, but for me—so I can move on with my life.

The people we cross paths with in life can either be a blessing or a lesson—and I'm finally realizing T.J. was both for me. He taught me that betrayal from the people closest to us feels like a knife stabbing you in the chest, depleting your lungs of the air necessary to breathe. He dug that knife deeper and twisted it in at a painful angle when I think about how I trusted him and he let me down, wrecking our life-long friendship *and* my relationship in one fell swoop. He was my best friend, the guy by my side since we were ten—the last fucking person I thought would betray me like he did. I mourned our friendship as if he died—because that's how final it felt. When I walked in on him and Natasha, it might as well have been a picture of his casket being lowered into the ground.

But he also gave me a gift—the love of a woman that he disrespected and didn't appreciate. Regardless of how crazy it is that Olivia and I were connected by T.J.—If he hadn't cheated on her and messed up yet another relationship in his life, she never would have moved back to Emerson Falls and I never would have met her. His screw up this time ended up being the antidote of my sorrow, the balm to soothe the ache that his disloyalty left in my heart. In a weird and twisted way, he both wrecked me and delivered the cure to my affliction in three years' time.

Regardless that he is partly to thank for bringing her here, Olivia is the one that has put me back together, dug her way into my heart, and there is no way I'll ever let go of her now. She's my treasure, the other half of my soul, the one person who makes me believe in happiness now, and I need to make things right with her.

"Take care, Kane. And take care of her too," he says on a weak smile before turning around and walking out of the door.

"Do you want me to heat up your food?" The waitress comes by once T.J. has left and I take my seat again.

"Yeah, thanks. And can I get a slice of chocolate cream pie to go?"

"Of course," she smiles and takes my plate, returning a few minutes later with my food and dessert.

By the time I leave the restaurant, it's raining outside, the water coming down hard on the asphalt as rivers start to form along the roads. Still lacking food in my house, I make a quick trip to the grocery store to grab the basics, but I never make it fully inside.

The moment I step foot on the tile through the automatic doors, an orchestra of crickets jumps across the floor right in front of my feet, hopping along to escape the torrential downpour outside.

And I smile, the kind of smile that you can't fight because it comes from a place of warmth and pure joy, a knowing feeling that the universe is sending you a sign you'd be stupid to ignore.

The kind of smile that the cricket-hating woman pulled me in with and then wove her red hair and fiery personality around my heart, bringing me back to life. And I take that as a sign of serendipity.

I turn right back out of the door, hop back in my truck, and race across town to the woman who hopefully still wants me as much as I *need* her.

# CHAPTER 40

Olivia

Today was one of the longest days of teaching in my life. My students sensed there was something wrong when they saw me, my face red and my eyes puffy from all the crying I did before I returned to my classroom from my talk with Drew.

"Miss Walsh, are you okay?" Daisy comes up to me, her wide brown eyes full of worry as I stare down at the young girl who probably hasn't experienced heartache like mine yet.

"Yeah, I'm okay, hun. I'm just having a bad day," I reply on a weak smile and then make my way around her.

"Did Mr. Garrison make you cry? 'Cause if he did, we'll beat him up for you," she exclaims as murmurs of promise filter through the class.

"What? Why would you think that?" I ask nervously.

"Come on, Miss Walsh. We all know you two were dating. It was so obvious by the way you made googly eyes at each other every time you saw one another around campus," she rolls her eyes as the rest of the students giggle and nod in agreement.

I shake my head and chuckle. I guess Kane and I weren't as stealth about our relationship as I thought we were.

"No, Mr. Garrison didn't make me cry. But relationships are hard and sometimes miscommunication can cause problems and disagreements," I sigh and attempt to start the class.

"But are you guys going to be okay?" Daisy begs for reassurance as she cuts me off. "You two are so cute together. The whole school wants you to get married. We even created a hashtag for you on social media," her wide smile blinds me as her look of hope stares me down.

"What?" I laugh as the kids start gossiping amongst themselves.

"Yeah, #WAG and #teacherlove," she beams and scrolls through her phone, showing me her Twitter feed comprising other students' messages about Kane and me. There are a few pictures of the two of us near one another—one of us from the pep rally that really seems to be quite popular—with captions guessing what we're thinking or talking about.

"What does #WAG stand for?" I ask, sitting on top of the desk next to her as the students talk and I resolve that not much learning will happen today.

"Walsh and Garrison," she grins, which makes me do the same.

"This is really sweet, and also kind of creepy, but I don't think it's appropriate to speak about our relationship with students. I appreciate your support though," I tease commanding the attention of the class and handing out the assignment for the day.

Listening to the kids talk about how perfect we are for each other just made the ache in my chest magnify throughout the course of the day—because I know we're perfect for each other. But I have no idea whether that's enough for us to move past the T.J. twist. Although I know it was important for Trevor to give me an apology, part of me wishes he would have just stayed in California and owned his mistakes, instead of bringing his turmoil here and spreading it around like wildfire. Apparently he's good at leaving a trail of ash and soot where he's burned those closest to him.

By the time I make it home, I'm exhausted. Between the emotional rollercoaster I'm on and the tiny human inside of me draining me of energy, I barely make it to the couch after changing my clothes. As soon as my head hits the cushions, I fall asleep, not even remembering when I closed my eyes.

I dream of Kane—his touch, his kiss, the feeling of being wrapped in his arms. I think back to that first night at Tony's, when all I saw him as was a decadent indulgence my mind and body craved. The morning he rescued me from the crickets will still remain one of my fondest memories though as I recall wanting to punch him and then climb him like a tree when his quick wit and banter made me furious and turned on at the same time. I replay the night at his house when he finally opened up to me and let me in—into his home, his mind, his body—and the victory I felt as his walls finally crumbled.

I thought that was it. I thought that after he said those words out loud—the reason he was so scared to open his heart up again—that all the obstacles we faced were out of the way.

Boy, was I wrong.

Now, I'm carrying his baby and he doesn't know. I'm completely in love with him, and he doesn't know. And I want him until the end of forever—and he doesn't know.

A sound in my dreams pulls me awake, until I open my eyes and realize the knock at the door is real, even though it felt like a part of the movie playing in my head.

Pushing myself up off the couch, I wrap my navy sweater around me and trudge to the door, yawning wide as I open it and freeze when I see who's there.

"Hi, beautiful," Kane says in that deep, sultry voice that I missed more than anything.

And I instantly cry, gut-wrenching sobs wracking my body as Kane steps inside and pulls me into his chest, wrapping his arms around me, and holding onto me with such force, it finally makes me feel like I can crumble and he'll be there to catch me before I fall.

"Shhhh, it's okay. I'm here, baby," he whispers against the shell of my ear, pulling me in close so we're touching on every possible surface of our bodies. He shuts the door behind us and walks me slowly back over to the couch while keeping me wrapped up in him. When he motions for us to take a seat, I nervously release him as if he'll run right back out of my apartment and I'll lose him all over again.

Once we sit, I crawl into his lap and he encompasses me in his chest, holding me so tight while I release all the sorrow I've felt over the past few days. I lose track of time and don't dare to speak—all I want is to soak in this feeling of being back in his arms again, where everything feels right.

"Liv," he finally breaks the silence, rubbing his hands along my back. "We need to talk, baby, and I want to see your eyes when we do," he softly consoles me, urging me to sit up.

I manage to push myself upright and wipe my eyes free of the tears clouding my vision as I take him in, this handsome man who is fragile and bruised, but sturdy and brave, and back in front of me, ready to face our challenges. His beard is longer than usual, his eyes darkened by his past and lack of rest. If he's been feeling anything like I have, I'm sure he's been missing sleep too. His lips curl up just slightly in a smile—a small sliver of hope that the discussion we're about to have won't leave me breathless and broken.

"Kane, I'm so sorry. I swear, I had no idea Trevor was your T.J.. He just showed up, and I..."

Kane places a finger over my lips, silencing me as he shakes his head. His eyes narrow while they bounce back and forth between mine.

"Don't you dare apologize to me, Olivia. You did nothing wrong here. I am the wrong one. I'm the one who ran when I saw T.J. and didn't respect you enough to talk to you about everything I was feeling. I just needed some space to gather my thoughts, but leaving you in the dark wasn't right, and I will forever regret that."

"Kane, it's okay... I just wanted to talk to you so desperately. I needed you to know that I was just as much in the dark as you were. And I had NO intention of taking him back, regardless of what he had to say. That wasn't the reason he was here, anyway, but I promise you, Kane... you are the man I want," I choke through my tears as Kane reaches up to brush them from my cheeks and push back my wild hair.

"Good. Because you are the only woman I want for the rest of my life, Olivia. I love you so damn much, and it took me understanding what I was really mad about to realize that."

"Oh, God... I love you too, Kane," I sigh before pressing my lips to his and kissing him for the first time in days. The feel of his mouth on mine again is like coming home, because Kane is my home now. He's the man I want next to me through everything life has to throw at us—the good, the bad, the messy.

I lose myself in him—the feel of his lips pressing lightly on mine, the sound of his murmurs when he changes the angle and pushes his tongue in my mouth, the urgency in the way his hands hold me, fighting to keep me close yet also make me feel safe. It's amazing, breathtaking—the only way I ever want to feel when I'm kissed by this man for the rest of my life.

When we part, Kane rests his forehead on mine as our breathing returns to normal. "I wanted to be strong for you before we spoke. I needed to be strong for you, Liv."

"You are strong, Kane," I tease him by squeezing his biceps, desperately trying to return things back to normal with us. I love that we can be playful after shattering each other's bodies in pleasure and love.

He shakes his head, pulling away so we can see each other's eyes again. "Muscles are only one part of it, baby. A man's strength comes from his ability and desire to be there for a woman—to put her above him, to keep her from falling when she needs to jump. I needed to make sure I could put you above everything else, Olivia. I had to make sure that what I was feeling—the palpable rage and hurt—wasn't directed at you. I was never mad at you, Olivia, please trust me on that. And it only took one smack of reality from my therapist for me to realize it."

"Your therapist?" I ask, shocked that he never told me this before. I know Kane's made hints of working through his anger and anxiety, but he never mentioned seeing a professional. And though some may find that alarming, my heart beats stronger for him. It takes bravery and acceptance to ask for help, to seek out the knowledge of someone else to guide us through the challenges in our lives. Knowing that Kane had that courage—it solidifies even more that this is the man for me. This is the man I want by my side.

"Yeah. I started seeing her right after the whole T.J. and Natasha thing. I had a lot of anger, resentment, and anxiety I was dealing with, so my parents suggested I talk to someone. It was the best decision I've ever made. I've learned to move past things, deal with my triggers, and open myself up again. If we had met before, there's no way I would have been ready to be this man for you. But I'm ready now, baby. This is it," he pulls on my neck so our faces are only inches away from each other again. "You and me, baby."

I close my eyes and sigh, breathing deeply before remembering the detail of our lives I've yet to tell him, the tiny, life-altering change that is quickly developing inside of me. "Well, not just you and me..."

His eyes snap up to mine and we part while he searches my face for clarity, questioning me with those whiskey-colored eyes I hope our child inherits from him.

"What do you mean?"

"I'm pregnant, Kane," I whisper as tears form again in my eyes and start to fall over.

The shock on his face is quickly replaced with elation as his lips break out into the most glorious smile he's ever given me, better than the one he first pulled me in with.

"Really? How?" He asks, his voice thick with emotion.

"I took antibiotics when I was sick a few weeks ago, and they counteract the pill. And with the way we've been having sex, your guess is as good as mine," I joke, but secretly fear that anger will replace his happiness. "I'm sorry, Kane. I promise, I didn't mean for this to happen..."

"Holy crap, babe. This... this is incredible! Why are you apologizing?" he says, which makes the worry disintegrate quickly.

"Really? You're not mad?"

"No, babe. Not at all. I mean, it's fast, but I know I wanted kids with you anyway. I want everything with you, Liv," he declares before pressing a kiss to my cheek, lingering there for a few seconds while I memorize his words.

"I was going to tell you Saturday when you came over. That's part of the reason why I wanted to see you," I confess as the realization hits him.

"But T.J. was here," he states as more of a fact than a continuation of my story. I nod. "So you knew this entire time and I wasn't picking up the phone?" he says angrily. "Christ, I'm such an ass. Please forgive me."

"It's okay. I understand why you were upset, Kane. I do, really. But I was also so terrified you weren't going to talk to me for weeks or possibly ever again, and I didn't get the chance to tell you. But I'm so glad you're here now," I whisper, still soaking in the fact that my secret is finally free and Kane is back in my world. The fear has been lifted from my chest, my heart is beating with purpose again, and the life we've created can finally be celebrated.

"I'm so sorry, Liv. But I am here now, and I promise, I'm not going anywhere."

I move to straddle him as his hands find my hips and I sink down in his lap, heating up my body instantly when I feel him grow hard beneath me.

"I missed you so much, Kane," I moan before kissing him and tracing the lines of his body through his sweater. "I love you, you beautiful, resilient man."

Kane breaks us apart, tosses his sweater and shirt off effortlessly, leaving him bare chested in front of me, while I catch myself drooling at the sight of him. I will never tire of this man and his sculpted body—and it's mine forever now.

"I missed you too, Liv. I love you so fucking much," he growls before crushing our mouths together again, showing me with his body how much I mean to him. But it's not just how he loves me with his body that makes me swoon— it's how he's opened his heart and soul to me, when he never thought he would again.

I lose myself in the twists and turns of our tongues, the moans coming from our throats, and the intense fire burning in between my legs. I relish in the feel of his skin under my fingers, his lips all over mine, and the love I know he feels for me.

Kane pushes my sweater off of my shoulders and down my arms, followed by my shirt up over my head, and then reaches around to unhook my bra—all with a slow and precise touch while his eyes memorize every inch of my skin.

"God, you're beautiful, baby," the deep rasp of his voice ignites goosebumps on my skin as he places kisses along my collarbone and down my shoulders as my head falls to the side. His lips find my nipple next, surprising me with the feel of his tongue as he swirls it around and pulls the sensitive nub into his mouth, handling the flesh with his hand simultaneously. And boy, the sensitivity is there already—a pleasant side effect of the pregnancy.

I start to pant, drawing quick breaths while Kane continues to lick and suck on my breasts, making wetness pool between my legs at an unprecedented rate.

"Kane, please..."

"What do you need, baby?" He demands while growing stronger and faster in his touches on my body. His hands are moving everywhere, gripping my hips and directing me up and over his hard cock still covered by his jeans.

"You, Kane," I breathe out and then quickly snap my head up and pull his face to mine. "You're all I've ever needed, Kane. Make love to me, please..."

I see the return of my love in his eyes as his hands tremble on their way up to caress my cheeks. "You're all I need too, Olivia. I love you," he licks his lips before kissing me deeply and then directing me to stand.

We both discard our pants and underwear and then settle back on the couch with him hovering over me, nestled between my thighs. I can feel him nudge my opening before pushing forward and burying himself deep inside of me.

I swallow hard and shiver at the force of his thrust, but then quickly immerse myself in every sensation his body is giving mine. Kane dives deep, again and again, extracting every tremor of pleasure from my body. I'm sensitive all over apparently, and Kane is taking full advantage.

While leaning above me, he latches onto my nipple again while he continues to drag his cock in and out of me at a slow and even pace. It's luxurious, tormenting, and not nearly fast enough for what I need from him.

But my God, does it feel good. It's a torture that I will gladly accept until I feel like I can't take it anymore and urge him to move faster.

"More, Kane. Please," I plead while he continues to move at a snail's pace. "Why are you torturing me? Oh," I moan, throwing my head back and closing my eyes as my vision blurs and the dull vibration of my orgasm grows stronger, spiking in intensity while Kane keeps up his movements.

"I'm making love to you tonight, baby," he whispers in my ear, kissing down my neck and continuing to agonize me. "This is slow and sweet love... we have all the time in the world for the fast and dirty. But right now, I want you to submerge yourself in the soft feeling of our bodies connecting. I want you to feel every inch of me as I slide in and out of you. I want you to come from the sheer pleasure of our movements."

And with those last few words, I feel the warmth of my orgasm overtake me. The luxurious wave of ecstasy washes over me in a constant ripple, lasting so long I don't think it will ever end. Roll after roll of pleasure shakes my body and I come—I come so hard and long that by the time my orgasm ends, I'm completely unaware that Kane followed me to the finish line as he found his own drawn out release.

Our breaths are ragged, our bodies are covered in a light coat of sweat, our minds so blurry that all we can do is lie there, our chests heaving together while we come down from the high.

This man makes me feel cherished, loved, and sated. He's everything I was looking for—and in some twisted turn of fate, we got tangled up in each other—and now I'll never let him go.

# CHAPTER 41

Kane

*Three Weeks Later*

"Do you need any more help in here?" I ask Olivia as I come up behind her in my kitchen. I place a soft kiss on her neck as my arms wrap around her waist and my hands rest on the flat part of her stomach covered in an evergreen sweater dress— hugging her curves and tight stomach, which won't be flat for much longer.

Olivia is having my baby, and I'd be lying if I said the thought of that isn't the most life-changing feeling I've ever experienced. I'm going to be a father, and now my sole focus will be doing everything in my power to protect and cherish Olivia and our child. My heart is beating for another—two other people now—and it's a clarity I never thought I would crave again.

But everything *is* clear now. Olivia. Our child. Our life together is all I see and all I want. I found my purpose again— a feeling I lost for years, but I slowly discovered it was waiting for Olivia to resurface. I feel mentally and physically stronger than ever, solid enough to handle this, and beyond grateful that I get to experience it all with her.

The feel of my lips on her neck spikes goosebumps all over Olivia's skin, which makes me ravenous for her. I love knowing I have that effect on her with just a soft brush of my mouth.

Since we reconciled a few weeks ago, we haven't spent a day apart. Olivia is planning to move into my house over our Christmas vacation and we approached Principal North about our relationship. She was beyond supportive and elated for us. Olivia also told her about the baby to prepare for her absence at the beginning of the next school year. She's due in July, but will probably take longer than six weeks off so she can bond with the baby.

"Could you grab the cheese and olives from the fridge, babe?" She asks while looking over her shoulder at me and flashing me that brilliant smile that hooked me that first night at Tony's. I owe that man more than I can every repay him for pushing me that night to talk to her.

"Absolutely," I kiss her lips before retrieving the items she requested.

"I hope there's enough food," she says while surveying the surface of my kitchen island, covered in snacks. A veggie tray, chips and dip, meatballs, and a charcuterie board are organized around the marble. I hand her the olives and cheese as she adds them to the wooden slab, surrounded by other morsels of food, and I laugh. There's enough grub here to feed an army.

"I'm sure there's more than enough. Plus, the ham is in the oven with the potatoes, macaroni and cheese, rolls and veggies. I think everyone will take home leftovers at this point."

She sighs. "I know, I guess I'm just nervous."

"Why are you nervous?"

"This is the first time all of our friends and family will be together under the same roof. I just want everyone to get along. I don't want any more drama in our lives."

I tilt my head at her, observing the worry on her face. Ever since T.J. came back and threw us for a loop, I've noticed the confidence Olivia usually exudes has diminished a bit. I've reassured her countless times that everything between us is fine, but she's explained she's nervous that something else will happen. When she mentioned the idea of having a holiday party, I encouraged it, hoping that the event would help her focus her attention on something else. And I thought it would be a great way to bring everyone together to share in our excitement. Also, I may be using it to surprise Olivia with something else.

But seeing her worry again makes my heart beat erratically, after I finally feel like things are back on track. I rest my forehead on hers. "As long as you and I are together, Liv, we can face it all. Now stop stressing, it's bad for the baby."

She pushes me away and swats a hand to my chest playfully before pulling me back to her by my shirt. She crushes her mouth to mine, moaning when our lips meet, igniting desire in my body. I swear, if we had more time, I would escalate this further with no question.

"Don't start something we can't finish, Liv," I growl against her lips before we part and I see the lust in her eyes.

"Who said I didn't plan on finishing it," she smirks before sinking down to her knees and reaching for my pants. As soon as she pops the button on my jeans, the doorbell rings.

"Fuck," I moan while throwing my head back, which makes Olivia laugh at me as she stands.

"To be continued," she eyes me over her shoulder as she makes her way to the door to answer it, swaying her hips in that teasing way, enticing me to ignore our guests for a few more minutes.

I look around my home, the place I never imagined letting a woman into, and see all the touches that Olivia has added for the party. Toasted marshmallow scent fills the room from the candle she has lit on the fireplace and evergreen garland drapes across the mantle with small pine cone accents. An epic Christmas tree stands in the corner of the living room in front of the expansive bay window, dressed in white lights and silver and gold ornaments—classic and breathtaking, just like she is. Red poinsettia plants sit atop every surface to complete the Christmas feel and the smell of the ham roasting in the oven screams holiday feast.

Olivia opens the door, greeted by Perry and her husband, and their two kids.

"Hi, guys! Welcome," she beams as they make their way through the doors and survey the room.

"Your house is gorgeous, Kane," Perry compliments while reaching out to hug Olivia and takes the coats from her kids. Perry is dressed in a red sweater dress that is as elegant and refined as she is. Her magazine ready family—dressed in coordinating outfits—follows in tow, making me question whether Olivia will make us match our baby at some point in the future. Dear God, I hope not.

"Thanks, Perry, but it's our house now. Come on in. There are snacks on the island and I have a movie and games set up in the enclosed patio for the kids. There's a heater out there too so they won't get cold," I explain while showing them over.

Perry and her husband usher their kids to the entertainment just as Olivia's parents arrive.

"My baby girl," her mom coos as she and Dan enter. "You look so beautiful, already glowing," she cups Olivia's cheek before hugging her and then shucking her coat.

"Thanks, Mom. Although, that just might be sweat," Olivia wipes across her forehead in jest. "I can't seem to get comfortable. I'm either freezing cold or burning up."

"That's because you are a human incubator," Perry chimes in as she comes back into the living room, followed by her husband, Nathan. "Just wait, there are plenty more side effects just waiting for you."

"I actually haven't been feeling too bad, just some nausea and exhaustion, mostly. But Kane has been wonderful in helping any way he can," Olivia beams up at me, which makes me want to puff my chest out with pride—but I refrain. Instead, I give her a chaste kiss on the lips.

"I'm just trying to take care of you, babe."

"That's all we could ask for," Olivia's dad chimes in, reaching to shake my hand. Having the approval of Olivia's parents means everything to me. I never want them to doubt my love for her. And after asking for their blessing to marry her last week, I know they don't. Her mom was thrilled and instantly started to cry. And her dad welcomed me to the family again, just like he did at Thanksgiving. He explained that within just the first few moments of talking to me, he knew I was the one for his daughter. Talk about feeding a man's ego.

If Olivia and I have a daughter, I hope I can detect the right man for her in the same way one day.

"Hey, man!" Drew yells from the door this time as he and Tammy arrive.

"Hey, bro. Come on in." I walk over to greet them, kissing Tammy on the cheek as they hang their coats.

"The place looks gorgeous, Kane," Tammy says while looking around, her blue eyes twinkling from the reflection of the lights on the tree. "See, I told you all you needed was a woman in your life and then everything would be magical," she winks at me as Olivia comes up to hug her.

'Tammy! Drew! Thanks for coming," she declares. I love the fact that my woman gets along so well with my closest friend and his wife. Drew and Tammy are the friends I needed to push and encourage me through the growth I've made over the last three years, and now seeing them accept and love

Olivia like I do makes all of the heartache and pain worth it.

These people are my true friends. There are no ulterior motives, not competition or pretense to uphold. They are honest and hardworking and I'm proud to call them friends and extended family.

"Of course. We wouldn't have missed it. And you look gorgeous, Liv. Pregnancy agrees with you. I can't say the same about me though," Tammy says and then catches herself, covering her mouth with her hand as her eyes goes wide.

"What? What are you saying?" Olivia whispers while the four of us huddle together.

Drew smiles and then puts his arm around Tammy. "Tammy's pregnant again. We just found out a few days ago, but didn't mean to say anything," he shrugs, but Olivia and I just smile at each other and then back at our friends.

"Congrats, man. That's great," I hug my friend while the girls do the same.

"I'm sorry, I didn't mean to say anything. It's still very early and we're afraid of losing it again, obviously. Plus, I didn't want to steal your thunder tonight," Tammy whispers and then I glare over at her.

"You wouldn't be stealing anyone's thunder, Tammy," Olivia reassures her, bypassing Tammy's slip, thank God. "But of course, we will keep this between us. And hopefully, every-thing works out and then we can have our babies together!" She quietly celebrates while both her and Tammy well with tears.

"That would be fucking awesome," Drew agrees before we all break apart.

"Come on! Walk, please," Amy demands as she shuffles through the door with two kids in front of her and one at-tached to her hip. Her hair is a mess from the wind and her son who's currently grabbing a huge chunk of it, her jeans have some sort of stain on the leg, and you can almost see the tears on the verge of falling from her eyes.

"Come here, Evan!" Olivia says with a motherly voice as she turns from Drew, Tammy, and myself and grabs the baby from Amy's arms when they stop in the entryway. Seeing her with a child on her hip does things to my heart and has my stomach flipping. She's going to be the best mom. I can't wait to watch her love and nurture our child.

Drew, Tammy, and I move away from the door as Perry comes forward to join Amy and Olivia.

"Where's John?" Perry asks Amy once she's directed the kids to the patio where the rest of them are. Perry's children are a little older so it's nice to know they're partially supervised while the parents can converse.

Amy's eyes find the ground as she drops the diaper bag on the floor and peels off her coat. "He's working late. There's some mad rush to get something finished before the holidays," she explains, but it seems she's more upset about that than she's letting on.

Perry shoots a knowing gaze at Olivia as Olivia shakes her head.

"Okay, well I'm glad you and the kids still came. Clara is working late tonight too, but she should be here soon. She insisted she had to finish a presentation before the weekend. But, come on. Let's go eat some yummy snacks," she smiles down at the baby in her arms while leading everyone into the kitchen around the food.

Everyone chats and nibbles on the appetizers while dinner finishes in the oven. The screaming and laughing of kids in the other room provides a glimpse of our future—but it doesn't scare me. In fact, it makes me anxious in a good way —a way that shows me what this next chapter of our lives is about to look like. It's scary but full of optimism—and my house full of people that care about us assures me we can handle it with everyone's support.

"Knock, knock," Cooper shouts as he comes in through the front door, dressed in his uniform, the tan and green fabric stretched across his broad chest. His radio clings to his vest, which holds a few other tools I'm sure he uses from time to time. The belt wrapped around his waist holding his gun and keys clangs as he walks further inside.

"Hey, Coop! What are you doing here?" Olivia rushes over to hug her brother with his surprise visit, ruffling his dark hair a bit. We knew he was working tonight, so we didn't think he'd be able to come.

"I had to stop by a least for a little bit. I'm on the clock, but one of the other patrol units is on standby in case we get a call. I wouldn't have wanted to miss tonight," he says, which makes my gut clench.

'What's going on tonight?" Olivia asks just as I shoot a wide-eyed look of death at Cooper.

"Uh, your party, of course," he tries to recover, but Olivia narrows her eyes at Cooper before directing them to me.

"You wouldn't just show up for some party, Coop. Why are you really here?" Her hands find her hips while she stares down her brother, making me sweat.

This wasn't how I planned this. I had it all mapped out in my head, and then fucking Cooper had to open his loud mouth. I feel retribution coming for my future brother-in-law in more ways than one.

"Uh... I...," Cooper stutters and then looks at me to save him. I point my finger at him and then mimic a punch in my hand, the sound pulling Olivia's attention back to me. Our friends dart their eyes across the room at each other, waiting to see how I handle this wrench in my plan.

"Kane?" She turns to me now just as I drop my hands and take a deep breath.

"Well, this wasn't how this was supposed to happen... but I guess since almost everyone's all here, there's no time like the present," I concede while walking over to the bags of gifts under the Christmas tree Olivia had wrapped in preparation for the white elephant game we were going to play later. The ring was ready to go in the gift I had strategically placed for Olivia to pick. She would have opened it to show everyone and I was going to drop down on one knee. But apparently life doesn't go as planned for us.

And in this moment, I realize that's okay. In fact, I willingly accept that life with Olivia will constantly be a path of twists and turns and tangled plot lines—and I wouldn't have it any other way.

I pick up the bag and retrieve the black velvet box, standing and turning around to see Olivia watching my every move. Walking up to her, her eyes glance down at the box and she sucks in a deep breath.

"Olivia," I say before dropping to a knee in front of her. I hear the shuffle of our family and friends around us, moving closer so they can see and hear. I hope Drew is coming through for me and recording this like I asked.

"Three years ago, my life was shattered. I was betrayed by the two people closest to me and I never thought I would bounce back from that. But when I saw you dancing away on that stool at Tony's, something inside of me pulled me to you. What started out as hot and passionate, quickly turned to something more meaningful with the help of a bunch of crickets."

Olivia laughs while everyone else around us chuckles. Our friends and family are all familiar with the cricket story by now.

"You showed me that opening my heart up again was worth the risk. And even though our pasts were intertwined, in some twisted up way, it was my tainted betrayal and your devastating disappointment that brought us together. We healed the cuts both of us had yet to recover from. And now, we're going to be joined together forever by the life we've created," I reach up to caress her belly.

"I love you more than I ever thought was possible. I need you and want you more than you will ever know. You've put me back together, built me up to be the man I always wanted to be, and I want nothing more than to be that man for you for the rest of our lives."

I reach down and open the box and extract the ring—a classic princess cut diamond with smaller diamonds on the band—before reaching for her hand to place the ring on her finger once she says yes.

"Olivia Walsh, will you marry me?"

Olivia's eyes are clouded by tears, but they never leave mine as she smiles down at me so wide, tears cascading down her cheeks, and her hand trembling before she nods.

"Yes, Kane," she says, choking out the words through the emotion clogging her throat—but those two words are all I needed to hear. I slide the ring on her finger as our friends and family clap and cheer, filling the room with celebration as I rise and pull her into me for a searing kiss—sealing our commitment to each other in front of everyone.

"I love you," I whisper when we part.

"I love you too, Kane," she whispers back, peering up at me with the most loving gaze, it makes my heart thump wildly in my chest. This woman is mine. She lured me out of the darkness and showed me the light in my life that was missing—the only light I could have found from her.

Olivia's parents interrupt us first, hugging us in congratulations while Olivia and her mom wipe each other's tears. Her dad pulls me in for a hug and pats me on the back. I wish my parents could have been here, but my dad hates driving in the snow. I told him we would make our way up there to see them soon.

Perry, Amy, and Tammy all come in next, pulling Olivia's hand in all directions to scope out her ring, while John, Drew, and Cooper all congratulate me with handshakes and side hugs.

"Sorry, Kane," Cooper finally says, hunched over a bit in embarrassment.

"Don't worry, I'll get my revenge one day," I wink at him, which makes him shake his head in laughter.

"I have no doubt," he replies, and I thank my lucky stars that I get to have a brother-in-law like Cooper. After he and Dan drilled me at Thanksgiving, the two of us have bonded and become friends. His relationship with Olivia is important to them both, and I'm grateful that I am accepted by one of the most important men in her life.

"Now we have wedding and baby plans to attend to," Perry exclaims, and I can already see the wheels turning in her mind.

The chatter filling my home brings a sense of peace over me while I admire our loved ones sharing in our moment. It's amazing how much my life has changed in just three months' time, and I wouldn't change a thing. Even though it was one hell of a ride to get here, I realize that the tangled mess I thought was my life actually turned out to be a woven masterpiece, with each thread coming together to create something truly beautiful.

I have the woman of my dreams, the home filled with love and laughter, and a family on the way. Nothing can ruin this.

*"219 this is 141. We've got a 12-72 at 1600 Lake Drive. Requesting back-up immediately."*

Cooper's radio echoes in the room, drawing the attention of everyone to him.

*"141, 10-4. On my way,"* he replies before looking around at all of us. "I've got to go. Congrats, sis," he says while kissing Olivia and then his mom on the cheek, hugging his dad, and then waving goodbye to everyone else before quickly turning and immediately running out of the door.

"Be careful, Coop!" Olivia's mom shouts after him just as the door slams shut.

"What's a 12-72?" Drew asks, his eyes bouncing around the room.

"Burglary in progress," Olivia's dad answers casually.

"1600 Lake Drive... isn't that where Pearson Advertising is?" Perry asks while looking at Amy and Olivia with worry etched on her face.

"Wait, that's Clara's advertising firm!" Amy shouts while the energy in the room shifts immediately.

"Oh, my God, Kane," Olivia reaches for me, burying her face in my chest. "What if she's hurt? What if Cooper and the other deputies don't get there in time?"

I rub her back while offering her whatever comfort I can—knowing that there's nothing we can do but hope and pray that the sheriffs get to her quickly.

"It's going to be okay, babe. Clara is strong and help is on the way. If anyone can help her, it's Cooper," I say confidently, even though I'm beyond terrified that a member of our tribe is in grave danger.

THE END

Want to know what happens to Clara?  Stay tuned for
_Enticed_, Clara and Cooper's story coming in early 2020!


If you LOVED Tangled, please consider leaving
a review on Amazon!

# Acknowledgments

I started reading romance novels in 2018 about a month after I lost my grandma (the same grandma Olivia refers to in this story—the details regarding her grandma are all real anecdotes from my grandma's life). At a time when I needed the escape the most, I turned to stories of overcoming loss, working past the obstacles life brings us, and believing in the happily ever after's. In January of 2019, I started toying with the idea of writing my own book, and started brainstorming ideas with one of my best friends. By the end of March, I had a story and I started typing. Six weeks later, Chasing Hope was done and I got the courage to self-publish.

My excitement for story-telling only grew from there, and now I am pushing publish on my fifth novel since March of this year!

Thinking back on this accomplishment brings tears to my eyes. I have found a creative outlet I needed desperately. I have strengthened friendships with people close to me. And I have "met" so many AMAZING people in the romance community through social media—dedicated and generous women who have supported my journey and helped introduce me to new readers.

I can't believe that this is where my life has ended up by downloading one book and turning the page. Thank you to every person near and dear in my life that has supported me in this! I would not be where I am right now without you! My husband, my children, my mother, and a few of my very close friends cheer me on from behind the scenes, and it makes me believe that anything is possible.

Adding the element of T.J. in this story stemmed from a betrayal I experienced from someone I thought was my best friend when I was nineteen. Even though the circumstances were different than the case of Kane and Olivia's story, I never fail to remember that the person I thought was my friend taught me one of the most important lessons in my life about trust. And if she hadn't made her decision, I never would have met my husband. Everything works out the way it's supposed to, and sometimes the people who hurt us the most can also help us in the most unlikely of ways.

I hope you loved Kane and Olivia's story as much as I loved writing it!

On to Cooper and Clara's story next!

## *More Books by Harlow James*

### *The Hopetown Series*

Chasing Hope

Destined to Be

A Simple Love

One Look, A Baseball Romance Standalone

Wanna keep up with my releases and connect outside of my books?

Follow me on Instagram
Follow me on Facebook
Join my reader group: Harlow James' Harlots

And if you LOVED Tangled, please consider leaving a review on Goodreads too!